A TOWN CALLED DISCOVERY

RR HAYWOOD

RRHAYWOOD

Copyright © R. R. Haywood 2020

R. R. Haywood asserts his moral right under the Copyright, Designs and Patents Act, 1988, to be identified as the author of this work.

All Rights reserved.

Disclaimer: This is a work of fiction. All characters and events, unless those clearly in the public domain, are fictitious, and any resemblance to actual persons, living, dead (or undead), is purely coincidental.
The inclusion within this story of the characters "Pea and Sam" are used as a prize in a competition and although to a degree they are based on the real persons they remain fictitious characters within a work of fiction and the author asserts his full rights to amend, delete or change those characters.

No part of this publication may be reproduced, copied, stored in a retrieval system, or transmitted, in any form or by any means, without the prior written consent of the copyright holder, nor be otherwise circulated in any form of binding or cover other than that in which it is published and without a similar condition being imposed on the subsequent purchaser.

Cover Art by Mark Swan.

A TOWN CALLED DISCOVERY

RR Haywood

PROLOGUE

In the beginning

She runs between the high hedges on a concrete path. Sprinting with sweat pouring down her face, and sodden, blue coveralls clinging to her frame. Her bare feet slap the path, and somewhere behind her, the dogs snarl and bark as they give chase.

Confusion inside. She has no self. No identity, but the terror she felt is now channelled into a burning rage that pushes her on to find him, to hurt him, to kill him.

Everything hurts, and she bleeds from her hands, from her arms, and from her feet, leaving slick spots of blood on the path she flies over.

The last corner. The straight section to the door. She screams out to summon energy, but she's so tired now, and her face pales with crimson blooms as her vision closes in.

The dogs breach the corner behind her, leaning into the curve, then coming straight to power on in her wake, scenting her blood and her fear, and she sprints with everything she has, not breathing, not looking back.

She can make it. She can reach the door, but there's nothing left to give after that. She can't do it all again. Please, not again.

The door slams open as she staggers out, readying for the drop, but she lands on a concrete path, yelling out at the shock of it and rolling quickly in expectation of the dogs savaging her, but they stop at the door, not crossing the threshold.

She rolls on her back, gasping for air as the foot presses down into her neck. She bucks and heaves, grabbing it with both hands and gurgling at the weight bearing down.

Cold, blue eyes, set in a rugged, handsome face, stare into hers. The same cold, blue eyes she has seen through all of this.

He smiles like a wolf and holds her pinned while staring into her hazel eyes flecked with green, and when he speaks, his voice is harsh and bitter, 'Well done, little Roshi... Welcome to Discovery.'

CHAPTER ONE

This beginning

A dream. A nightmare. He is falling through the air towards an ocean of huge, rolling waves. He has no self. He has no name. He screams to wake before he hits the surface, because everyone knows, if you die in a dream, you die for real.

He hits the surface and feels the bones in his legs snap from the impact. Saltwater fills his lungs, and where images of his life should be flashing through, there is only a void, and in his final seconds of life, he sees an open-topped inflatable boat go whizzing past, helmed by a figure in a hooded, waterproof smock, then he sinks down into the water, with his vision closing in as his body shuts down to die.

He screams because he died, but he is back to falling through the air, still not knowing who he is, and the next impact is brutal, breaking both his legs, and he drowns in agony, watching the bubbles in the water, formed from the spin of the propeller as the boat moves slowly overhead, but a heartbeat later, he is back to falling again and searches his mind for any trace memory of who he is.

It happens dozens of times. Over and again. Dropping through the air into an ocean that feels as hard as concrete, and each time the same boat is there, helmed by the same hooded figure watching him die. Fear and terror mix with utter confusion to create a hysteria he cannot break free from, and he slams into the water, breaking his spine but clings to life as the boat slows, and the hooded figure leans over the side.

'Getting boring now.'

A female voice, mocking in a tone, that only makes his terror worse, and he screams out, but the water rushes in to make him choke and gag, and drown, and die.

Back to falling, back to screaming, back to abject panic, but he spots the figure in the boat holding something in the air above her head. Two white scorecards, both printed with zeros, and the figure shakes her head as his scream goes past, only to cut off when he hits the surface, sending a plume of water into the boat. She leans forward, peering over the edge to watch him flailing in obvious agony from his broken limbs.

'Try not dying?' she shouts.

It repeats over and again, until he becomes driven to the point of insanity, clawing his own eyes out, punching himself, breaking his own nose and jaw and crushing his own windpipe to make it stop. He hurts himself for the sheer lunacy of it, desperate to do anything to break the cycle. Praying for it to end, but it never does. It goes on. Repeating. Over and again. Falling and dying, with each, an agonising death in perpetuity coupled with an absolute loss of his mind.

Then, in a split second of lucid thought between the

ravings of his alien mind, he spots the figure in the boat standing like a starfish, and an image of a skydiver rushes through his mind, except he doesn't know how he knows that.

Splaying his arms and legs slows the acceleration. He tries, and he dies, but gradually learns to angle and position to achieve the best deceleration, and the realisation comes that he needs to master *how* he hits the water.

A belly flops hurts like mad and near on kills him instantly, and headfirst is not a nice sensation as there is a split second of life *after* the skull pops open in which he knows his brain is on the outside.

He gains position and glides, then, at the last second, angles to dive into the water. The impact snaps his neck.

He tries again and breaks his spine.

'Oh my god, this is taking forever,' she yells, holding her arms out while swamped in the waterproof clothing.

Position, glide, tuck, and he dives into the wave, but he goes too deep, and the blackness surrounding him renders him unable to know which direction the surface is in. Pure frustration hits, but it's hopeless, and in seething fury, he sucks water into his lungs to reset and do it again.

Fall, position, glide, angle, and dive. He goes deep, and the second the force of the drop abates so, he starts to kick to gain the surface, but the pressure from the weight of water stays the same, and there is no discernible difference in light. His body demands air, sending signals to his mouth to open, and his lungs to breathe in. He kicks harder, using more energy, which makes the demand for air only greater. His vision starts closing in. He begs internally not to die again and fights to swim, to live as the urge to breathe in takes over his will, and as his mouth opens so, his head breaches the surface, and he gasps to suck pure, beautiful air into his body.

'Well done, honey pot,' the figure in the boat calls out, giving him a slow, sarcastic hand clap.

'Help me...' he gasps, spraying water from his mouth while treading water.

'Er... I just did?' she guns the engine and powers off as he screams out for her to stop, and the last thing he notices is the name of the boat.

Discovery.

CHAPTER TWO

Sharp stones cut and dig into his knees and hands as he crawls from the sea, desperate to be away from the waves that crash and threaten to suck him back into the water.

How he got here is a blur of rising and falling while being carried by huge rolling waves, growing cold and confused until the sea deposited him, with a nasty thud and scrape, over the shingle, and now he crawls, whimpering and bleeding as the waves slam him down and drag him back.

Finally, he gets far enough away to slump, sobbing, naked and terrified on a large, flat rock, to lie curled up under a driving rain, and his mind lessens the immediacy of danger, but he still doesn't know who he is. There is nothing before this. He can give the names of things, but when he looks to the back of his hands, he does not recognise them.

The shore is only a jut of land, with the ocean on three sides, and the cliff behind him. There is nowhere to go, and no sign of ships that he can wave to for help. No aircraft heard in the sky. Nothing. He waits, fretting, panicking, freezing, and terrified, then screams out in absolute dread on seeing a freak wave surging from the ocean that slams him into the rocks, before dragging him out to drown and die.

An instant later, he is back to life with his body scraping over the shingle and once more runs to break free from the waves trying to drag him back out. He stops at the foot of the cliff, gasping for air and desperately looking for a way out while trying to watch the waves crashing on the beach. There is nowhere to go but up, and so he starts to climb, weak, shaky, cold, and hurting.

He gets ten metres up, when his right hand slips, and he tumbles down to land with a crack of a leg bone breaking on the rocks below, crying out in agony and horror at his leg now at a right angle from the knee down.

'That wasn't very good, was it,' the same female voice comes sails, clearly from the top of the cliff.

'HELP ME,' he roars, but she doesn't answer. He bellows and begs as the rain falls, and his body heat reduces while his lifeblood pours over the rocks, and he doesn't see the huge wave coming again that once more rags him over the rocks before taking him out to die.

Sharp stones cut and dig into his knees and hands. He tries to run but slips, and the waves pull him back. On he goes, fighting and desperate to stagger away from the sea to the flat rock.

'Up you come, bubble-gum,' the voice sails down, the same one from the boat.

'WHO ARE YOU?'

'You've got to climb up, my brave bear.'

'TELL ME WHO I AM!' he screams so hard his voice breaks.

'Climb up before the wave comes...'

He starts climbing, but the screed is loose, the nooks and crannies wet and slippery when he tries to find purchase. He falls time and again, dying instantly, dying slowly, dying constantly, until the face of the cliff is memorised almost intimately, while all the time she mocks and goads until, finally, with teeth bared, he reaches the top and scrabbles to reach a hand over the lip, but the grass is too wet to grip, and so he tumbles back, screaming out with frustration.

'Oh, that was so close,' she calls out as he plummets, hitting the rocks to die in searing agony while looking up to a figure leaning over the cliff edge. 'Next time, buttercup...'

He reaches the top, grimacing with exertion as he drives his fingers into the wet earth to gain enough purchase to slowly inch his naked body over, with his bare arse facing the sky, and his naked legs dangling down. A surge of effort, and he rolls over the soaking wet grass, gasping for air before coming to rest on his back, then screaming in fear, and trying to get away, but it's too late.

'YOU KILLED ME,' he roars from the shore after running from the waves once more.

'Sorry,' she calls down in a sing-song voice, 'try again.'

'Why? What did I do?'

'Come back up, my brave tiger, and we'll chat.'

'NO.'

'The wave will come.'

With dread in his gut, he reaches the top to peer over the edge to a black-robed figure, with a heavy cowl over its head, staring down at gloved hands resting on the shaft of a woodcutter axe. The same axe that cut through his neck when he rolled onto his back. She doesn't speak or move, and with mere seconds to go before his grip gives out, he climbs over.

He waits at the base again, never realising there was

such pain as having his dick chopped off. It was worse than when he bit through his tongue. Worse than when his bones jutted from his skin. Worse than all of them.

'YOU CHOPPED MY DICK OFF.'

'Sorry!'

'My dick,' he mutters, climbing up again 'my actual dick…' He stops to look down at it, shaking his head at the surrealness and the abstract existence of whatever this is.

An idea forms, and he climbs faster, reaching the top to check her position before springing up to his feet, and grabbing fistfuls of the robe as the axe bites in his shoulder. The agony is searing but no worse than any other time he has died, and he throws himself backwards off the cliff while gripping the robe to take her with him, and as they plummet, so the cowl comes down, and his world fills with raven black hair and hazel, almond-shaped eyes, flecked with green, set in flawless skin, above full lips that smile to show a tiny gap between her front teeth, and the scent of cherry blossom fills his nose as she laughs without fear. 'Good try, handsome…' they hit the rocks, and death once more claims his mind.

He supplicates, but she kills him. He appeals to her femininity, but she kills him. He turns his back, but she kills him, and she never utters a word once he is at the top.

He learns to climb over and vault to his feet before she can strike and even gains enough time to flee, but she throws the axe, sending it spinning through the air to embed in his back, taking him down to squirm and weep in the mud, before feeling the press of her foot on his shoulder as she prises the axe free to finish him off.

The next time he does the same, climbing over to vault up, and runs for it, then veers sharply to the side as the thrown axe sails by that he scoops up to brandish in the pouring rain.

'FUCK YOU!' he roars out in victory, expecting to see fear, expecting to see worry, but she walks slowly towards him and thrusts her head back to flick the cowl off with a wry smile, then arches an eyebrow, and flicks her gaze down to his penis while waggling her little finger and widening her eyes as she forms a sensual pout, and in that instant, he feels an absurd sense of shame at being naked. 'Why are you doing this?' he asks weakly. 'What did I do?'

She shrugs and walks towards him, slow and sensual, with a sway designed to capture his attention, then flicks an eyebrow up, and smiles.

'Please...I don't know you...who am I? What's happening to me?'

'Tell you later, tiger.'

'TELL ME NOW!'

She tuts softly, showing a fleeting look of mock sympathy while pulling a knife from the folds of the robe.

'Stop it...please... I don't want to hurt you, just tell me who I am... Why am I here? What did I do? Stop...STOP! I'll fucking kill you...' he hefts the axe to show he means it, but she laughs softly, and again, flicks her eyes down to his penis.

'It is cold, isn't it...' she launches fast, coming in with the knife gripped, and a few seconds later, he drops to his knees to vomit at the side of her body while that goading smile remains etched on her face despite her insides being on the outside from the huge gaping wound across her gut.

Hot bile burns his throat, bringing tears to his eyes that he tries to blink away, before sitting back on his haunches, whimpering in state of pure anguish. He is dead, and this is hell. It is the only conclusion he can fathom or think of. He did something awful, something terrible, and this is the eternal retribution of spite from a god that has sent him to suffer damnation.

He moves away to see he is on a bleak, featureless plateau, with a gnarled hedgerow of vicious, barbed thorns that runs from cliff edge to cliff edge in a deep horseshoe with a single opening to a narrow track.

He can't stay here. Something will happen. Something painful and nasty. He looks around wondering what it will be. The sea is too far away now, and the ground seems firm.

A crackle. A buzz. 'That's not even funny...' the bolt scars the sky with a fractional searing of pure energy that burns his retinas and brings light to the world, before it hits his chest, exploding his heart and sending him flying metres back through the air.

From death to life, and he vaults to his feet, clutching his chest, and decides that being struck by lightning is nearly as painful as having his dick chopped off, and he lurches around, expecting to see her body, but it's gone, and he sets off towards the dark foreboding path while casting fearful looks at the sky above.

He pauses for a second before stepping in, staring down a long, narrow, straight path hemmed in on both sides by impenetrable thorn forest. A crackle in the sky, and in he goes, rushing forward with a yelp to start walking quickly, fearing and expecting the worst, but nothing happens, and he walks on without incident.

It's nerves that make him look back. A creeping, insidious horror that makes him look around to cry out at seeing the entrance to the plateau is but a step behind him.

He runs harder, with raw, primaeval fear in his gut, and snaps his head to look front to be sure he is running. He is.

The ground is going by, and his feet are gaining traction to propel him forward.

Then the scent of cherry blossom fills his nose, and the greatest fear of all comes when he looks back to see her right there, grinning at him. Just a step away on the plateau. Her injury gone. Her mouth smiling that taunting, mocking grin as those hazel eyes flecked with green sparkle in the grim light.

He faces forward, giving it everything he has to run and run, and never stop running, but the fear magnifies. He can sense her right behind him. He can feel her warmth, and when her touch finally comes, he screams out and tries to inject strength to get away, but her hands move slowly across his naked back, gently, softly, her fingertips tracing a route up and down his spine, and out to the sides.

'Keep going,' she whispers softly, then shoves hard, sending him sprawling down with a yelp in expectation of hitting the rutted path, but he lands on grass, sliding a foot before wrenching up to his feet to instant change of environment surrounding him, and he takes in the striped lawn stretching away to a mansion house, and the path he was on behind him with no sign of the woman.

He hears them before he sees them. Snarling dogs running fast on strong legs, coming into view at the end of the path, and without a second thought, he starts sprinting across the lawns. They take him down in seconds, launching into his back and legs, tearing him off his feet and ripping him apart.

The second the blackness of death comes, he is back at the edge of the lawn, sprawled out on the grass, but rises quickly with a frantic look behind to the empty path, and starts running.

He keeps looking back, expecting them to come any

second, and is hit from the front with an impact that takes him off his feet to land on his back, staring down to the arrow sticking from his chest with the word *discovery* in flowing script on the shaft and a length of silk ribbon tied on. *Haha, gotcha...keep your eyes up.*

He tries to rise, thinking a single arrow might not be fatal, but stumbles, and falls with a great sickening fatigue pulsing through his veins that makes every inch of his body writhe in agony.

A blink of an eye, and he's back to life at the edge of the lawn, springing up to run while watching the black sticks fly up from the direction of the house, arcing gracefully through the sky before reaching the apex of their climb, only to start dropping.

He dies again and again. Hit by arrows, and each one with a silk ribbon attached with words written that he reads in her mocking voice. *The arrows are poisoned. Don't let them cut you. Keep going, tiger. Attaboy, handsome. Almost there, my brave bear.*

The pain becomes secondary to death, and each death is but an ever-increasing frustration that prevents him reaching the end, and he doesn't notice that he runs faster and breathes easier the more times he does it. He doesn't notice his reflexes becoming sharper as his instincts and reactional speed become honed.

The dogs come when he reaches the halfway mark. He panics, loses focus, and is struck by an arrow to the shoulder, and falls to writhe and grunt, reading the silk ribbon on the shaft.

Don't worry about the dogs. Watch where you're going.

He gets closer to the house and spots the open door on the ground level. It's a big house too. Grand and high, with ivy climbing the walls, and a wide veranda running the length of the building.

A greater application of speed, breathing better, easier, his legs stronger. He reaches the stairs leading up to the veranda before the lead dog sinks teeth into his ankle, ripping him off his feet.

An even greater application of speed this time, and he leaps the steps to surge at the doors, crashing through, then turning on the spot to slam them closed, scrabbling to get the locks and bolts home before the dogs launch at the other side, making him stagger back while gasping for air, hardly believing he got away.

CHAPTER THREE

A clink of glass makes him turn from the doors, blinking in surprise at the seated men and women, dressed in formal dinner suits and exquisite ballgowns, holding masquerade masks to their faces. A servant in a bright red jacket serving wine from a bottle held in a white cloth. A baroque room lined with gilt frames and a low chandelier.

'Where am I?' he asks, 'What's happening?'

A young man giggles softly, covering his mouth and turning his head as though trying to suppress his mirth.

'Where am I?' he asks again, his voice louder.

Another low chuckle comes from behind. He twists on the spot, trying to see who made the noise, as more snickers roll around the room. He turns again, angry, freaked out and dripping sweat, while still naked, but every motion he makes seems to make them chuckle more.

'Stop that...STOP IT!'

Bosoms heave as women cackle, and the men bray deep while slapping their thighs in a manly fashion. He spots the door at the end of the room and moves off as the servant draws a pistol from inside his jacket and shoots him dead.

He staggers upright in the centre of the room and casts about at the silent faces staring at him through the masks. The servant is the killing thing this time, and his hand is already inside his jacket.

'Please...please tell me where I am...' the chuckles start. Low and soft, yet building, and he resists the bite of anger to keep his voice neutral, 'I don't know what's happening. Please stop laughing...please...' They laugh harder as shame starts to steal over him with a deep humiliation, and when he covers his groin, they scream out as though it's the funniest thing ever seen, and the anger bites as a chime from a grandfather clock at the edge of the room sounds out, and the servant pulls the gun to shoot him dead.

He staggers upright and runs at the servant who fires.

Several more times, he tries, but there is no way of covering the distance, either to the door or the servant, before the gun fires, and the abject humiliation carries on each time as they give mirth at his pathetic existence, and nothing is uglier than people laughing when a great sorrow is felt by one.

Desolation, grief, and confusion sink deep as he lives and dies, resetting each time in the centre of the room to be scorned and humiliated.

The grandfather clock chimes, the gun fires, and he resets to lower down, naked, forlorn, and lost, as they laugh and cackle, and in the last second before the clock chimes and the gun fires, he spots one of the women is closer to him than the servant.

He resets and holds his appearance of utter misery intact. They start laughing on cue, and he looks around slowly, as though moving for nothing other than the sake of it. He was right. She is closer than the servant. A woman in a simple black ballgown that is markedly different to the frills, lace, and extravagance of the others. Golden skin and full lips below the mask that form a wry smirk he has seen before.

A glint at the base of her neck catches his eye. A pendant hanging etched with a single word *Discovery.*

'See me now?' she asks quietly, softly. The same woman from the plateau. She purses her lips, giving that wry smile, and holds the mask to her face as her head cocks over. 'Did you like the dogs?' she asks as the clock chimes, and the servant fires.

He resets from the gunshot and looks over as the first ripples of amusement roll around the room.

'Tell me who I am,' he says.

She shrugs, 'Make me.'

His eyes flick to the ground between them, then to the servant, measuring the distance.

'Try it,' she urges as the room fills with laughter, 'next time.' The clock chimes.

From death to life. He runs at her and stops with a gasp at the knife in her hand buried in his gut, the shock of it, the pain of it. He reaches an arm out, bracing himself against the back of the seat while she lowers the mask to look up, through hazel eyes flecked with green. She moves closer, just an inch, but it drives the blade deeper. Another inch, and he cries out from the pain, with veins bulging from his neck and forehead, while she whispers softly. 'Move faster...' the gun fires.

Reset, and his hand goes to his side with a trace memory of the knife wound that is no longer there while she stares at him with a strange expression, like an expectation. The mask no longer covering her face, and her right hand hidden from view between her thigh and the side of the seat.

He moves fast, clumsily trying to block the knife, but she is quicker than he, and it slides deep while she searches his expression, seeing into him as though looking for something.

Death to life. He charges again, but the knife plunges in, making him grunt from the searing agony, and he slumps forward, barely bracing his weight with a hand on the back of the sofa as he lowers towards her. A moment in time, and the goading smile fades as she studies the contours of his face. 'Fight me,' she whispers in the second before the gun fires.

Death to life. He tries to block it, but the knife goes in, and once more he leans over her, searching for compassion, for humanity, for anything. 'Why?' he whispers, swallowing the agony.

She shakes her head, staring up, 'Not yet...you have to fight me.'

'I won't,' he says, squeezing his eyes closed from the agony.

'Look at me... You have to fight me... Do it...'

'No!' he snarls.

'COME ON,' she shouts, twisting the knife as the gun fires.

He resets with a spark of anger inside and charges at her, but the knife comes up and in, stabbing hard as her other hand reaches up to grip the back of his neck. 'You have to fight me,' she spits the words out, anger in her expression. 'Pathetic,' she sneers, 'you're not what I thought at all...'

The gun fires, but that withering contempt sparks a blind fury, and his body rams into her so hard the next time the sofa tips over backwards. She slews across the floor, with him on top, but she twists the blade into his side while he grips her throat, squeezing hard but seeing only delight in her face.

He resets and screams out, slamming her over in a vicious, never-ending fight while she urges him on, 'That's it, tiger... Attaboy!' They bite, rake, and claw with savage brutality as the rage builds to vent, but she shows only playful delight until, suddenly, the seething violence is gone, and he resets to stand sickened, ashamed, and bereft of hope, hating her but loathing himself more.

A flicker of a thoughtful expression shows for the most fleeting of seconds as she takes him in, before smiling slowly and cocking her head over. 'Oh,' she says with mock sadness, 'was that it?'

A snarl, and he charges. He loses count of how many times he resets. He loses all notion of time or anything other than attacking, to fight, to win, to hurt her for hurting him.

She stabs again, plunging the knife in, but the pain of it isn't the shock it once was, and his hand closes over hers, holding the hilt, and pulls it out to stab it into her stomach, sinking down on top of her as she gasps in surprise. 'Nicely done,' she whispers.

Reset, and he takes her off the sofa, wrenching her up and into the wall behind. She tries stabbing into his side, but he wraps his arms around her waist, squeezing with everything he has. She grunts and wriggles up, with the swell of her breasts pushing into his face, and her dress riding up, as her bare legs wrap around his body, and his world fills with the scent of cherry blossom, and the heat of her form, the shape of her, the narrowness of her waist. She grunts and wriggles as he jerks his head free to catch air, staring up as she stares down, both squeezing and holding on for dear life with eyes locked. She goes still, exerting all her strength into her legs, squeezing his mid-section. He tenses, feeling the muscles contracting, then she bucks and heaves to get an arm down between them, but he stays put, knowing he's got her. Then his eyes widen as the hand she pushed down grips hold of his penis and testicles.

'No,' he gasps, 'that's not fair...'

'Everything's fair in a fight,' she says, her grip tightening as he grimaces.

'I wouldn't do that to you...' he squeezes his eyes closed in expectation of the explosion of pain that doesn't come, and she looks down at him with a gentle frown.

'You really wouldn't, would you...' she whispers as the gun fires.

Reset, and a few seconds later, she lifts her head to look down her body, at the knife stuck in her belly while he lies at her side, his head but an inch from hers, while his hands clutch the stab wounds to his gut. She lowers her head and turns to look at him, their noses almost touching, their breaths blasting over each other.

He comes to know every pore and freckle on her face and neck, the flecks in her eyes, and the strands of hair that come loose to hang down. The creases in the corners of her eyes and the light wrinkles in her forehead. He also starts to win more than he loses and gets to the point he can grip her wrist and pluck the knife away, regardless of which direction or angle she stabs him from, and all the time, the room laughs with men slapping thighs and women cackling, but no matter how fast he gets, he cannot stop the servant shooting him, and she is the only one closest enough to reach.

He charges, tips the sofa, lets the blade sink into his gut, and scores a victory when she shows the first look of surprise at him not fighting back. He smiles at the quasi-victory as she tuts and chuckles at him. 'Getting tired?' she asks.

'Maybe,' he says, impervious to the pain of the knife sticking in his side, and reaches up to gently tuck the strand of hair dangling by her eye away with an action that makes her frown.

Reset, and he charges, tipping the sofa back and showing his speed learned by plucking the knife from her grip and sending it scooting across the room. She lashes out, but he grips her wrists, pinning them down while she bucks and heaves.

'Help me,' he says simply.

She goes to shout, to yell, and spit before huffing and looking up at him. 'Fine,' she says with a strange glint of mischief, of humour, or pride, of something he can't understand. 'He's only got one bullet, you idiot,' the clock chimes, and the gun fires.

He staggers upright and charges to tip the sofa, blocking her wrist and plucking the knife from her hand that he launches at the servant, knocking his aim off as he fires and kills an old woman on the other side of the room, that prompts everyone else to roar with laughter.

He presses the attack, vaulting the sofa to take the man down with punches that get harder and harder until she grabs him from behind, pulling him back.

'He's dead... Oh my god, I can't believe you didn't figure that out...'

'What?' he spins to face her, the rage ebbing fast as the confusion comes back. 'Who am I? What's...I don't...' he gibbers as she pushes the servant's gun into his hand,'What's that for?'

'You'll need it.'

'Tell me who I...' his words cut off as he looks down to her hand plunging the knife into his chest.

'Try thinking for yourself next time...' she says as he topples backwards.

She steps over him, placing one foot either side of his body, and looks down while the blood froths from his mouth, and his eyes form an unspoken question. 'Stick at it, tiger,' she cocks her head over with a sudden frown, 'are you looking up my dress?'

CHAPTER FOUR

He opens his eyes to what looks like an inner hallway of the mansion house, and he counts seven doors in a room shaped like a hexagon. Or is it a heptagon? He frowns while still lying down and remembers he is naked and everything that led to him being here, and it's only when he rises, that he realises the gun is in his right hand.

He looks at it. Feeling the weight and thinking of the woman, while also trying to think if he has ever fired a gun before? You just pull the trigger, right?

His ears ring from the shot, and he squirms, on the floor, pumping blood over the polished floor. A door opens, and the woman marches in, now dressed in simple, black jeans and t-shirt, with a pistol in a holster on her hip.

'What did you do?' she asks, staring down at him with dumbfounded shock.

'Shot my willy off,' he gasps, clutching his bleeding privates as she squats down to pick his dismembered member up, 'you said it only had one bullet.'

She tuts, stands, and pulls her gun to aim at him, 'You are so bad at this.'

'I didn't look up your dress...'

She fires.

He opens his eyes to stare up at the vaulted ceiling and rises slowly, making sure to aim the gun away from his body while still wincing at his poor penis getting so much abuse. A thought pops in his head that grows roots and evolves into an idea.

She marches into the room to stare down at him clutching his bleeding leg. 'Seriously? Again?' she asks, shaking her head at him.

He aims the gun up, earning a sharp look that quickly morphs into that wry smile, 'Nicely done, tiger...'

He pulls the trigger, shooting her through the leg. She drops with a grunt, pulling her own gun to shoot his already injured thigh.

'I didn't look up your dress...' he grunts and shoots her in the stomach.

She shunts from the impact and shoots him in the chest, 'Did...'

'I didn't,' he sends a bullet into her arm.

'Did,' she gets one in his tummy, and the floor of the seven-sided room becomes slick with hot blood that adds to the tang of metal and cherry blossom in the air as they shoot each other dead.

He opens his eyes to the vaulted ceiling and looks around the immaculate room.

'I didn't look up your dress,' he shouts out. He's chopped her with an axe, seen her corpse come back to life, stabbed her, strangled, punched, bit, gauged, headbutted, and he just shot her repeatedly, but it's important she knows he's not a pervert. 'I really didn't.' He frowns when no response comes. 'Hey...are you there?' he walks towards the door she came through, his hand stretching out to grab the handle as it bursts open, slamming into his face and making him stagger back with a yelp as a man in blue coveralls rushes in and kicks him hard to the stomach with a heavy boot.

He goes down with the air smacked from his body and feels an impact on the back of his head as the man lays into him with a big stick. He fires the gun, plucking the trigger and shooting himself in the leg again, and dies screaming in pain with his skull beaten in.

The gun aims at the door as he waits for the man in blue coveralls to come through, but the door behind him crashes open instead. He spins and starts firing in panic, sending the rounds into door frames, the walls, and doors. Through luck, he gets one into the man's leg, and he goes down as the other six doors burst open at the same time, with six more men in blue coveralls carrying the same black sticks running in. He fires and empties the gun, but goes down from the barrage of hits that break his arms and legs, before they start on his head.

Seven men. One always comes first, then the other six come at the same time. They're fast and strong too. Fit, healthy, and wearing big boots. He is naked, vulnerable, and completely outnumbered, and despite having a gun, he cannot shoot fast enough to stop them.

It becomes as bad as falling from the sky into the ocean. That same sense of hopelessness, and he gets the idea to shoot himself, but that just resets faster. He tries running through the doors, but they always reach him first.

He cries out for the woman, begging her to stop them, and that loss of her presence brings forth a crushing loneliness that saps his will to survive.

So, he stops and simply waits on his back, staring at the

vaulted ceiling, counting beams and studying the striations in the panelling while his body is broken by the men.

He starts detaching himself from reality and tries to think of nice things, except he has no memory, so there are no nice things to think of. Then, he remembers her hands tickling his back on the path, and the way he plucked the strand of hair from her mouth, and that one time she grabbed his dick and balls but didn't wrench, and his desperate, lonely mind twists those things into acts of kindness, giving him memories to hold dear, something to hold in his heart while the men break his body.

He learns that pain is a suggestion of a sensation. It is not real. He has nerve endings in his body that send signals to his brain that tell him something is happening to the body that should not be happening. He learns to switch that off until he is able to count the striations in the beams and look with disinterest upon his attackers while they beat and break him.

He dies and resets, and notices neither, but stares up at the beams. A door opens. He doesn't notice. Footsteps come, but he doesn't hear them. He stares at the beams and decides he is not here, and this is not real.

She appears above him, standing, once more, with her feet either side of his arms, with her hands on her hips to stare down like the strange devil angel woman she is, 'What's wrong with you?'

'I didn't look up your dress.'

'Fine. Whatever. Forget the dress. You need to get through this one.'

'Why?'

'Because you do. Get up and fight back.'

'I don't want to.'

'Why?'

'They're not you.'
'Stop being weird. Fight back.'
'Will you stay?'
'No!'
'I'm not fighting then.'
'You have to.'
'I don't want to.'
'It's taking ages. I'm bored...'
'What's your name?'
'Sally.'
'Sally?'

'No, it's not fucking Sally... Get up and fight,' she holds her hand out, stretching down and beckoning for him to take it. He stares at it for a second, watching her hand open and close, 'Take the hand!'

He takes the hand and feels her pull as he rises to his feet to stare down into those hazel eyes, flecked with green. 'You have to fight back,' she tells him, still holding his hand and thinking she should let it go.

'What for?' he asks with a wan shrug.

'Because we can't do the next one until you've finished this one... That's why.'

'Why did you leave me?'

'Right, listen, your mind is fucking up, but you and I...' she waves her hands holding his between them, 'are here for this, nothing else... Got it? I have to wait for you, so hurry up.'

'No.'

She goes to speak, to fire into him with more angered words but stops herself, and smiles that wry grin, 'You'll fight.'

'I won't.'
'You will.'

He shakes his head and sighs.

She finally drops his hand and marches out of the seven-sided room, and slams the door closed behind her. Seconds pass, and he waits for the men to come and thinks he'll count the striations on the third beam this time. Then she comes back, striding over the tiles to stop with her arms folded in front of him with a smug grin, 'You'll fight.'

'I won't.'

The first man comes. Booting the door open to charge in with his big stick.

'Bet you do,' she says as the stick slams into her head. She goes down with a cry, curling up into a ball as the six other doors crash open to disgorge the men who join the first in laying about the woman.

'HELP ME...' she cries out as her arms break, and her legs snap.

What a thing to do. What a nasty thing to do. Just because he inferred, he missed her. She doesn't feel pain. He knows she doesn't, because he's killed her enough times to know she doesn't feel anything.

'HELP ME...' one of her teeth flies across the floor. That's a shame. She has nice teeth. White and even, with just a tiny gap between the front two. It's nice though. It suits her. 'Please...' she gasps, her voice weaker, but it's still a cheap trick to play. Even if she did come back for him. Wait. She came back for him. She came to check and asked him to fight. She said she is waiting for him. 'For me...' she whispers across the room amidst the sound of bones breaking, 'fight them...for me...'

Something about it all triggers a reaction, and before he can stop himself or even think about it, he is firing into them. They turn as one to launch into him, and he goes down to look across the floor to see her broken and smeared with blood, but that smile etched on her face as he dies.

Reset. The first one comes and dies. The rest come, and he kills one more with the gun, then starts moving, taking blows where he has to but firing back when he can, learning to twist and move, and deciding, in the grand scheme of things, that having a pistol in such a melee is a bit shit. A stick is much better.

He learns to bend and move, flex, and twist, to rotate, and use his form to counter-attack. He dies many times, but each death brings with it a lesson until, eventually, his entire core becomes perfectly centred and calm, with his being entirely at peace with whatever this is, because he is not here, and this is not real.

Reset. He waits. Calm. Controlled. Detached. They come, and all seven are taken down, from start to finish, in less than a minute in a stunning blur of speed, with the room filling with the dull cracks of bones breaking and bodies falling, and as the last one drops, he exhales slowly while looking up at the striations on the beams above his head.

She strides in, looking about the bodies, then at him with her mouth open and a strange look on her face as he bends to picks the gun up. 'Oh, don't be a prick,' she groans. He shoots her dead.

Seven doors. Seven ways out. He chooses the one she came through, takes the clothes from one of the dead attackers, the pistol from her holster, and finally, leaves the seven-sided room.

CHAPTER FIVE

A room within a room. He walks around the outside of the seven-sided structure, it's just a mock-up. Like a set from a movie. Not that he can remember any movies.

The outer room is a grand, wide space with high ceilings. No internal doors. No furniture. One wall of windows with a set of French doors leading out to a veranda, and a small table outside with a red apple and a plastic bottle of water on the top. A small card propped against the bottle.

Have a break, my brave tiger.

He is thirsty and hot, and that apple does look delicious. His mouth waters just from staring at it, but he knows they, or she, want him to go outside and eat that apple, and drink that water so he can be savaged by wolves or bears, or ninjas on ropes, dropping from the roof with big swords.

What if he doesn't go out? What can kill him in here?

Damn though, that apple sure does look nice, and the condensation, clinging to the outside of the bottle, makes him swallow and lick his lips that have suddenly become very dry.

He needs that water. He has to eat that apple. It's so hot in here, and he sweats freely, swallowing while refusing to go outside, and the coveralls become sodden and cling to his frame, while his face flushed red as the air becomes thicker and hotter.

They're killing him with heat and thirst. What a foul thing to do. He tries to break a window for airflow, but the stick bounces off the glass.

HAVE A BREAK, MY BRAVE TIGER.

He deserves a break. He should have a break. He's died a thousand times, so he totally deserves a break now. To hell with it. He pushes the door and steps out to a sensation of relief he never thought possible, and breathes deep, relishing the shiver running down his spine.

A few strides, and he grabs the bottle, feeling the iciness of it, and twists the top off to drink deep, with a groan of pleasure at the chilled water cascading into his parched mouth and down his sore throat.

He drinks half in one go but feels his belly swell, and draws the bottle away to belch, and while waiting for whatever nasty thing will kill him, he decides he might as well eat the apple.

He munches the apple and looks ahead, over the fountains and flower beds, to the solid wall of the high box hedge enclosing him in, but with one gaping opening in the middle. That's it. The only way out of here. He has to go through that opening.

The hedge is dense, thick, and filled with barbed thorns and razor wire. Both sides of the veranda are the same. He couldn't get through with a big axe, let alone with a stick and a gun.

Never mind, the apple was nice, and if he resets anywhere near here, he can hopefully eat it again.

That thought stops him dead in his tracks. He is accepting this. He is accepting what this is. That's wrong. Whatever this place is, it is very wrong. He waits for the feeling of panic to rush back, but it doesn't come. The fear is there, but it's muted now, like buried inside. He berates his complacency, then readjusts his thinking that it's not complacency, but a simple acceptance that he cannot do anything else.

He's lost within minutes. He went in, walked straight, and came to a junction, and went left, then right, then he forgot which way he went from there, and now he is lost because this is a maze. Why wouldn't it be a maze? Of course, it's a maze.

The light starts to fade, and the shadows on the path grow deeper and darker. Day becomes evening, becomes twilight, and with low clouds in the sky obscuring any light from the moon or stars, it becomes near on pitch black. He keeps walking, using the fighting stick to feel his way forward.

Then he hears them. The feet drumming. The mouths blasting air, and the throats giving low growls as the dogs latch on to his scent. He starts running, then realises the folly of doing such a thing in the pitch dark.

He goes down hard, sprawling out with teeth clamped and ragging on his arm. Another joins in, snarling and biting his other arm. More on his legs, sinking teeth while he loses all hope of detaching himself from reality and dies screaming once again.

Hot, sweaty, and gasping. He wakes in the seven-sided

room to see he is still in the blue coveralls, but the bodies are all gone.

He goes out of the French doors to sigh with relief at the cool air and offers a smile at the bottle of water, and banana on the table next to the card.

That maze is very confusing, but try to do it right, my honey pot
It's so boring waiting for you
(You're a dick for shooting me)
(I hope you choke on the banana)

He almost does choke on the banana but from the involuntary chuckle as he reads the card. A split second later, he berates himself at the change in his mindset. This is not funny. None of this is funny. Well, maybe a bit funny.

It's not funny.

He stops to look at the flowers and knows they are called roses. He bends to sniff, inhaling the perfumed fragrance, and plucks the stem of a deep red rose curled in perfect form. He takes it back to the table. 'For the fruit and water,' he calls out, leaving it on the table, figuring being nice never hurt anyone, which is a complete lie because he spoke nicely to her loads of times, and she still chopped and stabbed him.

'I'm taking my rose back,' he calls out, feeling petty and striding off with a loss of dignity towards the maze. But then, she did come back for him in the seven-sided room. He goes back to put the rose down and takes another with him into the maze.

He's lost within minutes again. He memorised the route coming in, counting off the lefts and rights, then realised he had no idea where he was going, so what difference does it make where he came from? He thought that while walking and then realised it's important to know where he has been so he can learn which way to go in the future, but by that time, he was lost.

The day fades, the night descends with the same complete absence of light, and he lowers down to sit and smell the rose while he waits. He inhales deep, drawing the scent in and finding it akin to staring at the striations in the beams, and this time he doesn't scream when the dogs come.

You didn't even try!!!
Why are you giving me a rose? I hate you, my brave tiger.
Try and do it right this time.
(I actually do hate you)
(Do you like oranges?)

He does like oranges, and this one is big and juicy. He takes two yellow roses. 'Thank you for the orange,' he leaves one on the table and takes the other with him into the maze.

He tries hard. He really does but, still, gets lost, and the night comes, he lies down on his back to inhale the rose.

What the actual fuck was that???
Stop giving me roses. I detest you on a molecular level, my super soldier man.
Do it right this time!
(Phwoar, fancy a nice pair?)

He can't help but chuckle as he eats the pear that is utterly delicious in a way no other food has ever been delicious.

Day. Night. Light. Dark. Lost again, and he lies down to

savour the rose and ponders the subtle differences in fragrances they all have.

> *Roses are red. Violets are blue.*
> *You're a twat that isn't trying.*
> *I hate roses.*
> *Do it right!!*
> *(The melon is super nice)*
> *(I pissed on it, by the way)*

He sprays a mouthful of melon on reading the last line, then spins around at the sound of the muffled laugh coming from somewhere. He sniffs the outer skin of the fruit, not detecting any scent of urine, then tries to remember what urine smells like. An orange rose this time. 'Thanks for the melon.' He heads into the maze with an idea to leave a trail, so he knows where he has already been.

> *Oh my god. What is wrong with you?*
> *It resets!!! Breaking branches won't work.*
> *Dear me, you're not very bright, are you my sweet sugar plum?*
> *Do it RIGHT!!*
> *(Plum? Get it? I'm funny)*

He figures she left three plums because they're smaller. Rose left, and he sets off once again to see she was right, and none of his clues are still there. The thing is vast too and must span several square miles at the very least, judging by the distances he is covering each time he comes in.

> *Let me spell it out.*
> *R.I.G.H.T.*

Do it RIGHT!
(I'm starting to like roses, but I hate you more with each passing minute)

An hour later he stops, turns around, and marches back to the table to read the card again.

R.I.G.H.T.

He stays right. Going right and never left. Some do lead to dead ends, but he makes far greater progress than he has before, but not enough, not this time anyway.

Finally!
I was about to tattoo it on your dick
Take the grapes with you and hurry up, smarty pants
(Check your dick)

He takes the grapes with him and jogs into the maze. Staying right and remembering the route to take, and checks his penis for any tattoos, but thankfully, there aren't any.

Hours pass, he jogs as often as he can and only stops to recover his energy to keep going, then he reaches it. Turning from a path into a large circular opening with another table in the middle, and a bottle of water on the top. He snatches the card up, wiping the sweat from his brow as he reads quickly.

Discovery leads to salvation
Run

The lack of jokes and quips imbues a sense of urgency

that makes him look up and around. Multiple paths lead off. Several on the left, several on the right, more ahead. She said to stay right.

D

Right there, on the edge of one path. The letter D hanging from a branch. He reads the card again.

> D<small>ISCOVERY LEADS TO SALVATION</small>.

He runs.

They come within minutes. Barks heard in the distance. He drinks as he runs to slake his thirst and pounds on, cursing when he reaches junctions and has to waste time to learn which is a dead-end and grunting with satisfaction when he finally spots the letter **I** hanging from a branch at a big junction.

S on a branch.

C on a branch.

The dogs reach him. Snarling and sweeping along the path behind him, and he stops to inhale the rose, still gripped in his hands, that takes his mind from this place now.

He resets in the middle. Waking up to see the bottle of water on the table but no card. No anything. He grabs the bottle and goes on.

Where is O? He can't find O. The dogs are coming. Any sense of calm he felt before vanishes. The dogs reach him.

Up. Grab the bottle. O! He finally spots it hanging side on and knows with a stab of guilt that he must have run past it a dozen times at least.

V.

E.
R.

Exhaustion starts to hit. The sweat stopped pouring ages ago when he ran out of water. His legs feel like rubber, and his head hurts. Just one more letter to go. Left. Dead end. Go back. Go right. Scan the sides of the bushes. Look for the letter. They're so close now. The snarls, and feet pounding only a few twists and turns behind him.

Y! There it is. He runs into the lane, sprinting hard, but it's long and bends frequently, taking him through sweeping corners until it straightens out with a door at the very end. He gives it everything he has got, surging the last few metres to slam through the door with a sense of victory as the dogs skid to a stop and watch him dropping towards the ocean below.

CHAPTER SIX

Position, glide, angle, and dive.
'Keep going,' she shouts over the noise of the waves and wind, from the boat named *Discovery*, riding the waves as he goes to shout, to scream, and roar, but something feels different. The boots. They're filling with water and dragging him down. He tucks a leg up, pulling the laces apart to tug it and let it drop. Then the other one as he rises and drops on the waves, and when he looks around, she is gone.

The same as before, and he's dumped on the sharp stones that cut his hands, but he's done this before, many times.

His hands and feet find the first holds, and he starts going up the cliff with that fury rising inside.

'Where is she?' he demands of the seven men dressed in blue coveralls waiting for him with axes, but as before, they remain expressionless and silent.

They don't stand a chance. The violence within him becomes a cold detachment, and the space he has now is wider and bigger. He goes to work with his mind taking him back to the lessons learned in the seven-sided room, breaking knees, arms, and noses before snatching an axe, and swinging it around, cleaving another one in half.

He steps into the path with an axe and walks for five strides before looking back, but the plateau is now five strides behind him. Another foul trick. Another cheap thing done. Where is she?

He runs onto the lawn, ditching the axe to gain speed. The first arrow comes swooshing to thud into the earth. Then the rest sail down as he weaves and dodges before reaching the house to run through the door, slamming it closed behind him. A few strides across the room and he tips the sofa, blocking the knife coming into his gut and pulling the mask away to look into soft blue eyes and a fair complexion that isn't hers. He shouts in frustration, throwing the knife into the servant.

'WHERE ARE YOU?' he stalks through the group, throat punching the young man that always laughs first for good measure.

The seven-sided room, and the second he steps in, so the other six doors open, and they come running. He goes in to meet them, avoiding the fighting sticks swinging at his head as that violence within grows darker and stronger.

He strides out, sweating profusely, and snatches the bottle of water up to drink it down in one long gulp while reading the card.

Don't stop.

He snatches a rose and runs on. He is not here. This is not real. Pain is just a suggestion of a sensation.

The middle, and another bottle of water. The dogs are loosed, and he goes faster, willing strength into his legs, but he knows the route now and finds the letters with ease.

The straight path to the door. Please no. Please not again. Please. He inhales the rose and runs praying through to scream in rage as he drops through the air.

Position, glide, angle, and dive. He goes deep and swims up to gasp again. 'I can't,' he cries out, gasping for air.

'You can,' she says dully, watching him intently from the boat. She twists her hand to make the engine bite and powers away.

Shore. Cliff. A dozen men with axes. He kills them all and takes the path to run out across the lawn, and bursts into the room to throw a taken axe across the space into the servant, and throat punches the young man as he goes past into the battle of the seven-sided room.

Six come and die. Then another seven rush through, but they die all the same. His reflexes and instincts carrying him through while the heat rises, pressing down like a great weight.

He staggers out onto the veranda, leaning against the table to drink the water. while he sways on the spot, and reads the card.

Keep going

Rose. Maze. Run.
Halfway. Water. Dogs. Run. Door. Please no.
Position, glide, angle and dive.

He doesn't speak when the boat named discovery slows nearby. She doesn't either. She just pulls her hood back and locks eyes on his, without any sign of rage or anger, or goad this time.

Shore. Cliff. Kill the men. Plateau to the lawn, and the axe sails across the masquerade room before he steps inside, smashing into the servant. He takes it up as he passes and spins once with a vicious snarl to behead the young man as the women cackle and the men slap thighs.

The first seven come in the seven-sided room. He kills them and the next seven as the heat rises. He has no sweat to give now, he has nothing to give now. Another seven men in blue coveralls block the path from the seven-sided room to the French doors. No matter. He sways in the heat, shrugs, and goes at them.

There is no card at the table this time. No apple either. Just the bottle of water that he gulps down in one go while staggering to the flowerbed to pluck the stem of a red rose free, and he presses the velvet head to his nose and inhales. There is no pain. He is not here.

The maze is torturous. He falters and staggers into the hedges, cutting his hands and arms open on the thorns and razor wire. He loses focus for a long time, then comes to, crawling on all fours with his eyes fixed on the door at the end as the dogs walk behind him. Sniffing his feet and panting softly, but he has no knowledge of them. He has no knowledge of anything other than the door that he reaches and paws at, before falling through, landing face down on a concrete path.

He is falling in his mind. Position, glide, angle, and dive. He gets ready for the impact as she walks over, folding her arms and smiling at him humping the ground.

'Why on earth did you keep going?' she asks, not expecting an answer.

His movements slow, his arms and legs growing still. 'You told me to,' the whisper is almost lost on the last breath before he blacks out,

Roshi drops down to pluck the rose from his hand and inhales the soft fragrance, 'What a strange man you are, my tiger...'

CHAPTER SEVEN

'Help me...please...'
On his feet in a heartbeat to look round. A big room like a warehouse. Walls covered in grime and years of dust. The concrete floor broken and pitted, streaked with old oil stains, and the air stinks of damp and piss. He was in the maze, then on a path. Confusion hits once again.

'Please...' a pitiful voice, feminine, distressed, and child-like. He blinks as he scans, seeing nothing, then spotting a big central pillar and a small foot poking out from the other side.

'I want my mummy...'

Oh god, she's young. Blond hair in pigtails, a school uniform, and tear-streaked cheeks. Wires around her body that go up to a digital clock on the pillar with red numbers flashing as they count down. 4:50. 4:49. 4:48.

He drops down, blinking rapidly, 'What happened? Where are we?'

'I don't know,' she wails, bursting into tears, 'I want my mummy...'

This is sick. To torture him is one thing, but a little girl is something else, and he frets for a minute, not knowing what to do.

4:00. 3:59. 3:58.

'I want to go,' she tries lifting her arms, but the wires are too tight around her body.

'I'm right here,' he grabs the box, turning it over and seeing the hinges on one side. He pushes at the lip, flipping the lid over to see all the wires running into one end thread through to numbered connectors, each held in place by a tiny screw. A sequence of numbers printed on the underside of the lid with a small precision screwdriver and a set of tweezers stay fixed in places by plastic clips. He looks again at the sequence of numbers, then at the screws, understanding what he has to do.

2:33. 2:32. 2:31.

There are so many. Dozens of them and the clock is counting back. Less than two minutes now, and the girl weeps and begs as he rushes, snagging his fingers and dropping the tools from the haste in his motion.

'We're going to be okay,' he says calmly, 'listen to me… We're going to be okay. We'll find your mummy.'

Ten seconds. He snaps the wires out, cutting his fingers on the sharp edges of the box.

'Please,' she begs.

0:05. 0:04. 0:03.

He ditches the box and scoots to wedge himself between the explosives and the girl, wrapping his body around hers. 'It's okay… We'll be okay… I promise…'

A tick. A click, and the explosives detonate.

At the far end of the room, on a high up gantry hidden from view in the shadows, Roshi releases the breath she was holding at seeing him ditch the box and rush to protect the child with his body.

A blink of an eye later, and he's back on the ground, waking up with a jolt and a yell, surging up onto his feet.

Roshi remembers doing this. Everyone remembers this scenario. The difference is everyone else does this scenario after knowing why they are here. He is doing it without that knowledge, but he still covered the girl with his body.

A sob, a cry, and the girl calls for her mummy. The man runs fast, baulking as he spots the girl tied to the base of the pillar. A fleeting look of relief that she is okay, and the understanding that this is another one of the levels he went through before.

He works fast. This is the same as the ocean and the cliff, the same as all the others, but it's not just him this time. There's a child here. 'I know what to do,' he tells the weeping girl, 'It's okay... I'll get you out this time...' Wedge, snap, check the next number, wedge, snap.

It takes over four minutes to free all the wires, and he glances after snapping the last wire, expecting to see the timer frozen, but it's still going, counting backwards with less than forty seconds to go. He doesn't hesitate but wrenches the wires free from the box to unwind them from the girl, then snatches her up to start running.

Roshi bites her lip, watching him run underneath to reach the big, heavy door that he heaves back on old, rusty rollers that screech out.

A dozen children of the same age as the first. Boys and girls all sitting in a room identical to the last. Wires around their frames and over their shoulders that all lead to a big flat box, the same as before, and a clock on a central pillar.

0:05. 0:04. 0:03.

'NO,' he roars out and turns away, dropping down to shelter the kid in his arms as the bombs detonate.

Reset, and Roshi watches him surge up before his eyes

are even open properly. He runs fast, sprinting past the girl to heave the door back.

'It can't be done,' Roshi says from behind him. Snapping his head over and staying passive when his hand grips her throat, lifting her off the ground to hold pinned against the wall.

'THEY'RE CHILDREN,' he roars. 'I swear to God, I will make you suffer…'

She squirms in his grip, her face turning red. 'It's not real,' she gasps.

'Help me get them free…'

'I can't… It's not real… It can't be done…'

'You're sick,' he mutters and releases his grip, letting her fall to the floor, with a look of disgust etched on his face.

'I said it's not… Hey, wait,' she rushes up to her feet, grabbing at his arm, but he pulls free, stepping away as though her very touch is abhorrent. 'I said it can't be done. It's a flawed test… Save one, save many, try hard, but they all die anyway…'

He looks back at the children as something inside snaps, and he turns to the woman, ready to make her end it by any means necessary, but the space is empty, and when he spins back, the children are gone too. No clock. No bomb or wires. He staggers away, faltering for a second while she watches silently from the gantry, feeling a strange reaction to his disgust. She nods once, firm and solid, and a second later, a uniformed American police officer walks into the room below. Black shirt, black trousers, smart and official, with a utility belt brimming with equipment, and a radio fastened to his shirt.

'Hey,' the man shouts, recognising the uniform, but again, not knowing how, 'I need help…'

The cop pulls his baton and flicks his arm to extend it out as he stalks at the man.

'There were kids and...what are you doing? I'm no threat to you... Sir, I am not a threat... Please...' the man stops running to hold his hands out in front, placating the expressionless cop. 'Please... I need help. I've been kidnapped and...' the cop moves fast, running the last few metres to swipe at the man who dodges back out of range.

Roshi leans over the gantry to watch with interest. A cop is of a symbol of authority that represents law and order.

'Stop! Please...' the man dodges and weaves, staying out of range of the cop swiping his baton at him.

Another cop walks in. A third. A fourth, and the man finally gets it. His face changing, his whole manner and being changing as he recognises it for what it is. This is the seven-sided room again. He goes back and away but ceases the calls to stop, and focusses on the threat facing him.

The first cop lunges, and this time he goes in to meet the attack, blocking the swipe and twisting to roll the cop over his hip, dumping him on the floor, then snapping his neck, and reaching down to yank the pistol free from the holster.

Roshi watches him aim and pull the trigger, but the gun doesn't fire. He doesn't know how to operate the safety switch. He tries again, cursing under his breath when it still doesn't fire, and ditches it to take the baton up, and as he kills them, so she sends more in, but not just cops.

'What the fuck?' he says at seeing a priest running at him wearing shiny brass knuckle dusters. 'Stop it...' he dances back and away, hesitating for a second, 'Father... Seriously...'

Roshi smiles faintly on the gantry.

'Oh, fuck off,' he lunges in, driving the baton into the

priest's kneecap, smashing it audibly before flipping the man over onto his back as a scream from the door snaps his head up.

An old man in a woollen cardigan holding a knife. A pregnant woman with a baseball bat. An old lady with a meat cleaver, all screaming as they waddle towards him.

The man stands his ground, shaking his head in disbelief. 'Are you taking the piss?' he mutters.

'Yep,' Roshi can't help but reply.

'I'm not killing them,' the man says, looking up and around.

'Die then' Roshi says from behind him.

He spins to see her staring earnestly, the grip marks still evident on her neck.

'What's going on?'

'Threats come in all sizes and shapes.'

'The kids, were they real?' he asks.

'What do you think?'

'I think, if they're real, I'll be killing you now.'

'I see,' she says in a way that suggests he gave the right answer, 'they're not real… None of them are, but the point is, threats can come from anywhere.'

'Who are you? Who am I? Ouch!' he yells out as the pregnant woman finally reaches him, lashing out weakly with the bat that he blocks one-handed. 'She's not real?'

'She's not real,' Roshi says, grinning at the sight.

'Promise me,' he says.

'I promise you,' she says earnestly.

He snaps her neck, then moves quickly to the old man, killing him quickly, then the old woman, before turning to face her.

'I want some answers now,' he says plaintively.

'Do you, my sugar pot?' she asks, leaning over slightly to look past him.

'Oh no, no way... They're children,' he says angrily, pointing his baton at the thirteen children stalking into the room. They don't smile or weep now, but stare fixed and expressionless, devoid of anything, but sinister because of it. 'No,' he drops the baton, shaking his head, 'no more.'

'Threats comes in all shapes and sizes,' Roshi says again.

'I don't bloody care... Oh, shit...' he ducks from a chef in a big white hat trying to knock him out with a rolling pin and veers off with a comical look of horror, then spins again as a woman in an apron whacks his head with a frying pan, 'oh, my god...'

Roshi bursts out laughing at the sight and sound, 'They're not real...'

'They look bloody real,' he yelps, dancing away from the woman swinging the pan at him.

'Fight back,' Roshi laughs.

'It's a frying pan... She's got a frying pan.'

'It's still a weapon...'

'Who are you?' he yells out, ducking to avoid the frying pan again, then ditching his baton to snatch the pan from the woman, and a big donk sounds out when he hits her with it. 'Oh, god, I am so sorry,' he says quickly, wincing at the sound it made.

'Roshi,' Roshi gasps, covering her mouth as she laughs at the sight.

'Roshi?' he asks, downing the chef with the frying pan.

'Yes!' she laughs harder, wiping the tears from her eyes, at the trail of people chasing him around the warehouse.

'What's my name?'

She gasps, unable to stop laughing at the sight, 'You haven't got one yet.'

'Get off my leg, you little shit,' he shouts, trying to shake a child from his leg, 'I must have a name...'

'I have to name you... Watch that chef!'

'Got him... Can you make them stop now?'

'I could...'

'I've got a frying pan,' he says, brandishing it as he charges at her.

She bursts out with a fresh peel of laughing, waving her hand at him while losing vision from the moisture in her eyes, 'Okay, okay...'

A cessation of sound from the feet running behind him, and he snatches a glance back to see the warehouse now empty other than the woman

STILL LAUGHING. He could attack her now, but something stills his actions. A lessening of the threat. The malice gone.

'Okay,' she says, wiping her eyes with one hand while fanning herself with the other. 'I'm Roshi,' she studies him while steadying her breathing. Dark blond hair, dark eyes, and a brooding, pensive look. His nose is a bit too big, his eyes a bit too deep. He's not overly muscled either but athletic, and currently waiting for her to stop chuckling.

'Who are you? Other than a serial killer, I mean,' he asks.

'Serial killer?'

'You stabbed me like a hundred times...'

'Oh, that,' she says, waving a hand at him, 'it's cool though, yeah? You got the whole pain thing now?'

'Pain thing?' he asks.

'Pain is fear, or rather, the fear of pain is what makes it so bad. Humans are programmed to relate intense pain to death, but once you realised you'd come back, the pain wasn't so bad, was it?'

He goes to argue to tell her she's a psychotic, sick bitch, then realises, begrudgingly, that she's right.

'They're going to love you,' she adds with a frown, almost to herself.

'Who will?'

'In Disco.'

'What's Disco?'

'Hold your horses, my strange, little man...' she smiles again, holding her hand out with an expectation that he will take it.

'I'm not holding your hand,' he says bluntly.

She blanches slightly at the rebuke, 'It's a sign of trust.'

'Trust? I fell from the bloody sky, with you holding scorecards up while I drowned, then you chopped my dick off with an axe... Why are you smiling? That's not even funny...'

'Take the hand, buttercup...'

He stands still, refusing to do as told, then sighs, and takes her hand in his, with the full expectation that he will explode, or snakes will drop from the ceiling onto his face, but nothing happens. He's just holding her hand. The same hand he knows so well from the fights they've had. The same feel of it. The same essence of her.

'You can drop the frying pan now,' she says, then laughs when it drops from his hand with a metallic clang, 'coffee?'

CHAPTER EIGHT

He lurches a step as the world around him changes to a bustling coffee shop filled with noise and smells. The scent of coffee, perfumes, aromas of food, and the clacking of keyboards as people type on laptops at tables. Others talk on phones, pressing fingers into ears to listen above the din. A counter to his side with a glass display case filled with pastries and cakes, and jets of steam blast from a long coffee machine on the other side. Men and women in uniforms shout to each other, calling out names of drinks as customers give orders. Harsh New York voices mixed with foreign accents, and every skin colour known to humanity seems to be in that one big room.

He pulls his hand from hers to rub his face as the dizzying sensation of the immediacy of the change sweeps over him. A hand on his arm, rubbing lightly. 'It passes,' she says quietly.

'Whaddya want?' a harsh, grating voice snaps the words.

'Two lattes, please,' Roshi says.

He blinks and looks around again, seeing it's real. The warehouse is gone. 'Is this real?' he asks.

'Real enough for now, and the coffees here are awesome,' Roshi says.

'What kinda lattes you want, lady?' the harsh voice booms.

'The bloody drinking kind in a cup...'

'I gotta ask,' the man behind the counter shouts.

'Good for you,' Roshi says, scathing and glaring over the counter as the man attacks his cash register like he's trying to re-programme a satellite before the world blows up.

'Ten bucks.'

'What?! Ten bucks for two coffees?'

'You wanna coffee, you pay the fuckin' price or fuck off someplace else.'

'Daylight robbery,' Roshi hands over a banknote that he snatches to throw in the till before slamming it closed. 'Did you hear that?' Roshi asks, pushing him down past the till to the waiting area, 'Ten dollars?'

He looks down to see he's still barefoot and dressed in a blue coveralls, but not one person spares a second glance at him.

'You could wear a giant chicken suit, and no one would look,' Roshi says. 'I did once... Where's the lattes? I ordered them like an hour ago...' she shouts at the counter.

'It was thirty seconds, you dumb broad...'

'Fuck you.'

'Fuck you!'

'I love New York,' Roshi says. 'You can have the best arguments here, and no one bats an eyelid... Watch this... YOU FUCKING PIECE OF SHIT,' he blanches in surprise, stepping back at the animosity of her voice, but only the closest guy looks with a mild tut and goes back to reading his paper, 'couldn't do that in a tea shop in Hastings, could you, my angel?'

'Two lattes,' a new voice bellows from the serving section.

'About time.'

'FUCK YOU,' the man at the cash register yells.

'Fuck off,' she shouts back, grinning as she grabs the coffees and nods for him to lead the way outside.

Yellow cabs. Skyscrapers, and the air thick with fumes and so much noise. People everywhere. A cop on a horse walking slowly through the snarled-up traffic with drivers leaning on horns and gesturing from windows. An assault to the senses, and he walks barefoot with people barging into his shoulders, knocking him around, until Roshi guides him to the side of the pavement and hands him a cup.

'So, my brave bear,' she says as they walk slowly down the street, 'I guess you want some answers, yeah?'

'Nah, I'm fine,' he says weakly.

'Bit noisy here though,' she muses, 'fancy somewhere quieter?'

'Quieter?'

'Lake or beach?'

'What?'

'Lake it is.'

He squeezes his eyes closed as the noise and bedlam of New York is replaced with the sound of nothing, and the dizziness comes on again. Nauseating, and making it feel like the ground is heaving underfoot. She grabs his hand, steadying him as he looks around to the wide expanse of calm glittering water on his left and a grassy meadow on his right. A pebbled shore underfoot, and clean, pure air inhales through his nose into his lungs.

Roshi sips her coffee, watching him closely, 'Okay now?'

He nods and blasts air. 'Sorry, bit overwhelming,' he mumbles.

'It's fine. Most people puke the first time.'

'Most people?'

'Yep. I almost puked... I heaved a bit but then got into an argument in that same coffee shop, so it kinda distracted me.'

She waits for it. Seeing him digest and process what she just said.

He decides, at that point, that he doesn't like being baited so resists the urge to reference what she just said, and sips his coffee instead. He knows it's coffee. He also knows he has had coffee before, but it's all still blank.

'Touché,' she says with that wry grin, 'either that, or you missed my massive clue.'

'I didn't miss it,' he says.

'Good for you, lumberjack. Okay poky... Where do we start? It's a bit messed up, cos normally you do stage one and then go into Disco, have a chat, learn a few bits, then do stage two, but I changed it.'

'I don't know what any of that means'

'Look at me,' she says. He looks at her. Feeling the invasive reflex of someone staring hard into his eyes but finds himself absorbed in her hazel iris' flecked with green, and the freckles on her nose, and such is that familiarity between them, that only then do they both become aware she is still holding his hand from steadying him when the world changed to the lake.

She finally lets go and reaches up to feel the pulse in his neck, detecting the steady beat. He isn't sweating through panic or anywhere close to hyperventilating. He can take it.

'I'll tell you...' she says, 'you'll never know who you were or where you're from. You'll never know your name, or what life you had before this. None of us do. Every person in Discovery is the same. We've all been taken from lives we have no knowledge of and can never go back to.'

'Did you do that...' he falters, frowning as he thinks, 'the falling and...'

'We call it The Circuit. Everyone does it, kind of, sort of,' she winces, half smiling. 'Anyway, moving on... Most people do it once, you did it three times, unbroken. Like I said, normally you do the circuit, then you go into Disco for orientation, then...' she waves a hand in the air, 'I'm repeating myself, but I need you to know all this. I put you straight into the start of stage two... The warehouse with the kids? That's the start of stage two... I wanted to see how you'd react *without* knowing anything.'

'Why? I don't understand...'

'I'll explain in a little while. Do you understand what The Circuit is?'

'Yes, no... I mean... Where did I come from?'

'I just said we don't know. I don't know where *I* came from or anyone else. No names, no memories...no nothing. We're all the same.'

He listens intently with more questions that demand answers, and more demands that create more questions with claxons sounding in his head through the fog of utter confusion that none of this makes sense. Then, he remembers he has coffee and takes another sip through the hole in the lid while staring out across a beautiful lake. It's warm here. He can feel the heat of the sun and smell the scents of flowers, the water too, the humidity of it. He lowers to a crouch, picking a pebble up that feels completely real. He smells it. Scenting earth and stone. He feels the weight of it. The smoothness that suggests it was in running water for a long time, that has rounded all the bumps and ridges off. He drops it, hearing the noise it makes and the action as it rolls then settles. He picks it up again and throws it into the water, watching it climb as it should, then reach the apex of the throw where gravity takes over and brings it down to splash into the lake, and he sees the ripples gliding out in ever-increasing circles.

'That stone so needed to go back in the lake.'

He smiles at the absurdity of her comment and looks up at her. He's killed her. She's killed him, yet here they are.

'Okay,' she says, still staring at him, 'the world we are in now is a construct run by an artificial intelligence.'

The world changes again, and they're standing in central London with red buses going by, and black taxicabs tooting horns. Madame Tussaud's famous waxwork museum dominates the street they're in. Daylight, and a sudden change in temperature. It's chillier, with a biting wind that makes him shiver as he fights the nausea.

'Are you listening?'

'I am,' he whispers. 'I am,' he says louder, nodding at her to show he means it.

'We're all from either the twentieth or twenty-first centuries, judging from what we all know of the world around us. What we recognise, what we can name and label, and understand... We don't know when the AI exists. She won't tell us. Do you understand? Nod. Say something. I need to see you are...'

'I heard you,' he says.

'Look at me,' he does as bid. Her tone, now firm and formal, is such that it's nigh on impossible to not do as she bids. The world changes around them again and fills with voices shouting, phones ringing, and men and women in weirdly coloured jackets staring at huge screens on circular podiums in a vast area enclosed by booths. People everywhere, and he has to step closer to her for the press of bodies, and again her arm is there, holding him steady. 'Where are we?'

'Stock exchange,' his knowledge is instant, but with the frustration of not knowing where it comes from, 'New York, I think… Yeah…it says there…NYSE…'

He lurches into her as it changes to a wide-open place, and a tremendous heat bearing down. He swallows, grimacing at the sensation and closing his eyes for a second.

'Where are we now?' she asks softly.

'Taj Mahal, India,' he says, looking around. Another change. Another place. Nausea and dizziness. 'Italy… Venice…er…the square…Saint…Saint…' he clicks his fingers as she watches him, her eyes lingering on his. 'Saint Marks!' he looks to the tower at one end and the columned sides filled with men, women, and children, all going about their lives. It's so real. The feel of it. The whole of it.

'Are you listening to me, my tiger…'

'Why do you do that?' he asks, looking back at her, 'Why do you call me those things?'

'Because you don't have a name yet, my handsome little teapot, that's why,' she grins that grin. The one he hated when she was killing him, 'what you are seeing now is part of the construct…'

Another change, and they're back to the lake with the calmness it imbues.

'We don't know where our real bodies are. We don't even know if we have real bodies. We *think* we have real bodies because we exist, but it's not proven, and the Old Lady never answers a bloody question.'

'The old lady is the AI?'

'You got it, my smart little smarty pants.'

'What?' he can't help but laugh again, a soft chuckle,

and he widens his eyes, shaking his head slowly. 'Isn't there a movie or...' he searches his mind, feeling rather than thinking.

'Lots of movies, lots of books, lots of fiction, and all sorts of things from popular culture,' she shrugs, nonchalant and casual, 'life imitates art. Art imitates life. Is your head fucked yet?'

'Just a bit.'

'Guess what?' she says, leaning in to whisper as though sharing a secret. He swallows again at her closeness. Scenting that fragrance of cherry blossom in the air around her, feeling her breath on his cheek, 'None of that is the weird part. Want to hear the weird part?'

The world changes to a huge open area. Early evening. People everywhere. The nausea hits, the dizziness inside that makes his eyes clamp shut.

'Look up,' her voice in his ear. He looks up, squinting to see an enormous airship lowering through the sky. Nazi swastikas on the rear fins. Instantly recognisable. His heart races. His breathing coming faster as she moves closer, 'May 6th, 1937...'

'Hindenburg,' he whispers, and the thing goes up. It ignites, and suddenly, there is just a mass ball of flame eating the giant structure as it plummets to smash on the ground. He's seen this. He has seen this same thing, but something is different now.

'You saw it in black and white on old newsreel,' she tells him as people stream past, screaming in panic. That's it. He gets it. This is colour. This is real-life. He can smell the burning and feel the waves of heat wafting across the ground that make him take a step back.

'We're time travellers...'

'What?' his features become stricken, stress in the lines

around his eyes, and his mouth tightens with confusion and shock.

Then it's gone, and the lake is back. He staggers away, dropping to a knee and thinking he will vomit.

'Are you listening?'

'Minute,' he says in a strangled whisper.

'Not in a minute. Now,' she moves to his side, gripping his arm to pull him up. 'Humanity is fucked in the future. The Old Lady is fixing it. We don't know where she is situated or in what form. She might be a computer or a fucking toaster for all we know. Hell, we might be a couple of Japanese schoolkids pissing about in a virtual reality game in the local arcade after school... Look at me... LOOK AT ME! You need to know this. You need to hear this...'

A change, and they're back in the coffee shop, and Roshi strides off to the chiller cabinet, taking a bottle of water.

'Five bucks.'

'Five bucks for a bottle of water? Are you being a cunt on purpose?'

'Take it or leave it, lady...'

'Fine! Fucking bellend...'

Back to the lake, and his head spins, his mind spins, the world spins, everything spins, 'Come on tiger, drink some water...'

He glugs deep, relishing the cool liquid cascading in his mouth and down his throat, which isn't real. How is he feeling it? How is he tasting it? She takes it from him, upending to drink deep and earning a look from him in the process. 'Cost five bucks,' she says as though that explains everything and hands it back. 'Besides, we've shared just about every bodily fluid apart from semen and vagina juice... Whoa!' she jumps back when he sprays his mouthful.

'We have access to the real world but only through the Old Lady. We go to places, and we change things. Look at me... Show me you're listening...' she comes too close, grabbing the front of his blue coveralls too hard. He pulls away, but she goes with him, refusing to let him rest or give him time to think.

'I need you to focus,' she says. He slips on the pebbles, landing on his arse, but she goes with him, pushing him down onto his back to sit on his chest, like a child demanding attention. 'Look at me...' she taps the side of his face, annoying, irritating, persistent, and determined.

'I'm listening,' he says, prickling with a touch of anger.

'Don't get angry. This is bigger than your anger. Imagine a student in their final year of university...boy or girl, it doesn't matter. The student is gifted. I mean super smart. They could cure diseases or become a great politician...but one day the student walks across the road and gets run over by a taxi. Killed instantly. Great shame. Awful tragedy. What effect does that have on the world? What *could* have happened if that student didn't get run over? What *would* have happened if they lived? The Old Lady says the world didn't fuck up because of any single thing but a whole sequence of things. So, we go back into the real world, and we make sure that student doesn't get run over. Then the Old Lady assesses what impact that has and the changes it causes. She does that with every single living person in every single situation. Then she compares it, works it out, and sends us back to change something else. Little tweaks here and there. Small stuff. No great change. No great shakes, but those changes add up, and it's all of those things that the Old Lady hopes will stop us all from dying... Tell me you understand what I said. I need to see it in your eyes.'

He stays still, not knowing anything but knowing enough right now, 'It's not possible.'

'Good,' she says as though he said the right thing, which he did.

The world changes, and he's lying on a polished marble floor in the foyer of a grand hotel with Roshi still sitting on his chest. He looks around seeing opulence and wealth in the furnishings, the fixtures, the design, and in the clothes worn by the people. Men in suits with wide lapels and shiny, black shoes. Women in dresses and hats, and his mind immediately forms the judgement of being in the 1920's.

'See that woman?' Roshi asks.

He follows her gaze to a beautiful woman making eyes at a man in a military uniform, lighting the end of a cigarette held in a long, black stick that she sucks from seductively, inhaling the smoke to release in wispy coils.

'She has sex with that army guy tonight and gets pregnant...' Roshi says, leaning close and whispering in his ear, as though staying secret and quiet, 'their son grows up to become an evil shit that poisons loads of people. We could kill him, *or* we could get in the way of these two doing rumpy-pumpy in her room later and making a baby in her belly.'

He snorts a dry laugh at the way she speaks as another man in a military uniform, flanked by two armed MP's, strides past, and on a signal given, the two MP's rush forward to grab the arms of the guy talking to the woman, dragging him away while he protests and demands to know what is happening. The woman looks horrified at the attention, rushing away from the scene.

'We planted evidence that he's a spy,' Roshi says. 'Look

again,' she adds when he glances up at her. He blinks in surprise at the scene now reset, and the military man back to lighting her cigarette. Another woman walks past them, double-takes, and rushes to the man.

'John? What are you doing? Who is she?' she demands angrily, 'Unless you had forgotten we're getting married in a month...'

The woman with the cigarette blanches, rising from her chair to walk briskly away.

'Same end result,' Roshi says, 'we paid that woman.'

A blink of an eye, and it resets to the woman lighting her own cigarette and staring around as though bored.

'We slipped a very strong laxative in his coffee this morning,' Roshi says, 'he's currently shitting himself to near death...'

Reset, and the sofa is empty, 'We gave both of them laxative this morning... Are you getting the point, my happy little budgie?'

He frowns up at her in response to the new term of endearment as the world changes back to the lake. A question in his eyes.

'Go on,' Roshi says.

'Every action has a reaction, and if you change...' he says.

'It does,' Roshi replies, cutting him off with a pat on the head, 'who's a clever twat?'

'Fuck off,' he pulls his head away as she laughs.

'Let the Old Lady worry about those things. We're ground troops. End of. The Old Lady tells us the point we can tweak, and we get some freedom in how we do it, but yes, that tweak ripples out like that stone you threw in the lake...but then we tweak somewhere else, change something else, and on it goes. Got it? Say *yes, Roshi, my grandmaster and wonderful teacher of wisdom...*'

'I'm not saying that.'

'Ungrateful,' she says with a lift of one eyebrow.

'What the fuck!' he yelps at the huge explosion nearby that sends clods of earth raining down on them. Another change, and he flinches as men in camouflage, carrying assault rifles, run past, screaming orders and commands. A tank trundling behind them, and a fighter jet thundering down with chain guns blasting into the soldiers running by. His heart ramps again as the jet roars overhead, leaving a trail of destruction behind, and more explosions sounding near and far.

'We go to war often,' Roshi says, her voice suddenly hard, 'changes are easy in war. The Old Lady will always look to find a war she can use.' A body lands next to him, smouldering and torn into chunks of flesh, 'Get used to it, you'll see that a lot.'

He jerks his head free to see men on horseback wearing bright red tunics, charging across the field, holding swords out in front as they yell and scream. Behind them, march dense lines of more soldiers, and teams of horses pulling cannons on big spoked wheels. Smoke drifts over them, making his eyes stink, and he coughs as he twists to see men in blue tunics running from the other side. Seconds pass as the two armies charge, then the air fills with the awful, terrible sound of meat on meat, and the clang of weapons mixed with the screams of injured and dying.

'There are places men can go that women can't...'

He gasps when it changes, again, to a huge room filled with beds on which lie men, bleeding and broken, whimpering and crying out. Uniformed orderlies run here and there, carrying water and stretchers, while doctors, wearing thick blood-stained aprons, saw at legs and arms while more soldiers hold their patients down. A woman in a white smock rushes past, her arms filled with dressings. She stops suddenly to turn and look at them. Grinning a sudden wry grin and winking a hazel eye flecked with green, before rushing on.

'That's you,' he blurts.

'And there are places where a woman is better suited.'

Another change, and he squeezes his eyes closed, his mind struggling to compute and deal with it all, but her hand comes back to his chin, and she lowers to speak quietly in his ear while turning his head, 'Look...'

A bar. Music playing. The lights low. Discrete, dimly lit booths border the edges, couples in shadows sitting close to each other. He squints, frowning and trying to understand what he is meant to be seeing. Then, he spots her in the closest booth. Roshi in a low-cut black dress, staring lovingly into the eyes of a man with wide shoulders in a dark suit and slicked-back hair. An instant reaction inside him. A tensing of his muscles. The man's hand comes up to touch Roshi's cheek, and she smiles coy and bashful.

'There are things I can do that you can't,' she whispers in his ear, seeing his expression harden as he watches the couple in the booth, seeing Roshi over there while feeling the press of her warm body on his. 'We're trained in all ways to achieve our aims,' her words come in a warm breath over his ear, making a shiver run up his spine. He shifts underneath her, hating the way the man is touching her in the booth, and she notices his fist clenching when the man in the booth drops his hand to her shoulder.

'Personally,' she says in an entirely normal, conversational tone of voice, sitting up a little, 'I can't stand blokes being all grabby and pawing at me. They left that in as part of the training package, but I refuse to do anything like that. Unless he's like super fit and... I'm joking. Don't you ever be a grabby twat, my little bear,' she says at the look on his face.

The world blinks around them, changing back to the lake, and she smiles down as he shakes his head in wonder at it all. Trying to discern what's going on, why, how, and all the millions of things that he should be asking, but there's too many and too much.

'Lot to take in,' she says, 'think you've got it?'

'No,' he says wanly, with such a look of wretched confusion, she can't help but reach down to stroke his cheek.

'My poor pumpkin. Do you like whales?'

'What?' the world shifts underneath him, and there is motion where previously there was none. A raft in the middle of a flat sea. The two of them in the middle as it bobs up and down. 'What's happening... SHIT!' he tenses, flinching and ready to scoot back off the raft, but she grabs hard, laughing and holding him tight as the black and white killer whale flies free from the surface, just metres away, to hang glittering in the air, before slamming down with a huge splash that sends plumes of icy cold water over both of them. Another one comes up from the other side, flipping as it sails up, then hits the water. Then more behind and in front, all around them, and he marvels at the size and majesty of the creatures, so agile and graceful.

The show goes on for minutes, and in that time, he forgets everything and becomes mesmerised by the dance surrounding him. Laughing with delight and holding his arms round her waist as the raft bobs up and down. She watches too but glances frequently at him, until the whales move off, still diving up and sinking down as they continue their journey.

'Oh my god,' he says, grinning at her, before sinking

back to lie down on the raft, with his hands rubbing the water from his face, 'that was incredible.'

'And we're back,' Roshi says, she finally gets up from his chest and holds her hand out, 'up you come... I think we're just about done.'

'This is insane,' he says, taking her hand to get up, 'I mean...how...I...'

'Was I heavy?'

'What?'

'On your chest, was I heavy?'

'On my... No...not at all...'

'Feel like I'm getting a bit porkier,' she says, clutching her bum cheeks in her hands, 'feels a bit too padded.'

'Er...'

She turns to present her backside to him, 'Is it big?'

'What?' he says, barely able to keep up.

'My bum, is it too big?'

'No, it's... It's fine.'

'Just fine?'

'What? It's fine... It's nice. You're very beautiful.'

'Aw, my handsome tiger, that's so sweet,' she says, turning back to face him with an apologetic look, and for the first time since meeting her, she looks, suddenly, vulnerable and exposed, swallowing and biting her bottom lip, 'I hate not being first.'

'First? What for?'

'The women in Disco... They'll be all over you. You're really hot.'

'I don't...' his words cut off as she steps in quickly, pushing her hands around his neck to pull him down as her mouth finds his, with a hunger that makes him freeze, not quite knowing what to do, but the scent of cherry blossom fills his nose, and in that second, he gains conscious awareness of just how familiar she is to him now.

The time they spent together is immeasurable without the passage of a clock or the transition of day to night, but he knows it was a lot, he also knows she's killed, hurt, patronised, humiliated, taunted, tortured, and degraded him, so by rights, he should grasp her head and snap that slender neck, but he doesn't, because the kiss is rather nice.

The feel of her lips. The sensation of it. It's more than nice, and he softens into the kiss, making her gasp while her heart thunders, and a tremor runs through her hands that push through his hair as their bodies press on a pebble beach next to a glittering lake.

'I haven't named you yet...' she pulls back an inch, but he closes the gap and the kiss goes on. 'Gotta shoot you to reset,' she murmurs, pawing at the gun in her holster.

He mumbles something between the kisses, pushing her hand down to keep the gun in the holster, before reaching up to cup her cheeks, and the kiss goes on.

A minute. Maybe two, but finally, she pulls free, pushing against him to step back, breathing hard and fast, her hair tussled, her lips still feeling the press of his.

'Fuck,' she whispers, 'I wasn't expecting that...'

'What?' he asks, feeling almost drunk with everything that's happened.

'Nothing,' she pulls the gun and aims.

'Don't...'

CHAPTER NINE

A Town Called Discovery

He wakes flat on his back an instant after being shot, and in his mind, he's still there at the lake with the feel of her body against his, but his heart was booming before, and his legs were trembling. Now he just has the emotional reaction with no physical reverberations, instantly rendering the experience to a memory, which makes him think of memories, and how he didn't have any when he fell from the sky, but now he has rather a lot. Most of which are unpleasant.

'Discovery leads to salvation,' he murmurs, reading the old-fashioned signboard above him.

"Welcome to Discovery"

Bright, yellow lettering over a sky-blue top half and a grass-green lower half. It's big too, and bold, in a sort of retro kind of way. It's also very definitely American. Like the sort of sign on the outskirts of a small mountain town, or one near a big valley, or waterfalls. A place with one main road running through where everyone knows each other, and the sheriff drives a big, old four-wheel drive with a shotgun clipped in a frame on the rear-window.

He turns his head while lying flat on his back to see the main road running through the town, and the people within said town walking about their business, greeting, calling out, and stopping to chat, because, you know, they all know each other.

He pushes up to his feet, noting he is still barefoot and still in blue coveralls and also noting, with a dismayed groan, that his blue coveralls now have a new embroidered patch stitched over the left breast.

I am Bear

'No way,' he groans, looking about as though expecting to see her smirking nearby, but seeing only a rough track leading away to a dense treeline that stretches off in both directions as far as he can see.

He doesn't want to be called Bear. He doesn't know what name he *should* have, but only that it shouldn't be Bear, or Tiger, or Honeypot, or Buttercup, or any of the other names she called him. He ponders those names and decides that maybe Bear isn't the worst one she could have given him. Roshi is quite a cool name. Maybe everyone in Discovery has outlandish names.

'Maybe,' Bear says to himself and sets off to towards the town. He reaches the edge where the rough track gives way to smooth blacktop and hesitates, wondering what would happen if he didn't go into the town but walked off into the forest.

Dogs.

That's what would happen. Or Wolves.

He crosses the threshold and starts padding along the road as the air fills with the sounds of engines and voices calling out. High-fronted buildings on both sides in muted pastel colours or red brick. Striped awnings in bold primary colours over stores, and shops set back on wide pavements, and an abstract notion enters his head that Americans call them sidewalks, whereas he thought of them as pavements.

A junction further down the main road, and he remembers, without knowing how he remembers, that Americans call them intersections, but then Roshi said this is a constructed computer-generated world made by an artificial intelligence posing as an old lady that might be a toaster.

'Good morning to ya, welcome to Disco, don't be alarmed...head for the diner, buddy.'

His mind snaps back to the now to see someone walking past him. A man in blue jeans and a checked shirt smiling and giving a thumbs-up as he heads across the road. 'Diner... You hear me, buddy? Straight on down the road aways, and see Allie...' the man stops alongside a pick-up, opening the driver's door and clambering in, while gesturing for Bear to keep going.

He closes the door before Bear can reply, gunning the engine that coughs, sputters, and fires up with the sort of throaty growl one would expect from a pick-up in a small American town, driven by a guy in blue jeans and checked shirt.

Bear looks around, taking in the other people nearby, so similar in appearance. Blue jeans and checked shirts, blue jeans and t-shirts. Women in denim skirts or floral summer dresses. Men with baseball caps, some in cowboy hats, but they suit this place, only adding to the visual display. Men and women talking and going about their business, waving, and calling out to one another. An entirely natural scene. Organic and normal, but jarring, and displacing at the same time.

'Well, hello there,' a female voice says, making Bear turn to see a deeply tanned woman with big, brown hair and a big smile walking towards him. A floral button-up dress with the top buttons undone, showing a wrinkled mahogany chest.

'Now, don't you be alarmed, sugar,' she reaches his side, pulling a sad face and rubbing his arm. 'This is Discovery, and there ain't nothing to be alarmed about. Y'all just come with me to the diner, and we'll get you a drink. You just went through something called *the circuit*...' she nods at him, talking as though to a child but looking him up and down with a wolfish eye. 'Say, your mentor should be with you?' she plucks the front of his coveralls out, reading the embroidered patch. 'Roshi,' she spits the word with a foul look. 'Damn bitch... You had Roshi, didn't you, honey? Woman? Yay big, talks like a crack-whore on acid?' she asks, rolling her eyes and offering him a manicured and very tanned hand, 'I'm Tammy, it is a pleasure to make your acquaintance.'

'Thank you...'

'Oh my, you're British,' she says with delight, fanning her face as though suddenly flushed, but she stops and frowns, staring harder, 'are you British?'

'Er... I'm not sure...'

'Oh, now, oh yes, you are British, sugar. Damn Roshi, damn bitch... Y'all come with Tammy now, and we'll get you to Allie...'

She loops her arm through his, hip bumping gently, while smiling with very white teeth framed in her very tanned face.

'This is Discovery,' she drawls, waving her free hand about as they walk on. 'This is where we all live and work, but it's not all work. Bear *is* a strange name, now,' she says, glancing sideways at him. 'Damn Roshi. Anyways, y'all will find everything you need here, in our little slice of paradise, and we'll take good care of you, so don't you fret none... They'll go through it all with you in orientation, but I'll be happy as anything to show you around, when your settled that is, say tonight? I could come see you...'

'Er...'

'Aw, just you relax, sugar, and let us take care of everything. Tammy'll get you feeling right on at home, sure as anything. Not that you remember your home, but don't you fret about that...'

She steers him towards a plate glass window, etched with *Discovery Diner* in flowing script, then bustles ahead through the open door to an interior that is exactly how he thinks a diner in small-town America should look, not that he can ever remember seeing one.

Red, cushioned bench seats and chairs against chrome tables, and walls in cream and pale blues. Retro, twee, and clean, with a long counter running down the left side of the interior behind which stand shiny coffee machines and stacks of white, ceramic mugs. The place looks empty, save for one table at the back with three people sitting in silence.

'Oh, now, looky look,' Tammy says in glee, holding his hand in a vice-like grip as though worried he'll run off, 'y'all got some new friends.'

A woman in a white blouse with a black apron tied about her waist walks from the counter carrying a tray and lifting her head in greeting. 'Hey there, I'm Allie,' she says, holding a hand out to Bear with a glance at his embroidered patch and a smile less hungry.

'This is Bear,' Tammy says proudly, presenting her find. 'Roshi's,' she adds darkly, glowering at Allie, 'damn bitch just left him wondering about like a little lost sheep.'

'It's nice to meet you, Bear,' Allie says, shaking his hand. High cheekbones, blue eyes, and blond hair tied back. Late thirties, maybe older, but she looks tired and strained. 'Thank you, Tammy. I can…'

'He's British,' Tammy cuts in, moving closer into his side, 'just the most amazing accent…'

'We've got plenty of Brits here, Tammy,' Allie says through her smile, 'I'm British.'

'Oh, y'all don't sound like Bear here.' Tammy simpers, winking at Bear, 'Say? When did Roshi get back on the circuit?'

'The Old Lady ordered her.' Allie says, cutting in with an air of diplomacy, 'Pete told me.'

'Well, damn that little bitch, but she shouldn't be leaving newbies walking about on their lonesome.'

'Thank you, Tammy,' Allie says, ramping up the diplomacy, 'I'll take him now and…'

'I can stay and help.'

'I'll be fine, but thank you so much,' Allie says firmly. 'Bear, you come with me…' she stops to look at Tammy's hand, still clamped on his. Tammy grins. Allie waits. Bear looks from one to the other.

'Well, now,' Tammy says through a wide, forced smile, finally letting go. 'Be seeing you later, Bear,' she adds in a whispery, deep voice, widening her eyes at him.

'Bye, Tammy,' Allie says, not looking back. She walks him down the empty diner to the table at the back. 'That's Tammy,' she says quietly, 'just say no…and keep saying no.'

'No?' Bear asks.

'No,' Allie says, then pauses in step, 'unless you want to, of course...'

She reaches the table and guides him into the last remaining space on a cushioned bench seat, next to a black woman in blue coveralls opposite two white men, also in blue coveralls.

'Everything will be okay,' Allie says calmly, looking at them each in turn. 'You all look so terrified,' she adds, then frowns lightly at Bear. 'You not so much,' she murmurs. 'Chat, say hi...' she waves a hand at them and walks off as all four track her motion, two of them turning in their seats to watch her going behind the counter and out of sight, before slowly twisting back to face forward.

Silence reigns. A deep, awkward silence of four people in blue coveralls, trying to snatch discrete glances without being seen to be looking while their hands rest on the tabletop inert and stationary.

'Here we go,' Allie says. She lowers a tray on the table, loaded with a full jug of coffee, empty mugs, milk, sugar, and spoons, 'Help yourselves...food won't be too long.'

The arrival of the tray changes the dynamics, bringing a communal thing they can look at and focus on while really using the distraction as an opportunity to glance properly at each other.

Bear studies the man opposite him. White, big-boned, and solid, with an embroidered patch that reads *I am James.*

Bear looks right to see the other two doing the same thing, reading each other's patches, and takes in the man next to James. A white guy with wide eyes, a shocked expression, and *I am Thomas* on his embroidered patch.

Then the awkward bit comes. The bit where James and Thomas need to shift and turn to see each other's patches, doing it with polite nods and turning more than they have to for the ease of the other.

Bear glances at the woman next to him and leans forward to see her patch as she does the same, crumpling her own coverall. Bear smiles and pulls back, then both turn with over-motion to present their chests to the other.

'Bear,' the woman says, reading his patch.

'Zara,' Bear says, reading her patch.

They all shuffle to face forward again as Allie tuts to herself in the kitchen, peering through the gap in the door, 'Gonna be a long day.'

Silence reigns again, until Zara leans forward an inch. 'Smells so nice,' she says, inhaling the aroma. 'I recognise it but…cannot remember a bloody thing…' she speaks in a British accent that Bear recognises to be London without knowing how.

'Did you…' Thomas speaks ou,t then stops, his eyes wide, and his expression shocked. 'Er…the sky into the ocean?' he motions falling with his hand as he speaks.

'Yes,' James says.

'Me too,' Zara says quickly. 'And the cliff…' she motions up with her hand.

Thomas sounds American. James speaks in clear English, but with a trace accent.

'It's called the circuit,' Zara says, making all three look at her, 'my mentor told me…Pete…he's French.'

'Oh,' Thomas says, 'I had a guy called Jacob.'

'Larry,' James says when they look at him.

'Er,' Bear clears his throat, 'Roshi.'

'Roshi?' Zara asks.

'Yes, Roshi.'

'That's a nice name,' Zara says.

'HELP YOURSELF TO THE COFFEE BEFORE IT

GETS COLD,' Allie shouts from the kitchen, still spying on them through the gap.

They look at the tray on the table, at the four mugs, the milk, the sugar, and the full coffee pot.

Zara looks across at Thomas, then over to James, and finally turns to look at Bear, 'Shall I do it?'

'Er,' Bear says, 'sure...'

'Okay, Zara,' James says.

'Thanks,' Thomas says.

Zara tries reaching for the coffee pot, then stands on realising she can't reach, prompting a polite shuffle from Bear, James, and Thomas who all try and help at the same time, getting in each other's way. 'I'll do it,' Zara says. They pull back to watch as she pours the dark liquid into the mugs. 'Milk?' she asks Thomas.

He stares at her, then at the mug, 'I don't know.'

Silence.

'Try it,' Zara says.

'I'll try it,' Thomas says, picking the mug up to sip and wincing at the heat. 'I guess I could try some milk.'

'James?' Zara asks, 'Milk?'

James watches Thomas add milk to his coffee, then taste it again. 'Is it better?' he asks.

'Much better,' Thomas says.

'I'd like milk, please,' James says to Zara.

'I might try some sugar,' Thomas says, eyeing the sugar pot and the spoon poking out of it.

'Yeah?' James asks him as though this is the most daring thing he has ever heard.

'Milk?' Zara asks Bear.

He thinks back to the coffee shop in New York with Roshi. They had lattes which are made with milk. 'Yes, please,' he says, guessing they didn't get taken to the coffee shop in New York.

'What's it like?' James asks Thomas as he sips his coffee, now with milk and sugar.

'Nice,' Thomas says.

'Can I have sugar, please?' James asks Zara, who gives him a look before sliding the sugar pot in front of him.

'You sound British,' Zara says to Bear, 'I think I'm British.'

'Jacob said I'm probably American,' Thomas says.

'What about you?' Zara asks James.

'Larry said he wasn't sure what I am,' James says.

Zara squints at her black coffee, then at James's mug, 'Did you put milk and sugar in? Can I try it?'

'Sure,' Thomas says, offering her his mug.

'Urgh,' she says, pulling a face after taking a sip.

'I've only got milk,' Bear says, offering her his mug.

She takes a sip from his mug, thinks hard, then sips her own, and thinks hard again. 'Milk,' she decides, 'but no sugar.'

She sits down, and the silence, that was before, comes back, but it's heavier now from the absence of the conversation they just had. Seemingly awkward too, and Bear guesses each is locked in their thoughts of the things they faced and did while delving into their souls and hearts as they search for something to cling to, something to say, who they are, and why they are here, to give reason and cause, to give purpose and explanation.

'I like coffee,' James says.

'Me too,' Thomas says.

'It's nice,' Zara adds her voice to the general agreement on coffee.

'Okay,' Allie calls out, carrying another bigger tray from

the kitchen. She slides the tray onto the table, filled with quarter-cut sandwiches in white and brown bread. Four plates stacked up, and a pile of pure white napkins.

'Okay, so these ones are all cheese, nothing strong though, just cheddar. Those are chicken in mayo. Those are just salad, lettuce, tomatoes, cucumber. None of you know what you like or don't like yet, but the best way is to just dive in and find out. One thing, that is very clear in Disco, is that most allergies appear to come from perceptions. We've only got one person here allergic to anything, and that was only after he saw someone else almost die from eating crab in a restaurant in Naples...use a plate, James.'

'Shorry,' he says with a mouthful, grabbing a plate.

'Eat,' Allie says, motioning to the other three, 'your mentors have told you not to question anything and to wait, right?'

Three of them nod, while Bear blinks with a cheese sandwich half in his mouth.

'That's done for a reason, so you're not overwhelmed with information too soon. Everyone here has been through the circuit, the same as you...'

Bear stares at Allie in surprise, then around at the other three, wondering how they and someone like Tammy could learn to kill twenty-one men between the seven-sided room and the French doors, but then he guesses, if they just keep resetting, eventually anyone should be able to get through it. Mind you, Tammy really didn't look that capable.

'You went through it?' Zara asks.

'Yes, I did. Larry and Pete did it the same time as me, actually,' Allie replies.

'What is this place?' Zara asks.

'This is Discovery,' Allie replies.

'I know that... I mean...*where* are we?' Zara asks.

'Which state?' Thomas asks.

'State?' James asks.

'In America, which state?' Thomas asks again.

'Are we in America?' James asks.

'Seriously dude?' Thomas asks, blinking at him.

'What?' James asks.

'We're not in America,' Allie says.

'Australia?' Zara asks.

'We're not in any country,' Allie says.

'We're in a toaster,' Bear mumbles.

'What?' Allie asks.

'Nothing,' he says quickly.

'Why didn't we die?' Thomas asks. 'And this is definitely America,' he adds.

'It's not America,' Allie says, 'and you didn't die because...'

'Why did you say a toaster?' Zara asks, cutting in to look at Bear.

'Okay. This isn't a country or a physical place,' Allie says quickly, 'this is a computer-generated environment...'

Three people stop eating to stare in shock as Bear carries on chewing, earning another look from Allie.

'Our bodies are alive somewhere, but we don't know where. We're part of a very powerful system that has created this town for a specific reason which, you will learn later ...'

'That film,' Thomas says, clicking his fingers.

'Oh, I know it,' Zara says, looking from Thomas to Allie.

'It's not any film,' Allie says.

'What film?' James asks.

'Seriously, dude?' Thomas asks, 'the one with the guy who wakes up in the spaceship thing after eating the green pill.'

'He didn't eat a green pill,' Zara says.

'He did. He had the green pill and woke up in the spaceship.'

'He had the red pill and went down a rabbit hole,' Zara says.

'Rabbit hole?' James asks. 'Did you have a rabbit hole on your circuit?' he looks to Allie with an expression of instant worry, 'Did I miss one?'

'Listen,' Allie says, getting their attention, 'this isn't like any movie...'

'What about that...' Thomas starts to say.

'Or book,' Allie cuts in, 'or comic...or song, or anything, and even if you had seen a movie, book, or comic that was exactly the same, I wouldn't know what it was... Which will come clear later. Do you know what AI means?'

'Er...' James says slowly.

'AI means artificial intelligence,' Allie says, bringing their focus back again, while Bear wonders how much Roshi told him that the others haven't heard yet, an artificial intelligence system has brought you from wherever you are to be in this world. Going through the circuit is the only way to get here. We don't know how the...'

'I didn't like dying,' James says with a heavy sigh, 'hurts.'

'Right, yes, yes, it does,' Allie says, 'we don't know how it all started. Only that the AI manifests as someone we call...'

'The Old Lady,' Bear says.

'The what?' Zara asks.

'Bloody Roshi!' Allie snaps under her breath, 'The AI manifests as someone we call the Old Lady...'

'Have you been here before?' Zara asks Bear.

'No,' Bear replies.

'He hasn't,' Allie says.

'How did he know about the old woman, then?'

'Old Lady,' Allie says, 'he had a different mentor that… Let's just move on. Did you each die?'

'Dying hurts,' James says again.

'Yes, it does, but you reset, right?' Allie asks, 'If you die here in Discovery, you will also reset, *but* let me make this very clear… We do not allow people to die here. If you die and reset, you will be punished, if someone causes you to die, *they* will be punished exactly the same as in the real world. No murders, no suicides, no manslaughter, or death through negligence. All crimes here are investigated and dealt with by the sheriff, and the Old Lady's will – that life here should be as normal as possible – is absolute. Do you all understand?'

Three nods.

'James,' Allie prompts, 'did you understand?'

'Yes, Allie.'

'We have something called *True Death*. It's a random phenomenon that means sometimes people do not reset. They die, and they are dead. We don't know how or why, and we cannot stop it. Do you all understand? James, you need to nod or say yes.'

'What did you mean about a toaster?' Zara asks suddenly, looking at Bear.

'Eh?' he asks.

'Toasters are electrical like computers. Did you know about this?'

'Bloody Roshi,' Allie mutters.

'Toasters aren't computers,' Thomas says.

'They can be,' Zara says, 'some have microprocessors to determine cooking time and…'

'Thank you, Zara,' Allie says firmly, 'we're not in a

toaster... We're probably not in a toaster. No, we're *definitely* not in a toaster.'

'So, this isn't America?' Thomas asks.

'No, Thomas. The town is based on, what the AI determined to be, the best environment to live within that promoted harmony, tranquillity, and co-habitation within a close-knit community.'

Thomas nods, 'But it looks really American.'

'Okay,' Allie says with a forced smile, 'finished eating? I'll show you round.'

Bear looks at the mound of sandwiches left, and the look of panic flitting across James's face at missing out on eating them all.

'I have questions,' Zara announces, 'how old am I? Do you know where I'm from? Am I British? Do we have a choice about this? Can you explain how an AI has enabled us to...'

'In time, Zara,' Allie says, cutting her off as she stands up and motions for them to follow her, 'James? Take one with you if you're still hungry.'

'Okay, Allie.'

'This really looks American,' Thomas says.

'When will my questions be answered?' Zara asks.

'I need a new job,' Allie mumbles. 'Bear,' she pulls him ahead of the others and speaks quietly, 'I'm guessing Roshi told you more than them, but keep that to yourself for now...'

'But...'

'Wow,' Zara says from behind them at the sight of James walking from the table with a plate piled with sandwiches, 'hungry?'

'Want one?' he asks, offering the plate.

They go outside into the picturesque tranquillity of

Main Street, with Allie flipping the closed sign over on the door, before locking it securely.

'You have crime here?' Bear asks.

'We have normal people living normal lives here,' Allie says, ushering them on, 'which means we have all the issues and behaviours normal people bring with them.'

'Sheriffs are American,' Thomas says, suddenly remembering her earlier comment.

'And Scottish,' Allie says.

'But this is American,' he says, looking around, 'this is really American.'

'We're not in America!' Allie says, 'Hardware store is down there. We've got clothes shops, electrical goods stores…like I said and will keep saying, everything here functions as an entirely normal town…'

'An American town.'

'Okay, fine, yes, Thomas. An American town. We use electricity, and we have gas in our homes for our ovens. We have streetlights with bulbs that blow. We have drain covers that lift up when Main Street floods from heavy rain, and yes, we have all four seasons here. The pharmacy is down there…the schoolhouse is…'

'Schoolhouse?' Zara asks, 'For kids?'

'Everything functions as normal, including our reproductive organs, so yes, we make babies, which means we need a schoolhouse.'

'How is that possible?' Zara asks, 'You said we don't have bodies.'

'Zara, I just run the diner and do meet and greet. Sheriff's office is over there. The bars are further down Main Street…' she sets off, giving a running commentary while leading them across the intersection. Four barefooted people in blue coveralls following Allie, while one of them carries a plate of sandwiches.

'Knew it,' Bear says, seeing a police liveried four-wheel-drive vehicle parked outside the sheriff's office.

'Knew what?' Zara asks.

'Nothing,' he says, trying to see if it has a shotgun clipped in the rear window.

'You'll meet Sheriff Lars another time,' Allie says, leading them across the road. 'Hospital,' she says, pointing ahead. 'Yes, we need a hospital,' she adds as Zara draws breath to ask more questions, 'we get bugs, we have births and injuries...'

'How? It's not real. Bacteria doesn't exist in a made-up world. This isn't made up, is it? It's real, isn't it,' Zara insists.

'Did you die?' Allie asks her, coming to a stop on the pavement.

'Well, yes, but...'

'But you came back.'

'Maybe we didn't really die,' Zara says.

'My head came off,' Bear tells her, 'and my wrist bone went through my eye into my brain.'

'Ew, too much information,' Zara says, pulling back with a wince.

'We'll go in to see the doctor,' Allie says, pushing through the door.

'How did your head come off, dude?' Thomas asks in awe.

'This way please,' Allie calls out, shooting Bear a glance, before carrying on down a corridor.

'Morning, Allie,' a woman in a nurse's uniform walks past, smiling in greeting.

'Hi, can you tell me how we die if we don't have bodies?' Zara asks, 'And get pregnant and...'

'Nice to meet you too,' the nurse says with a grin, turning to look back as she walks off.

'No, I mean... Oh, she's gone,' Zara says, 'I just don't get it.'

'Okay, sit down here, and I'll see if the doctor is free,' Allie says, stopping to look at James still carrying the plate of sandwiches, before knocking at a door, and listening for the response. She goes in, closing the door behind her, leaving the four in the corridor sitting on wooden chairs.

'Sandwich?' James asks, looking at Thomas to his side.

'No, thanks... This hospital is American.'

'Zara? Sandwich?' James asks, leaning past Thomas to offer the plate.

'I'm fine, how can you get pregnant or get sick if you don't have a real body? I think she's lying. Do you think she's lying?' she asks Bear.

'Er...'

'Sandwich, Bear?' James asks.

'Thanks,' Bear says, taking one from the pile, while Zara studies the inside of her own wrist.

'I can see veins.'

'Oh,' Bear says, chewing.

'We're in America,' Thomas says.

'If I have veins, then I have a heart, and if I have a heart, then... But I died... Did you say your head came off?'

'Yeah, at the top of the...'

'Zara,' Allie says, walking from the room, 'you can go first.'

'What for?'

'For a preliminary check-up and to be aged.'

'Aged?' Zara asks in alarm.

'To see how old you are,' Allie says.

'Oh. Right. Fine. Maybe this doctor can tell me how I can get pregnant.'

'Have sex?' Bear says, making Thomas snort a laugh and Allie tut.

'I know how...I mean *how*,' Zara says. She walks into the room, closing the door behind her.

'Sandwich, Allie?'

'No, thanks, James,' Allie says, taking Zara's seat next to Bear.

Bear fidgets, shifting position a few times, before plucking the courage up to ask the question, 'Is Roshi here?'

'No.'

Bear nods and looks down the corridor.

'She doesn't spend a lot of time here,' Allie says at length.

'Why not?' Bear asks.

'What about Jacob?' Thomas asks, 'He spends time here?'

'Jacob? Yeah, lots. You'll see him during your training... and Larry,' she adds, looking down at James.

'I like Larry,' James says earnestly.

'Good,' Allie says slowly, nodding at him with a smile.

'But not Roshi?' Bear asks.

'Not Roshi,' Allie says.

'Why not Roshi?'

'I said. She doesn't spend a lot of time here.'

'Why?'

'I just run the diner and do meet and greet, Bear,' she says stiffly, shifting position slightly.

'How did your head come off again?' Thomas asks, leaning forward to look past Allie.

'NEXT!' a female voice calls from the room.

'Go through,' Allie tells Bear.

He moves to the door, knocking once before pushing it open, 'Where's Zara?'

'Out the other door,' a female voice says from inside as Allie motions for him to go in. He steps in and closes the door. Looking around to see a blue material movable screen next to a wide single medical bed set against the wall. Books and mock skeletal models adorn shelves and the sides, and a big wooden desk set to one side.

'Hello?' he asks.

'Have some patience' the doctor says, walking out from behind the screen while pulling a pair of latex gloves on. 'Get it? Patience? Patients?' she laughs as she walks over. Bright red hair, freckles on her nose, and a smile that seems to stretch from ear to ear. Beautiful too. Not just pretty but beautiful. 'Right, let's have a look at you... Name?'

'I'm Bear,' Bear says, looking down at his embroidered patch.

She pulls a face, cocks her head, and squints at him, 'Roshi?'

'Yes.'

'Makes sense. You sound British. Say *how do you do*.'

'What?'

'Say *how do you do*.'

'How do you do?'

'Deffo British,' she says, 'open your mouth... Yep, you've got teeth and a tongue. Aces.'

'Are you Australian?'

'G'day, mate!' she booms while looking in his ear, making him flinch from the volume. 'Strip off.'

'What?'

'Strip off,' she says, nodding at him.

'Er...'

'I need to check you over. Come on, don't be shy...

Behind the screen...what?' she asks when he stands gawping.

'Nothing,' he says, moving past her to get behind the screen. She follows after him, grinning as he grabs the zipper at the front of his coveralls.

'Need a hand?'

'S'fine,' he says, tugging it down.

'Go on, get yer kit off,' she laughs.

He winces, grimaces, and drops the coveralls to cover his groin with his hands, then remembers being in the masquerade room stark naked with everyone laughing at him.

'Nice bod,' the doctor says appreciatively, 'you work out, huh?'

'What?' he says weakly.

'Bad doctor,' she says suddenly. 'Didn't introduce myself. I'm Doctor Lucy. Nice to meet you,' she holds a hand out.

'Er...' he grits his teeth and holds a hand out to shake, trying to cover himself with his other hand.

'I saw your willy,' she says, shaking his hand. 'Oh, stop it. I've seen so many now... Come on, let's have a proper squint at ya... Arms out to the sides,' she prods and pokes, making noises and pulling mock-serious faces. 'Nice and trim fella, nice arse too,' she says, poking one of his cheeks, 'Roshi's a lucky bitch... I had some hairy old guy when I came through. He's dead now. I killed him.'

'What?'

'Joke! Right, let me see your tackle.'

'My tackle?'

'Your plums, mate. Need to do the old cough test,' she comes to his front, reaching down to cup his testicles in her hand. 'Cough...' he coughs. She squeezes gently, moving her thumb and fingers to probe. 'Cough,' he coughs again. She carries on, pursing her lips and looking him in the eye while juggling his bollocks. 'Bit awkward...' she says seriously, 'Say *ar*.'

'Arrrrrrr.'

'Say *do you do extras?*'

'What?'

'Joking,' she lets go to stand back as he covers himself again, 'nice testes though, mate, good and bouncy.'

'What the fuck?'

'Ah, mate, we just met, take me for a drink first. Oh, gee, sorry, I thought you said do you *want a fuck...*'

'I never said...'

'Twenty-five to thirty-five.'

'What is?'

'You are, mate.'

He shakes his head, baffled and lost.

'Your age,' she says, 'twenty-five to thirty-five.'

'That's not very precise.'

'You're not a bloody tree, mate, you don't have rings up your arse I can count.'

'Yeah, but...'

'You got a couple of grey hairs in your head, but your pubes are okay, you got lines round your eyes, but your belly hasn't gone wobbly. Probably more like thirty-five, but you know, could be an old guy that looks younger, or a young guy that...'

'Can I get dressed now?' he interrupts.

'No.'

'Why not?'

'I'm perving,' he grabs his coveralls, yanking them up to pull the zipper over his chest. 'Go out that door,' she says with a laugh as he rushes past. 'Nice arse...'

'Stop it,' he yelps, covering his backside with his hands as he goes out to see Zara sitting on her own in a small waiting area.

'NEXT!'

He scoots over to sit down, crossing his legs and folding his arms.

'You should report her for that,' Zara whispers angrily. 'That was awful.'

'You heard it?' he asks in shock.

'Every word,' she whispers. 'Completely unethical.'

'Wahay! Look at you, big fella,' the voice comes through the door.

'Must be James,' Zara says.

'What's your name?'

'I am James.'

'James,' Bear says.

'We shouldn't be hearing it. What kind of hospital is this? What kind of doctor is she? Do you know what she said when I asked about pregnancy? She said use a Johnny or make him splodge on my belly. That's not funny, Bear.'

'Sorry,' he says, recovering from the snort of laughter that came out of its own accord.

'Get behind that screen and strip off then, big boy.'

They both stare at the door. 'Did she say anything else?' Bear asks quietly.

'No,' Zara says with a huff, 'I said if we're not really real, then how does it work. She said she didn't know.'

'Oh.'

'And I'm twenty to thirty apparently.'

'Oh. I'm probably thirty-five.'

'I heard.'

'HOLY SHIT!' the doctor yells out from inside the

room, making Bear sit up in alarm and Zara stiffen. 'Your wonga is enormous, mate… You're like a human tripod.'

'Jesus,' Zara whispers, shaking her head.

'Be careful when you get your first stiffy, you might faint.'

'Bear,' Zara snaps, 'stop laughing.'

'It's so thick…and long too…like a…like a big, one-eyed snake. Can I take a picture of it?'

'Oh my god, this so awful,' Zara says, covering her face with her hand.

'Is it heavy? Jesus, mate, that's heavy as anything. Now, you go easy if you meet a nice girl, or a bad one, or a bloke, for that matter, but don't let Tammy know you've got that beast tucked down there. Get dressed and off you go…'

The door opens to the doctor staring wide-eyed at Zara and holding her hands out a dozen or so inches apart. 'Did you hear that?' she whispers loudly. 'This guy's willy is huge.'

'This is awful,' Zara snaps as James walks out behind her, still carrying the plate of sandwiches and looking entirely nonplussed at the fuss.

The doctor goes in, closing the door behind her, then wrenching it back open. 'Almost forgot, you're probably twenty-five to thirty-five, James.'

'Thanks, Doc.'

'Huge penis,' she says, closing the door. 'NEXT.'

James sits down and resumes eating, looking about the waiting room with idle curiosity.

'I'm reporting her,' Zara whispers.

'To who?' Bear asks.

'Hi, I'm Doctor Lucy… What's your name?'

'Thomas, ma'am.'

'Ah, mate, nice manners there. Yank, are ya? Last fella

through had the biggest dick I've ever seen... Let's hope you've not got a tiddler, eh?'

'Must be someone in charge,' Zara says.

'The old lady?' Bear asks.

'The old lady,' Zara parrots angrily. 'There is no old lady. This isn't real... I mean...I mean it is real, but it's not the real that Allie was saying...what I mean is...'

'I think I've got it,' Bear says. 'Can I ask a question, how many times did you die in the circuit?'

The door opens with a grinning doctor Lucy winking at James while Thomas scrabbles to get dressed behind her in full view of the others. 'You're all done. Out you go, Tomo.'

'Yes, Ma'am,' he whimpers, scurrying past, while pulling his coveralls up.

'Good manners, that Tomo. Right, use a condom if you have sex, because you can still catch nasties even here. You might get the shits over the next day or two, but that's normal for newbies. Just drink loads of water. Allie?'

'Behind you,' Allie says, walking through the doctor's office.

'All yours...Zara, the grumps, is twenty to thirty, Bear, the fittie, and Trouser snake Jimmy are twenty-five to thirty-five, and me mate Tomo is an old bugger at thirty to forty.'

'Great, thanks,' Allie says.

'I want to report this doctor,' Zara says, pushing up to her feet. 'She groped Bear and was very inappropriate about James's penis.'

'Huge,' Doctor Lucy mouths, staring at Allie, while nodding towards James, and holding her hands out again. 'You wouldn't get the tip in your mouth.'

'That is outrageous,' Zara snaps.

'I'm guessing grumps was a lawyer, see ya!' the doctor

goes in, closing the door as Allie heads wearily across the room to the exit door.

'Lawyer? Was I a lawyer? And why is she calling me grumps?'

'I don't know, Zara. I just run the diner.'

The next stop is the town clerk which is just a short walk from the hospital, albeit at a pace slightly brisker than before, but then, Zara does walk with her arms folded, demanding to know who is in charge, and why she was called grumps, and that she's not grumpy and will probably have a very good sense of humour when she remembers it.

'Town clerk,' Allie says, pushing through the door which chimes melodically from the old-fashioned bell fitted to the top, and once again, Bear feels like he's stepping into a museum or a film-set.

A high fronted, wooden counter fitted with ornate, curved bars on the top to one side, and a grand, wooden desk on the other, with ledgers and books piled up, and the man in the light-coloured suit he saw earlier glancing up as they walk in.

'This is Norman, the clerk,' Allie says. 'Norman, new arrivals. Zara, James, Thomas, and Bear.'

'Bear?' Norman asks, blinking over the top of his spectacles.

'Roshi's.'

'Oh,' Norman says with evident distaste. 'We do not like strange names here, Mr Bear.'

'Er...' Bear says.

'Are you in charge?' Zara asks, detecting the air of authority about the man.

'I am in charge of some things, yes. The smooth fiscal running of the town being one of them.'

'That doctor was awful. Who do I complain to?'

'Doctor Lucy?' he enquires. 'Not me,' he adds abruptly. 'I have enough to do without taking on matters of medical negligence,' he closes the ledger he was writing in and tucks it into the pile before selecting another one as the bell chimes behind them.

'Hey, Allie.'

'Hey, Terry,' Allie says. 'That's Terry, he works in the planning offices,' she walks over to chat quietly, leaving the four alone with Norman.

'First one,' the clerk asks, peering over his glasses to Thomas. 'Name, gender, age, and mentor...'

'I'm er...I'm Thomas, the doc said I was thirty to forty and er...Jacob was my mentor.'

'Gender?'

'Man?' Thomas asks, flapping his hands at the others.

Norman repeats his words to himself while scratching a pen over the paper in his ledger. 'Sign here,' he says, turning the ledger to look expectantly at Thomas.

'What for?' Thomas asks, his eyes back to wide and shocked again.

'First wages. Just put the letter T there...'

'I can spell Thomas,' Thomas says.

'Good for you, but I don't have all day to wait while you practise your new signature, so just put T. Next?'

Zara takes her turn, making a show of reading the ledger, before signing, and stepping back.

'What does it say?' Bear asks as James takes his turn.

'Shorthand. Couldn't read it,' Zara admits.

'Name, gender, age, and mentor?' Norman asks, looking at Bear.

'Bear. Male. Twenty-five to thirty-five. Mentor was Roshi.'

'Roshi,' once again that look of distaste crosses

Norman's face as he curls his tongue around the name. 'Sign B here.'

'What does it say?' Bear asks, seeing the lines of squiggle on the page.

'It is a contract fulfilling the town's obligation to your financial needs. You will receive a weekly payment, to be collected from this bank weekdays, between the hours of 9am and 12 noon, and then from 1pm and 5pm. If you are unable to collect your money, you can sign for a trusted person to collect for you, or alternatively, you can request a deviation of payment from this office after filing form DP1. Would you like to see the full contract?'

'No, it's fine,' Bear says, using a pen for the first time since he can remember but finding his hand knows how to hold the tool and make the shapes required.

'I would,' Zara says. 'I'd like to see the full contract.'

'One will be made available to you,' Norman says without any sign of being irritated by the request as he tears four slips from a duplicated perforated sheet under the page. 'Take these to the bank for your first payments.'

He hands them over in that curt, business-like manner, then goes back to his desk, puts the ledger away, and takes another one out. 'Anything else?' he asks, looking over his glasses when they don't move.

'The bank?' Zara asks.

'You are in the bank,' Norman says slowly, pointing his pen to the counter behind them.

Bear, Zara, and Thomas look to each other, unsure and lost, while James smiles at Norman.

'This way,' Allie calls out, 'go to the counter and see Mavis.'

The four duly file through the small swing door on the half partition wall and cross to the counter together, coming to a stop in front of a woman with greying hair in a woollen cardigan blowing her nose. 'Help you?' she asks somewhat nasally after shoving the tissue up her woolly sleeve.

'That man sent us over,' Bear says.

Mavis leans forward, following his outstretched hand to Norman working at his desk. 'Queue up, please.'

The four turn to see a red roped section with one end marked *queue here.* 'You go first?' Bear asks Zara.

The other three walk around the red rope to stand in a line, while Zara hands her chit over that Mavis inspects and stamps, before handing over a number of banknotes that Zara stares at.

'Bank of Discovery,' she tells the others, walking over to show them the money.

'Excuse me! You have not signed for that money, young lady.'

'Sorry,' she rushes back to sign another slip.

'Next?' Mavis calls out.

They take their turns, waiting quietly while Jen and Allie chat in whispers and chuckle at private jokes in a way that makes them feel even more forlorn and lost in an alien world, apart from James who remains as nonplussed as before.

'Done?' Allie asks with all four clutching banknotes in their hands. 'Great...let's keep going...'

Clothes from *Discovery apparel. Discovery fashions. Discovery for men,* and the day wears on with a blur of strange folk, greeting them either happily or showing complete disinterest, and to the last, they tut, huff, and roll eyes at Bear's name and, even more so, on hearing Roshi was his mentor.

'What's wrong with Roshi?' Bear asks as they traipse back down Main Street loaded with bags.

'What's right with Roshi,' Allie replies under her breath but says no more, unwilling to be drawn into further conversation.

Zara bombards Allie with questions, clearly sceptical, but getting the same increasingly tired and jaded response. *I just run the diner and do meet and greet.* Thomas stays wide-eyed and shocked, and of all of them, only James seems outwardly calm in a staring-round-in-wonder kind of way.

Finally, they walk from the centre down the long intersection road leading out of town, and the stores lining the street give way to houses. Terraced at first, then with spaces between that grow bigger and further set back, with manicured lawns and small white picket fences. Still American. Still tranquil and still jarring.

'What's outside the town?' Bear asks.

'Parks, cemetery, swimming pool, golf course, and forests,' Allie replies. 'Miles and miles of pine forests.'

'Can we leave the town?' Zara asks.

'Sure, but just not yet,' Allie says. 'It's very easy to get lost... Wait until you've settled in for a while first. Up there,' she motions to a junction stretching off uphill. Gardens on both sides behind high wooden fences, and grand houses glimpsed beyond, but the road goes up, twisting and bending with small thickets of trees taking over when the fence line ends.

'You seeing that?' Thomas asks from behind them after a few solid minutes of steady ascent.

The others stop to look through the gap in the trees to the town spread out beneath them.

'Bloody hell,' Zara says, wiping a film of sweat from her head.

The town isn't big at all and rests in a vast clearing,

entirely enclosed by towering trees forming the pine forest. The four roads running north to south and east to west so clear, and the vehicles, moving slowly on them, look like toy cars with stick figure people glimpsed on the sidewalks and crossing the intersection. The roofs of the buildings look normal too, with chimneys here and there, and telephone wires running from one to the other and across the road.

'Nice views from up here,' Allie says, slightly breathless. James exhales noisily, resting his hands on his knees and sweating heavily.

'How are you so fit?' Zara asks. Bear looks around, then realises the question is aimed at him.

'I don't know,' he says honestly.

'Just a bit further,' Allie says, her gaze also resting on Bear. 'Round that bend.'

The bend is long and sweeping, opening out to a view of individual single-story, white-walled buildings with terracotta tiled roofs dotted on a hillside in a tiered fashion with paths and walkways running hither and thither.

'That doesn't get easier,' Allie says, sucking air in from the walk-up. 'Okay, so...if you have a family and work to a decent position, you'll maybe one day get a house down there,' she waves behind her at the town. 'Everyone else lives up here...singles, couples... There's a footpath running at the back down to the town. Comes out at the end of Main Street and, thankfully, is nowhere near as steep as this...but,' she takes another breath and smiles, 'but you needed to see the road up too.'

'Could've just told us,' Zara groans, her bags hanging heavy at her sides. 'Or...we could have walked the footpath, then gone down this one...'

'Quit moaning, grumps,' Allie says.

'What did you say?' Zara snaps as Allie grins and holds her hands up.

'Joke,' she says. 'I'll show you your digs.'

'Digs?' Thomas asks.

'House,' Allie says. 'Accommodation...residence.'

They enter the paved walkways bordered by stone walls, varying in height from low to taller than James. People here, too, that nod and call out, friendly and, seemingly, at ease in their surroundings.

Colours start to show from deckchairs, tables, and seats with striped cushions arranged on small verandas outside each habitat. Curtains hanging from open windows, and music heard playing inside the small houses. Flowers drape and hang down the walls, with ferns and bushes creating more paths and narrow avenues.

'You've got to stay inside your houses during the hours of darkness until your trainers say otherwise... Don't ask, Zara, I just run the diner. James, this is yours... All of you, go in, as they're all the same, really. Front door into a lounge area, sofa, armchair...bedroom through there, single bed, table, wardrobe, and drawers. Bathroom, toilet and shower only. Only the bigger houses get bathtubs... Kitchen is through there. Basic but enough. You've got food to last a few days, after that, you have to buy your own.'

Basic and simple, with the small rooms made crowded by five of them looking around. Everything in shades of beige, cream, white, and greys in a symmetry flows to create a snug, yet clean, and comforting ambience.

'That's it,' Allie says, holding her hand out to James. 'Stay in tonight, rest, eat, relax... You'll be collected tomorrow. Stop by and see me in the diner in a few days.'

They move on, walking a few minutes until they stop for Thomas to stare wide-eyed and shocked at his new home, and a new look of terror crosses his face at the prospect of being alone. 'You'll be fine,' Allie says, rubbing his shoulder. 'Go on, get some sleep.'

Another short distance, and Allie stops to open a door for Zara, 'All yours.'

'What happens if I do go out?'

'You'll be in trouble,' Allie replies. 'Someone will report you to the sheriff who will request you go home, and failing that, you'll be locked in a cell, then fined, and punished.'

'Why?' Zara demands.

'In you go, Zara,' Allie says, motioning for her to go on.

'But...'

'Love,' Allie snaps. 'Everyone here has done the same thing. Just go with it. Relax, sleep... You'll find out more tomorrow.'

'This is bloody awful,' Zara seethes, storming into the house. 'What am I supposed to do all night?'

'I don't know! Hang your new clothes up. Have a shower...'

Zara flinches, clearly not expecting such a sensible reply, 'I'm reporting that doctor...'

'Goodnight, Zara, come and see me in a few days,' Allie says, closing the door.

'This way,' she goes ahead of Bear, leading him through another series of walkways between houses of near-identical structures.

'I'll forget this route,' he says.

'Takes a couple of days,' Allie replies. 'That's yours.'

He looks ahead to a building set next to the treeline marking the edge of the estate. The same as the others, with a small veranda outside the front door.

'Allie,' he says as she pushes the door open.

'I know what you're going to ask, but it's not for me to say.'

'What?' he asks, pausing, before crossing the threshold as though that will prevent her walking off and ending the conversation.

'Roshi,' Allie says simply. 'Go on, get some rest…'

'Everyone seems to hate her.'

'Bear, it's been a long day.'

'And the others don't know about the time travel thing either…'

'Bloody Roshi,' Allie groans, then holds a hand up, silencing him as he goes to continue. 'I'm not getting involved. I run the diner…did you know the meet and greet is part of the diner job? I have to do it. I don't even like doing it. I hate it. I actually hate it…oh, now I feel bad saying that. I don't hate it… It's just hard not to…you know… tell you more. Having said that, Roshi's already told you everything by the looks of it. Get some rest. Stay inside. Come and see me…whatever…you heard it. Goodnight, Bear.'

'Night, Allie,' she walks off, leaving him alone on the veranda outside his new home as the sun dips below the treeline, bringing forth a twilight on a hillside of strange houses in a strange town in a made-up world.

CHAPTER TEN

It's the same as James's house. Small rooms finished in subtly blending shades. A two-seat leather sofa in the lounge with a tiny side table and two wooden chairs against the wall, and as he stares around, so the shadows grow deeper outside, and the standing lamp in the corner of the room blinks on, bathing the room in a soft, yellow glow.

The bed is low and wooden framed, but the sheets are rich cotton and feel starched and new. A single pillow, neither plump nor flat. He dumps the bags and opens the wardrobe to see a full-length mirror on the inside of the door, and steps back with a jolt that makes his heart thud.

Him. Self. His own reflection. He blinks at the weirdness of it, not recognising himself in any capacity. There is no familiarity. Nothing. Dark brown eyes and short, dark blond hair. A slight stubble shows on his cheeks and jaw. No scars, no marks. Lines around his eyes and on his forehead that he crinkles and smooths a few times. Laughter lines when he smiles, and a thicker one that forms at the top of his nose when he scowls. Even teeth, but his nose is a bit too big, and his eyes a little too deep.

'What the fuck…' he flinches again at the sight of himself talking, feeling more jarred than ever, and the surrealness of it all makes him feel weird, like homesick, but for a thing or a place he will never know. He's quite tall by the looks of it and slim too, not bulky like James, and minutes are lost as he looks in his mouth and turns this way and that, like a child gaining awareness of self for the first time.

That thought resonates. Awareness of self. It's like there is a connection there, but he knows his mind is clutching to seek reason and find sense where maybe there is none. This is what it is.

'Bear,' he says his name, the name given to him by Roshi. It feels strange in his mouth. 'Bear.' The sound of it, the feel of it. She called him brave little bear and a hundred other things that sounded so natural when she said them. 'Roshi,' he says to the man in the mirror. Everyone else he's met here has entirely normal names. Maybe it's a thing for Roshi to give fucked up names to the ones she mentors. He wonders if she lives up here on the hill, and where she is right now, then he wonders why everyone tutted, scowled, swore, and looked like they'd accidentally tasted their own shit when they heard her name.

He goes back into the lounge and spots the phone on a shelf. An old-fashioned thing with a cord between the handset and the base which rests on top of a thick, hard-backed pad marked *Discovery Directory*. He snatches it up, flicking it open to see the names of the stores in alphabetical order and names of other places. Planning, recreation, sheriff's office. Further on, he reaches the personal listings that he was hoping to see. First names only. No surnames. He finds Allie and looks across to a seven-digit number, then flicks quickly through to R, and looks down. *Roshi*. His heart skips a beat, and he looks to the number to see the word *removed* printed in its place.

A tut, and he goes to put the pad back, then stops, and works through to the last few pages. Zara. She's in it already. He doesn't hesitate but punches the numbers into the base unit, and hears a click followed by a ring at the other end that goes on for several seconds.

'Hello?' she sounds alarmed and worried.

'Zara, it's Bear...'

'Bear!? Are you okay? I didn't know we had phones.'

'Yeah, I just found it. How's your er...'

'House? It's awful. How's yours?'

'Same, I guess.'

'Did Allie say anything after you left me?'

'Not really. She seemed tired, she said she hated doing meet and greets. Have you eaten anything?'

'You mean Discovery ham and Discovery cheese on Discovery bread with some Discovery coffee?'

He chuckles into the handset, *'Yeah, it is a bit much.'*

'A bit much? I'm surprised the pillows haven't got Discovery embroidered on them...'

He falters for what to say, his mind running too fast to process actual thoughts, *'Er...I just wanted to see if you were okay.'*

'Thanks, Bear,' her voice sounds tired and strained. *'Have you called Thomas or James?'*

'No, just you. Should I?'

'I can do it. Are the numbers in this pad?'

'Yeah, I don't know how they've done it so quickly.'

'The whole thing is weird,' she says as he hears her flicking through the pages of the pad. *'They've got pizza takeaway... Do you think James has seen that yet?'*

'Don't tell him,' Bear says. *'Zara, listen...did your mentor*

say anything about...' he stops at the knock at his door, '*er... someone's knocking.*'

'*You've got a visitor?*'

'*Yeah, hang on...*'

'*I'll call Thomas and James.*'

'*Yeah, okay, bye, Zara...*'

He puts the phone back with a sudden thought that it could be Roshi, and he rushes over with his mouth already forming a smile in expectation of hazel eyes flecked with green as the door knocks again, louder and quicker.

'Hey...oh.'

'Well, hello, neighbour,' Tammy says, grinning widely with a cup of sugar clasped in her tanned hands. 'Need some sugar, sugar?'

'Hi, Tammy,' he says, showing teeth through a forced smile.

'Aw, now y'all look so lonesome and lost,' she says, lowering her head to look up in a way about as bashful as a wolf staring at a lamb. 'Tammy thought she'd come and make sure y'all settling in...'

'I'm fine,' he says as she sweeps through into his lounge. 'Er, like, just got here and...'

'Oh, now I remember these places being new, so dull and boring,' she says with a scowl that quickly slides into a big grin when she rests her eyes on him. 'Now, why don't you make us both a drink, and we can get to know each other a little...oh, my, where are my manners?' she gasps at her own temerity. 'Here you are, all new and lost, and I'm being demanding...'

'I am quite tired actually...'

'I bet you are,' she drawls. 'You rest, and I'll make the drinks...maybe have a shower?' she suggests. 'You know how to use it? I'll be happy to show you where the knobs are...'

He swallows at the overt predation within her gaze. 'Drink! Drink would be lovely.'

She about turns and sways her way into the kitchen as he falters at the door, thinking he should close it but not wanting to seal himself in with her. He does close it, reluctantly and with a last hopeful look around for Roshi smirking in the shadows.

'I was going to bring a bottle of vino, but newbies are banned from the hard stuff,' she says as he walks in. He blanches again when she turns, seeing she's undone another button on the top of her dress to reveal more deeply tanned chest full of lines and wrinkles from over-exposure to the sun.

'No! Er…I mean…yeah, no…er…alcohol.'

'Shame,' she pouts, pulling a sad face, then bends forward opening the fridge door slowly while her tanned breasts dangle within the dress that he refuses to look at. Totally refuses. Denies even. He fell from the sky, he climbed the cliff, he did the path and arrows, he outran the dogs, and fought the men in the seven-sided room.

He looks. It's impossible not to. A tiny twitch of his eyes, and just enough to see the wrinkly mounds, and instantly hating himself and the whole of everything for doing so.

'Oh, my,' she says primly, suddenly pushing the material of her dress in. 'I do apologise to you, showing my assets off without a care in the world… What must you be thinking of me…' she rises with the carton of milk, holding it to her chest.

'So, er…what is it you do in er…here in…um…Discovery, Tammy?'

'Aw, now that's so sweet,' she purrs, finally moving the cold carton away to show one erect nipple pushing through the material of her dress. 'Y'all making small talk with Tammy. but you know we can't chat none about things, what with you being a newbie and all. No, sir. We'll just have to find something else to *discuss*,' the last word comes out slow and deep.

'Argh, er…why…um…so, why's that then?' he says in a voice several octaves higher than usual.

'It's the rules, sugar. But those rules don't prevent us *discussing* other things and *doing* other things…'

'Oh my god…er…listen, I'm really tired…'

'Oh, me too,' she says with a sudden stretch, pushing her chest out even more. 'So darn tired…maybe we should…'

'Fuck no! Haha! I mean…er…so, we can't talk about anything then?'

'No, sir, nothing at all. Maybe Tammy should tuck you up and…'

'Roshi said they do time travel,' he blurts, earning a foul look in response.

'Damn Roshi, she got no right telling you that before you do training.'

'Is it true?'

'Now, sugar, I just said we can't discuss that.'

'What can we discuss? Have you travelled in time? Have you met the old lady? What's she like? Roshi said you all see a lot of wars…' her look darkens, the body language changing as she stops pushing her chest out to stand normally with a hand on her hip.

'She's a whore bitch what Roshi is,' she spits.

'Why does everyone hate her?'

'I ain't telling you nothing, now, I come over here being neighbourly so…' she rallies for another try, forming a sensual pout and sway as she takes a step towards him in the tiny kitchen. 'Y'all seem stressed, maybe you need a rub…'

'Er…we saw the doc!'

'Uh-huh,' Tammy says, moving closer.

'She er…we heard and…'

'Sure honey,' she comes closer, not hiding her actions of reaching up to undo another button.

'James has a huge penis!'

'Say what?'

'Huge,' he smiles weakly, holding his hands out like the doctor did. 'Said it was like that big.'

She blinks at the spread of his hands, looking from one to the other.

'Poor bloke,' Bear says. 'I think he's really er…like…upset and…I just wish I could go and comfort him but…'

She looks from one hand to the other, her head moving left to right. 'Y'all can't go out after dark.'

'No,' he whimpers. 'Poor James.'

'Poor James,' she whispers as her hands drop from undoing the button. 'He really upset?'

'Oh, god yes.'

'Poor lamb.'

'He is a poor lamb.'

'Maybe I should go check'

'Oh, you should. You totally should.'

'But I came all the way over here to see you…'

'S'fine! Poor James,' Bear says, holding his hands still spread up a bit more. 'Doc said she's never seen one so big… I think it hit him hard.'

'You're right. Something like that will upset a man for sure.'

'Called him a human tripod.'

'A what now?'

'Nothing.'

'You're a good friend, Bear, telling me poor James is so upset right now...'

'Poor James.'

'I'll go check on him, being neighbourly and all.'

'Okay.'

'I can come back after and see you if you want?'

'What the fuck? I mean no, no it's cool...I'll get some sleep.'

'What about that other one? The doc say anything about his... Never mind... You take care now, sugar, and Tammy'll see you soon,' she kisses his cheek, pushing her breasts into his body, before walking quickly out across the lounge and through the door, leaving Bear gasping at the speed of her exit.

'What just happened?' he asks the silence of the room, but the silence of the room doesn't impart any wisdom. He moves to close the front door she left open in her rush to find James and feels a rush of guilt at what he just did. Is James a friend? A mate? Will James even mind? He didn't seem the slightest bit bothered with the doctor earlier. Still, it was a shitty thing to do.

He stops in the doorway to stare out at a sky of proper night filled with shining stars and an air that feels warm and sultry. He looks over to the other buildings, seeing lights on inside and hearing music and the sound of laughter that invokes another surge of homesickness and a sudden pressing desire to go out and walk round. Then, he spots a figure in one of the nearby houses staring at him through a window, raising a glass in greeting, and decides, on the balance of things, that being arrested wouldn't be the best start to his new life.

Tea is the nectar of the Gods. That is without doubt. It is not even arguable or worthy of discussion. This conclusion is reached while Bear sips from his newly made mug of Finest Discovery Tea with another murmur of deep satisfaction, and suddenly, everything doesn't feel quite as bad as it did a few minutes ago when he felt desolate and lost. Now it's just a bit shit.

The chore of unpacking his new clothes and putting them away passes quickly, with frequent sips of his new favourite thing to help ease it along.

Into the bathroom, and he brushes his teeth while staring at the weird bloke in the mirror. The shower is decent, the soap is nice, and he washes, rinses, dries, and walks into his bedroom in his new boxers to listen to the crushing silence of nothingness.

More tea.

He tests the sofa. The wooden chairs. Washes up his tea mug, finds the waste bin, and walks back into the bedroom to listen to the crushing silence of nothingness.

He gets into bed, then gets out of bed, turns the light off, and gets back in while around him the strange noises of the night grow magnified and abstract. He won't sleep. There is no way he'll sleep. He's too wired. Too stressed and freaked out, besides, he can't remember ever sleeping before, and sure as shit, he's not going to do it now. Then, as his eyes adjust to the gloomy light, he spots the faint spider web cracks in the plaster on the ceiling above him. Like striations in a beam. He inhales deeply. He is not here. This is not real, and pain is just a suggestion.

What woke him? A noise? There is no noise. The gloom is deeper now, the shadows darker. He pushes the sheets off, straining to listen, then rises to his feet, and moves silently towards the door. The curtained window on his left, the only source of light, and the illumination it gives is a mere lifting of the darkness, but he sees the hand coming from the depth of the shadows, and in the split second it takes to react, to position, to block, to catch the wrist, and turn it to snatch the blade free, he scents the air that is filled with the aura of Roshi and the scent of cherry blossom.

'What's up, buttercup.'

Her whispered voice cuts off as the blade taken from her hand presses lightly at her throat. She lifts her chin in defiance, and even then, even in that depth of darkness with a knife at her neck, he can see the taunt in her eyes and that wry smile.

'Nice undies, I was hoping you'd sleep commando…' He starts lowering the blade, but her hand comes up, pushing it back in place, 'Keep it kinky, honeypot.'

'What the fuck?' he snorts the unwilling laugh as that wry smile spreads to a big grin that shows the whiteness of her teeth.

'I was going to kill you,' she says.

'Were you?'

'I'm an assassin.'

'Is that right?'

'You snore so loud.'

'Do I?' he asks, genuinely surprised.

'Like an actual bear.'

'Why does everyone hate you?'

'Cos I'm shpeshal.'

'What did you do?'

'Zara's pretty,' she says, ignoring his question.

'She is,' he replies, feeling a subtle stiffening in her frame.

'You met the doc yet?'

'Yep.'

'She's pretty too.'

'Very,' he replies assertively, almost spitefully, and her

hand grips harder as she glares unblinking while the tension in her form flows into him.

He starts lowering the knife, but she grips harder, holding it in place. He exerts more strength, but so does she, forcing the blade into her skin, and the flesh peels with a tiny cut that forms a bead of blood that runs dark and fat over the blade. He wrenches back, his strength and speed greater, but with a hint that she is letting him win, toying with him, and the second he wins the blade to cast it aside, so she pushes out, getting her hand to his throat and turning fast to slam him into the wall.

'You're bleeding,' he says.

She gets a finger to the cut, scooping the rivulet of blood up onto the end of her digit that she lifts to take in her mouth.

A grunt, a motion, and her back slams into the wall with his hand on her throat. She tries to strike, but he blocks and grips her wrist, lifting it to hold against the wall above her head while her chest heaves, and her breathing becomes harder, faster, and deeper. Her knee rises, but he twitches to block with his hip. She tries again, but he blocks, and her eyes stay locked on his. Challenging and playful, but her hesitation and nerves show when she swallows and blinks. This isn't The Circuit now, and the tension between them is not born from violence.

She tries for the knee strike once more. He blocks and presses closer, preventing her doing it again, and she wriggles, bucks, and heaves, but he tenses, holding position, sensing and feeling the game underway. A minute of near silence passes, broken only by grunts and the sound of them breathing harder.

'I can get free,' she whispers, daring him to say she can't. Their faces but inches apart. His body trapping her.

'You can't,' he says simply, honestly, adding a smile of his own. 'Why does everyone hate you?'

She blinks, suddenly, flinching as though in pain. 'You're hurting me,' she gasps.

'Fuck that, Roshi…'

'My little bear,' she laughs but blinks nervously, and he detects the tremor in her body, 'I so thought you'd fall for that.'

'Why do they hate you?'

'Wanna see me get free now?'

'You can't.'

'Can.'

'Why does everyone…what are you doing?'

'Getting free,' she says, looking him in the eye as her free hand brushes over his groin again.

'That's not fair,' he whispers tightly.

'What's not fair?' she asks, as her hand passes over his groin once more, then stops to rub.

'You are so fucked up,' he says, then gasps when her hand pushes into his shorts.

'Give in, and I'll stop,' she whispers, her lips rubbing softly over his ear.

'Fuck you,' he whispers, swallowing but standing his ground as her hand starts moving up and down.

'Well, duh…that's why I'm here…unless you just want to cream your pants from a handjob.'

'No…no, I don't.'

'I said I can get free,' she takes his earlobe in her teeth, making him gasp and stiffen.

'Say I've got you,' he grunts, his face turning to kiss her cheek.

'You stubborn shit…' she breathes, turning so their lips brush.

'Say it,' he whispers, barely kissing, almost kissing, so close, so very close. Hearts booming, and bodies trembling with tension and desire, and fear of rejection. A second in time frozen for eternity. Their eyes locked, and a meeting of wills, of energies that refuse to be beaten or cowed.

'You've got me...' she whispers with raw honesty.

Their lips meet, and the thrill surges through them both. The glorious anticipation of the contact now made and rewarded. A gentle kiss. A soft kiss. An expression of emotion shared, then the urge comes back, and they can't get close enough or move fast enough. His hands drop to the hem of her top, pulling it up as they break to let the material go by before pushing back in to kiss again. Her jeans go down. His boxers tugged and shoved. He fumbles at her knickers, but she drives him back across the room to the bed, pushing him down onto the mattress as she steps over to straddle and reaches down to pull the material of her underwear aside before sinking down onto him.

'Oh, my god,' he gasps at the feeling, at the sensation, at the idea of it and, the sheer unbelievable rush of ecstasy inside.

She doesn't take him fully but lowers slowly, her eyes locked on his with that vulnerability showing in the shadows. She breathes harder, lowering to take him in, and pushes her forehead into his. 'It's been a while,' she says quietly.

'Does it hurt?' he asks, his whole world suddenly consumed with abject worry at causing her pain.

'It's fine...just don't thrust.'

'I won't thrust.'

'Good,' she gasps.

'I really want to thrust now you've said it.'

'Don't...not yet...'

'Okay…oh, my god!'

'Are you coming?'

'Fuck! Oh, my god…I can't stop it.'

'It's not even in properly…wow, you're still going…'

'Oh, my god, oh, my god…'

'Jesus…how much semen have you got?'

'Sorry,' he spasms underneath her. 'Kiss would be nice…' he grunts.

…

'I am so sorry,' he murmurs a few seconds later, savouring the press of her lips on his.

'It's fine, my trigger-happy little teapot,' she says between kisses.

'Um…'

'What?' she asks, pulling back a fraction.

'It's all the way in, I think.'

She wriggles and sinks down deeper, then deeper, pushing her groin into his, until the contact is full and absorbed wholly. 'It is now,' she gasps. 'You're still hard. Go again?'

'I'd love to.'

'Yeah?'

'Definitely. If you want to?'

'I'm pushing your penis into my vagina…do you think I want to?'

'Just checking.'

She starts moving slowly as their breathing deepens again, and his hands reach up to cup her cheeks, guiding her down to kiss so gently, so softly.

She moves higher, groaning as she rides him, while he feels the stiffen of her nipples within his mouth. They kiss more, unable to stop kissing, unwilling to stop kissing, and although his new life has been short and filled with terrible, awful pain, this makes every second of it worthwhile.

'You're better than tea,' he tells her between kisses.

She seems to understand the statement, the meaning of it, the intent of his words, and she stops to stare down into his eyes in the grey gloom of the room, searching for something and finding it there, seeing it within him, and she blinks with sudden fear and worry.

'What's wrong?' he asks.

'Nothing,' she says quickly. 'You're better than fighting.'

He seems to understand her statement, the meaning of it, and the intent within her words, and so they move, and they kiss, and so they couple as one in the creation of a thing humanity has ever longed to describe, but which will never be given justice, save for the experience of knowing it.

She orgasms with him inside. Building up from a deep, spreading heat that grows and blooms as she wraps her arms and legs around him, holding him close and closer, but never close enough, and so she spasms in a flow of ecstasy that tighten her muscles around his shaft, making him come with powerful surges that lift her from the bed still on his lap.

They rest and kiss, but they do not speak. They stroke gently, with fingertips dancing over skin that prickles from the sensation.

They rest, and the sweat on their bodies grows cooler to dry, but still they kiss, gently, slowly, sharing and giving.

The heat rises, and the kisses become passionate once more, and so the night passes, until they slump sore and exhausted with minds and hearts willing, but bodies unable to give or take any more, and so they curl into each other, pressed tight, clasped, and enclosed.

'Thank you, my handsome little stallion,' she whispers,

hearing his breathing deepen as sleep calls his mind. 'They can't know this happened…'

'Kay,' he whispers.

She blinks slowly, staring at the window and feeling the second when he passes from awake to asleep, and she snuggles deeper into him while a troubled look shows. 'I need you to believe in me.'

'Always.'

'You crafty shit. I thought you were asleep.'

'I was. Why does everyone hate you?'

'Cos.'

'Cos why?'

'Just cos. Be on my side…'

'You want to swap sides?'

'Twat. I meant…'

'I know what you meant.'

'Not now. When the time comes. When I need you. Be there and stand for me.'

'I don't know what that means.'

'Just swear it.'

'I swear it.'

'No matter what they say.'

'I swear it.'

'Just know I'm not bad.'

'Nothing you say makes any sense to me, Roshi.'

'It doesn't need to yet… Go to sleep, my little tiger…'

He drifts off, and she moves closer into him, feeling his body wrapped around hers, and in the darkness of the night, she brings his fingers to her mouth to kiss and blinks as the tear rolls down her cheek.

CHAPTER ELEVEN

'Damn,' Thomas says slowly, 'this is giving me déjà vu.'
'I keep on getting it,' Zara says. 'Are we in the right place?'

'It said training centre on the door,' Bear says,

'This is a high school gym is what this is, dude,' Thomas says.

Basketball hoops at both ends, and tiered bleachers on one side with concertinaed runners fitted to the ceiling for climbing ropes, and hooped rings to be pulled out, and their boots squeak underfoot as they walk across the shiny wooden floor, full of coloured lines denoting the courts, lines, and markings.

Roshi was gone when Bear woke to the sound of the phone ringing, and a curt male voice telling him to report at the training centre in forty-five minutes in blue coveralls and boots. Zara called a few minutes after, arranging to meet so they could walk down together. He washed, dressed, worshiped at the altar of tea, and felt a dull ache in his testicles while grinning stupidly to himself and inhaling deeply to smell the lingering trace of cherry blossom.

He then got lost in the labyrinth of lanes and paths, until finally, running over to meet Zara and Thomas before setting off to find James, also wandering lost but completely unbothered.

'Guess we wait, huh?' Thomas says, looking to Zara for confirmation.

'Guess so,' she says. 'How was your night?'

'Sucked,' Thomas replies dully. 'Yours?'

'Same,' she says. 'Bear?'

'Er, yeah, you know.'

'What?' Thomas asks.

'Just er...quiet really.'

'Are those scratches?' Zara asks, leaning in to tug his collar down and wince at the red welts on his skin. 'Ooh, looks painful.'

'Fingernails?' Thomas asks.

'Um...got itchy.'

'Itchy?' Thomas asks.

'Stress, maybe,' Zara says.

'Stress,' Bear says quickly, wishing he'd looked in the mirror before he left.

'You don't look stressed,' Thomas says.

'Brave face?' Bear suggests. 'Er...James, how was your night, mate?'

'I ate all my food.'

'What?' Zara snaps. 'All of it?'

He nods, amiable and unfussed. 'I was hungry, but then the lady came over to tell me how the shower works and...'

'What lady?' Zara asks.

'You had a lady come over?' Thomas asks. 'Jesus, dude... I didn't have a lady come over...'

'She was nice,' James says.

'Did you have a lady come over?' Thomas asks Bear.

'No,' he says in a voice too high, then coughs to clear his throat, 'I mean no, of course not...so, a gym, eh?'

'Bear,' Zara says slowly, narrowing her eyes and folding her arms. 'What's going on? You've gone bright red.'

A bang at the end as the doors slam open from an older man with dark, greying hair dressed in black coveralls walking in with a wince. 'Excuse me, I did not mean this dramatic entrance.'

'Pete!' Zara says.

'Bonjour, mademoiselle,' he grins holding his arms out as he strides over to hug her. 'It is good to see you, Zara...ah, Monsieur Thomas, yes?' he pumps Thomas's hand while giving a self-effacing grin. 'And you must be James. You are very big, no?'

'Hello,' James says, dwarfing the guy as they shake hands.

'And you,' Pete says, turning to Bear. 'Monsieur Bear. Roshi's, yes?'

'Yes,' Bear says.

'Sit, sit,' Pete says after shaking Bear's hand. 'All of you, sit, we will talk.'

'Bloody French always get in first,' a voice calls out.

'Jacob!' Thomas exclaims as another man walks in, dressed in the same black coveralls as Pete and looking the same age with receding hair flecked with grey and a heavily lined face.

'Thomas, how are you, old chap?' he shakes hands, smiling warmly. 'Zara, very nice to meet you, and you, James...I'm afraid Larry isn't here, but he'll catch up when he can. You must be Bear? Roshi's, if I'm not mistaken?' distaste shows on his features as he says her name. His voice cultured and as strong as his handshake.

'Sit, sit,' Pete says again, waving at the bleachers. 'Do

not panic or worry at what you see,' he adds, holding his hands out to capture and hold their attention with a comical expression. 'We shall show you wonders you never think is possible,' he trails off into a dramatic whisper.

'I say, old chap,' Jacob says, giving Pete a rehearsed look. 'What say we have a pot of tea before we bedazzle their minds.'

'Tea?' Pete says with a mock scowl. 'I am French, Monsieur. I favour coffee, *s'il vous plait*.'

'Coffee is for heathens,' Jacob says pompously, clapping his hands once. The blink of an eye. The beat of a heart, and the world around them changes, making the four seated newbies lurch to their feet in shock at the new surroundings.

'What the fuck?' Thomas gasps.

'Tea is for civilised folk,' Jacob says with a flourish, spinning around with his arm outstretched to show them the sumptuous surroundings.

A grand restaurant of round tables laid with white lace cloths and covered in silver platters filled with delicate pastries, cakes, and cucumber sandwiches. Men and women dressed in formal suits and dresses, and the ambience holds a muted yet elegant air, with the tea served by immaculate waiters into small china cups balanced on small china saucers.

Bear smiles. James stares at the food. Thomas and Zara blink, swallow and reel in stunned shock.

'No, no, this is too formal,' Pete says in dismay. The blink of an eye, the beat of a heart, and the world around them becomes a loud, rumbustious Parisian street café complete with bustling waiters shouting at each other, and customers talking in loud, animated tones. The air thick with cigarette smoke that mingles with the aroma of coffee and freshly baked breads. 'Yes?' Pete asks, grinning at the four in blue coveralls. 'This is much better, no?'

'I feel sick,' Zara says, bracing her hands on her knees.

'Good god, no,' Jacob says, aghast at the sight. 'A man needs peace and quiet to enjoy his tea.' A clap of his hands, a blink of an eye, and they're back in the posh tea rooms as Thomas reaches out to lean on Zara, both of them blowing air through cheeks. Bear feels it too but nowhere as strong as before.

'No, Monsieur! A man cannot smoke here, he cannot talk or express himself.' Pete claps his hands, taking them instantly back to the Parisian street café, making Zara and James gag and gasp for air, while Jacob's wide-eyed, shocked expression magnifies.

'Good lord, are you deranged?' Jacob booms in disgust. 'I am not drinking foul coffee from a mug washed in the gutter, served by the filthy cigarette stained hands of a drunkard!' Back to the posh tea rooms, and Zara stands up straight, glares around, then vomits on a table, spewing over a platter of pastries while the refined men and women continue drinking tea in their stony silence.

'Zara,' Pete groans, shaking his head while pulling a wallet from his back pocket, and plucking a Bank of Discovery note out that he hands to a grinning Jacob.

'Shit,' Thomas heaves, gags, then copies Zara a second later by emptying his stomach on the legs of a man drinking tea alone at a table. The man doesn't flinch or show reaction.

'It was the same time!' Pete says, trying to snatch his money back.

'Certainly, was not,' Jacob exclaims. 'Zara vomited first by a mile, old chap,' he folds the money to tuck neatly into his top pocket. 'James? Do you feel sick at all? Perhaps, if you wish to vomit, you could do it here before we move on.'

'I'm fine, thank you, Jacob,' James says politely, before bending double to puke between his legs.

'Bear?' Pete asks, giving him a studied look.

'I'm fine,' Bear says. 'Seriously…' he adds at seeing the two men watching him closely.

'Roshi,' Jacob mutters.

'I am so sorry,' Zara says weakly, wiping her mouth with the back of her hand. 'Please let me…' she grabs a napkin and starts smearing her puke across the tablecloth. 'I'm so embarrassed…maybe you could move tables or…'

'Sir, I've vomited on your leg…' Thomas tells the man he puked on who carries on drinking his tea as stiffly as before. 'Sir…'

'Good lord, old chap,' Jacob says, staring in horror at the pile of spew between James's legs. 'How much have you eaten? I rather think we should move on now, Pete.'

A clap, and the world changes to a place that makes Bear smile. A lush, green meadow bordering a pebble shore next to the glittering surface of the lake.

Zara yelps, tumbling forward at losing her balance from still leaning over the table to suddenly having nothing to support her.

'Somewhat dizzying,' Jacob says mildly. 'Take a moment now, chaps, breathe the air and get settled before we move on.'

'You have seen this place before, no?' Pete asks, inclining his head at Bear.

He nods in reply, looking around and remembering yesterday, being on his back with Roshi sitting on his chest.

'Bloody woman,' Jacob says under his breath.

'She is a spirit,' Pete replies.

'She's something.'

'What's going on?' Zara asks, inhaling deeply.

'The more you do the easier it gets,' Jacob says. 'You'll always feel a change or a conscious reset...' he claps his hands, taking them back into the High School gym. 'Feel it,' he says calmly. 'Inside,' he claps again, taking them back to the posh tea rooms, now devoid of puke. 'The more you do, the easier it becomes,' another clap, and back to Paris, and Bear feels it, like Jacob said. A thing inside. Like a lurch of his guts, but somehow the expectation of the change minimises the nauseous reaction.

'Stop,' Zara says, gasping to breathe. A clap, back to the lake. 'Please,' Zara pleads, holding her stomach as Thomas stares down at the ground.

'The more we do,' Pete says, clapping his hands.

James pukes, resting his hands on his knees. Thomas follows a second later while Zara turns away.

Pete move closer to Bear, resting a hand on his shoulder, 'Close your eyes, Monsieur...we go fast now, yes?' Bear closes his eyes. Hearing the clap and feeling the change. 'I place my hands on your ears,' Pete says softly. Bear feels the hands press lightly at first, then harder, reducing his capacity to hear. Sight and hearing now gone. He hears the faint clap and feels the change. Then a change without the clap. The lurch inside. Again. Again, and again, and each time he feels it while Pete holds his head between his hands.

Minutes pass. Maybe more, and they go through dozens, with Bear learning the sensation until Pete suddenly lets go and steps away.

'Open your eyes now.'

Back in the gym, with James sitting on the floor with his head between his knees, but the other two are upright and alert, if somewhat wan looking, but clearly coping better than before.

'This is a good start,' Pete says. 'The more you do...'

'The easier it becomes,' Jacob adds. 'James, are you okay?'

'Feel sick,' James mumbles.

Bear spots the look between Pete and Jacob. A message passed between two people that know each other very well, with intent and meaning loaded into a split second of shared eye contact.

'Pete,' Zara says, drawing a deep breath. 'You said we'd be told what this is.'

'We will, yes, yes,' Pete says easily.

'You done this before, huh?' Thomas asks, looking over at Bear.

'Er...my mentor, I think she did things a bit differently...'

'Okay, okay,' Pete says, getting their attention. 'Allie told you this is a computer-generated world, yes? Everything you see is part of that world, a programme, software, binary code,' the world shifts again back to the posh tea rooms. 'This is a training room... BONJOUR!' he shouts suddenly and loud, making the four in blue coveralls jump, but no one else does. No one else even glances over.

'I'm terribly sorry,' Jacob says, gently laying his hand on the arm of a passing waiter, 'what time is lunch served?' The waiter stays immobile, not answering or even looking at Jacob, but Bear has seen that lack of expression before. In the men who attacked him in the seven-sided room, and the cops, and others that came into the bomb warehouse.

'The quality is perfect, no?' Pete says, walking over to a table. 'Please, move around,' he urges the others, waving his hands while pulling a chair out to sit down. James gets to his feet, and for the first time since meeting him, Bear notices his affable expression is now gone, replaced with one of abject misery. He moves to a chair, grabbing it to pull out and plonks down heavily, while Zara and Thomas look to each other for reassurance, then to Bear.

'We can match anywhere we want,' Jacob explains as the three start moving about the room.

'Match?' Zara asks, bending over to wave her hand in front of a woman eating a cake who pays no heed but munches on.

'Well, yes,' Jacob replies. 'This is a real place, or at least it existed in the real world. We simply copied it, and when I say *we* copied it, I mean we said we wanted it copied and… well, it was done. The people are not real. They look real, they smell and feel real too… Go ahead, touch them… They're not people.'

Thomas and Bear watch Zara reach out slowly, gently brushing her hand on the woman's arm and gaining no reaction. She leans closer, inspecting the woman's features and watching intently as she chews, swallows, and lifts the pastry to her mouth to bite into. She watches the flakes fall, and the way the woman diligently pats her mouth with a napkin to rid any crumbs. 'She's breathing,' Zara says, taking the woman's wrist, 'pulse too… She's real.'

'No,' Pete says from his table, reaching out to take a pastry from the platter near him.

Zara places her hand over the woman's eyes and holds for a few seconds before drawing it away to study the pupil retraction. 'She's real,' she insists.

'There are degrees of realness,' Jacob says, walking over to join Zara. 'She has a heart, she has a nervous system and the same organs we have. She is entirely human,' he plucks the pastry from the woman's hand and flicks it at her face. She simply pats the spot with a napkin but stays otherwise still. 'But she is not human,' he takes her hat off, ruffles her hair, and puts the hat back on. 'She cannot feel, she does not have free will or the capacity to think. She is programmed to react in certain ways for the purposes of this training scenario. This woman existed, yes. We copied her from real life, but *this* woman is not human.'

'Jesus,' Thomas says.

'She is not Jesus either,' Pete says with a mouthful of food.

'There are many things we do not know,' Jacob continues. 'How it works, why it works, how it can be done... The Old Lady, you see, remarkable woman, a remarkable person, but she is not one to offer explanation.'

'Okay,' Zara says, stepping back, 'this is a training room. Training for what?'

'I told you, Jacob,' Pete says, grinning at his friend.

'You did, Peter,' Jacob says, turning to Zara. 'Pete said you are very, er...inquisitive.'

'I said nosy.'

'I was trying to be polite.'

'British are always trying to be polite,' Pete says, glancing at James to see him eating a cucumber sandwich taken from a platter.

'Is it okay to eat now?' he asks, a rabbit caught in headlights.

'Sure,' Pete says kindly, 'eat, James.'

'Training for what?' Zara asks again.

'I'd like to know too,' Thomas says, stepping closer to Zara and even adopting her stance of folded arms.

'Loyal,' Pete says, pointing at Thomas. 'Jacob said you are very loyal, Thomas. Loyalty is a great virtue in our world.'

'What world?' Zara asks pointedly.

'You, though,' Pete says, pointing his pastry at Bear, 'I do not yet know what you are, Monsieur.'

'What world?' Zara snaps.

'Persistence,' Pete grins.

'Irritated, more like. Confused. Angry. Weirded out... and I just threw up.'

'Nags too,' the Frenchman says with a mock grumble.

'Pete!' Zara snaps.

'Okay, okay,' he says quickly, 'we go slow to make it easier.'

'Spit it out,' she insists. 'What? Make what easier?'

'James, you'll need to stand up now,' Jacob says, motioning the big man to come closer. 'Pete? Ready?'

'Oui oui, I am ready,' Pete says, rising from his chair to move closer to everyone else.

'Listen closely to the end,' Jacob says as the world changes.

A grand building stands majestic in front of them. Young adults walk briskly with armfuls of books, while masters in black robes cycle or walk past. A place of learning, a centre of education. A road in front of them running left to right, and they spot the young woman with red hair running from the entrance to the building. She looks happy and full of life. Grinning broadly with her books in her arms. The other students know her and call out. She reaches the road, turning to acknowledge someone, and the impact is brutal when the car smashes into her legs, launching her across the bonnet and into the windscreen. The car brakes sharply, sending her flying across the road and coming to stop in a growing pool of blood with her neck very clearly broken.

Zara gasps at the shock of it. Thomas flinches, turning

his head sharply away, while James sways as though ready to puke again.

It's shocking to Bear too, but not in the same horrified and appalled way, more of a natural instinct to flinch at the sight of a human form suffering such instant trauma in that way. He also recognises the scenario from the example Roshi told him.

'That young lady is a very promising student,' Jacob says while the students and masters scream out in shock as they run towards her body. 'Or rather, she was,' he adds sadly. 'We shall never know her true potential…what she could have achieved…what she could have become.'

'What if?' Pete says gently. 'What if this young lady did not die?'

'Oh my god,' Zara says as the whole scene freezes for a second before everyone starts moving backward in rewind. The corpse animates, sliding across the road and defying gravity to lift up through the air into the front windscreen of the car, then down across the bonnet, and back onto the road, then to walking backwards on the pavement towards the front of the building. Then it pauses again with everything frozen.

'What if?' Pete whispers.

The world comes back to life with the red-haired young woman running down the path, calling out to the people she knows. She reaches the kerb, turning to acknowledge someone when an arm shoots out, stopping her from running out. She turns in alarm, staring into the face of a man with dark greying hair as the car goes past.

'My god…thank you,' she says in alarm.

'You are most welcome,' the charming man holding her arm says in a thick French accent before walking on.

'That's you?' Zara asks, looking at Pete.

The scene changes to the red-haired woman sitting in a big silent room full of people taking exams at desks. Another change to a graduation ceremony, and the same woman shaking hands with an old man on a stage to a round of applause. Another change to the red-haired woman studying in a laboratory, but she's older now, and her eyes have wisdom. Another change to the same woman at a desk surrounded by piles of papers and books. She looks up with an exaggerated lightbulb moment of profound shock.

'She just discovered the cure for a tropical disease that kills over ten million people each year,' Jacob says softly.

Another change to a hospital ward crammed with beds full of malnourished, emaciated people. Africa somewhere. Hot with insects buzzing, and nurses in white with masks over their faces rushing between the beds.

'And six months later...' Jacob says.

The same room but filled with a fraction of the beds. The walls clean, the nurses now without masks, the patients in plaster casts and splints with injuries instead of disease.

'One might think it is impossible to predict the future,' Jacob says quietly.

'But the Old Lady is from the future...where the human species is extinct,' Pete says.

'And she is determined to stop that from happening,' Jacob adds.

'It wasn't one single thing that caused it but many,' Pete says, picking the thread up with a well-rehearsed back and forth between the two men. 'Not one single person but many. All of our lives are entwined...'

'Six degrees of separation,' Zara says quietly.

'Yes,' Pete says. 'Billions of lives all connected. Tens of billions. Hundreds. It is not a thing a human mind can process, but an AI? Oui, an AI can see these things. She picks the threads apart and tells us what to tweak...so, we travel in time in the real world, and we tweak, and we change,' Pete finishes to a slack jawed Zara and Thomas, both stunned to the core.

'Planning offices?' Jacob asks Pete.

'Oui, I think so,' Pete claps his hands, changing the world about them to a small, empty room with a door at either end. 'This is room seven...come,' he walks to one of the doors, turning the handle that squeaks noisily as he swings the door in and steps out into a corridor lined with doors that feeds into a big, open-plan office filled with people. A T junction at the other end with a door marked *Operatives prep room.* They file after him, all of them gathering to look around.

'This is the planning offices,' Jacob explains, walking up the corridor. 'The numbered rooms are where we deploy from Discovery to the real world...' they walk behind him, seeing each door is numbered from seven down to one. 'Each set of operatives work under a handler, they have their own offices along that side, and this, this is the main office...everyone! Can I have your attention please...' he claps his hands, bringing the big open plan office to a sudden, hushed quiet as people working at computer terminals and bent over folders at desks all stop to look over. 'New arrivals,' Jacob calls out. 'Zara, Thomas, James, and Bear...'

Bear hears his name whispered a few times. Roshi's name too, with knowing nods and rolls of eyes.

'Ah, Martha,' Pete says as a tall, austere woman steps from a private office at the rear, 'Martha is the operations manager; she is the boss, yes?'

'Nice to meet you,' Martha says curtly, 'everyone back to work, we're still behind.'

Jacob and Pete lead the four back down to room seven, taking them in one door to cross the room and through the next that takes them into an art deco hotel lobby, sumptuous and retro, with a polished marble floor that Bear once laid on with Roshi on his chest, and he cannot help the grin that spreads when he spots the stunning woman holding the cigarette in the long, black stick. James, Zara, and Thomas blink heavily, the shock still etched on their faces as they look round.

'This is another training construct,' Jacob says. 'Now listen carefully...'

The scenarios play out the same as before, with explanations given by Pete and Jacob as they gently lead Zara, Thomas, and James through the same thing Roshi told Bear, but they go slowly, spelling it out over and again. Explaining the same thing so it sinks in, but Bear finds himself drifting off to think about last night.

'Questions?' Jacob finally asks.

'Er, just a few,' Zara states. 'You're telling me we exist in a computer-generated world while our actual real bodies might or might not be somewhere, but we can go into the *real world* to do *real things* to change time for an AI system to see if it will stop everyone dying. Is that right?'

The two older men exchange a glance, nodding at each other, then back to Zara.

'Yes,' they say together.

'Fuck off!' Zara says in disbelief.

'That don't make any sense,' Thomas says, rubbing his jaw. 'How?'

Pete shrugs, pulling a face in reply.

'There is no how,' Zara says, waving a dismissive hand at both of them. 'It's not possible.'

'Why?' Pete asks.

'Why?' she fires back. 'It defies the laws of...of physics and chemistry, and biology, and...and every law of nature... and the process of organic material...and...and just about everything. Do you think we're idiots? I'm not an idiot.'

'To be perfectly frank,' Jacob says, cutting into the conversation with a hard voice. 'It is not our job to convince you one way or the other.'

A chilling bluntness to his manner robs the venom from Zara's expression, making all of them fall silent as he continues.

Pete sighs heavily. Good cop, bad cop, and he takes his turn. 'You are not children. It is best these things are said straight. The Old Lady says what she wants, the planning office give the jobs to a handler who guides their operatives. I am an operative. Jacob is too, and Larry...' he adds with a nod to James.

'Is Roshi a real-world operative?' Bear asks.

'She is' Jacob says coldly. 'But do not think for one second that you have an affinity to that woman. Roshi holds no allegiance to anyone other than herself.'

'Jacob,' Pete says quietly as though warning him to stop.

'Roshi is reckless and dangerous. She has reluctantly performed her duty in the circuit, and it is highly unlikely, and wholly to yours and everyone else's benefit, that you will ever see he,' he stares hard at Bear, invasively studying for reaction.

Pete sighs again, a master of using body language and verbalised noises to imply mood and emotion, and without uttering a word, he conveys a great sadness at this awful truth.

'Indeed,' Jacob says darkly. 'Pete and I are operatives. As such, we do not have a great deal of time to spare with you, so we will make haste through the remainder of this initial assessment, after which you will be able to complete orientation and find a suitable role within the town.'

'Just,' Zara says, holding a hand up, then rubbing her forehead quickly, 'just slow down a bit?'

'Oh, I am terribly sorry, young lady. Please allow me to slow the world down and all that is in it so you can comprehend the simple facts I have given you...'

'Jesus,' Zara whispers.

'We only just got here, dude,' Thomas says.

'Times are hard. The things we do are becoming increasingly dangerous. We do not have time to molly coddle you. You are here to be assessed. After which you will be assigned a role within the town. Understood? Good. Glad we got that clear.'

'It's not clear,' Zara says, 'it's not clear at all.'

'Great stuff!' Jacob booms. 'Pete?'

'Oui,' the other man says sadly, deeply, rubbing a hand over his jaw as he offers a shrug. He goes to speak, then pauses, thinking of what to say. 'Good luck,' he adds simply, walking off with Jacob.

'Where are you going?' Zara asks.

'Remember,' Pete calls back, turning as he walks to the doors. 'It is not real...it is a test.'

'What is?' Zara asks as the lights go out.

CHAPTER TWELVE

'I can't see...' James whimpers in the darkness.

A scent in the air. A tang. A uniqueness of smell of oil and grease. 'Stage two,' Bear mutters.

The lights come on. Sudden, harsh, and making them all cover their eyes.

'What the fuck?' Zara reels back, lowering her arm to stare around at the huge warehouse. Walls streaked with grime. The floor pitted and broken. 'Bear!' she shouts at seeing him run off.

'I know this...I did it with Roshi,' he reaches the pillar, circumventing to the other side to see the same little girl sat on the floor with wires tied about her body leading to the box on the floor.

'I want to go,' the girl sobs.

'What is it?' Thomas asks, jogging over. 'What the...a kid? She's a kid...'

'It's a bomb,' Bear says, scooting to grip the wires running behind her to the box. He flips the lid, showing them the numbered clips, then pointing at the timer, and frowning at the numbers flashing red.

9:01. 9:00. 8:59.

'Bitch,' he mutters, 'she only gave me five minutes...'

'Hey, sweetie,' Thomas says softly, 'don't cry, it'll be okay...'

'She's not real,' Bear says.

'This is sick,' Zara says. 'Who are these people?'

'She looks damn real to me,' Thomas mutters darkly.

'Like the people in the tea rooms,' Bear says, 'like them... she's not real...there's another dozen in that room down there but...'

'What?' Zara snaps, spinning around to see the door at the far end.

'Down there,' Bear says. 'I had five minutes to disarm both bombs, but it couldn't be done... Even if the wires are pulled out, they still explode. Roshi said it's flawed...like a fake test. The bombs explode when it hits zero, then I reset...'

'Reset?' Zara asks. 'Back to life, you mean?'

'Yeah, like the circuit,' Bear says, looking from her to Thomas, still trying to offer comfort to the child. A gag behind them, a wretch, and they turn to see James, bent double, heaving his guts up once again.

'Okay,' Zara says, putting her hands on her hips to draw a sharp intake of breath. 'Two bombs, right? Show me how they disarm.'

'They don't disarm, but you can get the wires free...the numbers on the lid...see? They match the clips. I think you have to pull the wires out in sequence, but even if we did both, there's nowhere to go...'

'Bear, promise us this isn't real,' Zara says.

'It's not real,' he says honestly. 'I did it with Roshi... They reset each time.'

She looks back to Thomas, seeing him nod, wan and weak, but showing he understands.

'You do that one, Thomas…we'll get through it. Okay?' she says.

'Man, this is some fucked up shit,' Thomas grumbles to himself, dropping to his knees with the box.

'I want my mummy…'

'You're not real…' Thomas tells himself, 'not real…'

Bear and Zara run the length of the room, reaching the door to wrench it back on the squeaking rollers as Pete and Jacob watch from the gantry overhead hidden in the shadows. A look between them that shows Jacob's distaste at Roshi's cheating.

Zara gasps, seeing the dozen children sitting on the filthy, broken floor, all tied with wires leading to another box. A timer on the central pillar.

She runs to the box, flipping the lid to see the wires inside and the numbers, then looks through the open door to Thomas on his knees working on the box with frequent glances up at the timer above his head.

'Let me,' Bear says, taking the box from her hands. 'Tell Thomas to snap them out…there isn't time to unscrew them.'

She runs to Thomas, showing him the way Bear was doing it. 'Like this…snap them out.' She sprints over to James, bent double on the ground, groaning to himself. 'Up,' she grabs his arm, pulling hard. 'James, get up… We need you.'

'Feel sick,' he moans.

'We all do, get up…JAMES, GET UP!'

He rises slowly, ponderously, then yelps as Zara yanks him on, dragging him across the warehouse towards the door.

'How's it going?' Zara asks, pulling James into the room who stares aghast at the children and steps back as though ready to flee in horror.

'Won't make it,' Bear says, glancing up at the timer.

'Will the wires come off?' she asks, moving to the closest child to grip and pull at the wires wrapped around his body.

'Tried it, doesn't work,' Bear replies. 'Have to pull them from the box when they're all free...I never got these out. Just the girl with Thomas...'

She frowns at his back. 'How many times did you die, Bear?'

He shrugs and works on, 'Lost count.'

She blinks at the answer, widening her eyes and snatching a glance to James, now pale, drawn, and trembling from head to toe.

'Doesn't hurt, right?' she asks.

'What? Dying? You know it does.'

'But bombs, right? Quick, yeah?'

'Guess so,' he snaps a wire, checks the sequence, and keeps going. 'Not as bad as the blokes with sticks or that bloody axe...or the knife...or being shot in the guts, or the poisoned arrows or...'

'I, err...' she says slowly, looking again to an even more horrified James. 'I don't think we did the same thing as you, Bear.'

'Done it!' he snaps the final wire free, yanking the clutch from the box. 'Help me...' he shouts, rushing to the nearest child to wrench the wires away.

'James,' Zara says, lifting the child to carry over towards the big man, 'hold him...'

'What? I can't...'

'You have to...TAKE HIM...Tom? How are you doing?'

'TOO MANY...I CAN'T DO IT...'

'Okay,' she thinks fast, looking at the box, at the sticks of explosive, at the kids, at James, at the rooms, the distance, 'we'll reset, right?' Bear! We'll reset, right?'

'Yes.'

'You promise.'

'I promise.'

'Please, no, please, no....' James begs, his legs giving out as he sinks down with the kids to lie crumpled on the ground.

Zara pushes her hands through her hair, her face morphing with abject worry as Bear glances at the timer, shrugs, and stands up to stretch.

'Next time,' he says casually, earning a horrified look from Zara.

'I AIN'T DYING, MAN,' Tom screams.

'Not much choice,' Bear mutters, watching the timer.

Tears spill down Zara's cheeks, and her bottom lip quavers when she looks to Bear, but she forces a brave nod, steeling herself against the surge of fear and panic inside.

'Even if we get the wires from both bombs, they still detonate,' Bear says, watching the timer.

'There'll be a way,' Zara whispers. 'TOM? WE NEED TO MOVE FASTER NEXT TIME.'

'Aw, hell, no,' the American summons courage from the depths of his soul as the timer counts back from ten seconds. He moves to the girl, lowering behind her the way Bear did, shielding her from the bomb with his body as Pete reaches a hand to nudge Jacob, motioning for him to look at Thomas. 'It's okay, sweetie, we'll be okay, sweetie,' he murmurs to the kid, closing his eyes.

0:04. 0:03. 0:02.

A click. A boom. Another click. Another boom, and the

two rooms erupt with scorching fire that sears out, eviscerating everything in its path as three scream, and one waits silently.

Death to life. Three still scream. Still on fire. Still dying. Still feeling the wall of heat engulfing them, melting their skin as their lungs shrivel and burn in their bodies.

'UP,' Bear shouts, on his feet and pulling at Zara's arm. She lurches to her feet, screaming and dancing in panic on the spot. 'Zara...Zara...' he grabs her face, cupping her cheeks, robbing the air from her throat, and bringing her down from panic. 'Reset,' he says calmly, 'We've reset...'

'Reset,' she whispers.

'Reset,' he says, 'We have to move...get Thomas on the first one...okay?'

'Okay,' she gasps, pulling back as Bear runs off for the door. James screams and wails, curled in a ball and trapped in utter terror of what just happened. She grabs at Thomas, working fast to ease his whimpers, wiping the tears from his cheeks. 'We've reset...Tom, we've reset...we've got to move now...'

On the gantry, Jacob exhales slowly as the two older men track Bear running to the door. Another look between them. 'Tea break after this one?' Jacob whispers.

Bear starts work in the second room. On his knees, his hands steady, because this is not new to him. Movement at his side. Zara running down from getting Thomas started on the other bomb, her motion and gait jerky and uncoordinated, but she rushes in, breathing hard, and stares around at the children, at the pillar, and the sticks of explosive, then moves away out of sight of the door, and drops to her knees to puke, gasping for air and wiping the strands of spittle hanging from her mouth.

'You okay?' Bear asks, risking a quick look at her and the timer.

'No,' she whispers, her voice ragged and hoarse. The explosion was awful, the feel of it, the seconds of living that came after the blast when all around her was just heat and fire, and pain. She can't do it again. She won't do it again. She glances back to see James still curled up on the floor, crying hard. A big man he may be, but his fear has rendered him useless.

She moves to the pillar, grasps the sticks, and pulls, feeling a second's worth of resistance before they came away in her hands. 'Magnet,' she says, looking at the back, then at the metal plate on the pillar. A thought. A tight grin. A glint in her eyes.

'Almost done,' Bear says, seeing her form in his peripheral vision.

'I've got an idea,' she says.

'What?'

'Focus on that first,' she says firmly, her hands on her hips, and a weird feeling of being watched that makes her look up and around.

'Done!' Bear calls out, surging to his feet to start pulling the wires free from the box with a look to the closest child and making ready to start untangling him.

'No,' Zara says, rushing to the pillar, 'Get to Thomas, do his box...'

He falters for a second, thinking to argue, then sprints hard over the pitted floor to reach Thomas.

'Can I finish it?'

'Huh? You done the other one?' Thomas asks, handing it over.

'Yep...'

'What the...' Thomas says, getting to his feet at the sight

of Zara running towards him with the explosives and other box in her hands. 'Zara...what the...'

'We'll leave this bomb here and take the kid down to the other room behind the door...'

'Wow,' Thomas says, his mouth dropping open. 'That's really smart.'

'I am smart,' she says bluntly as Pete and Jacob share another glance on the gantry and lean forward to watch closer, 'Get James down there...;

3:58. 3:57. 3:56.

'James, get up dude...come on...' Thomas heaves him up, fighting against the bulk of the bigger man trying to sink back down, 'Get up, man... We've got to get out... Zara, he ain't moving...'

The final wire snaps clear, and Bear yanks the threads from the box, loosening the tangle to tug it free from the child still repeating the same few phrases, and now he's done it a few times, he can see the replay. Like a constant reset happening. The same motions and words in a set order. *Help me. I want to go. I want my mummy.*

He lifts her up into his side and sets off running for the door, sprinting past Zara and Thomas dragging James while Jacob and Pete lean over the railing on the gantry with intense scrutiny of the actions below.

'BEAR,' Zara shouts, turning to see only thirty seconds left on the timer.

Bear ditches the last two children at the side and runs back, seeing James crawling on his knees with his face streaked with tears and snot, and the other two heaving on his arms.

'They won't get James through the door,' Jacob says.

A burst of strength, an application of speed, and James starts moving faster from Bear wrenching him up from behind and driving hard knee strikes into the back of his legs.

Pete grips the rail tighter, his knuckles turning white while watching intently as Jacob glances at the timer, ten seconds, nine seconds.

They surge through, and Bear drops back to grab the handle and pull the heavy thing over the squeaking rollers, leaving Thomas and Zara to drag James bodily over the ground, both of them grunting and crying out from the exertion needed.

0:05. 0:04. 0:03.

The door slams, and Bear runs with everything he has to reach the others, diving through the air to cover their forms with his own body as the bombs in the other room detonate with two solid, percussive whumps that shake the walls and make the ground heave. The door rattles in the frame. The air becomes charged, but it holds, the door holds, deflecting the intense searing heat and raging furnace from getting through.

'Yes!' Pete says, clenching his fist with a look of victory, impervious to the raging fire broiling just metres below them.

'Flawed test,' Jacob announces, folding his arms, 'Roshi interfered.'

'Ah, this was good, they did good,' Pete says, gesturing towards the door hidden in the fires.

'Flawed,' Jacob repeats, 'They had an advantage.'

'Zara is smart, she would have worked it out.'

'We can hypothesise to our hearts content, but the fact remains that Roshi interfered,' he claps his hands, instantly killing the flames rolling beneath them that suck back and away as though simply removed from existence, leaving the room unmarked.

'Then we go on,' Pete says, waving a hand.

'We were going for a tea break,' Jacob says with a slight blanch at the concept of missing a refreshment break.

'No, we go on,' Pete says.

'Did it work?' Thomas asks, his voice muffled from being buried underneath Bear and Zara. He pokes his head up as the others turn to look. 'We did it…' he gasps, 'Dude… we did it…'

'Bloody hell,' Zara says, rolling free to sit up and look over at the closed door. 'I really didn't think that would work. What's next?' she asks Bear.

'I don't know. I never got this far.'

'The freaky-ass robot kids are gone,' Thomas says, looking around, 'This place is so messed up…'

'Understatement,' Zara mutters.

'You were smart, Zara,' he says earnestly.

'Thanks. You both did well…apart from you, James. You need to stop eating. You weigh too much…'

A squeak brings them to silence. A noise of a heavy door moving an inch on old rollers. Then it slams back hard, making Zara and Thomas flinch from the noise as a black-clad figure stands silently in the frame.

'A cop?' Thomas asks, glancing at Zara.

'Oh, shit,' Bear launches up, vaulting to his feet as the cop charges in, drawing his baton as he moves.

'BEAR!' Zara shouts. 'What you are doing?'

'MOVE BACK,' Bear shouts, running to intercept as the cop flicks his wrist, extending the baton that he pulls back, readying to strike.

'He's a cop,' Thomas says quickly, pushing to his feet, 'Bear, get back, man…holy shit!'

A sickening crunch of bone as Bear breaks his arm, then

snaps his neck with a noise like a dry twig, and the cop falls dead, with his head at an unnatural angle.

'What did you do,' Zara whispers, 'Bear…what did you do?'

'He's not a policeman,' Bear says, picking the baton up, 'It's one of them…the robot things…'

'Bloody Roshi,' Jacob mutters, waving his hand to create another two uniformed cops.

'You killed him, dude,' Thomas whispers.

'Well, yeah, those sticks really hurt…'

'But…dude, you killed him…'

'They killed me loads of times… Well, not the cops, but the men in the blue did…and…'

'What men in blue?' Thomas asks.

'Bear did a different circuit to us,' Zara says, unable to take her eyes off the dead man at Bear's feet.

'What?' Thomas asks. 'What circuit did he do?'

'LOOK OUT!' Zara screams as two more cops run through the door, both with batons held ready to strike.

Bear moves with a blur of motion. His instincts sharp from having done the same thing over and over through so many deaths. He goes low, feinting left, then darting right to slam his baton into the throat of one, making it drop with a gargle to writhe on the ground. The other spins into him, lashing out with vicious strikes that Bear blocks with his own baton, dancing back three steps before moving in with a knee to his groin, then a strike down to the back of the skull, and he clears back, creating distance while the two cops squirm in pain on the ground.

'Bitch,' Jacob snaps, waving his hand to create four more uniformed cops that start running the second they appear.

'Man, we're gonna be in trouble… You don't hurt cops,'

Thomas says, instantly back to fretting, 'Even pretend, freaky-ass robot cops…'

'How did you do that?' Zara asks, stunned to the core at what she just saw. Not just the brutal explosion of violence, but the speed of Bear. The way he moves, the fluidity of him, and the calmness exuding as he did it.

'Er…just kinda learnt, really,' Bear replies.

Zara leans over to look past Bear at the open door, and four more cops running through the other warehouse. 'Er… so…' she waves at the door, wincing politely, 'There's some more?'

'More?' Bear asks, turning to face the door.

'More,' she says as the four cops run in.

'Fuck, dude,' Thomas says. 'Fuck, dude…' he says again at the speed of Bear charging in to attack them head on. 'Fuck, dude,' he says when one falls dead with the point of a baton stuck through his eye.

'Ooh,' Zara winces when another one falls with a broken neck. 'Ew,' she flinches at the next bone snapping from Bear ramming his knee into the back of an elbow.

'Fuck, dude,' Thomas says as Bear throws the third cop into the fourth cop, then runs to attack them both.

'Ooh, that one's getting up,' Zara yells as a cop starts pushing to his feet, 'Bear…him…that one…oh, yep, he's dead now…anything we can do at all?'

'I'm fine,' Bear grunts.

'Sure?' she asks in the abject surrealness.

'My god,' Pete says from the gantry, as shocked as Zara and Thomas. 'What did Roshi do to him?' he asks as Jacob waves a hand to create another eight men in blue coveralls, each holding the bigger fighting sticks as they sprint the length of the warehouse towards the door.

Zara flinches, counting quickly, 'Bear? Can you do eight?'

'I can do eight,' Bear says.

'You can do eight?' Thomas asks.

'Yep,' Bear says, running to the doorway, 'Didn't you do this?'

'Do what, precisely?' Zara asks.

'These men in the Hexa...hepta...the room with seven sides?'

'Heptagon,' Zara says, her hands still on her hips while she holds conversation with a man fighting eight others, 'And, err, no, strangely enough. I had to go through a big bucket of keys to find the right one to unlock a door while it got really hot.'

'Same,' Thomas says.

'What?' Bear snaps, turning to glare for a second with three dead men in blue coveralls at his feet, 'Bitch...'

'Bitch,' Jacob growls on the gantry.

'She is a bitch,' Pete laughs.

'Who's a bitch?' Thomas asks, flinching and wincing at the mass slaughter taking place just a few feet away.

'Roshi,' Bear shouts.

'Damn, Roshi,' Jacob mutters.

'When did you die?' Bear asks, lashing out to fend two off, then grabbing a wrist to turn and snap while kicking into the side of a knee.

'At the beginning,' Zara says, sharing a look with Thomas.

'The parachute right,' Thomas says.

'Yeah,' Zara says.

'Parachute? Are you taking the piss?' Bears asks, snapping a neck.

'I woke up falling from the sky with Pete, obviously, I

didn't know he was Pete then...Just some guy screaming at me to pull the cord,' Zara says.

'You swim for the boat?' Thomas asks her.

'Yep, went to the cliff, used the rope to reach the top, and went down the path,' Zara says.

'Rope?' Bear asks. A crunch. A grunt. A snap. A body falls. A gargle, another snap, and Bear comes back to the doorway, breathing hard and holding a fighting stick in each hand, 'What bloody rope?'

'What?' Zara asks, looking completely confused. 'Did you have rope?' she asks Thomas.

'Sure did. Ain't no way up that cliff without rope.'

'Fucking bitch,' Bear mutters, shaking his head.

'Fucking bitch,' Jacob mutters, shaking his head while Pete wipes tears of laughter rolling down his cheeks.

'How did you get to the cliff?' Bear asks with a sudden sinking feeling.

'We just said...in the goddam boat,' Thomas says. 'How else we gonna get there? Swim?'

'I'll fucking kill her...again. I'll kill her again...what about the lightning?'

'What?' they both ask at the same time.

'Oh, my god,' Bear says. 'The path? You run down it but don't get anywhere while the...the...one you killed comes back to life and...why are you looking at me like that? Poisoned arrows? Dogs? A fucking twat in a red jacket with a gun in a room full of idiots in masks...'

'This is beyond reckless,' Jacob seethes.

'It's too much,' Pete says, bent double from laughing.

'Oh, I had the people in the masks,' Zara says.

'They were all laughing,' Thomas says.

'Yeah, at being naked, right?' Bear asks.

A howl of laughter from somewhere high and far away makes them turn to look.

'Naked?' Zara asks.

'Dude, were you naked?' Thomas asks.

'Were you not naked?' Bear asks.

'I wasn't naked,' Zara says.

'Me neither, man,' Thomas adds.

'That is unacceptable,' Jacob snaps.

'She made him...he...' Pete gasps for air, clutching his stomach.

'I was naked,' Bear says.

'Wow,' Zara says.

'Dude,' Thomas says.

'Naked,' Pete sputters, sinking to a knee from laughing so hard, 'He was naked...'

'How many times did you die, Bear?' Thomas asks quietly.

'I don't know,' Bear says with a shrug. 'Few hundred?' his head cocks over as a frown shows while he lifts a fighting stick to point behind them. 'There's a door.'

'Door?' Zara asks, spinning around to see a single plain wooden door now in the far wall, her head spinning from her mind trying to process too many things at once, 'Did you say a few hundred?'

'At least,' Bear says.

'Door?' Jacob asks in alarm from the gantry.

'Oui,' Pete says, wiping the tears from his cheeks and still chuckling, 'Naked...this is too good.'

'Why is the door there?' Jacob asks.

'They have passed stage two, no? They can go on.'

'No,' Jacob says, waving a hand, 'Absolutely not.'

'The door's gone,' Thomas points out at the sight of the solid wall.

'You are not the only one that can wave a hand, Monsieur,' Pete says, gesturing at the air.

'Sooo,' Zara says, looking from Bear to the door that keeps popping in and out of existence.

'That is operative training,' Jacob whispers angrily, 'They are not operatives...'

'They have passed stage two... They can go on.'

'Roshi needs to learn not to meddle,' Jacob asserts, 'These tests do not count...'

'It is not our job to punish Roshi,' Pete fires back as they wave at the air, making the door exist, then not exist. 'Ah, you leave me no choice,' the Frenchman adds, delving a hand into his pocket to pull out a shiny coin, 'Heads or tails?'

'Good lord, man! We are not deciding on the flip of a...' Pete lifts an eyebrow, giving his old friend a knowing look. Jacob narrows his eyes, firming his resolve, 'Fine! Heads.'

Pete grins and flicks it up to spin over and over before slamming it down onto the back of his hand as Jacob leans in. 'Tails!' Pete announces happily as Jacob tuts and huffs again.

'GO THROUGH THE DOOR,' Pete shouts.

'Not James, though,' Jacob says stiffly, 'He's clearly not suitable...LEAVE JAMES WHERE HE IS...'

A pause, a hesitancy. Bodies everywhere. Dead and broken. Zara exhales slowly, lifting her eyebrows, confused as hell, jarred and lost, but looking at Bear and seeing a strange quiet calm about him that in no way suggests he just killed over a dozen men with his bare hands. She should be terrified of him, of what she just saw, but it seems to fit this place, whatever this place is. She died twice in the circuit. Once on the first drop. She was screaming and panicking too much to pull the cord and died on impact. The second time she pulled it too late and broke both her legs, then drowned. Those were awful experiences, deeply terrifying, but to do it a *few hundred times* is beyond anything she can comprehend. 'I guess we go through then,' she says, looking from Bear to Thomas.

'Okay,' Bear says amiably.

'Sure,' Thomas whispers, 'Why not...'

CHAPTER THIRTEEN

'Curiouser and curiouser, cried Alice,' Zara mutters, staring around with a look of mild distaste at the small room laid with bare floorboards. The walls scuffed and marked, with a single grimy, opaque window. A scarred and battered table propped against the wall on which rests a thin paper folder.

'What's that from?' Thomas asks.

'Alice in Wonderland...'

'How do you remember that?' he asks, 'I don't remember anything.'

'Context.'

'Context?' he asks, watching Bear close the door behind them, both men blinking and looking at each other when it simply ceases to exist.

'You need context to remember,' Zara says, 'like in the diner when Allie told us what Discovery is, and you remembered that movie with the pills. You had context.'

'Oh,' he says, 'context.'

'Window,' Zara says, pointing at the window, 'What does that make you think of?'

'Curtains?' he says after a second.

'Or,' she says slowly, 'a computer operating system... Windows? Anyway, I suppose we've got to read that folder. It's filthy in here...stinks too...and that last place was grim. You'd think they'd clean up a bit. Right...what have we got here?' She goes quiet, picking the single sheet of paper out to turn and then looks back in the folder, 'Just one sheet... shall I read it out? Yes?'

'You should read it out,' Bear says.

'Totally, read it out,' Thomas says, the pair earning a quick look from Zara before she focusses back on the sheet and clears her throat.

'*Operatives Scenario Training*...that's capitalised at the top...'

'Ninja!' Thomas blurts.

'What is?' Zara asks, looking over the top of the sheet.

'Bear...with the,' he says, making small karate chops with his hands, 'Out there...ninja...context?'

'Oh,' Zara says, 'Right. Got it.'

'Just popped in my head,' Thomas says, looking from her to Bear.

'No, it's...er...great stuff,' she says, 'shall I read this? I'll read this...*Operatives Scenario Training*... Jacob said it takes years to become an operative? Why are *we* doing this?'

'Taster session?' Thomas suggests as Bear nods in agreement.

'Good thinking,' Zara says, 'Anyway...I'll read it out... *Operatives must be able to respond quickly, with limited information, and use their wits to achieve the objective. Your orders: Frank Delaney must not meet Gordon Berkowitz for lunch at 12:30 at the German Deli on Twenty-Eighth and Seventh...return here on completion.*'

'Okay,' Thomas says, 'And?'

'That's it,' she says, 'Seems simple enough. What's the time now?'

'Er,' Thomas checks his wrists, while Bear looks around at the bare walls.

'No clock,' Zara says, 'well, there's only one door out, so it seems obvious to me. Shall we? Bear, you go first.'

'What?' he asks.

'Might be a trap or something...'

'Right,' he says.

'Well. You know. You have already died a few hundred times...'

'Oh, right, yes, of course... I'll go first then.'

Another simple wooden door with a round twist knob that squeaks faintly when he turns it. He can even feel the grind of the latch pulling back and the point when the door swings free on the hinges that gives way to an alley strewn with litter, newspapers, cans, and tins, split bags of rubbish and rotten food, all giving a weirdly sweet, foul stench. A high brick wall topped with rusting coils of razor wire on the right, and on the left, he watches yellow cabs driving by on the main road full of people and noise.

'How's it looking?' Zara asks from the room.

'Fine. I think we're in New York,' Bear says, pointing a fighting stick down the alley towards the road, 'Yellow taxis.'

'Cali has yellow cabs,' Thomas says, having stepped out to look down at the road.

'Cali?' Zara asks.

'Wow, dude,' Thomas mumbles, shaking his head, 'California...I didn't know I knew that...'

'I told you,' Zara tells him, 'Context.'

'Early nineteen-hundreds, a car salesman had too many cars left, so he painted them yellow to stand out and started a taxi company...' Thomas says, his eyes widening as he speaks, 'but yellow cabs have been in use for years before that…and there was a study that determined yellow was the colour that stood out the most…holy shit! I know stuff…'

They reach the busy, wide road packed with traffic in a view that makes Bear think of the few steps he took with Roshi after visiting the coffee shop. He wasn't in a fit state to pay attention then, but it feels the same, the same vibe and ambience. High rise buildings on both sides, and it's hot and close. Summer in the city, and the back of his neck feels dirty and gritty. Deja vu passes through, jarring his mind once more.

'Twenty-Eighth and Seventh,' Zara says, staring around as a steady flow of people walk by. All of them so human, so normal, so individually massed in the way of city folk. Everything so real, so utterly detailed and flawed with the imperfections that make up life.

'It's a grid system, isn't it? Thomas?' Zara asks.

'Huh?'

'The roads, aren't they a grid system?'

'Er, yeah, the numbers are on the intersections.'

'You mean the junctions? Where the roads meet?'

'Yeah, intersections,' he says.

'Okay,' she bites her bottom lip, staring left, then right to work out which is closest, 'This way.'

She sets off at a brisk pace, striding confidently along, in blue coveralls and black boots, with Bear and Thomas jogging to catch up.

'There are no signs,' she states on reaching the junction, giving Thomas a look that conveys this is his responsibility.

'Why are looking at me?' he asks.

'You're American,' she says. 'Excuse me…' she calls out to a man passing by, 'what road is this?'

The man replies, talking fast and loud in a language none of them know.

'Hey, buddy,' Thomas says, stepping towards another man, 'what road we on?'

'Fifth.'

'Fifth Avenue?'

'No, fifth fucking city, you dumbass,' the man shouts.

'I think we're on Fifth Avenue,' Thomas says.

'What about the side streets? Which one is that? Which way do they go?'

'I don't know,' Thomas says at the onslaught of questions from Zara.

'Right, we'll keep going then.'

She strides across an intersection as the other two run after her, dodging and weaving around pedestrians, street vendors, and people carrying goods in from trucks and vans. Sirens fill the air as a small flotilla of police cars go screaming by.

'Twenty,' Zara says, reaching the next junction, 'so, this is Fifth and Twenty?'

'Yeah,' Thomas says, 'we need Seventh and Twenty-Eight...'

'We've got fifteen minutes,' Bear adds, nodding towards the shop window behind them displaying clocks and watches, all showing the time at 12:15.

They push on to the next junction, then curse and about turn on realising it's Nineteenth street. Then they start jogging, going past Twenty and Twenty-first. The crowds and intersections slow them down. Making them veer and weave as Zara and Thomas start breathing harder, their legs becoming heavy with sweat beading on their faces.

'Down there,' Bear says, pointing ahead to Twenty-

Eighth street. They take the junction at speed, with cars sounding horns, and drivers leaning from windows to yell angrily.

'Shit,' Zara gasps, coming to a hard stop to about turn, 'Other way…this is Fourth Avenue.'

Back across the junction to a chorus of honks and yells. Running faster now, with glimpses of clocks in shop windows.

'There,' Bear says, spotting the colours of the German flag painted on the signboard of the delicatessen window opposite them on a section of street that looks strangely empty of people, save for one bulky man in an ill-fitting, grey suit walking towards the deli.

'FRANK!' Zara shouts, making the guy start and look round, 'Are you Frank?'

'Who are you?' the man asks in a thick New York accent, scowling at three sweaty people in blue coveralls running across the road at him.

'You can't go in there,' Zara says between ragged breaths, pointing at the deli behind him.

'Who the hell are you? What the hell is this?' he backs away with a glance at the stick held in Bear's hand, 'Fuck off before I call the cops…'

'No, no,' Zara says, reaching for his arm.

'GET THE FUCK OFF ME.'

'You're not real,' Zara tells him. 'You're a robot thing in this…this messed up construct toaster, bloody whatever… I'm so hot,' she adds, fanning her face while nodding at him.

'What the fuck is wrong with you? Get the fuck away from me. Fucking crazy…you're fucking loopy…' he yanks a phone from a pocket, flipping it open, 'Callin' the goddam cops…'

Across the road, at a table behind the plate glass

window of the diner, Pete winces while Jacob gives a smug grin. 'Not so good now, are they, old chap,' he says with obvious relish.

'Is first time,' Pete says.

'Rather looks like he is telephoning the police to me,' Jacob says.

'Do not phone the police,' Zara snaps, pointing at Frank.

'You're fucking crazy, lady...' Frank says, backing into the wall of the deli as he thumbs three numbers on his keypad.

'We've passed, right?' Zara asks, 'What now? Where's Pete and Jacob?'

'GET ME THE DAMN COPS,' Frank bellows.

'Shit,' Thomas feels the situation worsening and scans the street and the windows, spotting a hygiene certificate giving a rating of the premises stuck on the inside of the door.

'City Health Department,' he says quickly, glancing from the certificate to Frank. 'Gordon called us...Mr Berkowitz, right? You're meeting him here? He found a rat in his food...'

'What?' Frank asks, pulling the phone an inch from his ear.

'Rushed him to hospital,' Thomas says. 'For er...for eating the dead rat...burger...thing...he's sick man, really sick. We're here to close the joint down. Goddam disgrace. Goddam rats in burgers, man,' he adds, glowering at Zara and Bear.

'Very disgusting,' Zara says, clearing her throat.

'Don't waste police time,' Thomas says, nodding at Frank's phone, 'We've got this now. Get down to see Gordon. He's not looking good...'

'What?' Frank gasps.

'He's gonna die, man,' Thomas says urgently, 'Rat poisoning. The dead rat had eaten rat poison… HE'S DYING, MAN!'

'Shit, Gordon?' Frank asks, closing the phone.

'We need to get in there,' Thomas says deeply with a steely eyed look at the deli. 'Goddam rat burgers…not on my watch. Get to Gordon, Frank. You have a nice day now.'

'Poor Gordon…' Frank whimpers, rushing off to hail a cab.

'Ah,' Pete says, watching Frank rush off down the street. 'Thomas, yes? That was good thinking.'

'That was luck and nothing more,' Jacob replies stiffly, 'and the first one is hardly what you'd call testing, by any degree.'

'This is an interesting day, is it not, my old friend?'

'It's something alright…'

'Oh, my god,' Zara says quietly, staring after Frank, 'That was so good, Tom.'

'Brilliant, mate,' Bear says, grinning at him.

'I saw the health certificate,' Thomas says, 'on the door… Context, right?' He bursts out laughing, shaking his head and bending over to rest his hands on his knees, 'I can't believe that worked.'

'I think I was just scaring him,' Zara says with a rueful look.

'You think?' Bear asks.

'You're a robot in a toaster,' Thomas says, bursting out laughing again.

'I never said it like that,' she says pointedly.

'You did,' Bear says.

'I bloody did not. Anyway, when you've finished mocking me, perhaps, we can go back.'

Pete sighs, sitting back in his chair to sip from his mug of coffee. 'What's next?' he asks, watching Jacob rifling through sheets of papers as the noise around them increases sharply from a waitress striding through with a birthday cake held in both hands, set with candles flaming on top. A sudden chorus of *Happy Birthday to you* from the staff ripples around, with patrons and families joining in. A young boy in the next booth claps his hands in glee, standing on the chair to watch the cake coming towards his table.

Pete looks around, smiling at the view, then notices Jacob saying something, and leans closer. 'I cannot hear you,' Pete says, motioning at his ear.

Jacob scowls and tries again, talking louder, but more voices join in the singing, drowning him out, while Pete laughs in pleasure at his irritation.

'ENOUGH!' Jacob snaps. Like a mute button pressed on a television, and instant silence is given, with people going on about their business without a single noise created.

'You are getting old and grumpy,' Pete chides.

'Couldn't hear myself think,' Jacob grumbles, 'I said how about we do the zoo next?'

'The zoo?' Pete asks. 'That is not the next one. The zoo is later, you know this, Jacob,' he leans forward again, resting his elbows on the table to fix his old friend with a studied look, 'It is not fair to punish them for Roshi's infractions.'

'Fair enough,' Jacob says, sitting back and holding his hands out, 'You're probably right, they wouldn't cope with it this soon. We'll do Mrs Jones.'

'I never said they wouldn't cope,' Pete says, pushing up from the table and leaning over the low partition wall to push a finger through the frosting on the birthday cake being served in absolute silence. 'Do you want a slice?' he asks with mouthful.

'No, I do not want a bloody slice,' Jacob says with a tut before pausing, 'Is it vanilla again?'

'It is always vanilla, and it will always *be* vanilla... Unless, of course, we change it. Maybe chocolate next time, oui? I think Mrs Jones is the same as Frank Delaney. Do the zoo, oui, yes... I think so. Do the zoo.'

'The zoo it is.'

CHAPTER FOURTEEN

'*Jimmy McConville is going to The Central Park Zoo with his mother to watch the sea lions being fed at 13:30 hours. He must not watch the feeding take place.* There's a bit more... *Operatives must maintain hypervigilance during incursions into the real-world and be able to self-extract while minimising contamination of other timelines...* This doesn't feel right, you know,' Zara says with a frown, reading the sheet again, 'It's like the terminology is aimed at people who know what they're doing... Self-extract? What does that even mean?'

'Get out?' Bear suggests.

'Well, obviously,' she says with a tut, 'It all feels a bit poorly done, if you ask me. Right, Tom...where's Central Park?'

'How would I know?' he asks. 'Fifth Avenue,' he adds, surprised at himself for knowing something he didn't know.

'We were on Fifth Avenue,' Bear says.

'They've obviously kept it local to make it easier,' Zara says. 'Shall we, then? Bear, you go first again, please.'

'You sound like a teacher,' Bear says, crossing to the door.

'Do I? Maybe I was? Do I look like a teacher?'

He pauses at the door, taking in her dark eyes and hair cut, short on the sides and back but longer on top, with tight afro curls. Elegant eyebrows, high cheekbones that all combine to imbue a sharpness with an obvious intelligence radiating with natural confidence.

'Could be...or a lawyer,' he says.

'I'd rather be a lawyer than a teacher,' she says, 'Right, come on...let's get it done. Do we have a lunch break? We should have a lunch break. I'm hungry. Are you hungry, Tom?'

From the alley to Fifth Avenue where Zara stands frowning for a few seconds with her hands on her hips, trying to decide which way to go before Thomas asks a passer-by.

'We don't even know what Jimmy McConville looks like,' Zara says, powerwalking along Fifth Avenue. Smaller and shorter than Bear and Thomas, but still generating a speed that makes them rush to keep up. 'How do we know what he looks like?'

'I don't know,' Bear says.

'We'll have to do it outside the zoo,' she says after another minute, raising her voice over the noise of the traffic, 'Zoo's always have admission fees, and we don't have any money to get in...so we can't stop them *inside* the zoo... If we go near a mother and child dressed like this, we'll get arrested...*and* this is America, so we'll probably just get shot.'

'That's racist,' Thomas blurts.

'Excuse me?' she snaps, coming to a sudden stop with her hands on her hips, 'It's not racist...'

'I didn't mean racist... I meant...'

'We haven't got time for this,' she says, powering on, 'But it's not racist.'

'I said I didn't mean...'

'Not now, Thomas. Think of a way we can stop a mother and child from going into a zoo...'

'We need to identify them first,' Bear says.

'Spare change?'

All three turn at the same time to see a homeless man on an old bedroll at the side of the pavement. A thick beard and filthy skin with rheumy, watery eyes, and his blackened hands hold a worn chunk of cardboard asking for money.

'Sorry, dude,' Thomas says, patting his legs, 'got nothing.'

They walk on in silence, glimpsing open air ahead with a hint of green that marks the edge of Central Park.

'What I want to know is why stop a kid from seeing animals being fed?' Zara asks as they cross an open space, 'How can that change time?'

'Anything can change time,' Bear replies, still holding the fighting stick that not one person looks twice at.

'Seems stupid to me,' she says.

'GET YA DAWGS HERE...DAWGS HERE...' the booming voice of a street vendor permeates the air, adding to the cacophony of sounds within the plaza bordering the park. Thick New York accents mingle with foreign tones and nuances that speak of zones and districts they've all heard in movies they cannot recall or remember without context.

They stride into the park and down the wide lanes, following the signs for the zoo and weaving past the thick crowds of tourists. Families everywhere. Mothers and children. Fathers and children.

'There,' Bear says, pointing ahead to three arches set in a brick wall giving entrance to the zoo. It's instantly obvious they can't go further without money to buy tickets, and they come to a stop with each looking around for ideas and watching the thick crowds streaming past.

Zara places her hands on her hips, thinking of the problem and also thinking to tell Thomas what racist means, when she spots a woman walking past, holding a brightly coloured map of the park that makes her think of the homeless man's cardboard sign, then the menus and signs they've seen everywhere else.

'Got it!' she says quickly, 'We need a sign…like at airports…you know when….'

'Nameboards?' Thomas suggests.

'Yes! We need those,' she says.

'Got it, hang fire here,' he rushes off back the way they came. Working against the flow of people to reach the plaza area and the vendors calling out with their goods and wares. A strip of cardboard from an old box. A borrowed pen, and he runs back with a grin, showing them his artwork.

Mrs McConville and Jimmy

'SHE MIGHT NOT BE MARRIED,' Zara points out.

'What?' Thomas asks, somewhat crestfallen.

'You've put *Mrs*… She might be Miss…'

'Aw, heck, do you think it matters?'

'It'll be fine… Right, stand in the middle and hold it up.'

'Me? Why can't Bear do it? He's taller.'

'Good point. Bear, hold this,' she says, plucking the

fighting stick from his hands to replace with the sign, 'Up a bit more... Yep, that's fine...'

'What do I say if they see me?' Bear asks.

'Worry about that when...'

'Say there, I'm Mrs McConville. Is there a problem?' a woman asks, holding hands with a stout and serious child at her side.

'No way,' Bear says, looking at the card, then at them, 'That was quick.'

'Hi!' Zara blurts. 'You can't go in.'

'What? Why?' the woman demands with instant New York aggression.

'Er...because...' Zara flounders for a second, then remembers what Thomas said earlier, 'There's poisonous rats...'

'What?' Mrs McConville snaps, pulling stout and serious Jimmy closer to her side.

'Hey, did you say poisonous rats?' a man asks, stopping as he walks by to stare in alarm at Zara, then at Bear, and Thomas also in blue coveralls. 'Honey, you hear that? The zoo's overrun with dangerous rats,' he tells his wife in a strong New York voice.

'No, I meant...' Zara says.

'Poisonous rats?' a woman asks, 'Did she say poisonous rats?'

'No, I just meant in the food...' Zara says.

'THE FOOD?' someone yells, 'The rats are in the food?'

'No! Just the diseased ones...'

'Diseased?' someone asks.

'I meant poisoned,' Zara says.

'What's going on?' another man asks.

'Goddam diseased rats in the zoo,' the first man replies.

'Diseased rats.'

'Dangerous rats...'

'Biting people...'

'Attacking people eating food...'

'I never said that,' Zara shouts, and suddenly, the crowd isn't streaming into the zoo anymore but clinging in alarm to the growing nucleus surrounding the three in blue coveralls.

'Mommy...I don't want to get bit by a rat,' a stout, serious, and now very worried Jimmy McConville says.

'He got bit by a rat?' someone asks.

'Who got bit?' a woman calls out.

'That kid... He's been bit by diseased rats.'

'Get him outta here... Hey, lady...get your kid away.'

'EVERYONE LISTEN,' Zara yells to be heard, but that increase in volume only makes everyone else get louder.

On a park bench, some several metres away, two men peer over the top of their newspapers. 'Ready?' Jacob asks.

'Oui.'

'OH, MY GOD, A RAT!' a woman screams as a pigeon trots by her feet, running back into another woman who shoves her away into a child that cries out at being knocked down. The domino effect starts with the mother of the child lashing out into the woman that knocked her daughter over. That woman fights back, screaming that it wasn't her fault. Their husbands wade in hard, and so the ripples spill out with an escalation of aggression rising by the second.

'HEY...HEY!' Zara shouts out, wading deeper into the crowd on seeing the two women still trying to fight despite being held by the men. She gets between them, using her body as a shield to try and keep them apart.

Thomas spins around, blinking at not seeing Zara, where she was. He turns this way and that, snatching glimpses between the dense ranks of jostling people, but the speed increases with shouts and calls in loud angry voices becoming ragged and hoarse. More people come piling in, drawn to the chaos, as the numbers increase, to the extent the two men reading newspapers on a nearby bench draw their feet under their seats to keep clear of the path.

'ZARA!' Thomas shouts, feeling a rush of panic, 'I CAN'T SEE ZARA...ZARA... SHE WAS RIGHT HERE...'

'Police... Move back...' the first cop arrives, swinging his baton up to start swiping at legs and arms, forcing a path into the crowd as more of his uniformed colleagues run in behind him.

Zara wedges herself between the two women still trying to fight each other. A hand on each chest. Feet braced. Her face grimacing at the press, but for a second, she gains order and sees a fleeting look of calmness flicker through both women and their husbands, and that split-second quietness rolls out, seemingly poised in the air, with everyone and everything balanced on a knife edge. 'Thank fuck,' she says with a breath of relief.

'Now?' Jacob asks quietly from behind his newspaper.

'Oui,' Pete whispers, 'Now.'

The two women being held apart by Zara scream with fresh rage as their husbands simply release their holds to go at each other with Zara trapped in the middle.

At that same second, so everyone else goes at everyone else with fists flying, heads butting, hands grabbing, and cops whacking anyone in reach with hard metal batons.

'Holy fuck,' Thomas reels back from the explosion of violence as the whole crowd collapses in on itself. He tries to run, to flee, but gets knocked this way and that, unable to find a path out, when he trips and sprawls across the ground, thinking all he can do is curl up and pray until a strong hand grabs the back of his collar, yanking him up and back.

'Stay behind me.'

Bear glimpses blue coveralls in a seething mass of people. A glimpse of tight, black afro curls. He moves on with smooth hand motions gliding people away with Thomas close behind. A flash of metal. A black uniform, and a screaming angry face. The baton comes in hard. Bear steps left, catching the wrist and forcing the cop over his hip, snatching the baton free. A fist swings at him, he dances back, then darts forward, hooking the baton behind the attacker's knee to rip him off his feet, and on he goes, snaking through the fight. 'There,' he reaches back, grabs Thomas, and heaves him forward into the mass of people rolling on the ground, 'Get her out.'

Thomas spots Zara's arm and dives in, using his shoulders to barge men and women aside.

'GET ME OUT,' Zara screams, frenzied with panic at being squashed under bodies, 'GET ME OUT, GET ME OUT...'

'Gotcha,' Thomas grabs her shoulders, pulling back hard to lift her through the press, 'Bear...BEAR...WE'RE OUT...'

Bear takes the lead again, forcing a path to reach the edge of the crowd and spill free to stagger and lurch away, gasping for air and turning to look around in utter shock at the way the riot is contained within such a small area of space.

'What just happened?' Zara asks, wiping her sleeve over her face, a bare few feet from two men reading newspapers. She blinks fast, breathing hard and seeing blood on her sleeve, 'I'm bleeding...oh, shit...oh, shit...'

'Where?' Thomas asks, grabbing her hands to hold her still, as he inspects her face and head.

'I'm bleeding…' she cries out, dancing on the spot with a fresh burst of panic.

'Hang on,' Thomas says, wiping his sleeve over her cheeks, 'It's not yours…'

'What?'

'Not yours… The blood ain't yours.'

'Ew, that's so gross…get it off, get it off…'

'I am, dude, hold still…there, it's gone.'

'Has it gone?'

'I just said it is, it's gone…' Thomas says.

'We need to go,' Bear says, looking around at the bedlam.

'Insane… This place is insane…' Thomas says as the three run back for Fifth Avenue.

CHAPTER FIFTEEN

Breathless. Grimy and coated in sweat, they reach the door in the alley and blunder into the dingy room, slamming the door closed and dropping to rest against the wall.

'What happened?' Thomas asks, 'How did it go so bad...'

'I think it's just part of it,' Bear says, 'Like seeing how we'll react.'

The others stare at him, focussing on his words and the way he breathes so much easier.

'I didn't like it,' Zara says. 'Being trapped like that... Everyone so angry and...' she trails off, looking drained and shaken.

'Another one,' Bear says, moving to the table to pick the folder up. 'Want me to read it?' he asks, offering it to Zara first with an unspoken and unrealised team dynamic already forming.

'I can do it,' she inhales deeply, steadying the nerves while opening the cover to read the single printed, dog-eared sheet, 'It's like at school or...or college, or something...

you know when you get old textbooks that have been handled loads... I mean, look at this room and this folder. It's all so old and worn.'

Bear looks around, seeing what she means. The scuffed walls. The worn floorboards. The thick layer of dust on the window, and the folders they keep getting are stained from being handled, and the sheets within have torn edges and creases from being folded.

'What's it say?' Thomas asks.

'The annual waste disposal business association conference is taking place today in city hall. You must stop the afternoon presentations session taking place...'

A BIG ROOM filled with the noise of men in suits talking loudly while stuffing their jowly faces from the two hour long re-supplied meat and carb heavy buffet provided in one of City Hall's conference rooms.

'How you doing?' one of the men asks, walking past the three standing in a row at the end of the buffet table, tucking into food from plates piled high. 'Didn't get the memo, huh? Meant to be smart clothes,' he slurs, plopping creamed potatoes onto his plate, 'Who's outfit you with?'

'Big John,' Thomas replies.

'Big John?' the man asks, giving them a hard look that sets Zara's heart booming, 'I heard he was in Vegas.'

'He is,' Thomas says, covering his mouth as he chews, 'Asked us to come down, but a job came in... You know how it is.'

'Damn right, I do buddy,' the man booms, 'Give my regards.'

'Will do, sir, you have a good day now,' Thomas says,

lifting his plate in greeting as the man rushes back to his table.

'You're good at talking,' Bear says, motioning to Thomas with his plate.

'Thanks,' Thomas says, shovelling more food in.

'Aw, look at you three,' a woman says, pushing a trolley along the buffet bar to replenish the stocks of food, 'You got busy, I guess?'

'Yes, ma'am, we were all suited up and ready when the PD called in for a scene clean-up…homicide,' he adds in a whisper with a wink.

'Too bad,' she says, 'you got a drink? You wanna drink? Lemme get you a drink. You wanna beer?'

'No, thank you, ma'am, back on it… Say, you got some water or cola?'

'Sure thing, I'll get you some colas, you eat up.'

'You're good at talking,' Bear says again, earning a chuckle from Zara, 'Wonder what you did before… Maybe a salesman or something.'

Thomas shrugs, chewing fast while looking around the room. 'What about you?' he asks, covering his mouth again, 'Any idea?'

'Nope,' Bear says.

'Cop? Soldier? They learn fighting.'

'I couldn't fight. Roshi made me learn… It was either that or just keep dying.'

'Three colas,' the woman says, rushing back towards them with three glass bottles, 'Just holla if you want more.'

'Thank you, ma'am. Say, you don't have any matches, do you?'

'Sure thing, honey. Bowl on the bar over there. You help yourself now.'

'Thanks.'

'What I want to know,' Zara says after swallowing her mouthful, 'is why we're doing all these things after that big speech by Jacob.'

'LADIES AND GENTLEMEN...THIS IS A FIFTEEN MINUTE WARNING FOR THE AFTERNOON SESSION. FIFTEEN MINUTES.'

A chorus of groans roll through the room as the jowly faced men in suits suffer mild panic at the prospect of ceasing their gorging.

'We'd better go,' Zara says, pushing another sandwich into her mouth, 'Sho mice.'

'Huh?' Thomas asks.

'Sho mice...' she says, pointing at her mouth, 'Food.'

'Ah...we taking the colas with us?'

'Mmmm,' she nods quickly, 'Take the colas with us.'

'I think we're taking the colas with us,' Bear says.

'Don't take the piss,' she mumbles.

'Okay, Grumps.'

'Don't call me that,' she snaps, giving him a one second glare.

'I'll go do it. Meet you outside?' Bear asks.

'Meet you outside,' Zara says, 'You go do it.'

'I just said that.' Bear walks over to the bar, nodding at the man serving drinks before plucking a box of matches from the bowl on the end, 'Toilet here?'

'Over there,' the man says, pointing across the room.

'Thanks.'

Thomas grabs the colas, Zara another egg sandwich, and Bear crosses the room to the toilets. Zara and Thomas walk slowly from the main room to the outer hall, skirting the wall while she eats, and Thomas pops a lid to guzzle the sugary liquid.

Into a cubicle, and Bear closes the door, drops the seat

down, and starts unwinding the toilet roll that he piles on the seat-cover as Zara and Thomas come to a stop with Zara taking a swig of cola, 'Christ, that's sweet.'

Match lit and pressed to the toilet paper that ignites with a small flame that grows fat and big, with fuel and air boosting its appetite. Smoke starts to waft up, thin tendrils at first, but Bear finds another roll from an overhead cubby and adds that too, while in the outer hall Zara takes another swig, and Thomas looks about.

Bear pauses, holding two more rolls in his hands and trying to decide if the fire is big enough without them. 'Stuff it,' he adds them too, then another three for good measure and exits fast, rushing from the stall past the urinals each filled with a fat jowly man in a suit trying to locate his penis by touch alone.

Into the main room and across to the doors, and out to nod at Zara who nudges Thomas who whacks the back of his elbow into thin glass covering the fire alarm that comes to life, filling City Hall with a wailing siren. The three walk off, down the stairs to the main entrance, reaching the doors as the sprinkler system activates, spraying gallons of water down over the jowly faced men in suits, all waddling soaked and grumbling from the conference room while thick smoke pours from the cubicle fire.

THE NEXT ONE is in London, and they all feel the change the second they go back into the room. *Malcolm Hanright will have a heart attack at 15:23 hours after exiting MacDonald's restaurant on Baker Street. He will die unless treated by paramedics within two minutes. He must not die.*

They exit the room to a new alley off Marylebone Road.

A short walk, and they find Baker Street. Another short walk, and they find the MacDonald's. A quick call from a telephone box at 15:18 with Zara dialling three nines and reporting a serious road traffic accident with multiple casualties. Several ambulances are dispatched, racing to the scene to find no accident just as Malcolm Hanright walks out from MacDonald's, coughs once, coughs twice, clutches his chest, and keels over right in front of the ambulance pulled over reporting back to control room that it was a fake call.

NEW YORK, and they step out into a harsh, biting wind of a city in mid-winter, and spend the next hour shivering in thin blue coveralls, working their way back to Central Park and the ice-rink where Zara concocts a plan for Thomas to distract the staff while Bear breaks into the electric room to shut the power off, thereby preventing Mario and Helen from ever meeting and falling in love, and so the day rolls on, with Zara emerging as a clear team leader, while Thomas deals with communication, distraction, and verbal coercion, leaving Bear to happily do anything that involves pain, risk, violence, or danger.

They become immersed in the fun of it. They don't know who they are. They know nothing of themselves, but they start to learn and evolve. They start to gain essences of characters and personalities that could be memories of who they were before or newly formed judgements and decisions based on what they see and do now. They gain history too, things to talk about and joke about with shared experiences as they discuss situations that could have been done better.

'So, perhaps, Roshi was right to push her recruit...' Pete says from a café on a London street, staring through the rain-lashed plate-glass window at Thomas delaying an Asian man getting the number 8 bus.

'Roshi is a reckless little bitch. That said, yes, I can see some value to this exercise.'

Pete nods slowly, watching the bus pull away as the Asian man flaps his arms in frustration at missing it, 'I think this could change things, yes?'

'Perhaps,' Jacob replies stiffly, going through the dog-eared sheets spread on the table-top between them.

'They are not worried at failing,' Pete says, 'They have no stress of this...no judgements.'

'Still, part of the construct,' Jacob murmurs.

'Oui, I know this, Jacob. Do Langdon,' he says, motioning at the sheets.

'Langdon?' Jacob asks with a bemused expression, 'Pushing it a bit, aren't you?'

'Is fine, Langdon. We do that next.'

'CLAIRE LANGDON WILL BE CONVICTED *of theft at Westminster Magistrates Court at 13:30hours. She will use a fire exit to make her way to the roof to commit suicide but will be stopped and talked down by court security officer Odoni Umbella. You must stop Mr Umbella from preventing the suicide of Langdon.* That's sick,' Zara says after reading it out, 'I'm not doing that. It's murder...'

'I don't think we have a choice,' Thomas says gently, 'They're not telling us to kill her.'

'No, they're telling us to let her die,' she fires back.

'I'll do it,' Bear says simply, remaining passive when the

other two look at him, 'It's not real. None of this is real... We came in that door from summer in New York and walked back out the same door into London in winter...'

They find the courts on Marylebone Road and find the court listings pinned to the wall and the court number for the hearing that convicts Claire Langdon. Within a few minutes, they spot Claire Langdon walking out of the courtroom, and never before has anyone ever been so bereft of hope and broken by life.

She stands out in the noisy crowd. Frail and timid. A figure of such abject pity that the mere sight invokes a desire to offer help and comfort, but they don't.

Instead, they watch as Claire Langdon walks from the court door to another older woman waiting with three small children, and they watch as Claire Langdon kneels down to kiss and hug them with tears streaming down her face before telling the older woman she needs the toilet and walks off into the crowd.

'Nana, where's mummy?' the smallest child asks.

'She's gone to the toilet,' the older woman says, her face etched with worry as she tries to see where her daughter went.

'Oh, god no,' Zara whispers, her hand covering her mouth, 'We can't...'

They watch with dread building as Claire Langdon comes to a stop by the wall. Wringing her hands while sobbing silently. Not one person notices or offers help. Not the staff or the people waiting. She is just another human being. Then a fire exit door opens, with a member of staff striding out who doesn't wait for it to close securely behind, and Claire Langdon slips out of sight.

The three then see uniformed security officer Odoni Umbella walking towards the door with a frown, and they know, if they do nothing, he will save her life. He will bring her back to her three children clinging to their grandmother's legs in the noisy, aggressive air of an inner-city court landing. What a thing to do. What a nasty thing to do. A heart-wrenching sight of a woman and her children, and the fact all three realise that it's designed to be this way does not lessen the effect.

'Now,' Bear says.

'I can't, dude,' Thomas says, stricken to the core.

'It's not real,' Bear says quickly.

'Man, there's three kids...'

'They're like the bomb kids... They're not real...'

'Just do it,' Zara says, urging Thomas on, 'Punch him...'

Thomas hesitates, even if it wasn't a woman with three kids, he couldn't punch Bear. 'Dude...I...'

'One of you, bloody hit me,' Bear whispers, seeing Mr Umbella almost at the door.

'Fuck's sake,' Zara hisses before walloping Bear around the face with a stinging slap, 'YOU SLEPT WITH HER?'

'Jesus,' Thomas says, flinching at the ferocious assault.

'MY SISTER! YOU FUCKED MY SISTER....' she slaps again, snapping Bear's head over.

'HEY,' Odoni Umbella calls out, his hand on the fire exit door.

'HE FUCKED MY SISTER...' Zara yells as the many women on the court landing draw breath while the many men wince and shake their heads. 'I'll bloody kill him...' she leaps at Bear, taking him down amidst flailing limbs, as the court security team rush in from all sides while on the top floor, Claire Langdon climbs out of the window to stand on the ledge with the weight of the world crushing her soul.

Zara, Bear, and Thomas are ejected from the court and told to piss off before the police are called, and they rush off away from the scene as Claire Langdon steps from the ledge to drop headfirst to the hard concrete below.

Zara and Thomas hear the impact, both flinching at the noise and the screams that come after.

'It's not real,' Bear says.

'They did it,' Pete says from across the road, 'Less than ten percent stop the guard from saving her…'

'I can see,' Jacob says, equally as stunned, watching the crowd gather around the ruined body.

There's nowhere to go from here. To keep going means to advance to more complicated scenarios, and to do that, they need to return to Discovery and report to Martha, but leaving it here, like this just isn't an option. It's too good. The uniqueness of it, and the lure to see how far they can push it.

'We go on?' Pete asks.

Jacob finally turns from looking at the body to stare at the Frenchman, 'Bloody right, we're going on…'

'Oui,' Pete says slowly with a wide grin forming, 'We will make history, my old friend.'

CHAPTER SIXTEEN

'Oh,' Zara says, coming to a stop after pushing through the door into the dingy room.

'What?' Bear asks, walking in behind her, 'Oh...'

'What?' Thomas asks, walking in last. 'Dude...' he grins at the sight of three leather chairs and a jug of coffee on the side table next to three mugs. 'Coffee break.'

'I'VE GIVEN THEM COFFEE,' Jacob says, striding along the sidewalk in Discovery with Pete at his side, 'It is remarkable. Truly remarkable. Raw recruits, Peter. They don't even have personalities yet. They're blank slates...'

'Oui, yes, I think we...'

'YOU TWO, STOP RIGHT THERE...'

They both blanch at the voice, spinning on the spot to see Allie marching towards them with a face like thunder, 'Why the hell is James in my diner?'

'Allie, my friend,' Pete says with a beaming smile, 'you

look radiant today, Mademoiselle. But James. He was sick. He vomit, yes? I took him there knowing you are a kind and caring woman.' His accent thickens slightly, softening his voice that becomes deeper as Jacob starts discretely sliding away.

'Stop flirting with me, Pete. And you can stand right there, Jacob... I know your bloody methods, you two. I do meet and greet. I am not a day care centre for sick newbies...'

'Allie, I can only apologise for this breach of etiquette, but alas, we have something very special underway right now.'

'And what am I supposed to do with him? I've got customers...'

'Get him washing up,' Pete says, waving a dismissive hand, 'The other three, they are remarkable, no? They're in scenario training and...'

'What?' she asks, blinking at him, 'Operative training? You've put them straight into operative training?'

'Well,' Jacob says, 'Peter and I decided to trial a new method and...'

'They have done Langdon,' Pete adds.

'Langdon!? Did they let her die?

'Oui, yes, they stop the security guard. They pass, one after the other. Frank Delaney, the zoo, ice-rink...and now Langdon, it is remarkable, yes?'

'It's something alright,' Allie mumbles, shaking her head at them, 'Oi...don't just walk off! You pair of sods...'

'Send him to planning,' Jacob calls back.

'He got lost going to the toilet,' she shouts after them before storming back to the diner.

'Where have you two been?' Jennifer asks, standing up from behind the reception desk, as the two men enter the planning offices, 'Allie called…she's got James in the diner, throwing up and…'

'Bonjour, Jennifer, you are looking very pretty today.'

'Aw, thanks, that's not creepy at all… Where are you going? Pete! Jacob…Fuck's sake…' she mutters, rushing out from behind the desk to follow them down the corridor.

'Zara, Thomas, and Bear have completed the first set of operative training scenarios up to Langdon…' Jacob calls back, 'We're going on…'

'What?' she snaps, running after them. 'You can't do that…' she comes to a stop as they push through the stairwell door, flapping her hands in the air before about turning and running on her heels back to the desk to grab the phone.

Two flights of stairs up, and the two men push through the doors into the large, open-plan office buzzing with noise, phones, and voices. A busy place with a hint of frantic energy hanging permanently in the air.

'Where the hell have you two been?' Martha demands, striding from her office.

'Oh, that's nice,' Zara says, sinking into the chair with a mug of coffee clasped in her hands, 'I wonder what the time is? Feels like we've been going for hours.'

'Gone quick though,' Bear says, taking a seat.

'Hmm, yes. Yes. it has. Fun too, apart from…you know. The suicide thing, and the big fight.'

'I can't believe this is happening, man. It's like my brain is going slower than everything else, that make sense?' Thomas asks.

'Totally,' Zara says. 'So, tell us again,' she says to Bear, 'What did you do on your circuit?'

'You've been gone all day, where have you been?' Martha demands again, the office falling quiet as everyone listens.

'They pass stage two,' Pete says, waving his hand at her, 'Roshi, she trains Bear, and he is something else. He killed over one dozen in the warehouse...'

'Over a dozen,' Jacob continues, knowing everyone in the office is listening.

'Zara, she thinks to move the bombs not the children.'

'Thomas works fast too, brilliant communicator,' Jacob adds. 'They passed, so we, err...' he trails off, glancing at Pete.

'We try a new thing. We try just one to see. Frank Delaney, yes? It is easy. We want to see, so we put them through. They do it. Oui. They do it well.'

'I don't believe this,' Martha says. Sharp eyes, sharp intelligence, sharp everything, but then, to make it to Operations Manager in Discovery means having a mind like a scalpel.

'Martha,' Pete says, holding his hands up while offering his charming smile.

'Jesus, Pete, I'm gay. It won't work,' Martha says, groaning in exasperation.

'I forget this,' he concedes, affecting his best puppy-dog expression.

'How? How can you forget I'm gay? You've tried it on like a thousand times and... Whoa, that was good,' she hisses, jabbing her finger towards him, 'You actually got me distracted then, you little shit. How far have you gone with them? Where are they now?'

'We did the zoo,' Jacob says, as though thinking hard.

'And the ice-rink,' Pete adds, also deep in thought.

'Er...the City Hall annual waste meeting...'

'How far?' Martha asks, her voice dropping several notches.

A pause. A hesitancy. 'Langdon,' she groans, rubbing her face.

'They passed,' Pete exclaims.

'You did Langdon with newbies. You actually did that,' Martha says, shaking her head in shock.

'Martha?' Jennifer calls out, rushing across the office towards the rear cubicle.

'What?' Martha snaps.

'I can't reach the Old Lady.'

'So?' Martha asks.

'I'm just saying,' Jennifer says with a huff, 'You'll have to make the decision.'

'Decision? What decision?'

'To go on.'

'On? Make sense, woman! Go on where...' she glares at Jennifer, then snaps her head over to the two operatives smiling nicely, 'No.'

'Yes,' Pete booms, waving his hands in the air, 'They pass, they must go on.'

'I said no.'

'I SAY YES!' Pete shouts in full passionate flow, 'It is unique, Martha. It is a thing of excellence; this breaks the ground, and we write new rules today... Give them a harder scenario. Let them see history... It is safe, no? It is just training, yes?'

'Martha,' Jacob says formally, 'They have no self or sense of character, they're blank slates, which means they have no preconceptions of anxiety. How many do we fail every year? Bloody Roshi was the last one through...'

'WE GO ON,' Pete booms, making his presentation to

the office at large, 'Three new recruits who want to succeed. They are hungry for this. They want this. They are fearless and bold. We have much work, yes? You are busy, and we are down on operatives, yes? WE GO ON!'

'So fucking dramatic,' Martha mutters, rubbing the back of her neck.

'Martha, Peter and I are getting older now. We cannot keep working at the pace you want. Three new operatives will spread that workload by a great deal, and may I take this opportunity to remind you that none of the operatives have had our allocated vacation time for the last three years...'

'Holidays? Are you taking the piss? I've never had a bloody holiday... Where's the Old Lady?'

'Er...I just said?' Jennifer states after a pause of being glared at, 'I can't reach her.'

'Say yes, Martha. Say oui, and we go on... We make history today.'

'My god, you are tiresome,' Martha says.

'Try working with him,' Jacob says.

Stunned silence. Heavy and charged as Bear sips his coffee. An exchange of looks between Zara and Thomas, both wide-eyed.

'She stabbed you?' Zara breaks the silence.

'Loads,' Bear says, nodding amiably.

'And you stabbed her?'

'Loads.'

'Fuck, man,' Thomas says, 'She sounds messed up.'

'God, yes,' Bear says, thinking back to last night.

'And you're okay?' Zara asks.

'Yeah, it was nice,' Bear says, still thinking of last night.

'Nice?!'

'What? Oh, I meant…I mean…er…yeah, not nice, but… bad, very bad but erm…so I mean, I think I'm okay.'

'Right,' she says slowly.

'Like, dude…you got urges to…you know…like kill people now?' Thomas asks slowly, eyeing the door.

'Only Americans,' Bear says seriously, lifting the cup to his mouth, then grinning in the silence.

'Dude,' Thomas laughs, 'but you are joking, right?'

'No, I'm being serious,' Bear says, letting the smile slowly fade as Thomas laughs again while still looking slightly unsure.

SILENCE. Heavy and charged as Martha glowers at Jacob and Pete while everyone holds their breath. Apart from Jennifer who tuts and taps her foot.

'Fine,' Martha says simply, striding from her office to a locked cabinet on one side of the big open-plan room, 'Someone organise a screen, I want to watch it…'

'Yes!' Pete says, punching the air.

'For the record,' Martha says, unlocking the cabinet, 'I did not know you put them into operative training in the first place…'

'It was entirely Pete's decision,' Jacob says.

'Oui,' Pete says seriously before realising what Jacob just said, 'You are a fucker, my old friend.'

'They can do two harder training scenarios, but I'm choosing them,' Martha says, running her fingertip over a line of thin manilla coloured folders on the middle shelf within the cabinet.

The air thickens and charges, and the tension mounts as everyone stares at Martha running her fingertips along the folders. She pulls one out, checks the cover, then seems to change her mind, and pushes it back in. Pete swallows, while Jacob's upper lip twitches with anticipation.

She draws two, opening the covers to read the sheets inside. Thinking hard, thinking long. 'How good are they?' she asks quietly as every head turns to look at Pete and Jacob.

'They're good,' Pete replies.

'Okay,' she says, pulling a folder out.

The air in the room changes from the dozens of people drawing sharp intakes of breath as they read the word across the front cover, while one snorts a dry laugh that she quickly hides when everyone looks at her.

'Sorry,' Jennifer murmurs.

'Jefferson?' Jacob asks.

'You said they're good,' Martha says, arching an eyebrow, 'Let's see how good.'

CHAPTER SEVENTEEN

'That's it,' Zara says, her voice trailing off as she reads back over the printed sheet.

The internal door reappeared while they drank coffee. One minute it was a scuffed wall, seamless in design, the next, there was a door.

'The door's back, dudes,' Thomas said mildly.

They went through it. Or rather, Bear went through it on request of Zara.

'Might be dangerous,' she said.

The warehouse was gone. Instead, there was an anteroom filled with rails of clothes and pairs of shoes laid in rows on the floor. A table in the middle on which the manilla folder waited for them with the word *Jefferson* hand-written across the front.

'Money,' Zara says, pulling three twenty-dollar bills from the folder clipped together with a small piece of paper, '*For expenses, retain all receipts*...Jesus...is this for real?'

'Read it again,' Thomas says.

'*For expenses, retain all receipts.*'

'Not that bit, the other bit,' Thomas says.

'The big bit?' she asks.

'Yeah, the big bit.'

'Read the big bit,' Bear says.

'*Bernard Jefferson will die of Typhoid Fever on May 28th, 1905 at his family home in Manhattan. Ensure he does not die. You cannot move him. Use the pen and notepad on the table to request your deployment date and location prior to commencing your incursion.*'

They look at the plain, black pen on top of the small, plain notepad on the table, then up to the clothes on the rails and the shoes on the floor, then back to the plain, black pen on the notepad, then finally back to Zara, holding the folder in one hand and the money in the other.

'Well, it's certainly a bit more complicated than stopping little Jimmy going to the zoo,' Zara points out.

'You think?' Bear asks.

'Yes, that's why I said it.'

'Seen this?' Bear asks, pulling two items of clothing from the rail. An old-looking, thick, woollen, brown suit jacket on a hanger in one hand and a modern, pale blue, checked shirt in the other.

'Ah, now that's interesting,' Zara says, 'Very interesting...'

'S<small>EE</small>!'

'Shush,' Martha snaps, waving a hand at Pete while everyone in the planning department watches the giant screen projected against one wall.

'I say she is smart. I said this, no?'

'So, that's Zara, right?' Jennifer asks.

'Yes,' Jacob says, 'That's Zara...the tall one is Bear, and the other one is Thomas.'

'Cool,' she says, 'Bear's kinda hot.'

'Er, that is not appropriate language for the workplace, thank you, Jennifer,' Martha says pointedly.

'Just saying.'

'Well, don't. He's not a piece of meat to be ogled.'

'I'd ogle his meat,' someone mumbles from the crowd of workers, earning a round of chuckles.

'Thomas is cute too,' someone else says.

'Zara's very attractive,' another voice adds.

'Enough!' Martha says, glowering at her subordinates, 'We are not gawping and grading on who looks fit.'

'I SEE,' Zara says, 'Right, we need to put modern clothes on first. You two, get changed in here, I'll go in the other room.'

'What?' Thomas asks.

'What?' Bear asks.

'Got an idea,' she says, grabbing armfuls of clothes, 'Get dressed, and I'll tell you on the way.'

'On the way where?' Bear asks.

'To what?' Thomas asks.

She pauses in the doorway, turning back to look at them, 'Nothing that stands out too much...come on, chop chop...work to do.'

'I LIKE HER,' Martha tells everyone, pointing at the screen.

'You said we're not to say that,' Jennifer says.

'I meant her attitude, thank you very much.'

'I like her attitude too,' someone mutters, 'She's got a fit attitude.'

'Bear's got a very nice attitude,' Jennifer says.

'Pack it in,' Martha says. 'Oh, right...er... Everyone, turn around!' she adds at the sight of Bear and Thomas tugging their blue coveralls off, 'NOW, PLEASE!'

'Done?' Zara calls out, tapping on the connecting door.

'Yup,' Thomas says.

'Right,' she says slowly after walking in and casting a visual inspection over their choice of clothes, 'We have identified a weakness.'

'Weakness?' Thomas asks.

'What weakness?' Bear asks.

'The ability to dress yourselves weakness,' she says, moving to the rails where she starts pulling hangers off.

'What's wrong with our clothes?' Thomas asks.

'Nothing... I'm sure brogues are great with tracksuit bottoms in some parts of life...'

'Huh?' Thomas asks, looking down at his brogues and black tracksuit bottoms while Bear smirks a grin.

'And you can stop smirking, Bear. You've put corduroys on.'

'What's wrong with corduroys?'

'They're green,' she states, looking at them while Thomas smirks. 'And they don't go with red training shoes, red and green should never be seen, remember that. Right, get changed and hurry up,' she adds, picking up the pen and notepad from the table before walking out.

'I bloody love her,' Martha states.

'She was good on the circuit,' Jacob says, 'Questioned everything. Nearly drove me mad.'

'Gosh, a strong woman asking questions caused you some issues, did it? Misogynist anyone?' Martha says. 'She's writing on the pad,' she adds as everyone in the room cocks their head over to see the words left on the pad. 'Clever bitch,' Martha whispers.

'Modern times New York?' Bear asks, reading the notepad in the dingy room while Zara checks them both over.

'We don't know what year we're in,' Zara replies. 'Tuck your shirt in, Thomas. You need to look smart.'

'What for?' Thomas asks, tucking his shirt in.

'Help you?' the man in the white lab coat asks, walking behind the counter while looking at a smartly dressed Thomas smiling warmly.

'Hi there. Are you the pharmacist?'

'I am the pharmacist,' the pharmacist says.

'I'm doing some research,' Thomas says.

'Research?'

'Yes, Sir. For a book.'

'A book?'

'Yes, Sir. I'm writing a book.'

'What book?'

'Er, it's about…time travel and…'

'Time Travel?'

'Yes, Sir. The main character has Typhoid Fever.'

'Typhoid Fever. He needs to see a doctor.'

'He's in olden times, like 1905...'

'1905?'

'Yes, Sir.'

'There was no treatment for Typhoid Fever in 1905.'

'What did people do if they had it? In 1905, I mean.'

'Prayed. Then mostly died.'

'It's a time travel book. He can travel to modern times and get medicine.'

'He can't travel anywhere. He's got Typhoid Fever. He's contagious.'

'No, I mean...he can get modern medicine from here and...'

'He's got Typhoid. He can't come here.'

'No, I mean...to modern times and...'

'He needs a doctor if he's got Typhoid. I don't want anyone with Typhoid coming here...'

'No, Sir. What I mean is he can access modern medicine.'

'He needs a prescription.'

'What for?'

'What for? You just said he has Typhoid Fever.'

'No, I mean...'

'Haven't you got the internet?'

'The internet? Shit...I forgot about the internet.'

'You forgot about the internet, and you're writing a book?'

'How did it go?' Zara asks as Thomas comes out the pharmacy.

'Yeah, we'll need another chemist...'

'Ceftria…Ceftro…' Thomas says as the female pharmacist smiles at him, clearly taken with the nicely dressed charming writer enquiring about treatments for Typhoid Fever.

'Ceftriaxone,' she says.

'Ceftriaxone,' Thomas says.

'Bingo, you got it,' she beams.

'Gee, thank you, Ma'am. I've been in a lot of pharmacists trying to work this one out. My computer broke, you see, so I can't get online…'

'That's too bad,' she says.

'How is it administered?'

'Injection, and then a seven-day course of tablets.'

'Seven days? Is that it?'

'That's it. Just an antibiotic. Same with the plague. Medicine has come a long way since 1905… What's your name?'

'Thomas, Ma'am.'

'Is that the name you write under?'

'Oh, I see…er…Thomas Hardy.'

'Thomas Hardy?'

'Yes, Ma'am.'

'That's your pen name?'

'It is, Ma'am… Say, do you know what will help…if I could see what they look like, you know, so I get it right. Readers are quick to judge when you get a fact wrong.'

'Sure. Ceftriaxone is used to treat bacterial infections… here we go…' she says, walking back with two small boxes. 'This one is for injection, the other is tablets…HEY!' she screams out when the man behind Thomas snatches the boxes from her hands and runs for the door.

'STOP! THIEF!' Thomas yells, bravely running after the robber.

'Unbelievable,' the pharmacist says, shaking her head, 'Did you see that?'

'Awful,' Zara says, stepping up to the counter, 'Cheeky sod. Hope you catch him.'

'Catch him? This is New York. We never catch anyone… Not even worth calling the police. Damn thieves… damn stealing… What can I get for you?'

'Oh, NICELY DONE,' Martha says with her hands on her hips while watching the screen, 'Very good, very smooth… Not seen it this good since Roshi.'

'Bloody Roshi,' Jacob mutters.

'Okay,' Zara says in the dingy room, 'We know what it is, we know how to treat it. All we've got to do is find the house, find Bernard Jefferson, get the medicine into him, then get back here.'

Bear and Thomas nod in agreement. Both dressed in period clothing of checked trousers, white shirts, waistcoats, and dark suit jackets, with bowler-style hats perched on their heads.

Zara purses her lips, thinking hard and looking down at her baggy, dark grey dress that just borders on the side of frilly. Figure hugging on her upper body and flaring out. A high collar, and a bonnet held in place with a hatpin through her tight curls.

'How do I look?'

'Great,' Thomas says eagerly, earning a look from the

other two before clearing his throat, 'Er…you look er…periodic and er…'

'Right, not awkward at all,' she says, 'Anyway, ready?'

'Yes,' Bear says, staring at the crimson blush spreading deeper through Thomas's cheeks.

They leave the room and walk up the alley onto Fifth Avenue to stare at the road packed full of yellow cabs, trucks, vans, and people walking by, gawping at their costumes.

'Arse,' Zara says, 'didn't change the date.'

Back in the dingy room, Zara takes the notepad from the table and writes *1905* across the front, placing it down as all three feel the lurch inside that signals the world just changed.

They go back out, into an alley markedly different from the one they saw before. Narrower and longer, with the brickwork rougher, and no plastic strewn on the ground. Smells hit them instantly. Animal dung, faeces, urine, body odour, coal, and wood-smoke. Strong and pungent, and that assault to their senses increases with each step they take towards Fifth Avenue.

'Oh my god,' Zara whispers at the view opening out in front of them, 'It's real…it's actually real…'

'I REMEMBER THAT FEELING,' Martha says in the silence of the planning office where every person studies the expressions on the faces of the three perched on the sidewalk of Fifth Avenue, New York City, 1905.

A WIDE ROAD flanked by grandiose high buildings, with each seeming to make a statement of wealth and opulence. First story flat roofs jut out with balconied gardens overlooking a street full of awnings, vendors, workers, and life.

Horses everywhere. Drawing coaches, and flatbed delivery carts. Huge, docile beasts fitted with blinkers with reins held by weathered men wearing soft caps and dark jackets. The odd motor-vehicle here and there. Noisy and spewing foul fumes, and still designed on the style of a horse-drawn carriages.

To think of a time so long ago suggests a lesser populace of the planet, where there is more space and less development, but what they see is a city bursting to life with human beings from every race, culture, and creed flooding the streets to carve a new existence. This is the America of old. The land of hope and dreams. The arrival point of European vessels, disgorging masses that run for the promised streets of gold, only to find them covered in horseshit and riddled with the stench of a city too new to have sanitation.

Disconcerting to say the least. Jarring. Upsetting. Confusing and weird, but also, it gives a buzz, a sensation of seeing something so wholly unique, even if it is a construct or part of a training package. It looks real. It is real. Down to the unique details. Down to the styles of clothing worn and the roaring hubbub of a packed, filthy, wealthy, dirt-poor city teeming with millions of people.

They see wealth everywhere. In the gilt lined coaches drawn by gleaming horses handled by liveried men with stern expressions. On the dresses of the women walking in flowing gowns of sumptuous design, with sunshades held perched on shoulders. They see it in the menfolk, wearing tailored suits and big hats, who walk with sticks, carving a path through the poor people dressed in rags. Starving and emaciated, with grimy faces and hands so filthy they look scarred.

A thing to see. A sight to behold.

'We need to go,' Zara says, striding as fast as before, with the two men rushing to keep up.

People start paying attention as they walk by, and even the handlers on the coaches and carriages cast eyes in their direction.

'Zara, slow down,' Thomas urges.

'Pardon?' she asks, looking back at him.

'Slow down,' he says again, 'People are looking at us.'

'I can bloody see that,' she snaps, glaring at a man walking by whose expression hardens on seeing the defiance in her face. 'Problem?' she snaps.

'Talkin' to me, nigger?' he asks, spinning to face her.

'What did you fucking say?'

'Whoa,' Bear steps in fast, blocking the man walking at Zara, 'Easy...'

'Fuck off,' the man says, trying to force past Bear, 'Damn uppity nigger...'

'HOW DARE YOU,' Zara shouts out.

'Zara, stop it,' Thomas urges.

'Stop it? He called me a nigger! Racist prick...'

'Fuckin' nigger whore,' the man growls, shoving a hand in his pocket.

It happens fast. Faster than the eye can track. The man pulls a knife out as he lunges at Bear who blurs with motion, gripping the wrist that he turns and breaks while snatching the blade free from the man's hand who suddenly finds his own knife held to his throat.

'Walk on friend,' Bear says quietly, looming over him. A second of eye contact, and Bear pushes him away before stepping to Zara, taking her arm in his, and walking on, leaving a few people standing open-mouthed and stunned.

'Fuck me,' Martha whispers in the planning office.
'We told you,' Jacob says.

'Did that just happen?' Zara asks, trying to look back.
'Yep, just keep going,' Bear says.
'He called me a nigger.'
'Everyone was looking at us,' Thomas says, falling into step on the other side of Zara, 'You were striding out too fast.'
'Too fast?' she snaps.
'Too fast for here,' he says quickly, 'We've got to blend in...'
'He was a racist fucking prick... I can't believe that just happened.'
Zara glowers, seethes and clenches her jaw with righteous rage. The words he used were one thing, but the hatred in his eyes was something else, and the speed in which he pulled a knife too. The fear starts to hit. The shock of it, and suddenly, the gleam vanishes, and what she sees are dirty streets and dirty people, almost feral in nature, with generational evolution separating whoever she is from whatever they are. She moves closer to Bear, clinging to his arm, as Thomas quietly steps in to flank her other side as they move on through a world that was never their own.
They find the houses they need, in a row that will be one day be demolished to make way for grand skyscrapers,

feeding the demand for expensive residences. A slight transition from bustling city to a quieter street that feels strange until they see the paper signs pinned to doors.

Warning. Typhoid Fever

'How do you catch it?' Bear asks.

'Bad water,' Thomas says, 'People not washing their hands after having a shit, sneezing, coughing... It's bacteria in human fluids.'

'Are we at risk?' Bear asks, suddenly thinking it might be part of the test and then also thinking that the guy with the knife was part of the test, and that everything they do is part of the test.

'I don't know, dude, I guess don't touch your nose, mouth, or eyes with your hands?'

'There's the house,' Zara says, pointing across the street to a gorgeously built Georgian town house of red brick, with a high, arched, gloss, black front door. 'Sign's there,' she adds, noticing the warning label pinned to the door.

'Explains why it's so quiet here,' Thomas says, looking about the deserted street.

'Right, let's get it done,' Zara says, 'Tom?'

'Yep, guess so,' he takes the lead, walking out across the empty road to climb the short flight of stone steps up to the gloss black front door to grip the heavy, solid brass knocker that thumps down, seemingly echoing a boom throughout the house.

Footsteps are heard. Locks are pulled back, and the door opens to a tall woman with dark hair staring out. Stern and imposing. A white apron tied about her waist, and her sleeves tugged up to show bare hands and arms dotted with flour that she wipes on a filthy rag. 'Got the fever here, so we have,' she says without preamble in a strong Belfast accent.

'Fuck,' Thomas mouths with an expression of abject shock, 'Mary?'

'Know you?' the woman snaps, her face hardening.

'Shit...Mary...' Thomas says again, pulling back.

'Aye, I'm Mary. What's it to you? The family is sick, so they are. The fever is here, ye best be going now...'

'We're from the city health department,' Bear says when Thomas stays quiet, 'We're here to check on the patients. How many have the fever?'

'They all do, so they have. What's it to you? We got the sign on the door, so we have.'

Bear falters for a second, unprepared for the passive aggression in her voice and the harsh glare.

'Yes, Ma'am,' Thomas says smoothly, jolting forward from a prod in the back from Zara, 'We're checking compliance ordinance in line with policy 108 subsection 2. You're aware of that policy, Ma'am. Are you the cook, Miss Mallon?'

'You know my name?' she demands as Bear and Zara look to Thomas.

'Of course,' Thomas says, 'You're the cook here. Our records are precise. We'll just need to see each patient please, and we'll be on our way. Stand aside.'

'I'll do no such thing,' Mary fires back, standing her ground.

'You'll move, Miss Mallon or my associate will move you,' Thomas says, locking eyes, 'Mr Bear...Miss Mallon is obstructing our passage.'

She finally moves back. Standing beside the open door. 'I'm a cook, no a housemaid,' she says through gritted teeth, 'I'll have no responsibility for this.'

'Yeah, I heard you don't like responsibility,' Thomas says, 'Where is the housemaid?'

'Dead,' Mary says flatly, eyeing Thomas for a long second while Bear and Zara exchange confused glances, 'What ye here for? To do what? They've got the fever, so they'll either die, or they won't.'

'Miss Zara here is a nurse. She will be checking the patients to assess suitability for a trial medication.'

'Her?' Mary asks, looking contemptuously at Zara, 'She's a nigger...'

'Now, Miss Mallon. We are on a schedule.'

'Right, ye are,' she says heavily, draping her rag over one shoulder, 'Up the stairs then...'

They move about the house without challenge. Hearing the groans and whimpers coming from rooms, with Mary giving the name of each family member in turn. That the Jefferson's are wealthy is obvious, but that they're all near death's door is also obvious. Most don't rouse, and those that do, barely open their eyes.

The experience becomes truly awful because each person they see is suffering near death from a disease for which they hold the treatment. They could ease pain right now. The vial of solution is big enough to give a dose to each and every member of the family, and that single dose might be enough to mean the difference between life and death. Except, they can't. They can only do one. Only Bernard Jefferson.

'Bernard?' Zara asks, standing next to the bed.

'I just said he is, so I did,' Mary snaps from the door, folding her meaty arms across her chest.

'Wait outside,' Thomas orders.

'I'll do no such thing...'

'You'll wait outside, or my associate will throw you from

the fucking window,' Thomas growls. She goes out quickly, easing the door closed.

'Thomas?' Zara whispers, 'What's going on?'

'That,' Thomas whispers back while pointing at the closed door, 'is Mary Mallon.'

'Who the hell is Mary Mallon?' Zara demands, looking at Bear who just shrugs.

'Mary Mallon?' Thomas says, looking at the blank expressions on their faces, 'Typhoid Mary?'

Zara blanches, pulling her head back and turning to look at the door the woman went through, 'Oh, my god... that's her?'

'Who?' Bear asks.

'Typhoid Mary,' Thomas whispers. 'She's a famous carrier of the disease... Moves from house to house being a cook and infecting every family she works for. She kills dozens of people before they lock her up in quarantine. Context, yeah?' he adds, looking at Zara.

'Jesus,' Zara says.

'Listen,' Thomas says, looking at them both in turn, 'We've got enough juice in that bottle to treat them all. And we can take her out...'

'No,' Zara says quickly, 'We're here for this.'

'But she kills loads,' Thomas says, motioning towards the door, 'Maybe, this is part of the test... Maybe all of this is like a moral thing?'

'No, no way. We do him, then we go,' Zara replies, her tone and manner firm.

'Bear?' Thomas asks.

'I'm with Zara, mate. The instructions are clear.'

'That's Typhoid Mary... She's a goddam serial killer.'

'This,' Zara hisses, waving a hand at Bernard Jefferson, 'We do this and nothing else.'

'Okay, okay,' Thomas says, backing down at her ferocity, 'Sorry, dude...'

'It's fine. Just get it done... Do you know how to do it?'

'Yeah, I think so,' Thomas says. He starts setting up. Pushing the needle through the rubber cap into the clear liquid within the vial, drawing back 4mg, a big dose, and more than needed.

'He's young,' Bear says, gently pushing the pyjama sleeve up the sleeping teenager's arm, 'Frail too...'

'Well, he gets to live,' Thomas mutters, pushing the needle into a vein to inject the solution. He covers the spot with a pinch of the pyjama top when he slides the needle out, holding it for a minute while Bear counts seven pills out from the bottle, leaving them on the bedside table under a slip a paper written with *one a day*.

Mary is gone by the time they leave, and they walk back through a near silent house to a near silent street without seeing her again.

'Okay,' Martha says, nodding to herself in the near silent planning offices, 'Okay. I see what you mean. They're good.'

'They are very good,' Pete says, motioning the screen.

'What's the backlog now?' Jacob asks.

'Sally?' Martha asks, looking over at a woman worker holding a clipboard.

'Er...nearly three hundred,' Sally says, checking her notes. 'The Old Lady is tasking more every day, and we just can't keep up. The operatives we lost to true death...the complexities of the missions...and er, the other side of course,' she drops her eyes for a second, remaining tight-lipped with a split-second of tension pulsing in the room. 'They all add up,' she adds quietly.

'We're sinking, Martha,' one of the workers calls out.

'Three new operatives,' Pete says, 'Is a big thing, no?'

Martha turns back to stare at the screen, watching Bear, Thomas, and Zara walk through Manhattan against a backdrop of horse drawn carriages. Seconds go by, and she thinks, biting her bottom lip, her arms folded, her feet planted until, eventually, she sighs with a heavy exhalation of air while shaking her head.

Jacob looks at the ground, Pete shrugs with disappointment.

'Get an RLI... Keep it simple,' Martha calls out, stilling all conversation. She lifts her head, eyeing the room and clapping her hands. 'Come on...get to it, and you two,' she points at Pete and Jacob, 'I want you armed and ready, in case. We'll see how good they are in the real world.'

CHAPTER EIGHTEEN

It is different. Immediately and instantly different. The intangible nature of something that can't be touched or identified because, whereas every scenario they have done so far felt real, this *is* real.

Zara stands flanked by Bear on one side and Thomas on the other. A classic, understated black dress clings to her frame, with the two men in smart black trousers and dark shirts, but they feel anything but elegant. Grimy skin, and greasy hands. Weary to the bone and drained from a long day in a constantly shifting landscape that makes them feel like they're barely clinging to sanity.

'We could just go,' she says quietly as the real people of the real world pass them on the street.

'Go where?' Thomas asks, watching the same thing.

'I don't know,' she admits after a silence, 'Bear? Would you go?'

Bear thinks for a second, weighing up the chance to go against seeing Roshi again. 'No, but you can if you want... I'll keep them back if anyone comes,' he speaks honestly, with an intense rawness of truth that makes Zara blink.

'Thomas?' she asks.

'Whatever you say,' he says.

'Me? I'm not in charge. What? Why are you both looking at me? Sod it... I'm too knackered to run away, and I'm actually looking forward to putting my feet up with a cup of tea in that freaky hobbit house... Let's just get it done and get back.'

A GREEN FOLDER with the letters RLI stencilled across the front was waiting for them on the table when they returned from New York 1905.

'You are hereby authorised to undertake a Real-Life-Incursion for the purposes of training. Your RLI has been evaluated to have a low prospect of true death, and you will be monitored at all times. In the event of an intervention from Discovery personnel, you will follow their instructions immediately and without discussion... Er...okay so,' Zara said, reading the folder, 'There's like a ton of information here, want me to read it all out?'

'Not really,' Thomas said heavily.

'Just the important bits,' Bear said.

'Er...August 7th. Carpe Diem restaurant on Seventh Avenue...Martin Alldis is celebrating his 50th birthday... basically he eats a bad lobster and dies from food poisoning. We've got to stop him eating it...the lobster that is. They've put in his description, the names of his party, his wife...even down to shoe sizes. It says the lobster he eats is the last one in the place. And they're giving us two hundred dollars for expenses...but they want receipts. That looks about it,' she said.

'So, what?' Thomas asked, 'We get there first, buy the last lobster and let birthday boy have the steak?'

'Err, yes, yes, I think so,' she said, 'Sounds like a plan. Let's get you two dressed then, shall we...'

They cross the road and go into the modern, warehouse-styled Carpe Diem restaurant, resplendently vulgar with exposed brick walls and misshaped tables, each with mix-matching chairs. Industrial style lights hang from rafters, and a light, funky beat plays softly from hidden speakers. Big potted plants add splashes of green, with works of ugly art on the walls. Repellent and fashionable at the same time.

'Table for three, please?' Thomas asks when a dark-suited, scowling waiter approaches them.

'This way,' the waiter says as though just the act of talking to them causes him physical discomfort. 'I'll get you menus,' he mumbles, waving a desultory hand at a table.

'No need,' Zara says, 'Three Lobsters, three colas.'

'Gee, I am so sorry, we've only got one lobster left,' the waiter says with acid dripping from his tongue.

'That's fine,' Thomas says quickly before Zara explodes, 'One lobster, two steaks, and three colas, please.'

'Whatever,' the waiter grumbles, walking off.

'He is so rude,' Zara says, shocked at the attitude.

Noise from the door. Jovial loud New York voices booming out as a thick set man with short, grey hair walks in, laughing with several other people.

'Alldis?' the waiter asks with a sneer.

'What the fuck's up with this guy?' a big man in the group says, stepping clear to motion a fat thumb at the waiter.

'I told you, Ronnie,' a woman says, nasal and loud, 'Being rude's a thing here. They do it here.'

'We're paying for rude?' the big guy asks.

'Er, hello?' the waiter asks, waving sarcastically.

'This guy,' the big man says, shaking his head at the waiter, 'What the fuck?'

'Food's great, Ronnie. You'll love it,' Martin Alldis says, motioning at the waiter.

'Fucking better be, Marty.'

'See,' Thomas says to Zara, 'It's a thing here.'

The place starts filling up with more customers, coming in to laugh in wonder at the acidic tones of the waiting staff who roll eyes, tut, and show utter disdain in everything they do. Menus are given out, drinks ordered, and finally, the waiters seek to establish what the Alldis group want to eat.

'Are you kidding me?' Martin Alldis exclaims on hearing the lobster is gone.

'Too late,' the waiter shrugs, pointing over, 'Greedy guts over there ordered it.'

'Hey, buddy, it's my birthday,' Martin shouts over with a grin, spreading his hands with an appeal to their good natures.

'Mine too, buddy,' Thomas laughs back.

Bear watches more customers arriving. A man and woman in dark clothes that glance over to his table with gazes that linger for a second. Behind them a party of four, also in dark clothes that do the same and look over for a second while being shown to a table.

'Lobster?' a waiter asks, plonking the plate down.

'Mine, thanks,' Thomas says, blinking at the whole lobster gleaming on the plate, surrounded by salad and fries. The steaks come next, taking Bear's attention from the customers to the food.

'I wouldn't risk eating the fries,' Zara says as Thomas takes one from the edge of the lobster plate.

He pauses, sighs wearily, and drops it back. 'Share?' he asks, nodding at her plate.

'Wow, this is thrilling,' Jennifer says, her voice breaking the studied silence of the planning office, 'And er... it's like way past six...I don't get overtime.'

'You can go,' Martha points out, 'You're not needed here.'

'Oh, it's fine. I'm still watching Bear's attitude.'

'Move the view left, Terry,' Martha orders. Terry taps away at his keyboard, studying the green code flowing down his screen. 'Good...pull back a little...great. All looks okay...' Martha frowns as the three newbies look up at something as the screen goes blank. 'What just happened? The feed's gone...'

'We've lost them,' Terry calls out, his fingers tapping frantically at the keyboard.

A DARK SUIT AND SHIRT. Blond hair cut short, with cold, blue eyes set in a rugged, handsome face. He stops at their table, making them all look up in surprise.

'Mind if I join you?' he asks politely, pulling a chair out to sit down.

'It's a private party, buddy,' Thomas says.

'I'm sure it is,' the man says, looking from Bear to Thomas, to Zara, his manner easy and relaxed, humour in his eyes. 'My name is Robert, it's very nice to meet you...' an English accent, clear and deep, 'Damned pity about that bad lobster. Poor Martin really wanted that tonight.'

'You're from Discovery,' Zara says with a sigh of relief as Thomas relaxes, 'Have we passed? Can we go back now? My bloody feet are killing me.'

Robert listens, nodding earnestly while leaning over the table towards her plate of steak and fries. 'May I? Haven't eaten a thing today. Now, let me see...you must be Thomas. You're obviously Zara? So, that means you must be Bear. Tell me, Bear...how is little Roshi?' he asks in a voice that makes Bear focus that bit more.

'We haven't seen her,' Zara says, 'Pete and Jacob are training us...'

'Pete and Jacob,' Robert muses, 'The last great bastions of Discovery. Good operatives too, very good.'

'Listen, we've been doing this all day. Can we at least get an explanation now?' Zara asks, clearly exhausted.

Robert smiles as though understanding entirely the day they are having, 'What do you think is happening?'

'I think we did stage two, and because Roshi gave Bear extra tuition or whatever, they chucked us into some scenarios... I don't know. We only got here yesterday...'

'I would say that makes a great deal of sense,' Robert says thoughtfully, eating more fries, 'But I'm not from Discovery... I'm from the other side...'

'Other side?' Zara asks, 'What other side?'

'The other side,' Robert says, covering his mouth as he speaks, 'I'm from Freedom.'

'GET A LOCK ON THAT LOCATION,' Martha shouts into the chaos of the planning office as she strides into her office, using a key to unlock a metal cabinet that she yanks open to reveal an armoury of black pistols.

'Martha...it's them...they're blocking us,' Terry calls out.

'Easy now, chaps,' Jacob booms, 'Stay calm...find the nearest workable location, and we'll go from there... Jennifer, get ready for a recall.'

'How many?' Jennifer asks, rushing across the room to a free terminal.

'Freedom?' Zara asks, looking at Thomas and Bear, as though to check if they know what it means, but seeing only blank looks.

'These are nice chips. Oh, we're in America, aren't we, so I should say fries. You're an American, aren't you?' Robert asks, looking at Thomas.

'Yes, Sir.'

'Always good manners, the Americans,' Robert says, 'Warmongering, greedy, fanatically religious nutjobs, but they do it with nice manners... Let me continue and forgive me rushing, but we don't have long. We've blocked the signal, you see. That means Discovery can't see us, and they don't have a lock on this location to deploy anyone...'

Chaos reigns in the planning offices, with keyboards clattering, and voices calling out in panicked tones. 'We've got nothing for over a hundred miles,' Terry shouts.

'Keep looking,' Pete says calmly, 'Sally...look for a back door, yes?'

'I'm trying, Pete,' Sally mutters, her fingers blurring over the keyboard.

'Jesus,' Zara says, rubbing her forehead, 'We've been going all day, and it feels like every twat and his dog is speaking in riddles and weird little clipped sentences that all mean something to you lot, but not to anyone else...'

'My apologies,' Robert says sincerely, holding his hands up, 'Let me explain. There are two AI's. They both want the same thing, but they have very different views on how that is achieved. Both reside in constructs provided by our AI's. Yours is called Discovery. Ours is called Freedom... Your AI is called the Old Lady. We have... Well, let's just say we have someone else. Is that clear so far?'

'Surprisingly, yes,' Zara says, 'Thank you.'

'You're very welcome,' he says, giving her a warm smile, 'We do things differently in Freedom, for instance, we tell our newbies exactly what's happening as soon as they arrive.'

'Oh my god, they need to do that in Discovery,' Zara says, 'Seriously, it was all like cryptic comments and go here, go there, here is your house, don't go out, this is a tearoom, this is a café in Paris...'

'Pete and Jacob,' Robert says with a nod, 'Same training script, god, that's old now. Do they still have those awful children tied to the bombs?'

'Yes!' Zara exclaims, leaning forward, 'That was horrible.'

'Freedom is...different,' Robert says, choosing his words carefully. 'Which is why I am here...to extend an invitation to join us. I'm told you three have done remarkably well, so I am shamelessly poaching. You'll have better housing, better facilities, better training, better everything... Think of it like this...Discovery is the British Army. They try hard, they work hard, and they're good at what they do but are largely ineffective, whereas Freedom is the US army. The biggest there ever will be and the best equipped. We have more, we do more...we work hard, but we also play hard. Discovery is a greasy, little café. Freedom is a five-star luxury resort...and one that doesn't serve poisonous lobster...I'm er...running out of analogies,' he says with a self-effacing grin, 'You only arrived yesterday, and no doubt, you went through the circuit and to the diner to see Allie, then the doctor? Who by the way is unfit to practise medicine, in my opinion...'

'Thank you,' Zara states, waving a hand at Robert, 'She was bloody awful.'

'We have proper doctors,' Roberts says, 'We have proper everything...'

'Er, hang on a sec,' Zara says, 'How did you know we were here?'

'Oh, I can't tell you our secrets...unless you join us, then I can tell you our secrets. Now listen, Martha will have her bods finding a back door any minute. So, how about it?'

'What?' Zara asks.

'Joining us,' Robert says, turning in his chair. 'Todd?' he calls out over the restaurant to another table filled with people in dark clothing. 'You were in Disco...which do you prefer?'

'Is this a trick question?' Todd calls back, making nearly every dark clothes wearing person in the restaurant laugh, 'I prefer Disco...joke! Seriously, choose Freedom, there's no comparison.'

'Hey, buddy,' the big guy with Martin Alldis' group calls out, 'go over and talk, huh? We're trying to eat a meal here...'

'Apologies,' Robert says, turning back on his chair,

'Todd was in Discovery until we rescued him. Anyway, there it is…and I do hate to rush you, but I must press for a decision.'

'Got the state,' Sally shouts, tapping furiously at her keyboard, 'Still too far out… going for the city…okay I can…I can get into the city…closest is Queens…'

'Too far,' Martha says, 'Queens is what? Thirty minutes by car? Get closer.'

'I'm trying…' Sally mutters.

'It's a strong signal,' Terry says, shaking his head, 'Strongest we've seen…'

'Martha?' Jennifer calls out, 'I'm logged in… How many do you want on recall?'

'Everyone,' Martha says, 'Get everyone.'

'An hour from now, you could be relaxing in a hot bath, with decent food, before you sleep in comfortable beds in a town you are free to roam in at your leisure, with a professional training package designed by the very best…'

'Okay, slow down,' Zara says, holding her hands out in a way Bear and Thomas now recognise as the precursor to a whole bunch of questions, 'How are you different? What do you do that's different? How can two AI's both be trying to change time, won't you be constantly undermining each other? It doesn't make sense…'

Robert sighs, flicking his wrist out to pull his sleeve so he can check the shiny gold watch on his watch. 'Good questions. You're smart, I like that, but we don't have time now. So, how about it?'

'How do we contact you?' Zara asks in a tired voice while rubbing her face, 'This is a bit much, to be honest...'

'You don't, is the simple answer,' Robert says bluntly but with an apologetic wince, 'It's now or never.' He leans forward, lowering his voice, 'But trust me when I say this...*not* joining us is the biggest mistake you will ever make...'

'I've got a back door in a deli on Eleventh Avenue! Go for room one...' Sally cries out as Pete and Jacob run for the deployment corridor and hold position outside the first door.

'LIVE,' Sally shouts the word that is taken and echoed by everyone else as the green lightbulb above the door pings on. The two men rush in, crossing the room to the door on the other side and through into the shockingly ice-cold air of a walk-in freezer in the back of a deli on Third Avenue as Jennifer types the message on her screen and hits send.

A brothel.
Mid-west America
1892.

She stares up at him. Tall and lean, with a thick, greying beard, tobacco stained around the mouth and chin. Leathery skin, and deep lines from years spent driving cattle across the plains. He stinks too. A pungent disgusting aroma of beer, whiskey, tobacco, cow-shit, and body odour.

That he's drunk is obvious. That's he's very horny is also obvious, judging by the bulge of his pants and the disgusting way he's rubbing himself over his clothes.

'I'ma gonna fuck you,' he drawls, reaching out to grope a breast but finding his hand swatted away.

'Stop being a grabby twat...'

'Playing hard to get makes me hornier than a dung beetle eating shit...'

'I'm playing impossible to get actually...besides, I'm still a bit sore from last night with Bear, so you've lucked out. Not that you'd get any even if it wasn't sore. Just so we're clear on that... Jesus, mate, you're not even listening...' she waves a hand in front of his face, but his eyes stay locked on her cleavage bulging from the dress. *The whore dress* as she calls it.

'I'ma gonna titty fuck you...'

'Ew, that's so gross,' Roshi says, pulling her head back in distaste, 'We've just got to wait here for a minute.'

'I'ma gonna give you the best damned minute of your life...'

'Wow, you're not even joking, are you? Get off! Stop pawing at me. Listen, grabby Magoo, Carlos is going to get caught cheating at the poker table in a minute. Jackson will call him out, and Carlos will have a big hissy fit to try and hide the cards up his sleeve... They all start shooting, and you're meant to get slotted through the head, so just be quiet and let me save your life...'

'I'ma gonna...'

'Pack it in before I break a finger...' Roshi says, glancing at the clock on the wall of the filthy bedroom in the filthy brothel that she suddenly started working at a few hours ago, 'Here we go...three...two...'

A shout. More shouts. A crash as a table is turned

over downstairs. Angry voices. She listens intently, pushing his hands away as they cycle through the air trying to touch her boobs. Even the gunshot doesn't stop him trying. Or the rest of the shots that let rip in a thunderous roar.

'I just saved your life,' she tells him.

'I'ma gonna...'

A bleep, and she arches her eyebrows at the vibration between her legs. 'Excuse me,' she hoists her skirts up, delves a hand into the darkness and pulls a bleeper from the Velcro strap on the top of her thigh. Squinting at the message scrolling across the screen.

TOTAL RECALL. THREE NEWBIES DOWN. RLI NY 7TH AVE. TOTAL RECALL. ALL UNITS. TOTAL RECALL.

'Come here,' the man growls with lust in his eyes at seeing her hitching her skirts. She grabs his thumb, snaps the joint and slams the flat of her palm into his nose, sending him reeling back as she yanks at the buckle of his thick, leather belt, pulling the strand free from the prong to whip it from his waist as he topples back.

She carries the motion on, swinging the heavy belt around her hips, looping the strap, and cinching it tight, before whipping the heavy six-shooter from the holster, while hoping to hell the grabby twat has kept it clean and oiled as she goes out the door and down the landing next to the balcony overlooking the people standing in shock over the bodies killed in the shoot-out.

'DAMN WHORE ROBBED ME,' the man roars, blundering from the room behind her with spurting blood from his nose as she starts down the wooden stairs.

'Oh, bugger...not now...' she runs on, going as fast as she can in the thick skirts.

'THERE...THE WHORE ROBBED ME,' he screams out, leaning over the balcony to point at her.

'You stand right still there, missy,' a man looms at the bottom of the stairs, a rifle held in his hands, and a gleaming tin star pinned to his shirt.

'Sure thing,' she says, holding her hands up. 'It was just a joke...' she reaches down slowly for the gun on her hip with her left hand, showing she intends to disarm.

'Damn bitch broke my nose...'

'I'm so sorry,' Roshi whispers before she flips the gun around and fires into the sheriff's chest. He flies back across the room as she drops to a crouch and palms the hammer back with her left to fire with her right at the men drawing guns on her. A world of noise and smoke. A world of screams, and five more men fall dead, but she's gone, snatching the Winchester rifle from the ground and the sheriff's pistol before running out into the night.

'Shit...shit...' Pete gasps, running behind Jacob, 'I'm too old for this...'

'Not the only one,' Jacob wheezes, powering on down the street. 'POLICE...MOVE...' he bellows with years of authority that make people believe his words, and they wilt back, clearing the path ahead, while across the world, across times and eras, bleepers vibrate and buzz with operatives pulling out and away from whatever they're doing to run for their exit points. A total recall has been ordered. Three newbies down in an RLI New York.

The door to room two bursts open as a blond haired,

blue eyed World War Two German Officer runs out. 'Who? Where?' he demands.

'Helmut! Thank god. Restaurant...Carpe Diem, Seventh Avenue...got a back door open on Eleventh...room one...go, go, go...' Martha shoves the semi-automatic pistol at him as he runs for room one, going through the same second as the door to room eight flies open.

'What's going on?' the new operative demands, his chef whites stained with food while the ladle in his hand drips onion soup on the floor.

Martha briefs, swapping the ladle for a pistol before sending him running for room one, and still they come. Men and women, postal workers, air stewards, beggars, priests, and everything in between lurching through numbered doors to be armed and sent back out, because they all know what a total recall means, and it could be them out there, it could be them waiting for the cavalry.

'Robert,' a woman calls over from the other side of the restaurant, making a show of tapping her watch. Robert checks his own, sighing heavily. 'We need to go,' the woman says.

'Yes, Beatrice,' Robert replies, emulating an expression of being nagged.

'Goddam,' the big man in Martin Alldis' group booms, 'quit the shouting, will ya...'

'Correction,' Robert says to Thomas. 'Not all Americans have good manners... Vile piece of shit,' he mutters darkly, casting a look at the Alldis table. 'Now I really do need an answer, but let me just say this... You don't *all* have to come,' he adds, looking only at Zara.

'We stay together,' Zara says firmly. The sharpness in her eyes now back as her senses kick in, reacting to his sneer, his arrogance, and the unhidden predation within his eyes, 'Thank you for your offer, but we respectfully decline.'

It's like she slapped him. Like she reached over and struck his face, and that rakish charm evaporates with his cold eyes hardening in a suddenly charged atmosphere as the whole place falls suddenly silent with tension ramping higher by the second.

'Bear, ask this man to leave, please,' Zara says, her voice carrying clearly across the room. Her unflinching gaze resting on Robert.

'You should go now,' Bear says, his voice flat and all the more threatening for the lack of tone.

Robert blinks once, blinks twice, and double-takes before turning on his chair to look around the restaurant, holding his hands up, and mouthing *what the fuck* with an expression that makes his group burst out laughing, and that split second reminds Bear of standing naked in the masquerade room, and he doesn't like that. He doesn't like that one bit.

'Robert, we really need to move,' Beatrice calls out with a chuckle, rising from the chair. 'What are we doing with them?' she asks, nodding at the Alldis group.

Robert pushes up from the table, shaking his head in disappointment. 'Such a shame,' he says to Zara. 'Kill them,' he calls out.

A hundred different things seem to happen in a hundred places at the same time in a stunning blur of motion as the world around Zara and Thomas explodes in surge of violence that everyone else seemed prepared for.

Bear drives up, grabbing the plate of lobster that he sends spinning across the room at Beatrice as she pulls the gun from the holster in the small of her back. As that plate spins away, sending the lobster and fries sailing through the air, Bear goes in, reaching out to grab Robert's wrist holding the gun he pulled from under his suit jacket, rotating around to snap the joint, but Robert goes with him, denying the break, the two locked as they turn at speed, while Robert plucks the trigger, sending shots past Bear's legs.

Beatrice goes down from the plate, smashing her front teeth out, and in the panic and pain of that same second, she pulls the trigger on her gun, sending a shot across the room into the surly waiter who staggers back into a table full of dark clothed operatives who burst up to their feet drawing weapons.

Thomas launches from his chair a split second after Bear, throwing himself over the table at Zara, intending to take her down with a heroic act of using himself as a human shield, but he misses, sailing by an inch from her side as she looks at the lobster and Beatrice's teeth seemingly floating in the air, and the waiter flying back, while the booming shots come from Robert's gun as he tries to shoot Bear while they dance on the spot.

'What the...' Zara flinches, looking down at Thomas groaning on the floor next to her as the lobster, teeth, and shot waiter all let gravity take over.

'DOWN,' Bear screams out.

Zara dives on Thomas, heroically using herself as a human shield while Bear simply pushes Robert away and spins around on one foot to kick the pistol from his hand, following through to shift balance and weight and sending his other foot up to kick into Robert's mid-section, smashing him back into the table that crashes down on top of Zara and Thomas.

A flash to his right, and Bear steps back, leaning away

from the blade slashing at his face. A grip, a twist, and he plucks the knife free before sticking it in the attacker's throat, ripping it across to sever the artery that spurts an arc of blood across the restaurant as the man spins away, and Bear spots the woman coming from his left, leaving himself open for a kick to the chest, absorbing the blow, but catching the leg, and twisting hard while kicking into the side of the knee on the supporting leg. The woman drops in abject shock. A second later, and her head wrenches over from Bear gripping her skull with a vicious show of power to the rest coming at him who falter in step at his absolute lack of fear.

'Shoot him, you pricks,' Robert shouts, floundering to get up from the broken remnants of the table.

'Oh, shit,' Bear mutters as over a dozen black-clothed operatives stop to draw guns. He starts to move, diving for a pillar a few feet off to the side as the guns let rip with rounds slamming the walls, the floor and splintering tables, chairs, works of art, and lampshades.

As the black-clothed operatives form a horse-shoe line to fire, so the huge plate windows behind them shatter into thousands of glittering chunks of glass that rain down from the bullets coming from Pete and Jacob as they sprint towards the restaurant.

A head blows out and a chest puckers with a red crimson bloom as the black-clothed operatives spin around to return fire.

Robert shouts out, vaulting to his feet as Bear does the same, running back at him as the man snatches a pistol from the ground to aim at Pete. Bear goes into him with hard kicks to his midsection, but Robert turns on the move, deflecting the blows and sending a vicious back-handed swipe that snaps Bear's head over.

'GET MORE,' Robert roars out.

Beatrice spits teeth and blood while huddled on the floor across the restaurant as waiters and customers scream in panic. She pulls a tablet from a pocket, smearing blood over the screen that makes her curse and rub it down her arm to clear it away.

'GET OUT,' Jacob booms, coming to a stop behind a car that slewed into a wall in panic at seeing two armed men shooting guns in the street, 'ZARA...TOM...GET OUT, GET OUT...'

'COVER ME...' Pete goes forward, with his pistol gripped double-handed as he vaults the ledge through the busted window to land squarely within Carpe Diem restaurant. He starts firing into black-clad bodies, while Jacob sends rounds in from outside, suppressing to buy the Frenchman time.

Beatrice hits send on the tablet and drops it to snatch her pistol up, aiming to send a shot at Pete, hitting him in the shoulder. He goes down with a roar, twisting to fire back as she sends more rounds in his direction.

In the street outside, the already panicked pedestrians and drivers freeze at the sight of a World War Two German Officer sprinting down the middle of the road, holding a gun. 'JACOB...PETE...' Helmut roars out.

'Pete's hit, three newbies inside...' Jacob shouts back, 'COVER ME...'

'NO!' Helmut tries shouting, but Jacob runs for it, diving through the broken window to land hard, whacking the air from his lungs, but he crawls on, desperate to reach his old friend, firing left-handed while his right clasps the bullet hole in his shoulder.

'Get them out, Jacob,' Pete gasps, changing magazine with a grimace at the pain.

'CAVALRY ARE COMING,' Jacob roars, 'HOLD ON…'

'SO ARE OURS,' Robert shouts.

'Roshi!' Martha cries out in relief, seeing the woman running from room seven.

'Where?' Roshi demands.

'I'm coming,' Martha says, taking the lead through room one to the cold freezer of the deli on Eleventh, running out into traffic as the two women build to a flat-out sprint.

Bear crawls to Zara and Thomas. Pulling them into a huddle as the three hunker down. Pete and Jacob behind a pillar, both bleeding and only taking studied shots to keep the others back as their ammunition depletes.

Helmut waves to the others arriving. Chefs, nuns, priests, hotel bellboys, and beggars sprinting flat out down Seventh Avenue with pistols up and aimed at Carpe Diem restaurant. 'THAT'S ENOUGH…' he shouts out, 'CEASEFIRE. CEASEFIRE…'

The call is taken up with Pete and Jacob repeating it until some of the black-clothed operatives stop firing, and a second later, a strained silence settles, only broken by the groans and whimpers of the terrified and hurt.

'Leave it, Robert,' Jacob calls out, 'You're changing history.'

'Go fuck yourself, old man,' Robert shouts back.

'Enough!' Pete yells, 'These are innocent people…we have rules…'

'We've got more coming, Robert,' Helmut shouts outside, 'Total recall. Stop this now.'

'You're not the only ones with a recall...' Robert calls out.

Helmut frowns as a plain door set within a wall bursts out with people pouring out. Men and women dressed as waiters, as hospital workers, as soldiers, and everything in between.

'Scheisse!' Helmut mutters.

The new arrivals react quickly, darting in all directions while bringing weapons up that start firing into the parked and crashed cars with a whole new firefight erupting.

'This is not good, my old friend,' Pete tells Jacob, wincing in pain as he cranes up to snatch a view of outside, 'I draw them out, oui? I run for Robert...you go to Zara and the others...yes? We do this.'

'Don't be an idiot,' Jacob snaps, 'Just hunker down.'

'TOO MANY,' Helmut bellows, seeing the Freedom operatives storm into the street as, behind him, more Discovery operatives reach the defensive line.

'Too many,' Pete says, nodding at Jacob, 'I go oui? I death charge now...'

'No bloody death charges,' Jacob says, pulling him back down again.

'No, Monsieur, I will death charge. It is my honour.'

'You think the British are going to be out-death-charged by the bloody French?' Jacob snaps.

'Then we will both death charge,' Pete exclaims.

'DAMN BLOODY RIGHT WE WILL,' Jacob roars.

'WE WILL DEATH CHARGE,' Pete booms.

'DO NOT DEATH CHARGE,' Helmut yells.

'Christ, those two are so old,' Robert mutters, shaking his head.

'DEATH CHARGE!' Jacob cries out.

'DEATH CHARGE,' Pete screams.

'NOBODY IS DEATH CHARGING,' Helmut shouts.

'Why aren't they bloody death charging?' Roshi asks, sprinting flat out towards the chaos at the end of Seventh Avenue, 'They should be death charging...'

'Fancy it?' Martha asks, while keeping pace at her side.

'Oh yes, fuck yes...FUCK YES! DEATH CHARGE!'

'Roshi,' Robert hisses, hearing her voice.

'Roshi,' Bear says, lifting his head.

'Roshi?' Beatrice lisps.

'Bloody Roshi,' Jacob grumbles.

'Roshi...no!' Helmut shouts, trying to run out as Roshi vaults the front end of a crashed car while firing the rifle at a Freedom soldier. Martha at her side, firing a pistol one handed as the two women spearhead the attack.

'Scheisse,' Helmut mutters, 'DEATH CHARGE...'

A call to arms as the Discovery operatives pour over the cars to charge at the enemy. Screaming out as Roshi spins the Winchester rifle over, with a grip on the trigger guard, taking another shot, before doing the same again.

'Fuck's sake,' Robert says at the scream going up, 'DEATH CHARGE...'

The Freedom operatives take their turn to give voice. Breaking cover to run at their sworn enemies as the street outside the Carpe Diem restaurant fills with men and women, all in varying costumes and clothes. All of them shouting. All of them running at the other side, with a ragged cacophony of gunshots ringing out before they come together to brawl and fight dirty, while those watching stand with slack-jaws and wide eyes.

Roshi aims and fires, leaping through the window into

the restaurant while spinning the rifle over to reload. She aims and fires, her dark eyes blazing, while her chest heaves in the *whore dress*. Turning on the spot with a swish of skirts, while flicking the rifle over to fire again as she spots Bear and grins that wry smile.

'Hello, my brave little tiger. Are you hiding or fighting?'

Another rotation of the rifle, but it clicks empty as she aims on a man bringing his pistol up. She doesn't hesitate but ditches the Winchester while moving left, and quickly draws the six-shooter, palming the hammer back to fire the heavy gun, and it's that point, right there in that precise second, that Bear knows he is head over heels in love.

In the carnage and chaos of that second and through the smoke, screams and blood of the firefight, he surmises that only by dying with someone so many times can you truly understand what love is, for they have held each other's hearts in their hands. Literally. After cutting with knives and ripping them out. Which was gross at the time, but now, actually, seems quite romantic.

Within that same second, and while Bear stares lovingly on, Roshi comes to understand that the problem with a six-shooter is that it only has six bullets. Hence the name, and six bullets don't last a long time. Robert counts them off, listening to the different sound the gun makes. Deeper. More thunderous, and on the fifth shot, while Bear sighs the sigh of a smitten man, so Robert grips his pistol and readies himself.

Roshi fires the last shot and drops the pistol to look for a new weapon as Robert surges to his feet a few metres to her side, 'Hello, little Roshi...'

She snaps her head over, her face showing instant rage at seeing him, but that expression morphs into fear when she clocks the pistol in his hand. A second of life left, and she snatches a look to Bear, her eyes wide. A second of life left. A second to mouth ***kill 'em all*** before the bullet enters her forehead and takes the back of her skull out.

Bear just stares. The world spinning around him. His mind back in the seven-sided room when the men beat her to death, and the felt rage inside at someone else hurting her because, although, what he and Roshi did to each other was sick and twisted, it was theirs, between them, and not for anyone else. She tortured him, but she took it back when he learnt to fight, and through those many, many hours, they shared something that was theirs and theirs alone. They held each other when they died and bled. She took him to New York and called him silly names, and took his rage without reaction in the warehouse, and sat on his lap as they watched the whales on the raft. She came to his room nervous and scared, and they made love as a man and woman. That was theirs. Theirs alone, and someone else just killed her, and so he is back in the seven-sided room, with a deep violent rage erupting inside that someone else dared hurt the woman he loves, while in his mind he sees only the words she mouthed.

Kill 'em all.

Robert doesn't stand a chance and feels the impact as Bear rips him from his feet. Slamming him down to stamp on his legs and arms.

Black suit wearing figures rush in and die. Someone stabs Bear in the gut, but he snaps the attacker's neck and carries on with the knife still there. He doesn't go down when someone shoots him in the back either but launches Robert through the single remaining plate glass window to land hard, sprawled and bleeding on the street outside.

Bear goes after him, leaping through as the glass still falls, and the Freedom operatives swarm in to die with broken bones. Bear's shot again but still keeps going, slamming them down and battering them aside to reach Robert, pulling the knife from his stomach to slit throats. To stab chests. To kill 'em all while that rage explodes within. There is no limit here. There was no limit in the seven-sided room. There was no limit on the circuit. Only death and violence. The same then. The same now. Roshi is dead.

Kill 'em all.

On he goes. Unstoppable within his rage. Seemingly impervious to pain as another knife is stabbed into his shoulder. He breaks the attacker's neck and lunges at Robert trying to crawl away. Heaving him over onto his back. Dropping over him. Pinning him to the ground. Slicing his gut open. Slicing deep.

'RETREAT...GET THE HELL OUT...' a Freedom operative shouts the words as those that can run break for their exit point while Bear hacks at Robert's mid-section to open the wound before reaching in to pull his innards out, wrapping them round Robert's neck to strangle him with his own intestines.

Mass panic all around. Chaos and confusion. Someone grabs at Bear who catches sight of a chef's uniform and lashes out, sending the man flying away. A priest grabs Bear's arm but drops from a broken neck. More come, clowns, doctors, nurses and pilots. All shouting and screaming with noise only to fall with broken arms, broken legs, or broken necks.

Someone shoots him in the arm, but he is not here. This is not real, and pain does not exist. Someone else shoots him in the belly, but that just makes him remember the time he and Roshi shot each other in the seven-sided room, and so he gets meaner, angrier, and faster, until Pete and Jacob, using each other as support, gain the street to take aim with pistols.

The two men fire repeatedly, sending bullets into Bear's chest, stomach, legs, and arms, but still, he roars until Pete lifts his aim and sends a round through his head. After that is only the familiar blackness of death that Bear knows so well.

CHAPTER NINETEEN

Six months later...

Monday

A BEAUTIFUL AUTUMNAL DAWN. Cold and crisp with an endless blue sky, and the ground a breath-taking vista of reds and browns from trees shedding their leaves that give a satisfying crunch from the overnight frost when he runs over them.

He takes Main Street to the intersection, running out of town past the big detached houses, *work hard to a decent position and one day get a house down there.*

Bear remembers Allie's words. He remembers them every time he runs through this end of the town, but he barely glances at the lawns and gardens, or the white-picket fences. He just listens to the leaves crunching underfoot and runs on, taking the junction that leads up the steep incline to the hobbit homes at the top.

He runs faster. Feeling his legs starting to hurt. Feeling his lungs working harder. His heart booming. He goes faster still, building to a sprint, with pain radiating out, but the pain isn't enough. It's never enough.

He reaches the top and takes hard lefts and rights down the alleys, rat-runs and paths, pounding past front doors, behind which the townsfolk of Discovery slumber at peace in their beds. He vaults benches and tables, leaping walls and dropping over heights greater than his own to land and run on.

He goes past Zara's home, noting her new curtains hanging on the inside and the nice new rattan patio furniture on her small veranda. A sprint past Thomas's home, smiling at the enormous gas-powered barbeque that could feed the whole of Discovery in one sitting.

He slows only when his own home comes in sight. Situated at the edge nearest the treeline, seemingly set aside from everyone else, like he is not part of it all.

A metal bar bolted to a frame fixed at the edge of his veranda. He jumps up, grabbing the cold metal, and starts the pull ups while looking at the rose bushes growing in pots, running alongside his wall. Thorny and gnarled, with twisting branches, and they won't bloom now until spring again, but that's okay. He can wait.

Pull ups. Push ups. Several sets of each, until he finally stands with sweat dripping from the end of his nose while lost in his own mind for a few minutes.

When he goes in, he does so to a place unchanged since the first night he stayed here. The same colours. The same furniture, and if he closes his eyes and inhales deeply, he imagines he can still smell her cherry blossom scent.

He drinks Discovery tea and eats Discovery toast covered with Discovery butter. He showers, dresses, and prepares for the day in silence, while elsewhere people wake nicely and listen to music as they prepare for their day ahead.

Jacket on, and he steps out to walk back through the alleys, rat-runs, and paths as the townspeople come out of their doors, turning away or even going back inside until he has passed. It doesn't matter. None of it matters.

He knocks the door and waits. 'OPEN, DUDE,' he goes in to see Thomas in his boxers, shoving a piece of toast in his mouth.

'Mate,' Bear says, rolling his eyes.

'I know, I know, man…' Thomas groans, rushing into his bedroom, 'So damn cold, I didn't want to get up…'

'Lazy shit,' Bear says. He likes Thomas's home and the way it's full of gadgets and appliances. Juicers, blenders, drinks makers, ice makers, everything-makers. Stacks of newspapers and magazines on the sides. Books everywhere. Prints, pictures, and paintings on the walls.

'Been for a run?' Thomas calls out.

'Yep,' Bear says, 'Come with me tomorrow.'

'Say, let me think. Sure. I could do that. Or, I could use the gym that has heating and running machines, and music, and nice women in tight clothes…'

Bear chuckles to himself, flicking through a pre-internet clothing catalogue from the 1980's.

'Ready,' Thomas says, presenting himself.

'You've trimmed it,' Bear says, nodding at Thomas's beard.

'Zara said a short beard makes me look trustworthy and authoritative.'

'Authoritative.'

'Nah, dude, it's authoritative.'

'It's not. It's authoritive.'

'Whatever, man,' Thomas says, widening his eyes, 'We going or what, huh? Waiting all morning for you.'

'Twat.'

'Holy moly, it's cold out here,' Thomas says when they step out.

'Morning, Tom.'

'Who's that?' Thomas asks, looking round, 'Oh hey, Norman.'

'Cold day,' Norman calls out, walking past while making a point of not looking at Bear.

'Sure is, I just said that to Bear,' Thomas says.

'You have a good day now, Tom.'

'Thanks, Norman,' Thomas says, offering a grim smile to Bear who just shrugs.

'Open up…it's the feds,' Thomas says a few minutes later, knocking at the door.

'Better have a warrant…'

They go into an exquisitely designed interior of soft browns and creams that all blend to create a beautiful home. Everything, from the rugs on the floor to the artwork on the walls, to the style and design of the furniture, is sublime, and if Bear likes Thomas's home, he loves Zara's. They both do. It's impossible not to.

'Well done,' she says with a nod at Tom's beard. 'Looks better.'

'Authoritive or authoritative?' Bear asks.

'Authoritative,' she says, walking off into her bedroom.

'Told you,' Thomas says, nodding slowly, 'And now you owe me ten bucks.'

'What? Fuck off…we didn't bet money.'

'One month ago, we made an agreement that all

disputes will carry a financial penalty for the loser…ten bucks.'

'Seriously?'

'Yup,' Thomas says, 'Ten bucks.'

'Zara?' Bear asks.

'The night Thomas got his new spaceship…I mean barbeque…you had a few beers and agreed it.'

'Fine,' Bear says, pulling a banknote from his pocket to hand over.

'I thank you,' Thomas says, plucking it away, 'I bet that hurt deep, you tight ass.'

'Right, come on then,' Zara says, bustling them to the door and out into the cold air, 'Work to do, chop, chop.'

They reach the diner on main street, with the morning sun bathing the town in gorgeous yellow light, and the air filled with the scent of pine from the forests surrounding them.

Zara goes in first to an early morning muted ambience of people sipping coffees and eating breakfast before they start work.

'Morning, Zara…hey, Tom.'

'Morning, Mavis,' Zara replies, showing displeasure in her tone at Bear being ignored.

Bear reaches the counter, moving into a gap between two men who suddenly decide to take their coffees to a booth instead.

'Ah, man, that's just rude,' Thomas remarks, earning rueful looks from the men.

'Doesn't matter,' Bear says quietly, 'Morning, James.'

At least James greets him warmly. A big smile on the big man as he looms massive behind the counter. A white apron covering his blue jeans, and checked shirt, and he serves the coffees with the speed of an elephant moving slowly.

'Pancakes?' Bear asks, looking at Zara and Thomas, 'Three for pancakes, James.'

'Okay, Bear.'

'Thanks, mate... Oh, and Tom is paying,' he says, grabbing his and Zara's mugs before stepping away to their usual table at the back.

'Hey,' Thomas blurts, 'You're so goddam tight.'

'Funny how life works out,' Zara remarks as they slide into the cushioned seats.

'Guess so,' Bear replies.

'Guess so, what?' Thomas asks, sliding in next to Zara. 'You're an asshole for that,' he tells Bear.

'I'll buy you lunch.'

'Where are you going for lunch?' Zara asks.

'We don't know,' Thomas says, giving her an open loo, 'Where are we going for lunch?'

'Good point,' she says slowly, 'Anyway, I was saying it's funny how life works out.'

'Yeah, like that morning I had ten bucks, and then I didn't have ten bucks...'

Zara sips her coffee, relishing the strong taste while thinking, 'It's the memorial thing this weekend...'

'Gee, bring the mood down, will ya,' Thomas says.

'Just saying,' she says, 'We have to go.'

'Correction. *You* have to go,' Bear says.

'We all have to go,' she says.

'Nope.'

'Bear, imagine how it will look if you ignore it.'

'It doesn't really matter either way, does it,' he says as James slides the tray of food onto the table, 'I go, and everyone hates me for turning up. I don't go, and everyone hates me for not going. So, I might as well not go.'

'We're going,' she says, 'Thank you, James.'

'That's okay, Zara,' the big man rumbles, thudding off back towards the counter.

'Listen,' she says, reaching out for a pancake.

'Uh-huh,' Thomas cuts in, shaking his head, 'It's breakfast.'

'I was just saying that...'

'Say it after,' he says, 'I'm having me some Monday morning carb loading without work talk.'

'Fine. But we're going.'

'Quit trying to get the last word in.'

'I wasn't. I was just saying we're going.'

'Dude. You're doing it again...'

The squabble continues as they devour the food and drink the coffee, with caffeine levels and blood sugar spiking quickly, animating their conversations as their voices grow that bit louder before heading for the planning offices, pushing in to see Jennifer lurching to her feet behind the desk.

'Morning, Bear,' she says brightly. 'And you other people,' she adds with a wave of her hand.

'Hey, Jen,' Bear says.

'He called me Jen,' Jennifer says, 'He wants me...'

'You look nice today, Jen...'

'Err, piss off, Tom... How was your weekend, Bear? I saw you running this morning. You looked like super-fast. I was totally thinking I should start running.'

'You should,' Bear says as Zara tuts, grabs his arms, and pulls him on down the corridor towards the stairs.

'So fit,' Jennifer mutters.

'We can still hear you,' Zara calls back.

'So? I said he's fit...he *is* fit.'

'At least someone likes me,' Bear says, going up the concrete stairwell.

'That's a whole wrong level of liking,' Zara says. 'Morning, morning,' she leads the way into the large, open-plan offices, rapidly filling with workers tugging coats off, logging into terminals, and hovering around the coffee machine.

'Big guy!' Terry says, beaming at Bear while dancing on the spot, throwing a few air punches, 'Saw you running this morning...'

'Err, yeah,' Bear says.

'Totally going to start soon,' Terry says earnestly, 'Got a tweak in the old calf though. Should rest it first.'

'Whenever you want,' Bear says.

'Morning,' Allie calls, walking towards them, 'You smell of coffee, how's my diner?'

'It's James's diner now,' Thomas replies.

'It'll always be my diner,' she says, walking off to grab a big pile off folders before following Zara into Martha's office.

'No middle ground with you, buddy,' Thomas remarks to Bear as he looks around the room, 'They either love or hate you, huh?'

'Is what it is,' Bear says.

'Personally,' Thomas says, 'I hate you.'

'Yeah?' Bear asks.

'Man, like so much...you know...like inside...there's so much hate right there...' he rubs his stomach. 'Or I might just need a shit...yeah, I'm going to deploy in trap one,' he rushes off for the toilets, leaving Bear to cross a room filled with people that either rush to say hi or ignore him completely.

'Morning,' he stops in the doorway, seeing Martha look up with a hand waving in the air while engaged in conversation with Zara and Allie. He leans back, resting against the frame and looking around, while thinking on Zara's words that its funny how life goes on and how things change.

Six months ago, this week, he dropped through the sky. Six months ago, this week, he met Zara, Thomas, and James in the diner run by Allie. Now James runs the diner, and Allie works for Martha in support of Zara. Six months ago, there was a backlog of over three hundred RLIs. Now there are less than fifty, and at the rate they are working ,that will be clear by the end of this month.

'I'll grab a brew,' he says.

'Sure,' Zara pulls back from her chat to nod at him, 'Where's Thomas?'

'Deploying in trap one.'

'That's gross,' she says, 'Briefing in five...'

He walks down the corridor lined with deployment rooms, to the end and the door marked "Operatives Prep".

CHAPTER TWENTY

He pauses to draw air before turning the handle. In truth, he's not all that bothered at being disliked, but this is the bit he doesn't like. The split-second when he walks into a room and sucks the life from it, robbing the conversations that instantly drop away with a shift in mood from jovial to hostile. It happens again when he enters, but he shows no reaction, and heads for the drinks machine.

Easy chairs here and there. Coffee tables and desks at the sides, with doors leading off to rooms filled with uniforms, period clothing, and equipment. Kit bags and parts of costumes dotted about. A busy room full of operatives getting ready for their deployments.

'Bear,' Larry says curtly, leaning past to get a mug.

'Ah, bonjour,' Pete booms, walking in from the changing rooms, 'It is suddenly quiet in here, is it not?'

'Hi, Pete,' Bear says, 'coffee?'

'I cannot drink coffee with you,' Pete says, his voice still loud, 'My peers, yes, they will ignore me if I am seen to be colluding...'

'Can it, Pete,' someone says.

'Or what?' Pete fires back, instantly passionate, 'I will talk to who I want. I am a free man...'

'Gee,' Thomas says, balking as he walks in, 'nice mood in here. That you again, Bear?'

'No, it is Marco...' Pete shouts, glaring at the man who told him to can it, 'He spews shit from his mouth like other people do from their backsides.'

An eruption of voices clamouring in anger as they lay into Pete who returns fire with equal passion. Jacob walks in from the changing rooms, his tweed suit dapper and neat, while he shakes his head. 'Like bloody children,' he grumbles, checking his watch, 'Briefing. Come on. Get to it.'

A mass exodus from the offices and prep rooms to the vast briefing room on the ground floor. Operatives, handlers, planners, and researchers clutching notepads and pens. Bear goes in with Thomas, Pete, and Jacob. Shuffling to find seats as Martha takes the front, shouting for quiet.

'Settle down. Come on, shush. Thank you...'

Thomas watches Martha speaking on the podium, with the lead handlers arranged in a neat line behind her, and Zara in the middle of them all. He stares at her, watching her closely and giving a cheeky grin when she spots him in the audience, chuckling when she rolls her eyes.

'The backlog is forty-eight,' Martha continues, 'which we aim to clear by the end of the month, and if we do, then it will be the first time in living memory that Disco has a clear worksheet, which gives us breathing space...'

Thomas snorts a laugh. Breathing space? Everyone else here already has breathing space because of him, Bear, and Zara. The hours everyone else works are already decreasing. They even get days off now if they want.

'The memorial is this weekend, and I repeat, we *will* have a one hundred percent turnout. I want our entire department at the event without exception… We will also show a united front,' she adds firmly, casting a hard gaze over the audience that all know exactly what she means. Bear drops his head, scratching his nose while Pete chuckles next to him.

'Something funny, Pete?' Martha asks when the murmurings start.

'We would be dead,' Pete calls out as the volume rises.

'I said, thank you,' Martha snaps, claiming an instant silence, 'We have a busy week, look after each other. Operatives, keep your beepers on you. Your handlers have your assignments. Everyone else, stay vigilant and do not…I repeat, do not fall into a false sense of security. Freedom has not gone anywhere. They will surface at some point.'

'It's fine, Bear can kill everyone again if they show up,' Marco calls out.

'GO FUCK YOURSELF, BUDDY,' Thomas shouts, surging to his feet with Pete.

'YOU GO FUCK YOURSELF,' Marco says, surging to his feet, while everyone else surges to their feet, while Bear and Jacob stay seated and nod amiably at each other.

'I think we've all got London this afternoon,' Jacob says over the shouting, 'Fancy meeting for lunch?'

'Sounds great,' Bear shouts back, giving a thumbs-up, 'What year?'

'Ask Zara,' Jacob mouths before getting up to help Martha quell the uprising.

CHAPTER TWENTY-ONE

M onday

It's too much now. He can't take anymore. The isolation has become unbearable. The loneliness. The sheer awfulness of being alone amongst so many souls that all seem happy and content. Everywhere he looks, people hold hands, chatting, talking, making connections. There is no one in the world for him, and there is no place left here for him to fill.

He looks up at the sky, waiting for the divine intervention that doesn't come. Tears stream down his cheeks, and his lips tremble with the utter heart-wrenching knowledge that not one person will miss him or even know he is gone.

All he has to do is take one step, and the pain will be gone.

His right foot comes out, hovering in the air as his weight starts to shift, and still, the divine intervention doesn't come, and the cars stream by, heedless to his plight.

Unseeing, uncaring, and rendered insentient for their lack of compassion and life. His foot goes further, and his eyes snap open with a decision made to do it, to end it, to choose death over the crushing emptiness of his life.

He drops to plummet to die, and such is the emotional outpouring, he doesn't feel the arms grip his chest until he's swinging through the air and then going up and over the barrier to come down hard on the metal surface of bridge.

'Easy…we've got you,' a soft American voice speaks into his ear, 'Easy, buddy, we've got you…'

'You're safe now,' an English voice, both deep and gentle. He starts to sob, to weep, and break apart, but they hold him fast, speaking soothing words into his mind.

'You're not alone,' Thomas tells the man, 'You're not alone…'

Sirens come closer. A cop car veering through the traffic, with the blue and red lights strobing to clear a path.

'It's okay,' Bear says, holding the man tight, 'You'll be okay, I promise you…'

Hank Peterson sobs hard, weeping from the first human contact in years. The sirens switch off, the wheels screech, and doors slam.

Hank blinks his eyes open, seeing through blurred vision to the woman running at him, the woman who drops to wrap her arms around the neck of her brother. Her brother who she lost contact with three years ago when he was laid off from his job and became a recluse from the shame of poverty. Her brother who she couldn't find until a phone call twenty minutes ago told her where he was.

'You know this guy?' the cop asks as Bear and Thomas draw back, leaving the man and woman clasped in tears on the floor of the bridge.

'No, Sir, just walking by,' Thomas says.

'Walking by?' the cop asks, frowning at them, 'In New York? And you ain't allowed to walk on Verrazano bridge...'

'Sorry, Sir,' Thomas says sincerely, 'we're not from here.'

'Sure thing,' the cop says, losing interest.

That act of kindness stays with Hank. It changes him. He reconnects with his sister and starts a charity that encourages lonely men to gather and talk, and a few years later, late one night, Hank is there when an angry young man finds a place to open up, which eventually stops his obsessive thoughts of taking an assault rifle into his former high school.

FATHER DONNELLY SMILES at the boy, reaching out to ruffle his hair, 'I'll see you on Sunday, Mikey...'

'Father, I can't thank you enough,' the mother gushes, her New Jersey accent thick and grating.

'It's fine, I love kids...' Father Donnelly says.

'Sunday school, Mikey,' the mother tells her son, 'You's be a good boy for the Father now, Mikey. You's do what he says...'

'Oh, I'm sure he will,' Father Donnelly says, rocking on his heels while resplendent in his black suit and white dog collar.

'Thank you again, Father,' the mother gushes, nodding, grinning, and thinking to make the cross, while not knowing how to make the cross, so sort of touching her head, and bowing a little bit. She takes Mikey by the hand, leading him out of the church. A beautiful woman with a fine figure. Shapely legs, and curves in all the right places, except the Father doesn't watch the mother, he watches the boy.

'Damn,' Thomas whispers, his eyes firmly on the mother, 'She was beautiful.'

'Help you?' Father Donnelly asks with a start, spinning around and wondering where the two men came from.

Thomas smiles sadly, shaking his head, 'You got women like that coming here, and you go for kids? That's fucked up, man...'

'What? How dare you! I have never touched a child in my...what are you doing? GET OFF...' he doesn't get to finish his sentence due to his spinal column snapping from Bear's hands wrenching his head to the side, and the paedophile priest falls dead on the cold flagstone floor of his church. Mikey doesn't come to Sunday School now. His mother takes him to the new military cadets place in which Mikey excels and joins the Marines. He is later awarded the Medal of Honor for saving an entire platoon during a firefight in Afghanistan.

'I'm so moving to New Jersey if they got women like that here,' Thomas says as they walk out into the sunshine.

JEAN STOLL LAUGHS at the message on her phone. She can't help it. Her husband can always make her laugh. It's just the way he words things, and the hundreds of private jokes they've built up from fourteen years of marriage. The phone beeps again, and she swipes to snort and giggle to herself, lost in the messages as she steps out to cross the road towards Old Holborn tube station in central London.

A hand on her shoulder pulling her back, and she cries out, thinking her bag is being snatched as the bus swooshes by an inch from her nose, the horn blaring.

'Almost,' Bear says.

'Oh, my god,' she gasps, looking up at the handsome man smiling at her, 'I was...'

'You take care now,' Bear says, walking off to join Thomas as Jean gasps from the fright, never knowing that her death would cause her husband to self-destruct and spiral into depression, until he tries gassing himself in their family home. An act that causes an explosion that kills the young boy next door. A young boy that will now grow to become a leading expert and government advisor on climate change.

'COLIN! SOMEONE, DO SOMETHING!' she grabs at his collar, pulling it away from his neck that seems to be swelling by the second. His face bright red, and the veins bulging as he gasps for air, clawing at his neck from his windpipe closing. Colin Jenson. Fifty-two years of age and suffering an extreme allergic reaction from the undeclared peanut sauce drizzled over his food. His wife panics, screaming out for an ambulance while waiters and diners gather in stunned shock.

'Move back,' Thomas orders, grabbing the woman's shoulders to guide her away as Bear stares at the epinephrine pen. 'Blue to the sky, orange to the thigh,' Thomas reminds him.

'Got it,' Bear says, plucking the blue lid off before driving the point into Colin's leg, 'It's not doing anything.'

'Give it a minute, dude.'

'Shit...have we got another one?'

'Dude, give it a minute...'

'OH, MY GOD,' Colin roars, suddenly able to breath.

'See,' Thomas says, 'He's fine.'

Colin isn't fine at all. But he does recover to guide his son into joining the US military as a combat engineer who later fixes a power supply into the comms system so Mikey can call for air support during the firefight in Afghanistan. A son who later develops a new way of creating longer lasting batteries that can drive engines. A system adopted by governments across the world after being convinced by a leading expert on climate change.

Mary Lieber peers through the peephole, frowning at the two uniformed cops.

'Who is it?' her husband barks, stepping from the huge living room into the vast hallway. A big man, stubbled and hard looking. Thick arms and legs from lifting weights. A dominant man who jealously covets his possessions.

'The police,' she whispers, pulling back from the door.

He scowls, marching over to push grab Mary's arm and yank her away before peering through.

'Open the door, please,' Thomas calls out, every inch the law-enforcement professional.

'Not a word,' the man hisses, squeezing his wife's arm as he opens the door with an instant change. Giving the two officers the same charming smile Mary fell for so many years ago, 'Can I help you?'

'Sir, we're conducting routine enquiries. May we come in?' Thomas asks.

'Can I ask what this is about?' the man asks politely.

'Sure,' Thomas says, lowering his voice. 'We're concerned for your neighbours, we wanted a quiet word,' he whispers.

'Oh, I see, yeah, sure,' the man says, a flash of relief in

his eyes. He steps back, making room for the two police officers to pass in. 'The wife,' he says, motioning to the woman who drops her head to hide the faded bruises around her eyes covered in make-up.

'Yeah, so, awkward situation,' Thomas says as though embarrassed, 'We heard your neighbour is beating on his wife.'

A look from the man to his wife who tenses and swallows. 'We, er…we've not heard anything,' the man says.

'Hey, I'm sure we're wrong,' Thomas says, 'Just that domestic violence is a big thing now. Folks go to jail and get done in the ass for that…'

'What?' the man asks.

Thomas laughs. 'You know, bend over in the showers… get a big guy called Buck whacking it between the cheeks, huh?' he motions a thrust while laughing too loudly as Bear smiles dumbly.

'I'm sorry,' the man says in a tight voice, 'I don't think that's appropriate to…'

'Joking buddy,' Thomas says, patting the big guy on the arm, 'Lighten up…it's not like you're beating on your wife, now, is it?'

'What? No! Course I…she'd…we'd never do that…'

'Good to hear, Sir. Only pussies beat women. You know, cowards…I mean real yellow-bellied shit eating maggots… say, can you show my colleague where your property overlooks your neighbour.'

'I don't think…'

'You'll be doing that now, Sir.'

'I really don't think…'

'Thank you, Sir. Knew we could count on you. Go with officer Bear now, and I'll get your wife's measurements…ha! I said measurements. I meant details. But say, she is pretty.'

'Show me please, Sir,' Bear says, nodding for the man to lead on.

He goes unwillingly, wanting to argue, but the mad glint in Thomas's eye makes him comply, walking off with officer Bear while casting looks back at his wife.

'Nice house,' Thomas remarks.

'Thank you,' she says quietly, her head still lowered, her arms across her chest, but he spots the bruises on her wrists and leans over to look down the hall, making sure they're not in hearing.

'The police can help you, Mary. They have refuges and support services. Your sister can put you and the kids up for a few days…' a sharp inhalation of air. A tensing of her body, 'Get a lawyer, he's a wealthy man.'

The man leads Bear through to the kitchen, his pride prickling, his sense of public duty fighting against his knowledge of the law and what the police are allowed to do. 'Listen, officer…I don't think you should be…' he turns as he speaks, yelping out and trying to jump back from Bear being right there, gripping his neck to take him off his feet across the kitchen table, knocking bowls and plates that smash on the tiled floor.

'What the…' Mary tenses by the front door, hearing the bangs and crashes coming from the kitchen.

'That's officer Bear,' Thomas says happily, 'It's fine…'

It's like the sound of a dry twig breaking. Distinct and crisp, and the man would scream out, but Bear's hand over his mouth prevents it as he grabs another finger and snaps it.

'You ever touch her again, I'll kill you…' snap. 'You ever hurt her again, I'll kill you…' snap. 'You ever threaten her, and I will kill you,' snap. 'If you do anything other than be nice, I will kill you,' snap, snap, snap.

'Seriously, you don't have to endure abuse,' Thomas

says softly, 'Get help, get support, you're worth more than this...'

'All done,' Bear says brightly, walking back down the hallway.

'You have a good day now, ma'am,' Thomas says pleasantly. Walking out the door after Bear. A few moments later, Mary slowly pulls a heavy skillet from the metal hook while eyeing her husband, writhing and crying on the floor from his fingers all being bent the wrong way. She kills him with the skillet but is later acquitted of murder by using the defence of a battered wife. The case gains international coverage, and Mary tours the country to speak out against abuse. She visits a high school and meets a man doing his own talk on abuse and anger, and depression. She listens to his story. He was abused too. He was angry. He was planning on taking an assault rifle into his old high school. Mary joins him for coffee after. They marry six months later, and the golden lines stretch forever on.

'I love Monday mornings,' Thomas says as they head off down the street from Mary's house.

'Yeah?' Bear asks, 'Why?'

'Pancakes,' Thomas says, holding his thumb up, 'and we only get easy jobs on a Monday morning... Did you know Marco's handler puts him into war on a Monday mornings.'

'That's bad,' Bear says.

'Bad? Who wants war on a Monday morning? You've got to warm up to a war...' they walk into the rear yard of an abandoned house and through the grass to the rear shed. Pulling the door open to step into room one and then out into planning office, and across the hall to Zara's office.

'Go alright?' she asks, double taking at the sight of them in uniform, 'Ooh, you both look good like that.'

'Holy shit,' Sally says, dropping her folders while walking past the office, 'He's a cop... Bear's a cop...'

'Fuck's sake,' Bear groans as Thomas bursts out laughing at the women of the office peering around the edge of the doorframe.

'What's next?' Bear asks Zara.

'Back into normal clothes...no, hang on, stay like that...' she starts rifling through the folders as the phone rings and snatches the receiver up. 'What? No! Sod off and get back to work...how much?' she looks up at Bear and Thomas. 'I'll think about it,' she puts the phone back and carries on going through folders.

'Think about what?' Thomas asks.

'I just got offered a hundred dollars to find a fireman RLI for you two...ah, no, the other cop one was given to Larry. Get changed, you're in London for the next few, until lunch... We're meeting Jacob and Pete at Covent Gardens 2016 for a bite... Well, go on, chop, chop, work to do...'

CHAPTER TWENTY-TWO

The Day After Carpe Diem

He wakes as before. Flat on his back, with the emotional vestiges of the rage still strong while immediately detecting his body is calm and relaxed. His heart rate spikes a little, but he has died many, many times before, so this is nothing new.

A concrete ceiling above him, and whatever he is lying on is hard and solid. He lifts his head to see three concrete walls and one made of bars and deduces he is inside a cell.

'You're in a cell,' the man sitting on the wooden chair on the other side of the bars says. A deep voice, gravelly and harsh, with a trace accent that hints at European. Grizzled and weathered. A thick beard streaked with grey, and a pump-action shotgun resting across the crook of his muscular arms bulging from his police issue shirt, 'I'm Lars.'

'Sheriff?' Bear asks.

Lars nods once but stays otherwise unmoving, while

Bear's mind suddenly fills with a stream of images and memories. He was with Zara and Thomas. They were in New York, then London, then New York. The RLI. Carpe Diem restaurant. Robert. The people in black. The firefight. Roshi! His heart booms, and his senses come to the fore as he twists lithely from the wooden bench to gain his feet, hardly noticing he is back to barefoot in the blue coveralls. He was in the restaurant. Roshi was shot. He went mad... what happened?

'Roshi?' he asks quickly. The sheriff doesn't answer but just stares impassively, 'Roshi? Is she...what happened?'

The sheriff rises smoothly to his feet with the shotgun still held across the crook of his arms. A pause as he studies Bear, then he walks to the water cooler at the end of the corridor, places the shotgun down, and slowly fills a paper cup while Bear thinks and tries to remember. He killed them all. He reacted to Roshi being shot. He killed Robert. It's all there, in his mind.

'What's happening?' he asks as the sheriff walks back.

Lars studies him again and lifts the shotgun one handed, bracing the butt in his hip while reaching out to hold the paper cup out in a steady hand. Bear takes the cup and drinks it down in one, relishing the cool waters cascading down his throat. 'Roshi?' Bear asks.

Lars shrugs.

CHAPTER TWENTY-THREE

Tuesday

A beautiful autumnal dawn, and each blade of grass stands stiff and frozen with the moisture hardened to ice that glitters and sparkles. His footsteps track across to the point he stands every morning. His breath misting fast from the run down here, and he drops to a crouch, lays it down with the others, sighs heavily, then pushes up to run on back to Main Street and the intersection that he takes at speed.

He passes the big houses, *work hard to a decent position and one day get a house down here.* To the junction. Up the hill to the top. To his home set back from everyone else. To his bar and the pull-ups, and press ups.

Discovery tea. Discovery toast. A hot shower, shave, and he dresses for the day while believing that, if he inhales deeply enough, he can still smell her.

He isn't greeted or acknowledged when he heads to

Thomas' house. Sometimes, he'll see some of the women from his office. The ones that smile at him at work, that look away when they're with their boyfriends or partners.

'Fuck's sake,' he tuts at Thomas yawning in his boxer shorts.

Another late finish, and it was full on night when the three finally left the planning offices. They were the last ones out too, but they're always the last ones out. Dinner was courtesy of James in the diner, before they trudged up the path to bid good night, with Bear retiring to stare at nothing and listen to nothing.

'Morning, Zara,' James says, greeting them with a smile as the three head into the diner. Monday was Thomas's favourite of pancakes. Tuesday is fruit and yogurt. Thomas's least favourite, especially when Zara nags him for trying to pour pancake syrup over his otherwise healthy food while knowing fully well that he and Bear will go straight for a café or diner on their first RLI to eat bacon and eggs.

'How was the run?' she asks.

'Fine,' Bear says.

'All good?' Thomas asks, glancing at him.

'All good,' Bear knows they're not asking about the actual run but the thing he does on the run. But it's okay, it doesn't matter.

'Ooh,' Zara says, waving her spoon at them, 'might have an overnighter coming up Thursday.'

'Wednesday to Thursday or Thursday to Friday?' Thomas asks.

'Duh,' she says with a look, 'Thursday to Friday... If I meant Wednesday, I would have said we might have a double coming up on Wednesday...'

'Gee, okay, Grumps,' Thomas says.

'I hate that,' she says with a mock glare.

'Okay,' Thomas says. 'Grumps,' he adds in a mumble.

'Grumps,' Bear mumbles.

'Idiots. First World War... We haven't got the details yet, but I think it's a protection job.'

'Ah, man, I hate that war,' Thomas grumbles.

'Everyone hates that war,' she says.

'Get Marco to do it, or Keith, or...'

'It's our turn... I'll keep you posted...' she says, trailing off with a wince. 'Don't,' she groans.

'Our door is always open,' Bear says.

'We operate an open sky ceiling thing,' Thomas says.

'We think outside box.'

'We give it legs and let it breathe.'

'We'll get our ducks in a row,' Bear says.

'Run it up the flagpole,' Thomas says.

'Keep me in the loop,' Bear says.

'Idiots, the pair of you...'

From the diner to the weird dynamics of the planning office and the strained disquiet of the *operatives' prep room* while they wait for the handlers to sort the daily jobs lists out and assign rooms.

That they undertake time travel is never really mentioned. That they do a thing of a magnitude, it makes the mind boggle at the mere thought is glossed over, and instead, they do what human beings have done throughout time and history and become bogged down in the details and facilitation of it all.

Besides. It's far more interesting to talk about who isn't pulling their weight or who is in trouble for pissing about. Who messed up. Who did well. Who is fucking who, and the intricacies of living rather than the concept of changing the course of humanity. They share news of places where the best meals are, the nicest beaches, the best time periods, with enthusiasts discussing cars, technology, sights, architecture, art, and every other manner of interest, and the forever ongoing discussion of where the most beautiful women and men are from.

'New Jersey,' Thomas tells the room, nodding earnestly. 'Dude, I'm being totally serious…she was hot…then we went out the church and like…every direction there were just hot women…New Jersey…'

'Was that after Bear killed the priest?' Marco asks.

'And before he killed everyone else?' Keith adds.

'HEY, FUCK YOU, MAN,' Thomas shouts as the room once more erupts into an all-out verbal brawl.

'Dear god,' Martha groans, shaking her head in Zara's office at the noise coming from the far end of the corridor, 'I'm sick of telling them…'

'I'll do it,' Zara says bluntly.

'Know what?' Martha says, 'Go for it… maybe they'll listen to someone else for a change.'

'Happy to,' Zara says, walking out from behind her desk to stride down the corridor while Martha goes to walk off, then stops with a sudden change of mind.

'Zara…' she calls out.

'Be fine,' Zara says, calling over her shoulder. She reaches the door, pushing hard to send it slamming against the wall with such a bang, it snaps every single head over. 'WHAT THE HELL ARE YOU DOING?' she thunders with a brutal raw authority that makes even Martha flinch in surprise.

The young woman strides deeper into the room, her expression furious. 'The whole bloody place can hear you… It is embarrassing, and it ends now… If it happens again, you will get suspensions and docked pay…ALL OF

YOU...problem, Marco?' she asks, seeing the look on his face.

'No,' he says quickly, 'sorry, Zara...'

'Good. Get to work...'

'Fuck me backwards,' Martha mumbles, sharing a look with Allie, 'Remind me never to piss her off.'

'Don't piss Zara off,' Allie says helpfully, 'Can we get docked pay?'

'No idea,' Martha replies.

'All done,' Zara says, walking back to her office. She goes in, sits down, and dives straight back into the folders.

Zara's methodology is sound. Starting each day with easier RLIs and making sure to put feel-good and positive jobs in with the negative ones to balance it out while keeping an eye on weather patterns, times of year, seasons, and places. She learnt the hard way how taxing it can be to have a series of jobs all in mid-winter New York with that biting freezing wind.

Her Tuesday rolls on with slightly more complex and involved RLIs for Bear and Thomas to deal with.

An infiltration of a water company in America to access the control panel to drain the storm tanks of a small town before a flood hits that evening.

Stop a Saudi Arabian prince bidding on a Picasso at an auction.

Prevent the robbery of a cash-in-transit van in Brooklyn.

Commit a robbery of a cash-in-transit van in Queens and throw the millions of dollars from the window of a high-rise in the city centre to clog traffic to divert the local news networks away from a controversial movie premiere that portrays Nazi Germany as the victims and denies the holocaust. She helps out on that one. Carrying the bags of money from the deployment position of a cupboard to five levels up and helping throw the banknotes from the window.

After that, she returns to Discovery while the other two disrupt a cocaine deal in a warehouse, posing as undercover cops to make all the dealers run off so they can corner and convince a young man not to embark on his criminal career.

They pick a fight with a street gang terrorising an inner-city London borough, well, Thomas picks the fight, then stands back as Bear actually does the fighting. She watches that one on the monitor in her office. Holding a mug of tea in her hands while tracking every move Bear makes while ignoring Sally and some of the other women peering around her door. Bear's abilities are staggering, the way he moves. Fluid. Graceful and so utterly brutal.

Her team are now processing four times more work than anyone else, hence, Allie being allocated to help, but still, there is a nag in the back of her mind that Bear is merely treading water, like he is waiting for a thing that will never happen. That's okay now, but what happens when he realises, the thing he is waiting for will never happen?

What then?

CHAPTER TWENTY-FOUR

The day after Carpe Diem

Lars comes back. Walking down the corridor to stop at the cell door. A uniformed woman behind him holding a pump-action shotgun. Asian, maybe Indian or Pakistani. Slight and feminine, but looking every inch the professional law-enforcement official.

'I'm deputy Prisha,' she says politely as Lars unlocks the cell door and moves in to stare down at Bear sitting on the wooden bench.

'Taking you to see the Old Lady,' Lars says, swinging the cell door in, 'You do anything, and we'll shoot you…then you reset here…'

'Okay,' Bear says.

'We got shackles,' Lars says, standing in front of Bear, unafraid, unflappable, and entirely stoic in manner, 'We need shackles?'

Bear shrugs, shaking his head, 'No…what's happening?'

'Not for us to say,' Lars says after a second of silence.

'It's been hours,' Bears says quietly, 'Where's Roshi? Zara? Thomas?'

'Come on,' Lars motions for Bear to go out, stepping in behind, 'Saw what you did in the restaurant...'

'Were you there?' Bear asks, 'Is Roshi okay?'

'Playback,' Lars says.

'Playback?' Bear asks, getting more confused.

'RLIs can be watched,' Prisha says from in front of him, leading them down the corridor, through a door, into a large room lined with desks and filing cabinets. An oversized map of Discovery on the wall, and Bear instantly takes it to be the sheriff's office, just off Main Street in the town centre. He looks to the windows, hoping to see out, but the blinds are closed, bathing the room in muted light.

'I thought it was the real world,' Bear says, still looking round, 'How can it be watched?'

Prisha goes to speak but stops as Lars shakes his head, then motions for the front door.

'We're walking you through town,' Prisha tells Bear. Her voice strong and confident, but the way she said it means something, like he should react.

'There's some people outside,' she continues.

'I don't know what that means...I only...we only got here yesterday. Was it yesterday? I've lost track but...'

'Means folk are angry,' Lars cuts in.

'Angry?' Bear asks.

'When we go out, you keep on ahead...'

'I...' Bear stammers, unsure of what to say or what's going on. 'Sure,' he whispers for want of anything else.

'Prisha,' Lars says, nodding at the door. She goes ahead, pushing the door open to prop open, before moving out of sight, 'Go on now.'

Bear follows her, feeling like a criminal in prison coveralls. His bare feet padding across the wooden floor and through the door to the sidewalk, and a bright sun glaring down that makes him wince and shield his eyes.

'This way,' Prisha says.

He blinks and gains his vision, seeing groups of people standing nearby, watching in silence. More down the street by the planning offices. Far more than he thought possible. He didn't realise Discovery had so many people. He hears mutters and low voices with dark angry expressions, while following deputy Prisha out into the road. Sheriff Lars walking behind with his shotgun across the crook of his arms.

He spots bruised faces here and there, and people with bandages and dressings milling near the entrance to the hospital. He looks up, seeing Doctor Lucy watching from a window.

'Murderer,' someone mutters from his right. The word is repeated as he walks down the centre of the road. He spots people with eyes red from crying that look shocked and in grief.

'He's a murderer,' someone else says.

'Exile him...'

'Send him back...'

'Scum...'

'Murderer...'

'What's going on?' Bear mutters, not understanding anything going on and wishing Zara and Thomas were here. 'Why are they calling me a murderer?' he asks Prisha.

'Just keep going,' she says from in front.

They walk on down Main Street to a part of town Bear hasn't seen before. Shops, stores, grocery places, and bars. The town is bigger than he thought. Deceptively so, and the groups of people still shout as they pass by, trudging on what feels like the condemned man's walk-of-death to the electric chair or the noose. He starts to get worried, his senses coming alive as he gauges distance to Prisha and turns his head to clock positioning of Lars, looking for ways out, for vehicles that he could use and deciding he'll run for the treeline at the far end of town.

'Don't,' Lars says from behind.

'Where's Roshi?' Bear asks, his voice stronger, harder. Prisha turns in alarm, seeing the change in the man, his head now higher, and those soft brown pensive eyes hardening by the second.

'HEY,' a voice calls out from behind them, breaking the escalating tension as they turn to see Doctor Lucy jogging towards them.

'What are you doing?' Prisha asks, moving to intercept her.

'Walking with him,' Lucy replies with a look that dares her to try and block the way. 'You're marching him down here like a criminal. Are you okay, Bear?'

'Lucy, you should…'

'Fuck off, Lars,' she says, brushing past to Bear's side, looping her arm through his. 'How you doing?' she asks gently, then leans closer to whisper, 'Lose the angry eyes, or they'll shoot you.'

He swallows, looking down and breathing in. 'What's going on?' he asks as they set off walking again.

'Carnage, mate. Had all sorts of injuries coming in. Gunshots, trauma…'

'Lucy,' Lars snaps.

'Ah, piss off. I'm not telling him anything…'

'Murderer…'

'SCUM…EXILE HIM…'

'Oh, hey, Jonesy,' Doctor Lucy calls out, waving a hand at the angry man shouting from the crowd. 'How's your crabs, mate? They cleared up yet? Try washing, it might help… Ignore them,' she tells Bear, 'Small town, something happens, and they all go mad.'

'Where's Roshi?'

She hesitates, pursing her lips, then offering a tight smile that doesn't reach her eyes. 'Speak to the Old Lady,' she says kindly, squeezing his arm, 'You'll be fine.'

CHAPTER TWENTY-FIVE

Wednesday

He places it down gently before running back through town, into Main Street, past the big houses, up the hill to his bar to the pull-ups and press-ups.

Tea. Toast. Shower, dressed and out to Thomas in his boxer shorts. To Zara and down to the diner for the Wednesday morning scrambled eggs on toast.

'How was the run?' Zara asks, sipping her coffee.

'Good,' Bear says.

'You've got psych eval this morning.'

'I'll go,' Thomas says eagerly.

'She's not that pretty...' Zara mutters.

'I was joking,' Thomas says, seeing the scowl.

A glorious cold, crisp day waits as they leave the diner, with Bear peeling off to the hospital.

'ENTER,' a mock deep voice, and he can't help but

smile as he walks in, snorting a laugh at the sight of Doctor Lucy behind her desk, wearing a fake beard and glasses. 'I am Professor Luciano,' she says deeply, 'Doctor Lucy is busy today.'

'Busy, yeah?'

'Yes,' Lucy says in that mock deep voice, 'She is putting on sexy lingerie to try and lure her next patient...'

'Fuck's sake...'

'Joking, mate,' she says, pulling the beard and glasses off, 'Or am I?'

'Where are we?' he asks.

'In the hospital.'

'Lucy,' he groans, 'in here or...'

'On the bed?' she asks, nodding at him with a wink, 'Get naked and comfy?'

'Oh my god, you're a sex pest.'

'Fact,' she says. 'I need therapy. Wanna be my therapist?' she asks, walking out from behind her desk, 'We could do that new saturation thing where we just fuck like mad until I get it out of my system...'

'What would you do if I actually said yes?' he asks, following her through the door at the end.

'Shit myself,' she laughs over her shoulder. 'Are you looking at my arse?' she asks, catching his eyes angled down.

'No,' he says simply, walking behind her into a small room with a sofa and two armchairs.

'Seriously, though,' she says, sitting down in one of the armchairs and looking jaw-droppingly stunning in a tight pencil skirt and simple green jumper, 'I probably would.'

'Would what?' he asks, losing the thread for a second.

'Have sex, mate. Gee, keep up, will ya...'

'I'm so reporting you.'

'Yeah, you do that,' she says, smiling as he sits down. 'So, how are you?' she changes instantly, her tone warm, soft, and genuinely caring. Her hands folded neatly on her lap.

'Fine, thank you,' he says politely.

'Good week?'

'Yeah, yeah, all good,' he replies.

'Busy?'

'Ah, you know... Zara keeps us working.'

'Gotta love that girl,' Lucy says, arching her eyebrows, 'She got over herself yet? How is the Fuhrer anyway?'

'She's fine. Zara's lovely.'

'No, mate, I'm lovely. Zara's an uptight bitch. Don't laugh at me...say it...'

'I'm not saying it.'

'Say it, say I'm lovely.'

'You're lovely.'

'Whoa, ethics here. I'm your doctor. How's James? Still got a huge penis?'

'I don't know. I never saw his penis.'

'I did. Huge, mate,' she says, holding her hands apart as though giving the size, 'Thomas okay?'

'Thomas is fine.'

'Great chat, Bear,' she beams, making him laugh before changing gear back down into the serious doctor again, 'How's the running?'

He nods, lowering his eyes, 'Good.'

'Have you thought about what we discussed? About decorating your place? Maybe getting some furniture...'

'Nah, it's...I mean...we've got a lot on...like really busy.'

'Tomo and Zara have done their places. Give me a key, I'll do it. You trust me, don't you?'

'Of course, I do.'

'Do you really?'

'Yes,' he says honestly, looking across the short distance to her blue eyes.

'Let me decorate then. It's time to move on.'

He squirms, shifting position and blinking with discomfort, 'Maybe.'

'And, I was thinking... Maybe I'll start running in the mornings...'

'Everyone wants to start running, I think,' he says, rubbing his jaw.

'No, Bear. People just want to get closer to you...'

'Lucy...'

'How about, I start running, and we change the route you do? How would that be?'

He swallows, his lips pursing. She reads him well, knowing she can push a little harder. 'Decorate, move on... change the route...' she leans forward, motioning for him to look at her, 'There are lots of single women here, Bear. Meet someone...go for drinks, you only eat in the diner with James... Try one of the bars or restaurants...'

He stiffens. His eyes hardening.

'Ah, mate,' she groans at his reaction to the word restaurant, 'you do RLIs in restaurants.'

'It's different,' he says curtly.

'Why? Because it's work? Okay, tell you what...as part of your therapy, I insist you take me to dinner.'

'Lucy.'

'Not like that, Bear,' she says calmly, 'No sex jokes now, I mean it...take Zara...go with Tomo or...'

'Ease up,' he whispers, inhaling deeply.

'No,' she says softly, shaking her head, 'It's been six months. We've eased up... We're not easing up anymore.'

THE DAY AFTER

'Take it easy, you'll be fine,' Doctor Lucy says, rubbing his arm as they walk down through the town. 'Could have given him some shoes, Lars,' she snaps, glaring back at the Sheriff, 'It's hot as hell out here, he'll burn his feet on the road.'

They approach a big house on a tree-lined lane. Wooden construction, and painted white, giving it a grand, colonial appearance. Willow trees in the grounds, and manicured lawns filled with bird feeders.

Doctor Lucy stays at his side, gently refusing to answer direct questions but giving comfort by her presence, and that alone stops Bear trying to make a run for it.

They don't go for the front door but circumvent the house, walking around the side towards the rear gardens.

'Bear!' Zara cries out, rushing over with Thomas. Both of them in normal clothes but looking drawn and exhausted. Zara pulls him for a hug, her arms around his neck, 'I was worried sick…'

'Dude,' Thomas says, his hand on Bear's shoulder, 'You okay? Zara kept telling them to let us see you…'

'I said you had rights…I said holding you like that was wrong…'

'Move on,' Lars says from behind.

'Give them a second, Lars,' Doctor Lucy says.

'Join the others,' Lars says, ignoring the doctor as he reaches to grab Bear's arm.

'Touch me, and I'll hurt you…'

'Whoa, easy now,' Doctor Lucy moves fast, pushing in front of Lars as Bear gives fair warning, his temper starting to prickle from the walk of shame he just endured and the lack of answers, the confusion, and a tight ball of worry starting to gnaw in his gut.

'Lars, old chap,' Jacob says, striding over, 'We're fine now, you can relax...'

'Oui, yes, it is okay now, Bear is okay now,' Pete says, his arm in a sling, his face covered in cuts and bruises. Jacob the same, with purple hues on his skin. Bear looks around, seeing the guy that was dressed in a German officer's uniform.

'That's Helmut,' Jacob says, 'The other woman is Martha...head of the planning offices.'

'Bear,' Martha says, studying him closely.

'Where's Roshi?' he asks.

'Easy now,' Lucy says, at his side, her hands on his arm.

'Where's Roshi?' Bear asks again.

'Maybe don't crowd in, eh?' Lucy says, looking around.

'I'm fine,' Bear says, his tone louder, his chin higher, 'Where is Roshi? SOMEONE ANSWER ME...WHERE IS ROSHI?'

Tension rises. Palpable and dangerous, because he is a dangerous man. Every person there saw what he did, but hands reach up to grip his face, pulling his vision down to dark eyes that show no fear.

'Listen to me,' Zara says, 'Stay calm. Do you understand?'

It shouldn't work. Her tone should press buttons and make him worse. The way she grips his head too hard, the pressure too great, but something in her hits the spot, making him nod.

'Do not hurt anyone,' she orders as Bear nods.

'Dude, we're right here,' Thomas says.

'Where's Roshi?' Bear asks again, his tone soft and

confused, his eyes filling with tears that spill out over Zara's hands. He swallows, his lips trembling as the emotion ripples out, with Lucy covering her mouth while Pete and Jacob stare at the ground with pained expressions.

'Well, now, you must be Bear...' an English accent, clipped and educated, coming from a middle-aged woman walking from the house, clapping her hands together as though to rid the dust from an unpleasant chore. Blue jeans, a white blouse with the sleeves rolled up, and the top few buttons left undone. Brown hair streaked with grey, pulled back in a loose bun, 'I'm the Old Lady...'

SIX MONTHS LATER.

'Bear?' Lucy asks, seeing the vacant look on his face in the therapy room.

'Yeah,' he says gruffly, clearing his throat as he draws his mind back from six months ago.

'Lost you for a minute. What were you thinking?'

'Just er...you know...the day...when we walked through the town...'

'Not a good day,' she says, watching him closely, 'but it was six months ago, Bear. Anyway. What do you think of my ideas? Good? Bad? Indifferent? Talk to me, Bear.'

'I er...' he looks down at his hands in his lap.

'I care for you, Bear...Thomas does, Zara does...lots of people do. We want you to be happy.'

'I'm fine,' he says quietly.

'It's time, mate,' she edges forward in the chair, reaching over to take his hands in a way to make him look up, 'Got to move on.'

'I don't want to move on,' a single tear forms in his eye.

Gleaming and swelling, readying to break free, but he blinks quickly, battering it away, 'I'm fine as I am…'

'Bear…it's time to accept it. It's time to stop running down there every morning…'

The Day After.

The Old Lady walks over to stand in front of him. That she has to crane her neck to look at him speaks of the size difference, and she frowns as she studies him, 'Handsome bugger, aren't you…'

'You're not old,' Thomas blurts, his eyes widening as he realises what just came out of his mouth.

'I'm very old,' the Old Lady says, turning to Thomas, 'but then, time is a dimension where everything happens in the same instance…so perhaps, I am not old.'

'Roshi?' Bear asks.

'Dead,' the Old Lady says bluntly.

A gut punch. A stab to the heart. He staggers back, unable to breath, unable to draw air.

'Leave him,' the Old Lady orders, and such is her tone that compliance is given instantly. 'That was a bloody mess,' she glowers around at everyone, 'What on earth were you all thinking?'

'It's entirely my fault,' Martha says, lowering her head in shame.

'No,' Pete says deeply, 'I did this…'

'Shut up,' the Old Lady snaps, silencing them as she stares at Bear looking shocked and drawn, 'If it wasn't for Bear, a lot more people would be dead, like Roshi…'

Bear tenses at her name. Thinking to rise and fight, and kill everyone but finding no strength to do anything.

'True death is an anomaly,' the Old Lady announces, looking to Thomas and Zara. 'Used to be rare. Now, not so. We lost several to true death from yesterday's...skirmish...' she says the word with distaste, pausing to think before turning away to walk briskly to a trestle table laid with a jug of clear iced liquid next to a glass. 'Six Discovery operatives were lost to true death,' she says, pouring from the jug, 'Roshi and five others...four of whom were killed by Bear when he reacted on seeing Roshi fall...'

Six Months Later

The hour or so passes with Lucy pulling back from pushing Bear to let a gentle conversation flow. She takes him back to her suggestions a few times and lets her humour show with jokes to break the tension every now and then.

'You alright?' she asks, checking her watch, signalling it's time to finish.

'Yeah, yeah, good...thanks.'

'Great,' she says, shuffling forward to stand up as he looks over at her, 'I so saw that.'

'What?'

'Looking up my skirt,' she says, her eyes twinkling, 'Devouring me with your hungry eyes...'

'Fuck's sake,' he laughs it off, thinking back to Roshi standing over him in the masquerade room, when she said he was looking up her dress.

'What time then?'

'Time?' he asks, following her to the door.

'Running in the morning. What time?'

'Lucy, you don't have to...'

'Ah, mate, I want to,' she says, whacking his arm, 'My arse is getting flabby from sitting down all day.'

'Your arse is perfect, we both know that...'

'How do you do that?' she asks seriously.

'What?'

'That? If anyone said that, it would be weird or pervy.'

'I don't know,' he shrugs, 'You do it all the time.'

'Yeah, but I'm funny,' she says as though this is fact, 'I am! Cheeky fucker...get out of my hospital... What time?'

'Lucy...'

'I'll come and sleep at yours tonight if you don't tell me...'

He looks back at her, smiling with a theatrical pause.

'Oh, my god, you flirted,' she says, grinning like a Cheshire cat.

'Ten to five.'

'Fuck off.'

'Okay, don't then.'

'Ten to five? For a run?'

The Day After

'I have questions,' Zara says urgently as the Old Lady pours water into a glass from a jug on a garden table.

'We all have questions, my dear,' the Old Lady says, 'For a start...how did Robert know we had three new recruits? How did they know where they would be? Who leaked? Hmmm? Anyone got any answers? I have. Or rather, Lars has. Seeing as he has been looking into this sorry mess all day with deputy Prisha.'

All eyes on the sheriff and his deputy. Both of whom remain impassive, waiting for instruction.

'For your information,' the Old Lady says, looking at Zara and Thomas, 'Lars and Prisha are skilled investigators...they are not just law-enforcement. What other roles do you have, Lars?'

'Compliance. Vetting. Dip-testing...amongst others.'

'Our Sheriff is a man of few words. Prisha?'

'Every completed RLI comes to us for compliance checking. We dip-test to make sure they've been done properly, and we conduct ongoing integrity testing and vetting of everyone in Discovery, especially those connected or directly involved in RLIs.'

'Keep going,' the Old Lady prompts, leaning against the trestle table.

A pause as Prisha and Lars look to Bear, both seemingly evaluating the risk and threat. 'Roshi sold out,' Lars says bluntly, shifting the aim of his shotgun to point squarely at Bear, 'Switched sides...'

Silence. Stunned and heavy.

'I'm terribly sorry,' Jacob says stiffly, 'I do not like Roshi one bit, but she is loyal.'

'No,' Lars says deeply.

'I rather think you need to watch what you say, dear chap,' Jacob says as Pete lays a gentle hand on his arm.

'Stay calm, my friend, Roshi would not do this.'

Prisha continues, 'We found the messages from her IT account. She deleted them, but we ran a recovery programme. Messages about Bear, Zara and Thomas...even down to the RLI at the Carpe Diem restaurant.'

'She was on a mission,' Martha says, 'How would she have known? I sent her to 1892 earlier in the day...'

'We're still investigating,' Prisha says, 'But we do know Roshi was planning on switching sides to Freedom. She'd accessed her reset function and changed it to New York at the back of the restaurant ten seconds after being shot. The whole thing was planned.'

Bear shakes his head, it doesn't make sense. None of it makes sense.

'Excuse me,' Zara asks, 'How do you know she hasn't reset?'

'We are in a computer programme, my dear,' the Old Lady answers, not unkindly, 'Simple code… We can see the reset of everyone in Discovery, and Roshi has not reset.'

'But…' Zara says, the questions forming too fast to be spoken.

'Roshi planned to get shot, reset there, and go with them,' Prisha says, 'After that, we wouldn't be able to see her. True death has a unique coding. She's dead. She probably arranged it the night before…'

'The evidence is clear,' the Old Lady states, 'However. On reflection, I rather feel we have *all* played a part in this mess. I, for one, ordered Roshi into the circuit. She hated the circuit, and I ordered it knowing that fact, so I have to take responsibility for her actions towards Bear, which we have all now seen, was barbaric to say the least. Torturous and degrading…but it was done, and that led Bear, Thomas, and Zara to Jacob and Pete and…well, on it went…we all played a part, unwittingly, I grant you, but nonetheless there it is…'

Bear can't speak or think. His mind closes in with a great and terrible fear growing inside while simply not believing it.

'None of this makes sense…' Zara says, 'You're all full of shit…'

A lurch as the world around them changes to an abject blackness, with each person seemingly illuminated from within. Each of them glowing within a void.

Zara's mouth drops open, Thomas swallows, hardly able to keep up with it all, while Bear just looks on, stricken to the core.

'Shit!' Thomas drops away as a bright, golden light shoots past him, leaving a glowing trail behind. It soars off into the distance, stretching as far as the eye can see. Another one flies overhead, weaving slightly with gentle undulations. A third passes, like shooting stars with solid trails. Mesmerising and stunning. Then a fourth, a fifth, and more, until dozens go overhead with a speed too great to track. They become hundreds. Thousands, tens of thousands, and more.

One passes underneath their feet, giving the effect they are weightless. A second, a third, and more, and more. On it goes, with bright, arcing lights, each with a never-ending trail stretching behind. The whole thing three dimensional with a depth they could never fathom or grasp, and within seconds, they are all surrounded by countless golden, glowing lines that overlap and go through each other, and at each point they meet, a brighter dot forms.

An incredible, breath-taking thing to see, and even the hardened ones, Pete and Jacob, Martha, and Lucy, and the two officers stare up and around in wonder.

'Each line represents a person,' the Old Lady's voice carries clear, 'Each dot represents the point of a decision, where something occurred, where something happened...'

'It's beautiful,' Zara whispers.

One of the lines sags down towards them, seemingly sinking away from the others to stand out.

'Focus now,' the Old Lady says. The line changes to a stream of images of a life seen through the eyes of a human. From waking in the morning to brushing teeth, washing, and on, through a day of work in an office with a stream of motion that is over within seconds. Another one does the same, drooping down so they can see a life lived through one day in series of silent, moving images. Then another and more. All from different parts of the world.

'One day...' the Old Lady says. 'What you are seeing are the lives of the people on the planet Earth during one day...' she pauses, letting each of them stare around in wonder. Even those that have seen it before gawp with their mouths open. It's impossible not to. A thing to see. A sight to behold.

'That is one day....and this is all of the days...'

As she speaks, the lines all drift away as though going further into the distance, but more join in, adding and multiplying with millions of shooting stars scorching across the blackness, all at the same time, to join those already there. It becomes impossible to track, with billions of connecting dots as the whole of the thing grows in a scale too great to understand, and through it all, there is a forward motion, as though all of the lines are being carried ever onwards. It gets faster, propelling at a speed that makes them feel dizzy and jarred until, suddenly, it slows down, and the lines start to break away, crumbling and ending. Shrinking, getting less, getting fewer, the density receding, the populace growing smaller, and still, they move on, but far fewer now, thousands instead of millions, hundreds instead of thousands. That it's dying, is obvious. Dwindling away to nothing until only a few lines remain that slow and stumble until they, too, fade out to nothing.

'Humanity dies. Not from one single act but from many. From climate change. From war. From minds poisoned by diatribe and evil. From ignorance, from emotional reactions...there is no one single thing to fix...' the forward motion ends, and they all gain the feeling of going backwards until they are back with the vast scale too great to comprehend.

'Because there is no single thing to point at, I assess everything and seek where to tweak and change. Right now, I am working through your time periods, which is why you are here. You are all very small cogs in a very big machine... so forgive my lack of emotional outpouring for dear Roshi, but as you can see, I am really rather busy...'

A blink, and the world around them changes back to the hot garden of the big weathered house with the Old Lady leaning against her trestle table.

'I declare now that no person here has responsibility for what happened. Bear will *not* be held accountable for his actions. He had no knowledge of who he was killing inside or outside the restaurant. He is a product of all of our stupidity, but he has skills that we will use. Zara, Thomas, and Bear will commence work immediately and undergo training as they work...'

'Am I fuck going back into that mess,' Zara says.

'Quite right too,' the Old Lady says primly, 'You're a handler through and through, young lady. Martha will train you. That is all. Get back to work...'

'But...' Zara sputters.

'Zara,' Martha says, a quiet warning to her voice.

'No, I want to know...where are our bodies? Who was I? What about my life before? And if humanity has ended, are we in your past? I mean *when* is this now, and how can two AI's both be doing the same thing? You'll just be undermining each other, and who made you? An AI has to be made, right? Who set your parameters and programme?' she trails off, staring at the Old Lady who smiles as though to a demanding child, 'I have questions...lots of questions...'

'We all have questions, my dear,' the Old Lady says,

walking back to her house, 'One day, we might even get answers...'

CHAPTER TWENTY-SIX

Thursday

A beautiful autumnal dawn. Cold, crisp, and clear. Bear slows from a jog to a walk. His breath pluming clouds of mist that roll up and away, disappearing forever into the sky, and each step he takes leaves a darkened spot on the frozen surface of the grass.

He stops where he always stops to look down and, once again, feels the sadness within, a great and awful sadness.

Roses litter her grave. Roses brought back from eras and times from cities and towns, from florists, and parks. Some bought, some cut, some stolen. Some grown in the tubs and planters outside his home.

He did it before. They had a thing. Only that one time, but it meant something. It had meaning. He left roses before he went into the maze on the circuit, and she left notes in return.

Roshi didn't die. Not Roshi. It was a game, a trick. She

told him that night to believe in her, and he said he would. He held her in his arms, the woman that tortured and killed him, that made him promise he would stand for her. Even when the Old Lady said she was dead, it wasn't real. She'd come back. Bear knew she would. He'd go for a piss in the night and find a blade pressed to his throat, or he would come to graveyard to find a note one morning, or a rose missing, or a sign, something only he would notice.

It never happened though, and it will never happen because Roshi is dead, and it's time to move on. It's time to change his running route and not bring a rose to the grave every morning.

Motion behind him from feet crunching over the frozen grass. Lucy drops down at his side, placing a hand on his shoulder to steady herself into the crouch.

'They're beautiful,' she says honestly. He half-expected a joke, but she reaches out to pick a stem up, gently fingering the frozen petals of the red rose he brought down yesterday. 'So many,' she whispers, looking over the grave, to the roses spilling out on the sides. She looks around, seeing the other five graves of the killed operatives, centrally positioned to give honour for the sacrifice made while Roshi was put at the far side, away from view, away from everyone else. Exiled in death if not in life.

He lays the rose down, knowing it will be the last one, and when he stands, he expects to feel a rush of freedom, or a great relief, something that will mark a change in his mind and outlook, but it's the same as before. She's not dead, and he's waiting for her to stroll out from behind a tree and say *what's up buttercup.*

'She was indestructible,' Lucy says, rising slowly, 'That's part of it all. Someone so vibrant and strong, so alive… nothing could hurt Roshi. Jesus, mate, I saw your circuit…I saw what you did to each other so...so, yeah...how can she die after you both did that?'

He nods. Feeling empty inside. Feeling numb.

'She groomed you, Bear,' Lucy says softly, reaching out to touch his hand, 'Last time?'

'Last time,' he says.

She nods, studying his profile, 'It's the right thing.'

'I can't believe you turned up,' he says, offering a smile.

'Fuck, it hurt,' she says with a groan. 'Getting out of bed in the dark? I was like *bloody Bear, stuff that, I'm going back to sleep...*' he laughs at her accent that always comes back stronger when she slips into funny mode. 'Nice though,' she adds, looking round, 'The dawn, I mean...I can see why you do it. Peaceful...'

'Yeah, you ready then?'

'We walking back?' she asks.

'Walking? We're not walking, Doctor Lucy.'

'Ah, shit...' she groans, walking after him as he turns away from Roshi for the last time. Her blue eyes sweeping over the grave, over the roses, the tip of her nose pink from the cold. A pause as her head turns to track Bear walking away, studying his form, the shape of him, 'Cracking arse, mate...'

He turns to smile, motioning with his head, 'Come on... We've warmed up now...'

From the graveyard, down the lanes and avenues, to the wide road into town, to Main Street that he takes at speed with Lucy at his side. They pass the big houses, the nice lawns, and picket fences, one of which she owns and lives in, and he reaches out for her hand, pulling her towards the junction of the steep hill.

'Sod that,' she says, shaking her head as he laughs, 'Bear...no way...'

'Yep,' he goes behind her, his hands on the base of her spine, driving her up and on while she bursts out laughing at the propulsion given. She starts running, trying to outpace him, but tiring quickly from the steep ascent. He catches up, breathing easily as he once more starts pushing her up the hill. She giggles and laughs, gasping for air while trying to swear at him, then blinks when his hands drop down past her backside to grip the undersides of her thighs.

'What are you doing?' she laughs.

'Running for you,' he starts pushing his arms forward, making her walk like a puppet as she bursts out laughing, trying to whack his arms away.

'Mate...stop! I can't...'

They reach the top, laughing and giggling, then hushing each other as they pass the silent homes on the hillside, taking the rat-runs, alleys, and paths to his house set away from everyone else.

'What's that?' she asks, gasping for air while pointing at his pull-up bar.

'Pull-ups.'

'Yeah? We doing them?'

'Do you want to?'

'Yeah, go on then...what do I do? I can't reach it.'

'Jump up.'

'I'm not a kangaroo, mate...give me a boost.'

'Okay, ready?' he comes in close behind, his hands gripping her waist, 'One...two...up!'

She grips the bar, hanging dead, 'What now?'

'Pull up,' he says, laughing at the sight.

'How?' she asks.

He goes back to her, his hands on her waist again, 'Pull...that's it...' He lifts her up as she pulls on the bar, rising to the top, then back down again. She does a few, then drops, and turns, grinning proudly.

'Your turn,' she says.

'Nah, it's fine.'

'Don't be shy,' she says, whacking his arm, 'I'm a doctor, and I've seen your willy.'

'Lucy!'

'Go on, give me the gun show…'

'Fuck's sake.'

'Yeah,' she says slowly, watching him jump to start the pull-ups. 'Jesus, how many? You're strong as an ox… Need a hand?' she goes in close, copying what he did for her but shamelessly grabbing his backside to push him up, grunting with the effort while he bursts out laughing again.

'Get off!'

'Go on…do more…I gotcha, mate…' she grunts and pushes, laughing herself while his grip gives out, and he drops down. 'Enough,' she says, wiping her eyes, 'I'm freezing, make me a coffee?'

'Come on,' he leads in through his door, stepping aside to let her through, then dropping his head with a sudden rush of shame at the sparseness of his home.

'I would look away if I were you,' she says with a smile, glancing back at him, 'You need some colour in here…'

'Yeah it's…'

'It's fine, we'll get there,' she slips into doctor mode, calming, soothing, understanding, 'Baby steps. You did the big thing letting me come with you so just change the route tomorrow, we can run somewhere else. If I'm able to walk that is…'

He smiles at the joke, getting two mugs from a cupboard, 'You can rest, I've got an overnighter…'

'Anything good?'

'War,' he says mildly.

'Gee, good info there, mate, thanks for the convo. Which war? Where?'

'We in therapy again?'

'It's called a conversation. It's what normal people do with their pie-holes when they're not eating.'

He snorts, adding a teabag to his mug, 'Tea or coffee?'

'Coffee.'

'First World War, Ypres in Belgium... Heard of it?' he asks.

'Yeah, course, everyone's heard of the First World War but not the other bit.'

'Battle of Passchendaele? I don't think that's changed... The other operatives have heard of it...'

'I'm a doctor not a historian, mate, go on... What's the job then?'

'November 1917, Ypres in Belgium. Big fight over two days that ended with a charge from the British straight into machine gun fire...thousands killed in minutes, then the Germans dropped mustard gas to hamper the medics getting to the injured.'

'Jesus,' she says, grimacing while watching him make drinks. She pulls the zip down on her running top, tugging it off to show the tight sports vest top underneath, 'At least you've put your heating on...'

'Only because you were here,' he says.

'Ah, the old turn the heating up trick and make her get naked, got it, like it...good thinking.'

'No, I was just...'

'Yeah, whatever, go on...so the Krauts killed the Tommies... What's the job?'

'Corporal John Simmonds dies at some point over the

two days...exactly when is unclear, hence, the overnighter, but the Old Lady wants him alive.'

'Ah, gotcha, he in the trenches, is he?'

'No, medic...like three miles back from the front line. Should be easy enough. Thomas can talk us in, then we just keep an eye on him. It's really nothing exciting. We've done a few wars now... Not in the fighting bit...just on the outskirts.'

'Interesting,' she says, holding his eye contact when he passes her mug of coffee over. 'So you'll be in uniform?' she asks lightly, lifting an eyebrow.

He smiles, looking away with a shy blush.

'I heard about you being a cop...'

'Did you?'

'Oh yes, got all the girls going, that did...you er...kept the uniform anywhere?'

He shakes his head, smiling over the rim of his mug, 'Nope.'

'Shame,' she says, smiling over the rim of her mug.

He blinks away from the intense eye contact, not knowing what to say or do, 'Listen er...I need a shower, you okay here?'

'Yeah, go for it. I'll drink my coffee and steal your er...' she looks around for something to steal and shrugs comically, 'I'll just try not to think about you in the buff...unless you need urgent medical attention, of course?'

'I'll shout if I start drowning...'

A strange energy fills his insides as he turns the shower on and strips off in the bathroom. Like an expectation hanging in the air. A foreknowledge of a thing that will happen. A sense of it. An instinct. He thinks to stop it before it happens, maybe ask her to leave or lock the door, but instead, he steps in under the flow and lets the hot water drum on his skull to blot his senses.

'Thought I heard a cry for help?' she rushes in with a smile that makes him start laughing, 'Are you drowning? Hang on, mate...I'm coming...'

She undresses quickly, cursing at the tight sports clothing twanging noisily that makes him laugh more while thinking he should tell her not yet, another time, not now, it's too soon. She's his doctor. It's not ethical. It's not right, but he doesn't say those things. He hears her step in behind him and turns around, swallowing at the sight of her flawless, perfect body but seeing only Roshi in his mind, but Roshi is dead, and it's as though Lucy can detect the thoughts in his mind with a sudden raw vulnerability showing in her eyes.

They come together a second later, with mouths and bodies pressing. They move back under the flow, feeling the sensuality of the water pounding their bodies as they kiss hard and long, because Roshi is dead, and she's not coming back.

He stiffens quickly when her hand goes down, gripping to rub as his moves down over her stomach to slip between her legs. A sense of urgency. A sense of rush. A need, a hunger. His fingers move softly, feeling her stiffen and grow wet before he slides in while her hand grips harder before pushing him back and dropping to her knees. She takes him in her mouth, her head moving up and down with her red hair plastered back, and her wide blue eyes watching him staring at her, because Roshi is dead. She's not coming back. This is real.

He lifts her up, gripping her hard and turning to press her back into the shower wall, hooking her legs up and around his back, and slides deep inside her. She arches, straining at the sensation as he starts to move. Her fingers on his back, raking harder and harder, her mouth biting his neck and ears.

Roshi is dead, and he fucks Lucy in the shower, because she is not coming back. Emotions swarm inside. This is wrong. All of it is wrong. Everything is wrong. It's a game, a trick, Roshi told him to stand for her, and now his dick is inside someone else. He starts to wilt but grunts, and moves harder, refusing to let it overtake his desire to change.

'Roshi groomed you,' that's what Lucy said during all those sessions, one a week for six long months, '*She took a newbie with no character, no memories, no personality and made you what she wanted. She manipulated you to fall in love. She tortured you and made you believe it was right...like a game... She groomed you, Bear. She used you.*'

'Fuck me,' Lucy gasps in his ear, her voice adding to the memories of the sessions of therapy. 'Harder...' she clings tighter, driving him into her. 'Oh, god...' she kisses his neck, his ear, and they angle to find each other's mouths, kissing deep as she climaxes, her body shuddering with spasms running through. A second later, he comes hard and fast, driving deep with an action that can never be undone, but it doesn't matter now. Roshi is dead. She's not coming back.

They kiss for a long time. Holding each other in that position under the shower until he does finally wilt and slip from being inside her. They wash each other, gently and slowly, with the awkward after-moments of the first time lingering in the air.

He goes out first, leaving her to rinse and going through to his bedroom to the wardrobe, and drops down to take a clean towel from the bottom shelf, and as he rises, he sees the glint of metal under his bed catching the morning sun streaming through the windows. He leans closer, trying to see what it is, then stretches his fingers under the frame, groping about, before feeling something delicate and small that he draws out and stares at while his heart skips a beat, and his stomach lurches. A fine silver necklace with a pendant attached, and the word *discovery* in flowing script.

CHAPTER TWENTY-SEVEN

Bear blinks, snapping back to the now, panicking with the notion that he was just asked a question, but everyone is nodding at whatever Martha just said. He reaches out for his mug, looking around the office at the people gathered.

'...three miles out in this village where the command structure is based,' Zara's voice permeates his mind. Her hand pointing at a map on a monitor. Pete and Jacob lean forward, studying the terrain while Thomas reads the set of identification papers in his hands.

'...they'll question both of you, so, Bear, be ready in case they separate you from Thomas...' Zara trails off.

'Got it,' Thomas says, studying the papers held in his hands, 'I'll get us in.'

The necklace jarred Bear to the core. Finding it there. Feeling it in his hands, and suddenly, he was back in the masquerade room seeing it for the first time. *See me now?* That's what Roshi said. Goading, taunting, mocking him while he stood naked and terrified. She groomed him. She used him. Played and manipulated him.

Was it always under his bed? How could he not see it before? Was it a sign or an act of pure serendipity?

'Keep your training in mind,' Jacob says, bringing Bear's focus back to the room, 'Language, behaviour, don't eyeball officers…just because they are not technologically advanced, it doesn't mean they are not intelligent.'

'Got it,' Thomas says again, looking at Bear who nods quickly.

'Sure,' Bear says, shifting in his chair.

'Bear, you okay?' Zara asks, glancing over.

'Uniform is uncomfortable,' he says, tugging the tight collar away from his neck.

'Say that again,' Thomas says, doing the same. Both in standard issue battle dress for the First World War. Stout boots with leggings wrapped around their calves to their knees. Thick trousers, shirt, tie, and woollen tunic. Webbing belts over the clothes. Lee Enfield .303 bolt action rifles rest against the office wall, each with a steel *soup-bowl* shrapnel helmet wedged on the top.

'You'll get used to it,' Jacob says as Pete snorts a dry laugh.

'You will not get used to it,' the Frenchman adds.

'They're stretched, strung out, under pressure, and desperate, so as long as they don't suspect you of being a spy, you'll be fine…' Zara says.

'The papers are real too, from dead soldiers serving in the Africa campaigns…' Martha cuts in.

'Great,' Bear says, shifting again.

'Okay,' Zara says. 'Locate and identity Corporal John Simmonds…' she taps the black and white photograph of a man in uniform on the screen, 'That's him. Royal Army Medical Corp…your papers declare you as from a rifles company, so actually getting close and staying close will be down to you on the ground...'

'I can do that,' Thomas says.

'Now, onto the time of deployment... You'll arrive a few hours before the shelling starts...'

It's not a sign. It's not. It's pure fluke. He only ever uses one towel, and he never looks under his bed. It's just a fluke. A one off. It's not a sign.

'...and at some point, during all of that, Corporal John Simmonds is declared as *killed in action*, what's not clear is how or when,' Zara says.

Roshi is dead. Lucy is nice. It's not a sign.

'...that's a good question, but as with all RLIs, it has to stay fluid...' Martha says.

Christ. Why can't they just get in and get it done? Stop talking about it and get it over with. Actually, this is what he needs. Something hard and difficult. Something physical to get his teeth into. Yeah. He needs this. Roshi is dead. It wasn't a sign.

'Okay, I think you're probably good to go, questions?' Zara asks.

'Nope,' Bear says, his voice louder and firmer than he intended, making everyone turn to look at him.

'Bored, then?' Zara asks, smiling as the others chuckle at the man of action, ready and willing to get stuck in. Thomas pats Bear's arm, pushing up from his chair to grab his rifle and helmet.

'Bear, Tom...quick word,' Zara says, nodding at the others to go, 'Pep talk with my team.'

'Good luck, chaps,' Jacob says brightly, patting Bear on the back as he follows Pete out.

Zara holds still, watching the two men get kitted up as

Martha goes out of the room, pulling the door closed behind her. 'Bear? What's wrong?' she asks immediately.

'Nothing…'

'My arse nothing. Spit it out…you kept zoning out. Are you up for this today? I can put it back if…'

'I'm fine…honestly. Don't give me the look,' he groans, 'I just had a weird morning.'

'With Lucy?' she asks as Thomas's eyebrows shoot up.

'I forgot, man, how was it?'

'Yeah, good, er…you know…running and…we did running…um…'

'You totally had sex, dude!'

'Did you?" Zara asks, blinking at him as he blushes furiously.

'You did! You had sex with Lucy…' Thomas says, grinning widely.

'Er, we, er…'

'Oh my god, Bear. You went for one run with her…' Zara says, shaking her head in shock, 'How fast do you move?'

'What? We've been speaking for like six months now…'

'She's your bloody doctor, right…well…is that what's freaked you out?'

'No, I found this straight after,' he says, pulling the necklace from his pocket.

'A necklace?' Thomas asks.

'Roshi's necklace.'

'Roshi's?' Zara asks, 'You've seen her?'

'No! It was under my bed from…you know…that night she stayed.'

'Oh…oh, okay. Sheesh, dude, I thought you'd seen her. I was like…what the fuck!'

'No, at least…I mean…I think it's from that night.'

'Ah,' Thomas says, nodding with understanding, 'the roses huh? A sign? It's not a sign, dude. It dropped off when you fucked and...'

'Don't say fucked like that,' Zara says with a tut.

'When you made love then...either way, it stayed under your bed because, buddy, you are a filthy shit that doesn't sweep under his bed.'

'It's just coincidence,' Zara says, 'I'd be freaked out too. But are you sure you're up for this today?'

'Yeah, course, I'm fine,' Bear says, pushing it back in his pocket.

'Okay,' she watches him for a second, studying his reactions and expression, 'I'll keep the live link on to watch when I can.'

'I'll be fine. Just a weird day.'

'Weird day? Man, this is a good day, Lucy is like the hottest woman in Disco...' Thomas says enthusiastically, looking at Bear while detecting the glare coming from Zara. 'Other than Zara,' he adds, still looking at Bear, 'who *is* the hottest woman ever, like...'

'Twat, she's not that great,' Zara mutters, 'but it'll do you good to...' She flaps her hands, floundering for a second, 'Get it out of your system? Is that the thing to say? Whatever. Go save John Simmonds, and we'll dissect it when you get back.'

'Lucy is like the second hottest woman, man,' Thomas continues, holding a mock serious look.

'Sod off, the pair of you,' Zara says, ushering them out of her office, 'Sally? Room one?'

'Good to go,' Sally shouts back, 'Good luck, Bear! And Tom, of course...'

'Gee, thanks for the after-thought,' Thomas shouts back,

pulling his steel hat on. 'Do me up?' he asks, lowering his chin towards Zara.

'Ask Lucy,' she says, grabbing the strap to hoik under his chin, snorting a laugh at the look on his face. 'Bear,' she reaches up, getting his chinstrap in place with a fleeting eye-contact held between the two, and for a second, it looks like she will say something, but then it's gone, and she steps back, 'good luck, go on…see you both later…'

CHAPTER TWENTY-EIGHT

Ypres, Belgium, 1917

They step from room one into an old barn. The door behind them giving access to a storeroom, now a portal with a live link back to the planning offices. A moment to adjust kit and peep outside before they stroll out onto an overgrown path and head east for the village.

Early winter, and the air is cold with a drizzling, soaking rain falling from low clouds. A few miles to the village, then a few more to the edge of the battlefields, but already, they can hear the booms of artillery guns firing in the distance. Solid, percussive bangs that roll around the green and peaceful countryside.

'Thomas Smith. Private. 8th battalion, Hampshire Regiment...Isle of Wight rifles. British by birth, but I lived in the states for a few years...dude, are you listening?'

'Yeah, course.'

'What's your name?'

'Brian Jones?'

'Regiment?'

'Same as yours.'

'Which is what?'

'8th battalion, Hampshire rifles, Isle of Wight regiment.'

'What the fuck, dude? Wrong way round. Hampshire regiment, Isle of Wight rifles…where were you born?'

'I don't know…Oldport? Newport?'

'Newport, listen, just stay quiet and act thick.'

'Okay.'

'Which means act normal.'

'Fuck you.'

'Just, you know, be this big, lumbering guy that's all brawn and no brains.'

'Fuck you.'

'That has sex with hot women after going for like *one run*.'

'That bit is true.'

'Where?'

'Shower.'

'Shower?'

'Yeah, the shower.'

'Then you found the necklace after?'

'Yep.'

'I see. So…how did Lucy actually get in the shower?'

'She stepped in.'

'No, I mean…'

'I said I was going for a shower, and then she followed.'

'You didn't ask her?'

'No.'

'She just came in?'

'Yeah…she made a joke that I was drowning and needed help.'

'Man,' Thomas says, tugging the collar of his tunic away from his neck while stretching his neck from the chin-strap already rubbing his skin while tilting and leaning to shift the weight of the trench-tools, bayonet, water-bottle, and gas mask, all hanging from his body with what must be the worst designed weight-distribution ever.

Bear does the same. Fidgeting as he walks. Tugging the trousers from going up his arse while shifting, leaning, huffing, and tutting.

'So, you played hide the sausage with Lucy in the shower, and now you feel like shit because you found the necklace from the dead girl you played hide the sausage with that one time *after* she groomed and made you into a killing machine...'

'Noise ahead,' Bear cuts in, straining to listen. A general hum of noise made of many things that grows louder as they walk. Then they breach the corner and stop dead to stare in stunned awe.

A wide road, once a grand artery lined with trees leading to the beautiful ancient town of Ypres, now a muddied sea of greys and browns, filled with teams of horses pulling wagons loaded with the mangled remains of uniformed corpses. More horses pulling artillery guns that slip and slide through the mud on big metal spoked wheels going the other direction. Wagons of supplies and ammunition. Officers on horse-back cursing and shouting for everyone else to make way.

Thousands of men on foot, and every single one in a uniform of a degree. Some look new and shiny like Bear and Thomas, but wan, shocked, and stunned as they head towards the distant booms of the guns, passing the flotilla of corpses going past them, and long lines of bandaged men shuffling with their hands on the man in front. Some with faces entirely covered with filthy dressings. Others can barely walk. Some laugh and grin manically, and nearly every single one has blood stains coming from their ears.

Thomas and Bear absorb into the mass. Earning a few half-interested looks, but within seconds, they are simply part of the flow and contra-flow that both feed and drain the front-line of human fodder.

The going becomes harder. The road boggier, with thick mud that clumps and clings to their boots, making each step heavy and cumbersome. They stay quiet too because no one else is talking. The only voices heard are those from the men driving the horses or the officers on horseback shouting for room to get through.

The edges of the town come into view. A skyline of broken chimneys, and a church tower now half the size of what it should be, with jagged spikes like broken fingers stretching into the sky.

Engines behind them, and the ripple effect of men turning to look sweeps down the road. Heavy tanks. Huge beasts with solid metal riveted sides and massive caterpillar tracks, with turrets bulging out from the sides, and the muzzles of guns poking out. They churn through the mud with ease, rocking and bouncing, but going ever forward, while spewing choking fumes. Big wheeled canvass covered trucks in between them, and suddenly, the vast scale of this war hits both of the men, and this is just one road to one battlefield.

They stand aside to watch the tanks go by, staring at the old technology and the trucks that follow.

'Lot of moustaches,' Thomas mutters.

Bear snorts a laugh, seeing what he means. Moustaches everywhere. Huge drooping things, bushy ones, some neatly trimmed too, and even a few Hitler style ones, worn by men with no idea of what that image will come to mean.

A dig in his ribs, and Bear follows Thomas's gaze skywards to a bi-plane flying in the distance, the noise lost from the cacophony of sound coming from the road, and still, above it all, above everything else, are the big booms of the huge artillery guns firing unseen.

They reach the town muddied, sweating, and looking at a hand-painted sign rammed into the mud. **This way to Hell...**

'Hey, you! Private...yes, you...'

Thomas and Bear lurch back from the huge horse coming to a stop in front of them. An officer on the top. His green flat cap so neat above his perfectly trimmed moustache, 'Remove that sign.'

'Sign, Sir?' Thomas asks, confused.

'The bloody sign, man!' the officer points at the hand-painted thing, 'Go on, get rid of it...the men don't need to see that.'

'Sir,' Thomas says, rushing to grab and pull the sign free. He goes to turn, to ask the officer what he should do with it but finds the horse and man gone, so shrugs, pauses for a second, and pushes it back into place to a low chorus of chuckles coming from the lines of men walking past.

'WHICH REGIMENT ARE YOU BOYS IN?' a big man asks, sergeant stripes on his arms, and a thick wooden cudgel wedged in his belt. Scars on his face, and his voice booms.

'Hampshire, Sir. Isle of Wight rifles...' Thomas replies.

'SPEAK UP,' the sergeant bellows.

'The constant shelling renders most men deaf', Jacob had told them before deploying.

'HAMPSHIRE, SIR. ISLE OF WIGHT RIFLES...'

'YOU A YANK?'

'BRITISH...LIVED THERE FOR A FEW YEARS... WE NEED TO REPORT TO CORPORAL SIMMONDS...'

'WHAT?'

'CORPORAL SIMMONDS...'

'THAT WAY...DOWN THERE AND SPEAK UP, SON. STOP BLOODY MUMBLING.'

They break off down another muddied track between rows of broken, ruined buildings where men gather in the torn-down eaves to rest and sleep. Small fires here and there. Water heated to make tea, and everyone looking hungry and drawn, with sunken cheeks and days of thick stubble. The stench, a ruinous smell of unwashed bodies, animal and human dung mixed with smoke, chemicals, and bad meat.

They find the Field Headquarters within minutes. A low building engulfed in sandbag walls, with men coming and going from the narrow entry point guarded by yet more soldiers. Open-topped cars wait outside on the roadway next to trucks and horses tied to posts. Men in groups, talking and smoking. Others resting against low walls, dozing, or staring vacantly.

'Papers,' a soldier guarding the entrance stops the two men, his eyes running over their kit and studying their faces, 'Don't know you...'

'Just arrived,' Thomas says.

'Just arrived, *sergeant*,' the man says.

'Sorry, sergeant.'

'Yank?'

'British. Lived there for a few years.'

'Name?'

'Thomas Smith. Private. Hampshire Regi...'

'I don't need all that bollocks. I meant your first name.'

'Gee, sorry, Tom. That's Brian.'

'Papers say you're assigned to Corporal Simmonds. Go around the building and across the back to the medical bays. On your way, now.'

They follow the path down through the churned-up grounds to a vast outbuilding constructed from stone and surrounded on all sides by men in blood-stained dressings crying out in agony. Men writhing from bullet wounds and shrapnel strikes to legs and bodies. Men with limbs shorn off from shell blasts. Another one with a German bayonet sticking from his chest, staring up in shock at two men arguing whether they should pull it out or not.

'Jesus...' Thomas swallows, his mind already reeling from seeing so many truly awful things.

'Help you, chaps?' one of the men, standing over the soldier stuck with the bayonet, calls over.

'We're looking for Corporal Simmonds...er...Sir?' Thomas ventures, not seeing a rank on the blood-stained white coat but hearing the cultured voice.

'Oh, he's inside somewhere,' the man says, waving them away, 'I say, now, chaps, don't suppose either of you are triage trained, are you?'

'I've done first aid,' Thomas says before he can stop himself.

'First aid? Whatever's that? We're just deciding whether to pull this blasted bayonet from this chap...'

'Are you doctors?' Thomas asks.

'Doctors? God, no. We're vets. We look after the horses...the General decided we should come and help tend the injured, and as grand an idea as that is, the horse does differ from the human form somewhat.'

'Leave it in,' Bear says, 'Withdrawing could rupture an artery...'

'Ha! Told you, Curly old chap,' the man booms, clapping his veterinary colleague on the arm.

'It does hurt a bit, Sirs,' the man gasps, still clutching the blade in his gut.

'Oh, you'll be alright there, Private. Eh? What, what. Chin up now.'

'Come on,' Thomas leads them on, treading over and around the broken bodies to venture inside the building. Beds everywhere, made from doors and planks of wood propped on anything that can hold them. Surgeons and aides working frantically in a putrid, wet heat amongst the buzz of flies and the cries of men.

'Corporal Simmonds?' Thomas asks a uniformed man rushing past.

'No. Over there...book in and get kitted for triage,' he rushes outside, a canvas bag over his shoulder, and a white armband around his arm.

They go deeper into the horror, past a surgeon pushing the innards of a stomach back into a cavity with a scowl, 'Dead. Next.'

'There,' Bear whispers, getting Thomas's attention to the same man he saw on Zara's monitor. Ruddy faced, and the neatly clipped moustache seen on the image now grown out and bushy. A green flat cap wedged on the back of his head, and he looks as exhausted as everyone else.

'Corporal Simmonds?'

'Yes? What?' the man snaps, glancing up while injecting a man in the arm from a syringe.

'Reporting for duty,' Thomas says smartly, 'Thomas Smith and Brian Jones, privates. Hampshire Regiment Isle of...'

'What? I don't need rifles here. I need medics,' Corporal Simmonds says gruffly, easing the syringe out, 'Get to the trenches... You'll just be in the way.'

'We're er...we're triage trained, Corporal,' Thomas says, remembering the words the veterinary surgeon used.

'A likely story, I'll say. Listen, chaps. The trenches are no fun, I'll grant you that, but you can't hide in here...'

'Sir, we have papers, we're seconded to help you,' Thomas asserts, reaching into his pocket for his papers.

'Good lord, I don't need to see papers, man! I need medics and stretcher bearers who can triage...'

'We can triage, we can carry stretchers, Corporal...we're here to work with you.'

'This is highly irregular,' he snaps, walking off before turning sharply. 'Come on, with me...' he leads them outside, casting a desultory glance at the papers while striding towards the outer fringes of the thick crowds of injured men. 'Him,' Corporal Simmonds says, pointing at a silent man staring into the distance, 'Triage him...'

'Sheesh, er...his limbs look unbroken, he's smoking... blood from his ears, his eyes are unfocussed...'

'I don't need his life history, man! Triage him. Urgent. Not urgent. Walking wounded...what is he?'

'He looks shell-shocked,' Bear says, dropping to lift the man's chin, seeing the vacant look. He clicks his fingers in front of the man's eyes, gaining zero response.

'That one,' Corporal Simmonds says, pointing to another one.

'Er...he er...he looks dead,' Thomas says, peering down.

'He is dead. That one...triage that man there...'

'This one? His arms been blown off, Corporal, he needs urgent care...'

'Right. Good enough. Back in with me. Rifles, eh?

Listen, chaps, you won't know everything, but you're not expected to. Just do your best. A few kind words is often all we can do. Pray with them if you have time. Tell them they'll be okay, that sort of thing. Dressings, splints, and everything you'll need is in that back room. Food is later, maybe...we don't always eat, you see, we're not a fighting unit, and they need it more than we do. Got it? If they die, get rid of them quickly. Bad for moral to have the dead knocking about. The worst wounded are brought in and kept away from the walking wounded, again, that's for moral. We don't want those going back into the trenches to see just how bad it is. Got it? The gas station is over the way...'

'Gas station?' Thomas asks.

'Gas victims, we can't have them in here with everyone else... The gas clings to everything. Get rid of 'em. Got it? We've got tons of Morphia so don't be afraid to use it...got it? On you go then, chaps. Mark them up urgent, walking wounded, and no good, I mean, obviously, don't tell them if they're looking to go for a duck...'

'Duck?' Thomas asks.

'Going to die, private. Don't tell them they are going to die. Dose them up and let them go peacefully. Best of it, eh? Do shout if you need help...got it?'

CHAPTER TWENTY-NINE

Discovery

Prisha leans in through the doorway to Lars' office. 'I'm going over. Need anything?' she asks.

'No,' he replies, thinking for a second, 'Cake.'

'You want a cake?'

He thinks for a second, 'Yes.'

'Help me out, Lars...what cake do you want?'

'Surprise me,' he says, leaning back to push a hand into his pocket.

'It's my turn,' she walks off through the main office. Grabbing her purse from her bag to draw a Discovery banknote before pulling her thick winter uniform coat on and stepping out to look up and down Main Street, so golden and rosy in the autumnal afternoon, lifting her hand in greeting to deputy Matias walking across the intersection.

'Prisha,' he says, drawing closer, 'going over?'

She nods, 'Lars wants cake.'

'What cake?'

'Said to surprise him. Want one?'

'Yeah, surprise me…' he says as she rolls her eyes in humour and starts walking off, 'Prish? I just heard Lucy was out running with Bear this morning. Norman saw them coming out of Bear's place too…said she looked flushed.'

Prisha pauses, turning back to nod, 'Okay.'

'Want me to do it?'

'Nah, it's on the way…get the cakes though?' she walks back, holding out the banknote, 'It was my turn.'

'What do you want?' he asks, taking the money.

'Surprise me,' she walks off, crossing the street and heading down to the front doors of the hospital and through as the reception staff look up with interest, 'Lucy in?'

'Her office,' one of them replies, 'I'll tell her you're coming.'

'Great,' Prisha walks on through the corridors, her utility belt fastened securely around her waist. Her boots treading firmly, with solid steps to the door that she knocks once.

'Yep…come in.'

She goes through, looking around the medical room and seeing Lucy washing her hands at the sink in the corner, 'Prisha, how are you?'

'Good,' Prisha says, still looking around.

'How can I help?' Lucy asks, walking behind her desk to switch the monitor off just as Prisha looks at it, 'You here for personal reasons or…'

'Nope, work,' Prisha says, sitting down on the wooden chair to stare over the desk at Lucy. The woman is stunning beyond words. Flawless even, and Prisha can see why Bear would go with her.

'Bear?' Lucy asks.

Prisha nods, using silence to encourage Lucy to speak.

'Ah, the tittle tattlers have been busy, have they?' Lucy asks, smiling over, 'I was going to come over after work.'

'Okay,' Prisha says.

'We had sex,' Lucy says openly.

'Right,' Prisha replies without reaction.

'Done,' Lucy beam, 'I have declared my romantic interest with an operative as per the rules. Was there anything else, Prisha, or do you want to sit in silence and see if I'll admit to a murder or something?'

Prisha laughs, she can't help it. Lucy is funny, and Prisha likes the way the accent comes back when she jokes, 'Just doing my job, Lucy.'

'To be honest, he can probably finish the therapy now,' Lucy says, the humour easing as her tone becomes serious, 'I mean...if this was the real world, I'd be sacked and out the door but...'

'It's not the real world,' Prisha says, standing up, 'You'll work it out...listen, Lucy...I have to say this bit.'

'Go on,' Lucy says, sitting back in her chair.

'Do not question an operative about RLIs. Do not seek information or try, or attempt to try or, in anyway, do anything to influence the work they do. If your romantic connection ends, you must inform us. The Discovery Sheriff's department does not wish to be intrusive in your private life, and anything said will remain confidential, but we will be kept informed of anything relating to operatives and those connected with RLIs...and we will be dipping your accounts to check...'

'Great speech, mate...you know operatives are the worst gossips ever? They can't keep their gobs shut about the stuff they do, and everyone knows they've got a first world war overnighter on...'

'Gotta say it,' Prisha says, holding her hands up, 'Catch you soon.'

Deputy Prisha goes out and down the corridor, through the hospital, and out the doors with a nod and a wave at the reception staff who descend into instant gossip the second she goes.

'Hey,' Prisha says, walking into the planning offices.

'Prish,' Jennifer says, glancing up over the desk, then dropping her head straight back down.

'What you doing?' Prisha asks, peering over to see Jennifer painting her nails, 'Bored then?'

'Always bored,' Jennifer mutters, 'What do you think?'

'Nice,' Prisha says, reaching over to pick the bottle up, 'Pink suits you.'

'Passes the time. Bear fucked Lucy this morning.'

'I heard,' Prisha says.

'Has she declared it?'

'Can't tell you. I'd have to kill you.'

'Tell me later. You coming over?'

'Could do.'

'Lucky bitch,' Jennifer sighs, looking up at the deputy.

'They'll make good babies, that's for sure,' Prisha says.

'Oh, my god, is she pregnant?'

'What!? No! It's a saying...when two beautiful people get together...'

'Is it? I never heard that. I'd make good babies with Bear.'

'You would.'

'Oh, you know what...you and Bear would make gorgeous babies...like, with your skin tone...'

'You think?'

'Totally,' Jennifer says, 'but he's mine next when him and Lucy don't work out.'

'I'd better get on. See you later...' Prisha walks off to the door, then up the stairs to the planning office, pushing through the door to the noise and chaos of the main room that falls that little bit quieter when she walks in.

'IT'S A RAID!'

'Very funny, Terry. Never gets old.'

'Prish,' Allie says, walking from Martha's office.

'Allie.'

'I've got them ready,' Allie says, motioning for Prisha to follow as she walks off towards her desk in Zara's office.

'Hey,' Prisha says, nodding at Zara who looks up with the startled gaze of someone very absorbed in their work.

'Prish, you okay?' Zara asks, sitting back to stretch and yawn with a yelp that brings moisture to her eyes that she blinks away before looking over at the second monitor showing Bear and Thomas carrying a stretcher filled with a man holding his guts in his hands.

Prisha looks over, wincing at the sight, 'First World War?'

'Yeah, Ypres, 1917,' Zara says grimly, 'Overnighter... unless they get it sorted earlier.'

'Joining in drooling over Bear in a soldier's uniform?' Allie asks, twisting around from her desk.

Prisha smiles, chuckling quietly.

'Lucy declared yet?' Allie asks.

'Can't say,' Prisha replies.

'Tell me later. You coming over?'

'Said I'd go around Jen's, coming?'

'Might do,' Allie muses, 'Zara? Fancy it?'

'Can't,' she says, pointing at the screen, 'Watching them...unless you want to bring a takeaway here and keep me company?'

'We can do that,' Allie says, 'We can all drool over Bear

then while we cry into our Chinese at the thought of him and Lucy making beautiful babies...'

'I just said that to Jen,' Prisha says.

'Ah, well,' Allie says. 'If anyone was going to get him...' she hefts the armful of folders up, passing them over to Prisha.

'Yeah, she is something else,' Prisha says.

'She's bloody not,' Zara snaps, 'She's not! It's all make-up and that accent and...'

'Yeah, you tell yourself that,' Allie jokes.

'See you tonight,' Prisha says, walking back across the office and down to the reception desk, 'We're having take-away here with Zara tonight now.'

'Who is?' Jennifer asks, peering over her desk.

'We are. Zara's on an overnighter. Allie said we'll keep her company.'

'Ooh, the war job, can we ogle Bear in a soldier's uniform?'

'Oh, yes,' Prisha laughs, 'Laters.'

She goes out and up the street, nodding here and there to the people of Discovery that pass by. Into the Sheriff's office, and the sight of Lars and Matius stuffing big, fresh cream cakes in their mouths, 'They look nice?'

'They are nice,' Matius replies with a mouthful.

'Lucy?' Lars asks.

'Done,' Prisha replies, dumping the folders on the central desk, 'Confirmed. Sex this morning.'

'Lucky man,' Matius mumbles.

'Cake,' Lars says, holding the box out for Prisha.

'Thanks,' she takes the last one out, biting into the long donut filled with cream and jam. 'We doing them today?' she asks, covering her mouth while nodding at the folders she brought in.

Lars nods once, walking over to grab a third of the folders that he carries into his office as Prisha spots the forlorn look on Matias' face at the prospect of a day spent dip-testing RLIs. 'Come on,' she says, 'sooner we start, sooner we finish...'

She logs into her screen, reading the subject name in the folder, finds the date, the location, and accesses the data systems. How it works, is beyond her. How the Old Lady retains live network connections to so many different systems, in so many different countries, across ever-changing time periods, is simply unbelievable, and the single, biggest reminder that they are not in the real world.

Why they do it, is also a question they've never had answered. The Old Lady can access every single life ever lived, so why ask three human beings to dip-test the few tweaks done by a few more human beings? Why rely on a fallible system? Why rely on deputy Matias skimming through his work to get finished quickly so he can go strut up and down Main Street in his police uniform?

There are more questions than answers, and although, ninety-nine percent of the population of Discovery are happy to go along with it, she and a few others, including Zara, still want to know how the finite details work.

CHAPTER THIRTY

Ypres, Belgium, 1917

The hardest thing is not knowing what kills Simmonds. They can't stay next to him without arousing great suspicion. Nor can they leave him out of sight for any length of time, so, while running back and forth with stretchers, while triaging, while rushing to grab clean dressings, while giving morphine and doing a dozen tasks, they have to watch him constantly.

They work hard through the evening to night and the hours of darkness, clearing the grounds of men waiting to be examined, then tasked to load the dead on the returning wagons. Stacking mangled bodies under an ever-falling rain that soaks them to the skin, and when they finally finish, they stand heaving for air, with flushed faces, shirt sleeves rolled up, and braces hanging down as the last of the wagons rolls away.

'My back,' Thomas groans, arching his spine.

'Stop bending over then, lift with your legs,' Bear says.

'*Stop bending over*,' Thomas mimics, '*lift with your legs...I'm Bear...I have sex with doctors that look like models...*'

'Fuck off,' Bear groans, wiping the sweat from his forehead with the back of his arm.

'*I'm all brooding and mysterious and...*whatever, man, damn this is hard work. Why can't someone try and kill that dude already...hey, I got a plan. You try and kill Simmonds, then I'll stop you, and we can go.'

'How does that do it?'

'Duh? If you're the one that kills him, and I stop you, then he doesn't die. Time travel man. Get with the programme.'

'I told you it confuses me,' Bear says.

'Everything confuses you. Tying shoelaces confuses you...hey, you hear that?'

'Hear what?' Bear asks, listening intently.

'Shelling has stopped,' Thomas says.

'Get orf, you filthy bugger...'

They turn quickly, seeing a bloodied man waving his hand at a fat, greasy rat licking the blood-stained dressing on the stump of an unconscious soldier. A helmet is launched, whacking it off, but the thing scurries through the mud, delighting in this land of plenty, so full of blood and flesh.

The rats are everywhere. The sheer number of them boggles the mind. Unafraid for the most part too and left to squeak and squabble with each other, and only swatted away when they start eating bodies.

'Chaps! Over here, quick as you like,' Corporal Simmonds calls out, striding from the medical building, 'Orders have come through...'

'Orders?' Thomas asks.

'We're going over the top with the push at dawn.'

'The what?' Thomas asks.

'The attack,' Simmonds says, too tired to question Thomas's lack of knowledge, 'We're attacking at dawn. It's my turn for this one.'

'Into the trenches?' Bear asks.

'That's the fella,' Simmonds says, trying to hide his own fear with a jaunty tone. He swallows, looking terrified for a second, 'Big one by all accounts. The Generals want it done...big advance on the German lines...'

A look between them. From Thomas to Bear at the complexity involved in keeping a man alive during a battle.

'You've not seen it, have you?' Simmonds asks, a faraway look in his eyes.

'No,' Thomas says.

The corporal tilts his head, 'Won't forget it, that's for sure... quick brew, then we'll go, it's a bit of a trek from here, I'm afraid.'

'You DIDN'T DRINK the coffee, Prish,' Matius says, looming next to her with his civilian coat on.

'Huh?' she looks up, blinking, 'You going home?'

'Gone six, you finishing?'

'Err, yeah, I'll finish this one and get going.'

'See you tomorrow,' he says, walking off.

Footsteps behind her. The heavy tread of Lars walking from his office. 'Don't stay late,' he walks out and away, his gruff manner making her smile.

'Bye, Lars,' Prisha says to thin air. 'Who's next?' she glances at the next folder in the pile to be dip-tested, reading the name. 'Hank Peterson...' suicide from Verrazano bridge. New York. 'Assigned to...Zara, Bear, and Thomas. Okay, Hank...let's see you living a long and happy life...'

She finds the right database, opening the screen to bring up the form, and types his name and date of birth into the sections. 'Hank Peterson...Hank Peterson....' she frowns, checking his date of birth again, 'Stop being awkward, Hank. I've got a takeaway waiting...'

They sit in the back of a canvass covered truck bouncing down the pitted track. Bear at the back, staring out to a moonlit landscape that grows steadily worse the further from the town they go. Banks of raw earth, and the ground undulating on both sides with coils of barbed wire stretching in every direction, with the silhouettes of dead and broken tree trunks the only remaining sign of a once green and fertile land.

Thomas next to him. Corporal Simmonds opposite, looking sick to the stomach, licking his lips, and swallowing constantly. That the man is terrified to the core is obvious, but then so is everyone else. Bear looks down the bench seats, seeing the admin and medical staff, ordered from the relative safety of the town to the trenches, ready for the big push. All of them the same as Simmonds. Scared witless and gripping hardly used rifles with trembling hands. Bear looks at Thomas, seeing the tension is getting to the normally jovial American. The chances are, they will reset in Discovery if they die here, but the risk of true death is very real, and with it comes the fear everyone else is feeling.

A boom in the distance as the artillery guns start back up. Sudden and frightening in the darkness, and now they hear the detonations too. The booming whumps of the earth juddering, and the tension in the truck ramps higher with lips growing thin. Men start praying and making the sign of the cross as Bear looks out, trying to see the shells going overhead.

The truck stops, slowing and skewing in the mud before the engine cuts out. 'THAT'S IT...FAR AS I CAN GO...' the driver yells.

'Every...' an officer in the back starts speaking, but fear makes his voice break and crack. He clears his throat, trying again, 'Everyone out, chaps...'

They jump down to slide in the mud, huddling together as a solitary figure looms from the darkness.

'THE LAST LOT, ARE YOU?' the sergeant from earlier stalks towards them with his cudgel now gripped in his hands, with his rifle slung across his back.

'Shush!' the officer hisses, 'Why are you shouting?'

'He's deaf, Sir,' Corporal Simmonds say, 'The shelling, you see...'

'FOLLOW ME,' the sergeant booms.

They fall in behind as he veers off across the muddy bank as the shells soar overhead to blow with bright orange flashes in all-too-close-distance.

'Jesus, dude,' Thomas stays close to Bear who stays close to Simmonds. His hand within grabbing reach of the man they have to protect. 'Trenches...' Thomas mumbles the word as they drop down a shallow decline, and then they are in it. Inside a trench.

They go on, losing all sense of direction and distance. The doglegs, the junctions, the zigging and zagging. Some are deeper with high sides shored up with sandbags, and lit lanterns giving a soft, orange glow to the faces of the men trying to sleep, play cards or smoking in silence.

They pass dugouts filled with officers still planning the big assault, and thousands of men simply waiting to die.

The further they go, the worse the conditions become. The mud deeper, the side walls rougher. Rats everywhere. Running alongside and scampering over their feet and alongside the shelves and divots in the walls.

It gets worse still. The shells exploding closer. The noise of them now a deafening roar, and they have to shout to be heard while the ground quakes with each strike, juddering and trembling. They slip and slide, pulling each other on as they descend into a living hell.

'Ah,' Prisha says to herself. 'Makes sense now...' it does happen sometimes. It's not normal, but then it's not rare either. Hank Peterson was saved from suicide on Verrazano bridge by Bear and Thomas and left in the care of his sister but died a day later after being run over by truck. 'Unlucky sod,' she mumbles, switching programmes to write a brief report ready to send back to Martha who will decide if the Old Lady needs to be updated, or if another tweak should be done.

She startles at the phone ringing next to her, lifting the receiver, 'Sheriff's office. Deputy Prisha...'

'It's Jen. What do you want to eat? Allie said she can do a run into New York and grab something.'

'Er, that is strictly forbidden,' Prisha says firmly, 'but I'll have Thai in that case.'

'Thai? Okay, come over in about twenty?'

'Yep,' Prisha puts the receiver down and finishes the report, printing it off to attach to the folder and thinking to take the completed ones back with her when she goes to meet the others. 'One more,' she tells herself, grabbing the next folder.

THE WALLS SHAKE. Crumbling, with mud sliding down that is scooped and pushed back by soldiers cowering with their heads between knees. Others rock back and forth. Driven mad by this constant noise as flares give phosphorous light to a landscape, twisted and torn apart.

They stopped walking minutes ago and were told, by way of being pushed into the walls, to stay here, and the big sergeant shows no fear to the noise or the horror but walks up and down, glaring at anyone looking like they might try and flee. His cudgel gripped and ready in his hands with obvious intent at what he will to do deserters or cowards.

Simmonds slides down on his haunches. His medical canvas bag hugged like a comforter. His eyes clamped shut. His cheeks wet from the tears falling out.

Thomas feels the fear. The horror. It gnaws inside him. Growing with a sense of dread. At least he has a chance at living and resetting back in Discovery, but still, it gets to him, the shelling, the noise, the flares, the fear hanging in the air.

'I'M OFF,' Sally says, leaning into Zara's office. 'Everything okay?' she asks, looking at the monitor.

'No,' Zara says glumly, 'They're in the bloody trenches waiting to charge the enemy...'

Sally winces, pulling a pained expression, 'Easy thing to say, but try not to worry...'

'Right,' Allie says, walking in, 'Jen and Prish want Thai. You happy with Thai, Zara?'

'Yeah, that's fine,' Zara says, leaning back in her chair to rub her face.

'Joining us?' Allie asks, seeing the stunned look on Sally's face that a programmer is being asked to share a meal with handlers and managers.

'Pardon?'

'We're doing a run into the real world for takeaway to keep Zara company.'

'Seriously?' Sally asks, 'Yeah, okay, you sure I'm not, like, in the way or something?'

'It's fine,' Allie says, 'Just don't tell anyone.'

'No way,' Prisha says, blinking at the screen. She looks away, shaking her head, then reads again before checking the details. Jean Stoll. Danish by birth but living in London. Steps in front of a bus but is saved by Bear. Zara's report indicates it was successful, but the systems show Jean Stoll was stabbed to death in a street robbery less than a week later. Two in one go isn't right, and the hairs on the back of her neck prickle with alarm as she reaches for the next folder.

BEAR'S PLAN IS FORMED. He'll shoot Simmonds in the leg the first chance he gets. Easy and simple. Simmonds won't be very happy for sure, but he'll stay alive.

He fidgets in position, pushing his hand into pocket to pull the necklace out, fingering the delicate links and the word inscribed on the pendant. *Are you looking up my dress?* He smiles at the memory, because that's all it is, just a memory of someone he once knew. Did she groom him? Probably. Does he care? Not really. Would he do it again? Yes, without doubt, but it's gone now. He must look to the future, and he decides, at that point, to buy Lucy flowers and ask her to go to dinner with him.

Another whoosh overhead, and the shell hits with a huge boom, with every soldier wishing it would end while hoping it never ends, because the end means they have to charge.

PRISHA READS through files and systems, flicking back and forth between the lives of the people targeted in the RLIs carried out by Zara's team.

Hank Peterson was killed the day after being saved. Jean Stoll was knifed in the heart during a robbery a week after Bear prevented her stepping out in front of a bus.

Colin Jenson was saved by Bear and Thomas giving him Epinephrine, he was meant to live and guide his son into the army, but he died two days later while alone at his house.

Mary Lieber. American housewife, and domestic violence victim. She was beaten to death inside prison while awaiting trial, but she was meant to live too.

Prisha punches deeper into her system to hunt for the flow. There's nearly always a flow when missions are done back to back this way. It's how the Old Lady works. Doing a batch of tweaks that all *seem* random, yet are all interconnected.

Hank Peterson *not* committing suicide means he later

opens a charity. That charity eventually stops a young abuse sufferer from gunning down dozens of students at his old school. That same young man then later marries Mary Lieber after she is acquitted of the murder of her husband. They have a daughter that marries a leading scientist and climate change expert. A man that should have died as a child when Jean Stoll's husband gassed himself and caused an explosion. A scientist that convinces governments to switch from fossil fuels to a new battery system developed by a former combat engineer, the son of Colin Jenson. And that combat engineer was meant to be saved by a US Marine called Mikey who went to military cadets instead of Sunday school.

The flow is right there as Prisha visualises the golden lines and the glowing dots as those lives entwine and shape the future of humanity.

Except, they don't happen. Hank Peterson is killed. Jean Stoll is killed. Colin Jenson dies too. Mikey still goes into the firefight in Afghan, but without the combat engineer, he never calls for air support, and he dies too. That means the new battery system is never developed, and Mary never marries the former angry young man. They don't have a child that marries the climate change expert. There is no climate change expert, because Jean Stoll still dies, and her husband still gasses himself and blows the street up.

'What the hell...' Prisha mutters as she rushes to Matias's desk to check through the RLIs done by other operatives. Marco, Keith, Helmut, and others.

All fine. No issues.

She goes into Lars's office, checking through his and seeing Pete and Jacob's work is fine. The same with Kathy. All of them are fine.

Only Zara's team are being targeted.

You know operatives are the worst gossips ever? They can't keep their gobs shut about the stuff they do, and everyone knows they've got a war overnighter on...

Lucy's words come back. Someone is feeding everything they are doing to Freedom. Zara has to get them back now. She has to recall them. Prisha runs across the office, grabbing her jacket and the folders before running for the door with the sudden realisation that Bear and Thomas are being tracked.

CHAPTER THIRTY-ONE

Teams of men for every gun. Fifteen-inch Howitzers lined up with gangs of exhausted soldiers working like demons to load and fire each shell that weighs over six-hundred kilos, winching the pulleys by hand to load the giant metal beast while more men turn the wheels to adjust angle and position. The other Howitzers fire down the line, expending their ammunition, but this one on the end is the last of the night, and as the dawn lifts, and the world turns to bring day, so the men run back and away to cover their ears as the huge thing fires with a noise that cannot be imagined.

The missile soars through the sky at over one thousand feet a second to cover the two miles to the front line where it swooshes over the trenches filled with thousands of men who stare up with fear etched on their faces.

That last shell drops over the heads of Bear, Thomas, and Corporal Simmonds. Landing metres beyond the first German trenches, detonating with yet another ear-splitting explosion of mud and screaming metal that flies out to embed in tree trunks that set to flame from the supercharged fragments.

After that, comes the silence. The awful, terrible, drawn-out silence as the senior officers check watches and pass word that the attack is to go as planned.

'UP...GET UP...' the sergeant with the cudgel booms, striding up and down his section, heaving men to their feet, 'MAKE READY...'

Officers emerge from dugouts, dry and clean after a night under cover, while around them, the freezing men shiver from the cold and terror, gripping their rifles and trying to kick the clinging mud from their boots.

Bear grabs Thomas, pulling him in close, 'Soon as the attack starts, I'll shoot him in the leg...you react and scream out...call me a cunt or...'

'I don't think they use cunt here...' Thomas says.

'Whatever then, whatever they use...'

'Okay, want me to shoot him?'

'No. You're an awful shot...'

'Hey, fuck you, man,' Thomas says, 'What if they make us go over?'

'LADDERS...' the sergeant screams. Wooden ladders are grabbed and propped against the trench wall. Pushed into place with a weird, bizarre action of men not wanting to go first but not wanting to be seen as holding back. A pushing starts with people trying to look like they are going for it while letting others push ahead.

'GET ON THEM FUCKING LADDERS...' a whack into a leg from the cudgel, a smack in the head from a big hand.

'Sir...' Corporal Simmonds calls out for a pale-faced officer emerging from a dugout, 'Medics, Sir, we don't go with the first wave...'

The officer blinks, confusion in his eyes. He's only been here for three days and has no clue what he is doing. A murmur sounds down the trenches, with some men grumbling at the medics trying to hold back while others agree the medics don't go first.

'FACE THAT WAY...' the sergeant moves fast, pushing at Simmonds to get him back into position.

'I'M A MEDIC,' Simmonds shouts back, pointing at his armband, 'HOW DO I GIVE TREATMENT IF I'M THE FIRST OVER?'

'DO NOT EYEBALL ME...' the sergeant marches off, either unable or unwilling to hear reason.

'Okay chaps...make ready now,' the officer calls out weakly, trying to work out how to hold his pistol and pocket watch and put the whistle in his mouth all at the same time, 'When the call comes...we'll go over what? Up and at them, I say...every man do his duty now...'

'FOR QUEEN AND COUNTRY,' the deaf sergeant roars, thinking the officer has finished speaking.

'Queen and country,' a wan, weak response ripples down the line from soldiers with bleeding ears, rendered deaf and dumb from the onslaught of shelling.

'QUEEN AND COUNTRY,' the sergeant roars again, stamping his feet and slamming his cudgel into a plank of wood. 'WE'LL HAVE AT 'EM...FILTHY KRAUTS... FILTHY BASTARDS...FILTHY FUCKING BASTARDS...' spittle flies from his lips, his face reddening from the strain of yelling.

'I say, sergeant,' the officer says primly, 'won't have that language here, you know...'

'FILTHY CUNTS...' the deaf sergeant screams.

'They do use cunt then,' Thomas tells Bear.

'Jesus,' Zara says in her office, shaking her head at the monitor, 'I don't think I can watch.'

'Don't then,' Allie says, 'Sit here, and I'll keep an eye.'

'Is Prisha coming?' Sally asks.

'Said she was,' Jennifer replies, pulling the lid from a carton.

'This feels wrong,' Zara says, 'We're eating takeaway just before witnessing mass murder...'

'Don't overthink it,' Allie says. 'Come on, swap seats.'

'ZARA!' Prisha's voice shouting through the office as the deputy bursts through the door from the stairwell.

'In here,' Jennifer shouts, leaning out the door. 'We started...what's up with you?' she asks, seeing the deputy's wild eyes.

'Something's wrong,' Prisha says, pushing into the office, 'All of your RLIs have been undone...get them back now!'

'What?' Zara asks, midway through standing from her chair.

'Your RLIs...Hank Peterson...he was stopped from suicide...'

'Yeah, Bear and Thomas called his sister,' Zara says, glancing at Allie.

'He died the next day,' Prisha blurts.

'That does happen,' Allie says, 'I mean it's rare but...'

'Jean Stoll? She was knifed in a robbery a few days after they stopped her being run over...that one in the restaurant...Colin?'

'Jenson,' Zara says calmly, her eyes fixed on Prisha.

'Him. He ate the same thing he is allergic to at home on his own. Kills him...and Mary Lieber? The battered wife? Beaten to death while on trial. I checked the flow. They're all connected, but none of them live or do the things they were meant to do, and it all means a climate change scientist doesn't tell the governments to use batteries. Listen, none of the other RLIs have been touched. You've been targeted. Get them back. They're being tracked.'

Zara nods, her mind running clear. 'Sally, send a message to Thomas's bleeper to get out now...' they all freeze as the lights go off with the computers, monitors, and electrical systems all shutting down, plunging the room into darkness and silence. 'What the fuck just happened?' Zara whispers into the silence.

'THIRTY SECONDS, CHAPS!' the officer shouts, lifting his whistle to his lips.

The call is repeated down the line as men mutter last minute prayers, trapped between being killed for cowardice and being shot by German machine guns.

'Ah, man...this is gonna hurt,' Thomas grumbles, 'You ready?'

'Yeah,' Bear looks at his friend and starts positioning to shoot Simmonds, thinking to wait until the man is on the ladder and hoping he can get the bullet clean through the thigh without hitting bone.

'Good luck,' Simmonds says, nodding at Bear and Thomas and looking wretched to the core.

'NOW!'

Whistles sound for miles along the trenches as thousands of men give voice and start moving for the ladders while the sergeants and corporals scream at them to get going. The fear and tension so thick you could spoon it from the very air, and as Simmonds shuffles towards the ladder, so Bear glances down the trench to see Todd from Carpe Diem restaurant staring back at him. His heart lurches. His stomach flips, and he blinks to look again. It's him, and he's staring right over.

Bear looks about, casting his gaze over the terrified faces of the soldiers and seeing more Freedom operatives spread through the trench, some he recognises, others he marks for looking cleaner, healthier, and from the fact they are all staring at him with serious intent.

Freedom are here. They're in the trench. They've been tracked and targeted.

Everything on instinct now. The whistles blowing. The climb to go over the top already underway. There are too many to fight here in the trench, and if Bear shoots Simmonds in the leg, those Freedom operatives will be on them instantly. They have to go over. He counts quickly, seeing more than a dozen spread through the trench. They spot him looking, with eye-contact held as they all shuffle for the ladders while above them the German guns start firing.

Bear moves closer to Thomas, watching the sides and all around, 'Freedom are here...don't react...go over the top and get Simmonds down.'

'Jesus, dude,' Thomas says, staring ahead, 'How many?'

'Lots...'

'Fucking job is getting worse by the minute,' Thomas mutters, placing a hand on the corporal's shoulder.

A scream above them cuts off as a private reaches the top of the ladder only to fly back with his brains spraying out.

'GET OVER...GET OVER...' the deaf sergeant roars, pushing men at the ladders, whacking legs with his cudgel to get them moving while his colleagues do the same.

Simmonds gains the ladder, gripping to rise, with Thomas pressing as close as he can behind. A wet feeling on Bear's face. He frowns, touching his cheek to feel mud, then spots a tuft of an explosion a few inches in front of him and turns to see one of the men from the restaurant sliding the bolt on his rifle to take another pot-shot in Bear's general direction. Bear twitches his own rifle, keeping it low at his waist and plucking the trigger to send an unheard and unseen shot back at the man. It strikes the base of the ladder as the man fires back while still they shuffle forwards.

Bear glances up to see Simmonds and Thomas breach the top to go over. His turn now, but that means leaving himself exposed to the guy shooting him. He looks across, the two poised as though waiting to see what the other will do. Bear goes for it, surging up the ladder one handed while holding his rifle as the guy does the same. Both racing up, staring at each other.

'THAT'S IT...LIKE THEM...GET UP THERE...' the deaf sergeant roars as they race with eyes locked to clamber from the trench to a whole other world, and the second they gain the top, the second they both dive to roll and aim with rifles. The guy misses. Bear doesn't and gets the round through his shoulder, sending him flying off, then he's up, running forward and feeling the jolt from the view that greets him.

Thousands of men pouring from the trenches into the brutal barrenness of no man's land. Churned mud and deep craters filled with debris and corpses. Dead tree trunks here and there, and banks of fog and smoke roll thick across the ground as bullets whip by his body. Men drop either side of him, torn apart from machine guns lacerating their flesh while others are cut down from single shot rifles fired by German snipers.

He spots Thomas running up behind Simmonds, slamming into his back to drive the man down out of sight, into a deep crater. Bear runs for them, shouting out when a round hits the ground in front of him. He runs fast, diving headfirst into the crater to see Thomas fighting to keep Simmonds down.

'GET OFF ME, MAN!' Simmonds roars, trying to break free.

Bear lands on his stomach, sliding down the steep sides, headfirst into the wet, gloopy mud at the bottom and sinking deeper than he anticipated. He struggles to get out, his head submerged as thick mud fills his mouth, blotting his hearing and eyesight. Floundering, flapping his arms and legs, and finally, feeling something to grip to drag himself out, pawing at the corpse of a German soldier. He sucks air, shaking his head to clear his eyes and spotting a man leaping over the edge of the crater, and sliding down the steep sides towards the pool at the bottom.

Gunfire and smoke. Chaos everywhere, and Bear flashes a hand out to grip the soldier sliding down the crater wall, trying to stop him landing in the pool. The soldier grabs Bear's arm, then twists, and pulls a knife from his belt, screaming out as he tries to stab Bear in the chest. He blocks the stab, sliding on his back as both men go down into the thick gloop. Another one launches over the side of the crater, sliding down towards the fight while pulling his own knife.

Without grip or purchase, with eyes stinging from the mud, with airways clogged, Bear fights the first, disarming and shoving his head into the mud, then leaning back from the knife of the second man, fending him off while another one comes over the lip of the crater. Another, and more pouring down with knives drawn.

'What the hell is wrong with you?' Simmonds demands, 'We'll be shot...'

Bear stabs and slashes, drowning one second, then breaking free to suck air and stick the blade into legs and chests, into throats and bodies. They become unrecognisable. Each coated with mud so thick they can't tell each other apart. Bear presses that advantage, screaming out *not me, not me* to make two attackers falter long enough to kill them both.

One of them breaks free from the gloop to go for Thomas and Simmonds, his bayonet gripped and ready.

'FUCK OFF,' Thomas screams at him, desperately looking for his rifle but seeing it yards away. The man keeps coming, murder in his eyes that show white through the thick mud on his face. 'Oh, hell...' Thomas steps back, sliding in the mud, then tripping over Simmonds, but as he goes down, he gets a foot up into the attacker's groin, crunching his testicles and making the man drop with a scream of utter agony. Thomas starts scrabbling away, his instinct and experience telling him to leave the fighting to Bear, but this isn't a normal job, this is beyond normal, this is way beyond normal. He yells out, grabs his rifle and charges at the man writhing on the floor to drive the point of the bayonet deep into his heart. He wrenches it free, slams the bolt back, and shoots the man through the head before staggering to launch himself once more at Simmonds still trying to get to his feet.

SILENCE. Profound, deep, and heavy. A silence born from a lack of machines humming, from a lack of fluorescent tube lights vibrating, from a lack of life in the devices around them. No emergency lights either, no lights at all, save for the silver light of the moon shining through the windows.

'Okay,' Zara says, flicking through a dusty safety manual taken from a shelf in Martha's office. '*Each deployment portal has an emergency back-up power supply that will last approximately three hours, this time being deemed sufficient to allow a recall of the operatives...*' Zara trails off from reading. 'How?' she snaps, 'How do we bloody recall without power? Where does the power even come from? Is there a generator?'

Silence from the others who shake heads, not knowing the answers.

'The phones are dead,' Prisha says, lifting a receiver. She moves across the corridor to the window, 'It's not just here...'

Zara rushes over with the others to stare out to a town in darkness, and not a light showing anywhere, 'Jesus...the whole town...has this ever happened before?'

They look to Allie, the oldest of them and the longest here. She shakes her head, 'Never heard it, never seen it...it can't happen...'

'WE CAN'T STAY HERE...' Bear reaches Thomas and Simmonds and screams to be heard, 'THE SHELLING. WE HAVE TO GO...'

Simmonds pushes Thomas away, thinking to flee, then spots the bodies poking from the gloop in the base of the crater. 'Help them...I have to help them...' he sets off, lumbering and slipping as Bear grabs his arms and twists him round.

'GO...UP...WE HAVE TO GO UP,' Bear pushes them

on, all three ducking down as another shell hits the far side of the crater, heaving the ground beneath them. 'UP...' he goes again, driving Thomas and Simmonds to get up into the horror of the wasteland where they run on past men screaming with limbs shorn off.

'BEAR!' Thomas screams the warning at a soldier taking aim with a rifle a dozen metres away. The three go down, diving into the mud to take cover as the round passes unheard above them.

With their own weapons lost in the crater, they crawl to reach the body of a young British soldier, still clutching his unfired rifle, as another round hits the mud, adding to the chaos of the awful barrage. Bear grabs the body, rolling him on his side to use as a shield to protect Simmonds and Thomas before getting the bolt back on the rifle, and rising up to aim and fire back, striking the soldier in the leg. Bear rises, sprinting hard to cover the distance before the other man can gather his wits to fire back.

He dives the last few feet, slamming into him as the guy draws a standard issue Army revolver from a leather holster and tries getting a shot off before Bear headbutts down, breaking his nose.

'Why are you here?'

'Fuck you...' the man bucks and heaves, fighting to get the pistol aimed at Bear who grabs the wrist, snaps the joint, wrenches the gun free, and shoots the man through his kneecap.

'WHY?' Bear roars.

'KILL ME...GO ON...'

Bear kills him, firing into his head at point blank range. He grabs the rifle and pushes up, wedging the revolver into his belt as a shell lands too close, sending him flying off his feet from the pressure wave to a few seconds of ringing in his ears, and his mind trying to grasp the now.

When he comes to, he lumbers up to his feet with his sense of direction lost, and the man he just shot now rendered to molecular form from the shell strike. He looks around, turning on the spot, trying to find Thomas and Simmonds.

'COWARDS…GET UP…' a roaring voice. One he knows. He heads towards it, slipping and sliding through the choking smoke to see the deaf sergeant lifting his cudgel to whack into Thomas and Simmonds, both unable to get to their feet from the slippery ground beneath them, both pleading for the man to stop, their arms raised in surrender and supplication. 'FILTHY COWARDS…' the sergeant hits Thomas in the arm, making him scream out in agony as Simmonds dives to protect him with his own body, and still, the sergeant lifts his cudgel to strike again.

Bear fires the revolver. Sending a shot into the sergeant's side. He spins around, incensed at being shot, to see Bear running towards him, 'COWARDS…'

Bear fires again, hitting his chest, but still, the big man roars and lifts his cudgel. Bear shoots the last two bullets from the revolver, then casts the weapon aside to bring his rifle up, aiming for the head that he blows out with a solid hit.

'TRAITOR!' another cry, Bear spins, seeing a line of British soldiers running from the smoke and mist towards him. All of them seeing him shoot the sergeant, 'TRAITOR. SHOOT HIM!'

'Fuck,' he drops to rush on, scrabbling to reach Thomas and Simmonds, grabbing them up to run.

'Okay,' Zara says calmly, swallowing while thinking, 'Jen, run down to the Old Lady…tell her what's happening. Prish, go for Martha and Lars, get them back here…'

She stops talking at the noise of a door slamming open. Their heads all turning from the window to the corridor leading down to the deployment rooms. Another noise. A soft thud.

'What's that?' Jen whispers.

Zara shakes her head, staring down into dark shadows of the corridor, 'Who is out on deployment?'

'Just Bear and Thomas,' Allie says.

They frown and listen to a creaking sound that Zara, Sally, and Allie know very well. The door handle to room seven. The one that creaks and needs fixing. The noise ends suddenly. A poise. A bunching of energy of something coming, with an instinct hitting the five women.

The handle turns fast, with red laser lights shining out as black clad figures pour from the room into the corridor.

'DOWN!' Zara shouts the warning, her and Prisha snatching at the pistols on their hips as Allie, Jen, and Sally dive away from the guns letting rip with both sides firing sudden and deafeningly loud.

'GO!' Prisha shouts to Sally and Jen, 'GET OUT… GET LARS…'

Zara fires back at the figures now diving into doorways for cover with muffled voices calling to each other, 'Allie… get to Martha's armoury for magazines…'

'Here,' Prisha throws a spare one from her belt to Zara, firing to give cover for Zara to change. She hits an attacker, making him scream out in agony as the wooden door frame and ceiling above her splinter with rounds coming back.

'How the fuck?' Allie mutters, crawling across the office towards Martha's office.

Sally and Jen make a run for it, lurching up to run for the stairwell door, prompting a fresh surge of firing with a round whipping past Prisha to hit Sally square in the back, sending her flying into a table of computers and monitors. Jen screams, turning to run back as bullets hit her chest and stomach with an impact that takes her off her feet.

Bear spots the German trench ahead. The helmets within so distinctly different to those worn by the British.

'WHAT ARE WE DOING?' Thomas screams, seeing the trench coming closer and a whole big bunch of German soldiers staring in shock at the three men running away from their own comrades. 'Ah, hell, this is gonna hurt...' he lowers his head, screaming out to build speed to charge forward.

Simmonds sees the trench right there. He's made it. A medic from The Royal Army Medical Corp has charged to breach an enemy trench. That he will be dead within the next five seconds is also in his mind, and he screams with Thomas, lowering his head as the three sail through the air over the heads of the Germans pressed into the wall of their trench. They land in a recess built into the far side. Thomas and Simmonds crumpling in a heap of arms and legs while Bear tries a deft roll and ends up slamming into several soldiers, bowling them over, then he's up, rising fast and back in the seven-sided room with a mind clear as his hands go to work.

A soldier runs at him, intending to skewer him with the bayonet fixed to his rifle that Bear sidesteps and neatly pushes the soldier on, making him stab his mate instead. He grabs a knife from a belt and cuts the throat, then backstabs into a chest before dropping to rise with a stab into a groin. Drop the knife. Grab a leg, snap the knee, dive, and rise up, grab a head, snap the neck. Sidestep, take the blow from a heavy stick. Take the heavy stick. Hit back with the heavy stick.

Thomas and Simmonds cry out, untangling themselves to stagger up with utter shock at what they just did. Both of them seeing Bear taking on a whole trench of angry Germans on his own. They look at each other. Both scared. Both terrified. Both nodding and roaring, and running to fight to help Bear and do what they can. An American that fell from the sky, and an exhausted medic that has no clue what is going on.

The attack buys time. It breaks a chink in the armour and allows more British to reach the trench to dive down and into the melee, sliding down the banked walls to land and fight, and only then, do the Germans realise and send the call to alarm as men start rushing to fix the breach.

'BLOW THE ROOMS...' a voice from a black-clad figure shouts an order, followed by a huge boom coming from room five as an explosive charge detonates, blowing the walls out with plaster, brick, and debris flying through the air into the street and main office.

'STOP...' Allie shouts, pressed into Prisha's side, with a pistol now gripped in her hands, 'We've got operatives deployed...please don't do it!'

Room four goes, exploding the walls out to render the thing useless as more bricks sail down into Main Street.

'STAY BEHIND ME,' Bear grabs Simmonds, pushing him into place.

He sets off through the trench. His heavy stick in one hand. A snatched German pistol in the other. Chaos everywhere. British soldiers pouring over the lip to drop into the trench to press the attack none of them thought was possible. Bear fires into the face of a man lunging at him, then wades forward, swinging the club left and right to batter a path.

He spots the junction ahead and the thick lines of German soldiers pouring into the forward trenches. He looks left, seeing more British breaching the lines to charge in and down to fight.

'Yes!' he mutters to himself, seeing the bag hanging from a hook next to a dugout, and rushes on towards it, whacking left and right. Clearing the way to the stick grenades. He grabs one, pulls the ceramic knobble hanging from a wire in the base that ignites the fuse within, and chucks it inside the dugout. Another one, pull the wire, throw into the junction. The first one explodes. The second one explodes. He throws more, launching them ahead as he runs on, clearing a path of death and destruction.

JENNIFER DIES SLOWLY, with blood frothing from her mouth. Sally dead, and the situation worsening by the second with Prisha, Allie, and Zara pinned in place, listening to room six detonating. They can't stop it from happening. The attackers are too many, too fierce and moving too fast. They'll get to room one and sever the live link for Bear and Thomas. They'll be trapped in 1917.

'DOWN!'

The three drop as the mortar hits the lip of the trench, blowing earth and men sky-high that rain back down in bloodied chunks. Carnage everywhere, and the trenches clogged with men fighting hand to hand. They can't get through, and even if they did, where can they go? Bear thinks fast, working out what to do. Going further into the German lines is too dangerous, and going back to the British lines means being shot for desertion.

He grabs Simmonds, heaving the man up to his feet to propel up and out of the trench, dragging the witless medic past skirmishing fighters.

'Where we going?' Thomas gasps.

'Road,' Bear shouts back, glancing up to see a speck of a black object dropping from the sky. He propels into Simmonds and Thomas, ripping both men off their feet into the deep mud of a crater as the shell hits where they were stood. On his feet a second later. Ears ringing. Eyes stinging. Throats burning.

'GAS GAS GAS...' a shout further away that rolls down and through, with every man able to yell repeating the words. Some drop to start tugging gas masks on, others carry on fighting, unable to stop and take action.

Bear doesn't hesitate but runs on, dragging Simmons and Thomas behind him, forcing them to move, with boots made heavy by the sticky, clinging mud.

He runs deeper into no man's land, his eyes strobing the view while still hearing the shouting, warning for gas, but not seeing any sign of it.

Thomas and Simmonds struggle to keep up, staggering instead of running. Their fitness way below Bear's. Pain everywhere. In their legs, chests, heads, and limbs. It goes on forever. It will never end, but Bear can see the edge now. He can see the coils of barbed wire and runs at them, letting go of Thomas to stoop and grab the body of a dead German, dragging him through the mud. He bunches power, heaving the corpse over the coils of razor wire, using the cadaver as a bridge to cross to reach the bank where the three slide down to the rutted road they came in on.

He gives them seconds to gain air. Mere seconds to ease their heartrates before grabbing them to keep going, heading back towards the town.

'THERE!'

They spin to look back, hearing the shout and cursing at the sight of the men pouring over the corpse bridge, not knowing if they're Freedom operatives or British soldiers chasing deserters.

AT LEAST TWO ATTACKERS KILLED, but room six still blows out with a huge boom that seems to suck the air from the offices, creating a pressure wave that makes ears pop. Spent magazines litter the floor. Chaos and confusion as to what is happening and why.

Marco races up the stairwell. The first to hear the noises and run for the planning offices. He bursts into the room, charging towards the armoury as the rounds slam into his torso, spinning him around to sprawl over Jennifer. Helmut a few metres behind him, running out, then dropping straight back from the ferocity of the gunfire. Rounds hitting the walls and doors. Striking computers and smashing windows.

'What the hell!' Jacob shouts out, running from the

stairwell as Helmut takes cover against the wall in the corridor.

'They're blowing the deployment rooms,' Helmut shouts as Jacob risks a look, then quickly snaps back from the rounds tearing chunks out of the doorframe and plastered walls.

'Jacob!' Pete calls, running into the landing as more Discovery operatives pour from restaurants and bars to sprint through the darkened town towards the planning office. Shouts in the air. Windows blowing out. Gunfire and explosions. A fireball coming from a first floor window, sending chunks of masonry into Main Street. People screaming in fear and trying to run away as the operatives aim for the noise and danger.

'We need weapons,' Helmut shouts from across the door to Jacob and Pete, and the others rushing in.

'The armoury's in there,' Keith yells back, pointing at the door.

Jacob curses with frustration and impotence. A need to do something. To get inside and fight back, but the glance he risked was enough to see the bodies gunned down inside.

'The sheriff's office!' Pete calls out with a sudden idea, 'Lars has weapons.'

'Go!' Helmut shouts as the next deployment room within the planning offices blows out.

'STOP!' Bear screams, holding his arms up over his head as he runs at the open-topped staff car filled with officers, making it brake hard to slew in the mud of the churned-up road.

'What the bleedin' hell you playin' at?' the sergeant at the wheel demands.

'Why are you here?' a man in the back demands, tall and broad, with a thick handlebar moustache and flat cap wedged neatly on his head. Emblems and officer's markings on his neatly pressed tunic.

'Deserters, I bet,' the sergeant snaps, pushing the door open to jump out. 'Watcha doing on the road? Running, are ya?' a thick London accent, and the man looks tough, stalking at Bear as Thomas heaves for air, glancing back down the road.

'Ain't got time for this, Bear…' the American gasps the words while Simmonds reels back, too confused to think.

'I said why are you here?' the tall officer demands.

'Answer the general,' the sergeant orders, pulling a service revolver from a holster that he aims at Bear.

'Need your car…'

'What?'

Bear moves fast, leaning left while his hands blur up to snatch the pistol from the sergeant, his foot coming up to boot the man away, snapping the lanyard clipped to the pistol's butt leading to his belt. 'Need the car,' Bear says again, aiming the gun at the officers in the car, 'Drop your guns and get out…'

'I'm the General, you fool!'

Bear fires the gun, aiming past the General's head, but the noise is enough to get them moving. The furious officers tugging their belts holding their sidearms off as they jump out into the thick mud.

'You'll be dead within two hours,' the General says calmly, staring daggers as Thomas grabs the belts and guns and drags Simmonds to the car, 'Cowards…hear me? COWARDS…'

'I'm not part of this...I'm not!' Simmonds cries out, 'Sirs...this is kidnap...it's against my will, it is...'

'Get in,' Thomas pushes him into the back as Bear gets into the driver's seat, staring at the controls with a foul utterance spilling from his lips.

A roar as the engine bites, making the wheels spin in the loose mud for a second before gaining traction as the shots come down the road, making the officers and sergeant dive for cover. Bear grips the wheel, grunting with the effort of turning the wheels without power-steering to help as Thomas and Simmonds duck in the back with the medic still claiming innocence.

The car starts moving. Gaining speed and distance, with Thomas risking a peep over the back seats to see the chasing men reaching the corner behind. They fire rifle shots, wild and un-aimed, as Bear increases the speed, fishtailing the car on the slick surface.

'No way,' Thomas mutters, shaking his head in disbelief at getting away. 'No fucking way...we did it, dude,' he grabs at Simmonds, pulling him close, 'We saved your ass...'

'I'll be shot for treason,' Simmonds wails.

'Better than...' Thomas stops talking to look back down the road, then up into the sky at the biplane dropping down to level out with a clear motion, 'Are you kidding me right now?'

The plane lifts for a second, showing the underside, and the big black Germanic cross on the wings then steadies to gain aim on the nice, juicy staff officer's car roaring down the road. 'I hate this job...' Thomas slams into Simmonds pushing him down into the footwell as Bear risks a glance over his shoulder, his mouth dropping open at the muzzle flashes of the machine gun on the German fighter showing clear.

Rounds hit the bank, sending divots up as Bear twists the heavy wheel, forcing the car to slew left and right while pushing his foot hard down. The plane fires again, sending rounds mere feet in front of the vehicle. The pilot grinning like a fiend as he steadies the aircraft and drops a bit lower.

Bear cries out when the seat next to him peppers with holes that go down the side, and the biplane soars overhead, roaring with noise from the propellers. So low that Bear could jump up and touch the fixed wheels. He watches the road ahead, sparing glances up to the plane, banking to make a run back as they reach the town, and the sentries on duty aiming rifles at the car coming in too fast.

They shout warning to stop. Firing shots into the air, then aiming lower at the car as the plane opens up with its gun again, strafing the sentry position and the front of the car as it swooshes through, turning hard into the lanes and avenues of the ruined town. More shots ring out, hitting the car as men spot the General's car obviously stolen by deserters.

ZARA CRIES OUT IN FRUSTRATION. Bear and Thomas are trapped. She can't leave them. She can't. She has to do something, and she stares at the door to room one.

'Don't do it,' Prisha calls out.

'They're my team,' Zara says firmly, rolling onto her back to change magazine in her pistol, 'Cover me.' She launches up to make a run as Prisha reacts on instinct and rises to run with Zara. Allie leans out, firing down the corridor to give what cover she can as the heat grows, and the red lasers flash through the smoke-filled air.

'FUCK YOU!' Thomas screams, aiming the revolver at the biplane, his arm bucking with each shot taken while he stands in the back of the car, driven at speed through the town to break free out onto the exit road. 'YEAH MOTHERFUCKER,' he yells as the plane roars overhead again, firing the last shot into the tail that makes absolutely no difference to the aircraft's handling or flight. 'Gimme another gun,' he shouts at Simmonds.

'I'm just a medic...'

'Yeah, and I'm a yank that fell from the sky and lives in a toaster...now, give me another goddam gun.'

'HE'S COMING BACK,' Bear shouts from the front, twisting the wheel to keep the vehicle slewing side to side. Crazed and sickeningly violent, but enough to stop the plane getting a firm bead in his sights.

Thomas aims, closing one eye and trying to do what Bear does by breathing deeply while the plane roars closer, dropping down to level out.

'Fuck,' Bear mutters. 'FUCK,' he shouts. 'FUCK!' he screams as the plane comes at them, the guns opening up with that ratatat noise, and the muzzle flashing as the rounds start hitting the road.

Thomas fires and misses. He grunts, fires again, and misses. He curses, pouts, and fires a third that sails harmlessly past the plane. 'Goddam it,' he really focusses now, plucking the trigger to send the fourth bullet underneath the aircraft. 'Ah, man,' he takes a quick fifth shot that also misses. He tuts, frowns, scowls, and fires the last shot overhead, sending the round through the underside into the pilot's foot who screams out in agony, yanking over too hard.

'Holy shit, I got him,' Thomas mutters. 'BEAR, I GOT

HIM...I SHOT THE PLANE...' he grins manically, staring at the plane as it fights for control, dipping and rising before seeming to tip over and slam nose down into the road behind them with a soft, dull thud that sounds out before the fuel ignites, sending a fireball scorching into the sky.

'Did you do that?' Bear asks, twisting to look round.

'I shot a plane down!' Thomas whoops in awe, 'WATCH THE ROAD!'

'Fuck!' Bear wrenches the wheel over, turning away from the bank but going too hard, slewing the car over towards the other bank. They hit side on, bouncing off, and the world around them spins and twirls. They hit the other side again with a bone-jarring crunch that sends Thomas and Simmonds up and out to land sprawling in the mud as Bear anchors on the brakes, bringing the heavy car to a stop, to sit with his eyes squeezed closed, and his head still spinning.

'Bear? BEAR? YOU OKAY?' Thomas yells, standing drunkenly in the mud.

'I'm a medic,' Simmonds whimpers.

'Aw, hell no,' Thomas shakes his head at the sight of a truck coming to a stop beyond the burning plane. Soldiers jumping out with rifles, going deep into the banked verges to get past the flames and heat. 'BEAR! Gotta go, buddy... come on, up, up, up...' he grabs at Simmonds, pulling him on yet again as Bear tries re-starting the car and curses loudly.

'Car's dead...we're on foot,' he shouts down to Thomas.

A PERILOUS THING TO DO. A most stupid action to take, to run at the danger with rounds flying past their heads and bodies. Fire and heat everywhere. Ceiling tiles hanging down. Red lasers flashing through the smoky air. Voices shouting. Noise and chaos, and every step seems to take a lifetime. Time slows, every action so clear and visceral.

Zara and Prisha run for room one while a black clad figure dives towards the door of room two, with an explosive charge ready to be thrown in. If that charge goes, it will blow through the walls to room one.

A round skims Prisha's arm. Another grazes Zara's thigh. Another hits the doorframe next to Allie, sending a splinter of wood into her cheek. Blood is spilled, but still they scream to shoot back as Zara and Prisha dive for the door.

They reach the junction, turning into the lane they walked down yesterday. The ground harder, less muddy, less clingy. Speed gained, with lungs bursting, and legs hurting. Shouts behind them. Guns fired. Rounds whizzing past.

Bear slows for a second, turning to aim a Webley service revolver, pulling the trigger with a snarl to send six shots back at the chasing soldiers. He hits one, making the man drop with a scream as the rest scatter to the sides.

He catches up with the other two, pushing them on with hard vicious shoves to their backs. 'RUN…KEEP GOING…' his voice shouts, strong, deep, and full of rage. He re-loads on the move. Taking the small bullets from the webbing pouches slung over his shoulder, pushing them into the little slots. He re-holsters that gun, re-loads another, then pauses to fire both back at the chasers, once more sending them scattering.

'There,' Thomas says, seeing the old barn ahead in the

distance. He glances to Simmonds as though suddenly realising the man is still with them, 'Oh, shit...Bear?'

'What?'

'What we doing with Simmonds?'

'No idea...'

An immense application of energy and force. Zara and Prisha charging across the corridor as the explosive charge is thrown into room two, both knowing it will blow through the wall.

Bear, Thomas, and Simmonds sprinting for the door to the old barn, with rounds striking into the ground about their feet.

Zara and Prisha slam into room one together, whacking the air from their lungs. Blood running down their faces and arms from the splinters, ricochets, and bullets skimming them, but they have barely a split-second to blink. The door to 1917 is right there. The door to Bear and Thomas. They have to make it.

Bear gives it everything he's got. Propelling Thomas and Simmonds over the last few yards to the barn door, using their combined body weight to smash through it. They hit hard, snapping the old wood in a shower of splinters.

The charge in room two detonates, supercharging the air that blows up and out, sending a pressure wave into the joining wall, blowing chunks of masonry into Zara and Prisha, lifting them off their feet to sail through to another time and place, with flames licking their backs at the same second Bear, Thomas, and Simmonds smash through the barn door.

All of them sprawling out over the filthy straw covered earthen ground. The noise of the explosion carries through for a second longer, then simply ends, ceasing to be as the connection is severed, and the door behind them once more leads to the storeroom.

Everything happening so fast. Everything on instinct. Prisha snatching a view of the room as she tumbles down. Bear the same. A strobing glimpse, but enough to see five black-clad figures with ski-masks pouring into the barn through an old doorway giving access to another storage area. Now another portal. Another live link, but if it's not to Discovery, then it must be to Freedom.

'AMBUSH!' Prisha shouts the warning, snapping Zara's head up to see the new threat as Bear rolls to vault up with a revolver gripped in each hand. The five figures in black react just as quickly. Snatching views to Zara and Prisha, then over to Bear and Thomas. Instinct and reactional training kick in as they all surge towards the middle of the barn with weapons up and ready. Positioning to aim. Gaining locks on targets, with steady hands and fingers pressing down on triggers.

'Got one and two,' Bear says, aiming his revolvers.

'Third,' Prisha shouts back, instantly understanding his order of view.

'Got Bear,' the black-clad figure closest to Bear says.

'Fourth,' Zara shouts.

'Lock on,' another shouts, aiming at Prisha.

'Lock on,' another yells out, aiming at Zara.

Two seconds and no more, for every person holding a gun to find a body to aim at as they all come to a stop in a sudden stalemate, with an intrinsic and absolute knowledge that if one trigger goes, they all will.

Zara and Prisha breathing hard. Their faces bathed in sweat and grime, with cuts showing on their arms and cheeks. Bear coated in thick mud, splashes of blood and gore all over him.

'Holy fuck,' Thomas staggers to his feet, gasping for air as he tugs a revolver from his belt to wave around at the people in black, 'Who do I aim at?'

'The fifth one, you twat,' Bear snaps.

'Fuck you...I shot a plane down,' Thomas retorts, waving his gun about, 'Which one is the fifth?'

'My end,' Zara calls out.

'Got him,' Thomas says.

A second in time passes. Everything on a knife edge, and fingers pressed so hard a blink of an eye could set them all off. Bear takes them in, gauging position and distance. Working out where each will move when the bullets start flying.

Noises from outside. Footsteps moving down the sides, and the clunks and clicks of rifles and weapons being made ready. 'YOU INSIDE...' a voice shouts. Rich, strong, and cultured, 'WE HAVE YOU SURROUNDED...COME OUT WITH YOUR HANDS UP...'

A stiffening from all sides. A tensing of muscles, with knuckles growing white from pressure. The tension ramps. The air charging with threat and malice as the immediacy of the situation comes to the fore.

There's only one way out now. It will happen. It has to happen. Bear readies, thinking to fire into the first two while moving right to take the other three, knowing he has to go fast.

'We know you're in there...Come out before we open fire...although, personally, I hope you stay there...'

'I think we pissed them off a bit, dude,' Thomas says.

'You think?' Bear asks.

'We've kidnapped a medic, crashed the General's car, and shot their angry, deaf sergeant...'

A snort of air from a figure in black aiming at Bear. A blast of breath as though in humour, as though in jest. A hint of cherry blossom in the air, and Bear's heart thuds loud in his chest as he locks onto the hazel eyes framed within the mask. A second to absorb it. To realise what it means. To see the intent, with her eyes that narrow and glint with mischief. A second, and no more. 'Now.' A whisper given. Unheard by anyone else.

A blur of motion, and the two of them move so much faster than everyone else. The woman leans back, flicking her aim over to shoot the fifth man in black as Bear's two Webley revolvers fire into one and two who spin away from the impact, both plucking wild shots. The small figure drops and turns, aiming to fire at the fourth as Bear lets rip with his two revolvers, and the last man flies off his feet from the force of three bullets hitting his centre of mass. The gunfire erupting so loud and awful in the confined space.

'FUCK!' Thomas shouts in shock at the speed of it. At everything in a blur of movement. Dead bodies on the floor. Shouts from outside. Ears ringing from the gunshots.

'Jesus,' Zara gasps, 'What just happened?'

Bear stares across at the last figure dressed in black who just killed her own team. At the hazel eyes flecked with green. His revolvers coming up fast as he turns from his last kill. She moves too. Anticipating his motion, stepping left as he steps right. Bringing their guns to aim at each other while circling on the spot.

'See me now,' she whispers the words he remembers so well. The mansion. The masquerade room. The taunt within her tone. Motion from his right. Figures coming through the door, dressed in black. They both turn and fire, and once more, the bodies drop as they rotate to aim back at each other. Circling like wolves, ready to fight or fuck. Ready to kill or mate. Ready for whatever happens. Both so poised within that second of pure life where every nuance and movement seems to mean something.

Neither fire. Neither back down until they complete a full rotation, and she starts edging back to the door.

'Bear!' Zara calls out, aiming at the figure backing away. Prisha the same. Both ready to fire. Both ready to kill but seeing Bear holding still. Not knowing why, only that he is. The figure reaches the door. Her pistol still locked on Bear. Her eyes still glued to his. She moves a hand to her tac-vest and draws a tablet. A press of a button, and she motions her head to the wall behind them. To the door leading into the storage room. To a door now leading to another location in time and space. 'Fuck,' Zara gasps, blinking at it, at what it means. She turns back to ask how. To ask why. To ask the questions always ready in her mind, but the figure stares at Bear as she steps back through the doorway with a last whisper given.

***K*ILL '*EM ALL*, T*IGER*.**

CHAPTER THIRTY-TWO

'They're all blown,' the operative shouts as they hunker down at the far end of the deployment corridor. Thick smoke filling the air, and the town of Discovery now in darkness.

Beatrice nods in response. Her face streaked with thick, black camo paint. Her sub-machine gun held ready, but she spots the looks of worry in the others as they glance about. 'I said don't worry. Bear isn't here. He's getting buried in a crater in 1917. Got it? We're going to punch out and take this fucking town. Kill anything that moves. Kill everything. GO!'

'Fuck!' Allie mutters, snatching a view down the corridor to the black-clad figures at the far end. Red lasers strobing out. Flames gripping the deployment rooms. Windows blown, and she can hear the shouts from outside in Main Street as people run towards the noise and chaos. Towards the fires and explosions. Another snatched glance, and she spots the figures starting to move.

It's a simple plan. Freedom have obviously got a mole in the town and made sure to attack when Bear is busy on an overnighter, and the amount of firepower they're laying down means the Discovery operatives can't get to the armoury. They can't slip into another time period and get weapons either because the deployment rooms are blown.

A simple plan, for sure, but brutally effective.

'ALLIE!' Helmut shouts from the outer corridor. 'Get down and find cover. We're getting weapons,' Helmut risks a lean into the door as more rounds slam into the wall and doorframe. Making him wilt back.

'DRIVE IN!' Beatrice yells out as the attackers start surging through the deployment corridor, towards the planning office. The guns firing again. Peppering the walls with rounds. Shooting through windows to cause damage. To create carnage. To cause maximum fear and shock.

'Scheisse!' Helmut mutters, banging the back of his head against the wall. 'SCHEISSE!' he roars out and bursts out to go low through the door, diving to roll as the fire rate intensifies. Allie spots him coming and rises from behind a desk, firing her pistol into the attackers as Helmut scrabbles to keep moving. A scream from Allie as a round hits her arm.

'ALLIE!' Helmut runs for her, seeing her go down with blood spraying out. Snatching the pistol up to return fire while grabbing her wrist to drag her behind a desk.

'TAKE THE FUCKING TOWN!' Beatrice screams as they swarm into the planning office. Booting desks over. Smashing tables aside, and rifle butts slam into the cabinet holding the RLI files waiting for deployment. Wrenching them out with liquid sprayed from a small bottle. A flame given. Another fire started.

The gunfire and explosions are heard throughout the town. Travelling far on the gentle wind and reaching the grand colonial house at the end of a tree-lined avenue. A fire burning in a hearth. A chair next to it. The window open, and the Old Lady sips from a glass of sherry while listening to the detonations and gunshots with a look of intense concentration on her face.

'FALL BACK,' Helmut shouts from the planning office as the room starts swarming with figures. 'GET OUT OF HERE...THERE'S TOO MANY,' he yells to whoever is outside. Telling them to flee. Telling them to hide as he spots more figures streaming along the corridor, running between the ruined deployment rooms. More figures dressed in black, clutching sub-machine guns fitted with red lasers. More figures firing into the walls. Into the desks and computers. Blinding muzzle flashes. Smoke and heat from the growing flames now licking the holes in the walls. A dozen attackers already in the room. Another dozen coming, and no doubt, their link is live and ready to disgorge more into the fray.

The horror hits. That there's nothing they can do. The armoury is kept in here, and the attack is too great. The town will be taken.

Jacob and Pete burst into the sheriff's office to see Lars and Matias already taking shotguns from their gun cabinet. Matias looking stricken and panicked. Lars as stoic as ever as he throws shotguns over to Pete and Jacob. A box of cartridges, and they set off through the door, back into Main Street. Back into the dark town where the glazed storefronts reflect the orange flames in the blown-out walls of the planning office. Debris on the road. Rounds pinging off the tarmac from attackers shooting through the windows. An operative goes down, crying out from being shot. No time to stop. No time to give aid, and the four men run on. Shouting out for the operatives clustered at the door to the planning offices to give way. To make room for them to get through.

'There's too many!' someone shouts in darkened bedlam as the four men run through reception, towards the stairwell. The ground floor door bursts open. Red lasers seen flashing. Something thrown.

'FLASHBANG IN,' someone shouts. The four men burst to take cover and get distance as every operative in the reception area cries out in warning. A huge boom. A blinding flash. Men and women fall back. Instantly disorientated by the flashbang. Another comes after it. Another bang. Another flash. The attackers press their advantage. Pacing into the reception, having breached the planning office and taken the stairs.

'Fall back!' Jacob shouts out, firing his shotgun to cover the others. Lars takes his turn, covering for Jacob while wrenching a terrified Matias behind him. Pushing him away.

The rounds start coming back. Fast firing from automatic weapons. Rounds striking the windows and desk. Wood and plaster breaking apart. Glass shattering. Someone goes down screaming. They don't know who. There isn't time to stop and think. Only to react and retreat into Main Street.

Four shotguns and two sidearms. That's all they have, and back they go. Beaten away by the ferocity of the attack.

In the planning office, Helmut drags Marco behind the desks where Allie clutches her bleeding arm. Marco still alive. Shot through the stomach and chest.

'Shoot me,' he gasps, grabbing at Helmut, 'I'll reset.'

Helmut casts him a look, shaking his head, 'I'm out of rounds.'

'KEEP GOING,' Beatrice screams out from a few feet away, 'We've taken the stairs. Get out into Main Street. I want the town. GO, GO, GO!'

Another dozen figures in black swarming through the corridor into the large room. Another dozen automatic weapons.

'Scheisse!' Helmut says.

'Shit,' Jacob says outside in Main Street.

'Oh, shit,' Thomas says in the barn in 1917 as they all turn towards the door to the storage room.

'YOU HAVE THIRTY SECONDS,' the voice outside the barn shouts, 'THEN WE OPEN FIRE.'

And in the grand colonial house, next to the fire burning in the hearth, the Old Lady's knuckles turn white as she squeezes the wooden arms of the chair. Her face a mask of focus. Her eyes blazing from the reflection of the flames.

In Main Street, Pete curses foully, spewing forth a foul tirade of words in French while the flames and shadows dance over his features. 'Again. Oui. We go again. We do this.'

In the planning office, Helmut nods grimly, locking eyes with Marco who grimaces at the pain as he slowly rises. Allie nodding at them both. Knowing what must be done. Knowing what they have to do.

'TEN SECONDS,' the voice outside the barn shouts out as Bear, Thomas, Zara, and Prisha all stare at the door. Knowing what must be done. All of them knowing what they have to do.

The Old Lady inhales sharply. Her eyes narrowing. Her grip tightening.

'WE DO THIS,' Pete shouts in Main Street as he glares at the operatives taking cover. All of them knowing what must be done. All of them knowing what they have to do.

'FIVE,' the voice outside the barn shouts.

'Ready?' Helmut says to Allie and Marco.

'FOUR.'

'ARE WE READY?' Pete yells.

'THREE.'

'I'm not fucking ready,' Thomas says, gulping air in the barn.

'TWO.'

The Old Lady's chin rises. Her gaze hardening. Her breath held.

'ONE!'

'DEATH CHARGE!' Helmut screams out as he rises from behind the desk with Allie and Marco.

'Oh, you are shitting me,' Beatrice groans.

'DEATH CHARGE!' Pete roars out in Main Street as the call is taken up, and the road swarms with operatives giving voice as they charge towards the planning office.

'What the fuck are they doing?' the Freedom team leader says in the reception area, shaking his head at the sight.

'FIRE!' the officer outside the barn shouts as the rifles start up and tear chunks out of the wooden boards.

'FIRE!' the Freedom team leader in the reception area shouts as his team lift weapons to take aim at the ragged line of Discovery operatives charging towards them.

'FIRE!' Beatrice yells in the planning office as a dozen red lasers take aim at Marco, Allie, and Helmut trying to charge across the room.

'Hey, douche bags!' a shout from the deployment corridor. An American voice calling out.

Everyone in the room snaps their heads over to see Thomas grinning at them from the end of the corridor. 'Death charge, bitches...' he flicks a finger up and steps aside for Bear to sprint past who thumbs the hammer back on his Webley revolver to pull the trigger to send the bullet that flies down the corridor into the first operative who falls back with his skull blowing out.

A thing to see, and a sight that will stay with Helmut, Marco, and Allie forever, because in that second, in the heat and smoke, with flames licking the walls, they watch as every attacker seems to move in perfect synchronicity. All of them twisting on the spot to aim into the corridor as another attacker drops with a blown-out skull. Then another after that.

'SHOOT HIM!' Beatrice screams the order. Bear fires his last shot and throws the gun, and before her brain can send the signal to duck, it slams into her mouth, and she drops while spitting teeth and blood once more.

'GET 'EM, BEAR!' Zara yells out from the end of the corridor as Bear slams into the first attacker. Wrenching him off his feet to pin in front, using him as a shield as the other Freedom operatives fire their sub-machines guns. Sending rounds into their own mate who screams out from the rounds striking his body.

Bear strides in to launch the now dead guy at another attacker. The weight of the impact sending the two bodies through a blown-out window. They drop fast and land hard with a crunch of bones, only to be shot by the rounds coming from the team in the reception area.

'SHIT!' the Freedom team leader shouts out as his unit stops firing.

'Shit!' Pete says, coming to a stop with the rest of the Discovery operatives as they look from the two bodies in the street up to the blown-out window.

'What the...' the Freedom team leader says.

'What the...' Pete says.

'GO ON, BEAR,' Zara's voice screaming out, 'KILL 'EM ALL!'

And the Old Lady finally releases the breath she held. Gasping it out as her eyes glint in the fire burning in the hearth while in the planning office, Bear grabs an attacker and turns him about to fire his automatic weapon into the others.

Chaos ensues. Noise and motion everywhere. The red lasers, suddenly, dazzling their own eyes as Bear goes deep into the thick of them. Snapping a knee joint with a foot to the back of a leg. Grabbing a neck to twist and break. Grabbing a rifle from a sling that he slams into a nose before twisting and launching the body out of the same blown-out window.

He's back in that zone. In the mindset drilled into him by Roshi who took a man with no name, who fell from the sky and groomed him. She tortured him. She made him beg and weep. She watched as he shit himself through fear and pain. She stood over him without mercy. Goading him. Taunting him. Berating his weakness. Cruel and heartless. A terrible thing to do. A most awful thing to do to another person.

See me now.

She whispered the words in the mansion. She made him see her.

'Tell me who I am,' he begged and pleaded.

'Make me.'

He tried to attack her, but he was slow and weak. She had a knife. She stabbed him and told him to move faster. He tried again. She killed him over and over, and still, he begged. Still, he pleaded, but there was no mercy to be given. No apology either. She needed him to be strong. *'This is no place for the weak.'*

He didn't understand. He couldn't understand. He had only what she told him. What she made him believe.

Death to life. Life to death. Over and over. Repeating it until the pain became a part of his existence. Until the pain became somehow less.

'Fight me,' she said. He refused. He wouldn't do it. *'Look at me...you have to fight me...do it...'*

He remembers those words. The way her eyes glared into him. Those hazel eyes flecked with green. The passion in her voice. The need for him to fight and be strong. He said no. She shouted at him. He died again, but when he came back, he did so with rage and fury, and that was the spark she needed. That was the spark she was trying to ignite all along. That thing inside.

'That's it, tiger... Attaboy!'

Those words repeat in his head now as he moves in to grip an arm that he twists and breaks before flipping the body over to boot away into another attacker. The savage violence born in the masquerade room erupts again as he takes a knife from a belt and slices it across a throat. As he steps back and stabs the point into a gut, then throws the blade into a head. As he kicks. As he punches. As he breaks limbs and sends bodies through the blown-out window.

But the masquerade room was just the first part. That was just them. That was just learning to deal with pain. The real training came after. When he woke in a room with seven-sides. When seven men came in with sticks. When he learnt to use the space around him and the momentum of those coming against him. A shift of a foot to slide away. A palm to a nose, sending bones up into the brain. A fist to a rib, sending shards into lungs. A foot to a knee joint. An elbow to a throat. There is no pain. He is not here. This is not real.

She groomed him.

She tortured him.

She did those things. But she did it to weaponise him, and as he throws the next body through the blown-out window, as the flames roar and the heat grows, as the violence erupts to a sickening level, so Beatrice tries crawling away, only to be stopped by a boot stepping on her hand. She looks up, toothless and bleeding once more, into the face of Zara aiming a pistol, 'I won't let this go. Say hi to Robert.'

The gun fires. The death charge resumes, and the Discovery operatives swarm to the bodies thrown out into the street. Snatching up sub-machine guns strapped to bodies and pistols from holsters.

'Oh, fuck...oh, fuck...OH, FUCK!' the Freedom team leader cries out as the rounds start coming back.

'DEATH CHARGE!' Pete yells out, the words taken up again.

'DEATH CHARGE!' Helmut screams out in the planning office, running into the fray with Marco and Allie as Bear storms from the room and out into the corridor. Into the stairwell. Hitting and hurting. Breaking and busting. Biting. Gouging. Slicing and killing.

'DEATH CHARGE!' Zara yells out with Thomas and Prisha. All of them charging into the mayhem. Into the battle. Into the heat and smoke, and in the grand colonial house, at the end of the tree-lined avenue, the Old Lady smiles wryly and sips once more from her glass of sherry.

CHAPTER THIRTY-THREE

The dawn comes. The sky growing lighter as he trudges past the houses with white picket fences.

'If you have a family and work to a decent position, you'll maybe one day get a house down there.'

He thinks of those words every time he passes by. The first day he met Allie. The first day they were here in the town.

Into the bend and up the steep hill. Into the lanes and avenues running between the little hobbit houses. A place now quiet and seemingly devoid of life. A place now empty with everyone down in the town. Drawn to the noise and commotion. Drawn to help and douse fires. To organise food and water. To do what's needed after such a thing.

A long night has passed. A long day before that. Bear doesn't know exactly what happened. Only that his team's missions were targeted. He doesn't know why Freedom did that.

What he does know is that they were tracked. Zara said that. Prisha too. They said Freedom wanted Bear out of the way so they could attack Discovery. They saw what Bear can do in Carpe Diem restaurant in New York.

Martha was there by then. She was outside with the others when they death charged. She said they'll need to review the way they operate and how they store weapons. That was while everyone was standing in the ruined planning offices staring about at the carnage.

'And can someone tell me why the hell there is a first world war medic treating our injured,' Martha then said, staring over at Corporal Simmonds wrapping a dressing around Allie's arm.

'Um,' Thomas said before offering a wan smile as they all looked at him, 'I shot a plane down…woohoo. Go team!'

'We can't send him back now,' Zara said, staring at Simmonds, 'They'll shoot him for desertion.'

'Well, we can't bloody keep him here,' Martha snapped, at which point Bear slipped away. Keeping his head down. Out into Main Street where the debris was being swept aside. Where the people of Discovery were gathered. The people that fell silent as he walked through.

'Bear,' Marco called out. Bear stopped to look back. Seeing the man now fully healed after being shot by Lars so he could reset. The town fell silent. Everyone looked over. Even the people in the planning offices fell quiet as they stared down onto Main Street through the holes in the walls. Marco paused. Swallowing once as he looked about, then back to Bear, 'That was good. What you did. Thank you.'

Bear nodded, 'Anytime.'

That was it, and he walked on as a few more people said thank you. As a few more said his name. People that had hated him for what he had done in Carpe Diem. People that wouldn't accept him because he was a monster.

That's what they said. They said Roshi had made a monster. He shouldn't be here. He shouldn't be allowed to be here.

'Interesting times,' Martha said quietly, watching Bear walk away, 'Now, what the hell are we doing with that medic?'

Now, Bear walks through the empty lanes to the last house at the end. The one closest to the forest. The pots of roses outside. His pull up bar fixed to the ground.

When he goes in, he does so to a place unchanged since the first night he stayed here. The same colours. The same furniture, and if he closes his eyes and inhales deeply, he imagines he can still smell her cherry blossom scent. It's dark though. The dawn not yet strong enough to get light through the drawn curtains.

Into his bedroom. Aiming for the bathroom. Needing to wash. Needing to be clean. Needing to rest and think, but he sees the hand coming from the depth of the shadows, and in the split second it takes to react and snatch the blade free, so he scents the air that is filled with the aura of Roshi and the scent of cherry blossom.

'What's up, buttercup...'

His heart lurches. Too many emotions inside. Relief. Denial. Anger. Joy. Too many things happening. Too many thoughts, but he moves in. Ready to do it all again. Ready to fall for it all once more. Ready to be groomed and tortured for eternity, but she pulls back at the last second. Her eyes fixing on his. A look of pain within them. A show of emotion. Of feeling. He frowns, unsure of why, unsure of what it means.

'Why the fuck is Lucy's sports bra in your bathroom?'

'Oh, shit...'

And in the grand colonial house at the end of the tree-lined avenue, the Old Lady lies down in her bed. Not that she needs to sleep. She's an AI.

But it feels nice to get into bed. She understands why humans like it so much. The softness underneath. The weight of the covers. The symbolism of sleep.

Not that Bear will be getting much sleep. Not with that one to explain, and even the Old Lady wouldn't want to be on the receiving end of Roshi's wrath, and as she closes her eyes, so she smiles once more as Bear's front door explodes in shards from Bear slamming through it. Scrabbling up to his feet as Roshi storms out.

'YOU FUCKED LUCY!'

'SIX MONTHS, ROSHI.'

'I SAID TO WAIT. I SAID THAT.'

'FOR SIX FUCKING MONTHS? WHAT THE ACTUAL FUCK?'

'Dear me,' the Old Lady says, tutting gently as Roshi steams into Bear, trying to hit his head and body as Bear blocks, and they start fighting once more. For anyone else, that would be a terrible thing, but perhaps they need to get it out of their system. It is how they formed a bond after all. However, it would not be good for everyone to see them fighting. Not good at all. Especially, with just how violent those two can be.

No. It would be best all around if they had some privacy.

'Six months, Roshi!' Bear shouts out, backing away as Roshi charges at him, 'You could have left me a sign!'

'I did! I left my necklace on your pillow, you fucking fuck!' she charges fast. Like a wolf ready to fight or fuck. Ready to kill or mate as Bear stops going back and charges towards her. Ready to fight or fuck. Ready to kill or mate, and the ground drops out. Simply not there. Only ocean below as they fall through the sky towards the rolling waves. Both glancing at each other. Both knowing exactly what just happened, and both knowing they are already too late to try and position to glide to get the angle to dive.

They hit the water. Things break. Things hurt. Saltwater is sucked in. Death comes.

CHAPTER THIRTY-FOUR

Couples Therapy

Death to life. Darkness to light. From the void of nothing to opening his eyes at the same time as his mind starts running, and his senses kick in. Giving depth to his vision and range to his hearing.

Softness underneath him, and he sits up to see he's naked on a single bed. An old-fashioned, wrought iron thing with curved metal ends. He gets up and moves to the door, looking about and thinking this feels like the top floor of the mansion house. The beams above his head. The old style windows. The bare floorboards. Wooden doors to rooms on his left and right, and a kitchen area in front of him. A simple table. Two chairs. Two pistols on the table. Both black.

A noise to his left. A door opens, and Roshi rushes out, then stops dead on seeing him. Both of them naked. Both staring at the other until they turn their heads to the table holding the two pistols. A big sheet of paper propped against a vase next to the pistols. Words on the sheet. Handwritten in a flowing script.

I strongly suggest you resolve your issues before you return to my town x

'That's fucked up,' Roshi says as Bear nods at her, agreeing wholly that this is, indeed, very fucked up. But then, everything here is fucked up. Like all of it. The whole of it. Every bit of it.

'Six fucking months,' he says.

'You fucked Lucy!'

They glare again. Both naked. Both filling with anger. Two pistols. Both black. They run for it. Both reaching at the same time. Both snatching them up to turn and fire, with rounds hitting heads that blow out as they fall dead.

Death to life. Darkness to light, and Bear vaults from the single bed to stagger out through the door as Roshi bursts from hers. Their dead bodies still on the floor, leaking brains and blood. The pistols back on the table. A new note on the top.

Best to thrash these things out while they are fresh.

Death to life. On his back in the bedroom, and he vaults up, running out and not blinking at the sight of two dead Bears, one dead Roshi, and one living Roshi aiming the gun at him.

He charges, and she fires, getting him in the chest, but he gained enough momentum to charge and land on her, both screaming out as they fight and bite before she gets the gun aimed and fires again, killing him outright, then a second later, she fires again, shooting herself through the temple.

From death to life, and they both wake in their rooms to vault up and charge out. Bear grabs the table to throw, but she dodges and grabs the kettle, swinging it hard to clang into the side of his head, spilling hot water over her hands. She grabs his leg and sinks her teeth into his naked thigh. A knee to his groin, and he flies off. She rises, grabbing the handle of a drawer, and yanks the whole thing out, that spills blades and kitchen utensils across the corpse littered floor.

'Shit,' she curses as he looks over. A second's worth of eye-contact where either could say *hey, hang on, let's stop now,* but neither do, and they lunge to grab whatever they can reach.

She stabs him with a corkscrew, while he slaps her head with an egg slice.

Reset, and they both wake to rush out. 'Just give in...' she calls over her shoulder, 'Go and fuck Lucy again.'

He goes to say something mean and awful, and terrible and sucks air. 'FUCK YOU,' he shouts instead.

'Try working on your vocabulary,' she says, reaching down to throw a severed arm at him.

He dances back, slapping the arm away, then grabbing it as he chases her into the masquerade room to see her wrenching the gun from the servant and moving back behind the sofa as he advances while holding the severed arm like a club.

'Put that down...Bear, you put that down...that's gross. Seriously, there's a line.'

He screams a gargled yell and runs at her as she lowers the gun and shoots his dick.

'Stop going for my dick,' he yells, clutching at his bleeding privates.

'Put the arm down then.'

'Fuck you!'

Death to Life. Both running from their temporary reset rooms allocated to them for use during their couples' therapy. Another chase. Another explosion of violence, but then, this is how they bonded. Pain is secondary. Death is not what it was, and although, violence can never be the right way to communicate, it seems to work for them. Especially, when they find a room filled with guns and explosives. And especially, when Roshi pulls the pin from a grenade and launches herself at Bear, wrapping her legs about his body, with the grenade held between them. 'I missed you,' she shouts.

'I missed you too,' he yells back, and the grenade explodes.

A SHORT WHILE LATER, on the veranda, outside the mansion house, the Old Lady looks mildly at the blown out French doors and the explosion marks caused by multiple grenades detonating, and steps over the dead bodies of Bear and Roshi, carefully treading between chunks of gore and flesh.

More bodies inside. Bullet holes in every wall and in every door. Bodies shot down and, in the lobby, the Old Lady finds another dead Bear skewered on a sword on top of another dead Roshi and more dead Bears, and more dead Roshis.

Fire in the gun room, with flames licking the walls, and

the stench of many weapons being fired many times. Bullet casings everywhere.

She tuts mildly and walks towards the stairs, marvelling at the door to the masquerade room, hanging off the hinges, with thick smoke billowing out, and several of the laughing mask-wearing people now on fire.

Up the stairs. More bodies. To the landing and over yet more bodies, then into the corridor to see them lying side by side. Hands entwined. Heads touching. Knives in both of their bellies.

'Hey,' Roshi gasps, trying to wave a hand before dropping her head back down.

'Feeling better?' the Old Lady asks, peering about at the carnage, then back down to their blooded bodies.

They both nod. Glancing at each other. Hurt in their eyes. Pain and worry too, but the love is there. The Old Lady can see it.

'Good,' she says quietly, 'Because I need you both ready.'

'Ready for what?' Bear asks, croaking the words out.

'For our revenge, of course,' she says as they both look up at her, 'Now, get ready. We're going after Freedom…'

ALSO BY RR HAYWOOD

A Town Called Discovery

The #1 Amazon Time Travel Thriller

A man falls from the sky. He has no memory.

What lies ahead are a series of tests. Each more brutal than the last, and if he gets through them all, he might just reach A Town Called Discovery.

*

EXTRACTED SERIES

EXTRACTED

EXECUTED

EXTINCT

Blockbuster Time-Travel

#1 Amazon US

#1 Amazon UK

#1 Audible US & UK

Washington Post & WSJ Best-seller

In 2061, a young scientist invents a time machine to fix a tragedy in his past. But his good intentions turn catastrophic when an early test reveals something unexpected: the end of the world.

A desperate plan is formed. Recruit three heroes, ordinary humans capable of extraordinary things, and change the future.

Safa Patel is an elite police officer, on duty when Downing Street comes under terrorist attack. As armed men storm through the breach, she dispatches them all.

'Mad' Harry Madden is a legend of the Second World War. Not only did he complete an impossible mission—to plant charges on a heavily defended submarine base—but he also escaped with his life.

Ben Ryder is just an insurance investigator. But as a young man he witnessed a gang assaulting a woman and her child. He went to their rescue, and killed all five.

Can these three heroes, extracted from their timelines at the point of death, save the world?

*

THE WORLDSHIP HUMILITY

#1 Audible bestselling smash hit narrated by Colin Morgan, star of Merlin & Humans.

#1 Amazon bestselling Science-Fiction

"A rollicking, action packed space adventure…"

"Best read of the year!"

"An original and exceptionally entertaining book."

"A beautifully written and humorous adventure."

Sam, an airlock operative, is bored. Living in space should be full of adventure, except it isn't, and he fills his time hacking 3-D movie posters.

Petty thief Yasmine Dufont grew up in the lawless lower levels of the ship, surrounded by violence and squalor, and now she wants out. She wants to escape to the luxury of the Ab-Spa, where they eat real food instead of rats and synth cubes.

Meanwhile, the sleek-hulled, unmanned Gagarin has come back from the ever-continuing search for a new home. Nearly all hope is lost that a new planet will ever be found, until the Gagarin returns with a code of information that suggests a habitable planet has been found. This news should be shared with the whole fleet, but a few rogue captains want to colonise it for themselves.

When Yasmine inadvertently steals the code, she and Sam become caught up in a dangerous game of murder, corruption, political wrangling and...porridge, with sex-addicted Detective Zhang Woo hot on their heels, his own life at risk if he fails to get the code back.

*

THE UNDEAD SERIES

THE UK's #1 Horror Series

Available on Amazon & Audible

"The Best Series Ever..."

The Undead. The First Seven Days

The Undead. The Second Week.

The Undead Day Fifteen.

The Undead Day Sixteen.

The Undead Day Seventeen

The Undead Day Eighteen

The Undead Day Nineteen

The Undead Day Twenty

The Undead Day Twenty-One

The Undead Twenty-Two

The Undead Twenty-Three: The Fort

The Undead Twenty-Four: Equilibrium

Blood on the Floor

An Undead novel

Blood at the Premiere

An Undead novel

The Camping Shop

An Undead novella

www.rrhaywood.com

Find me on Facebook:

https://www.facebook.com/RRHaywood/

Find me on Twitter:

https://twitter.com/RRHaywood

Printed in Great Britain
by Amazon